Elysium

By
Diane Scott Lewis

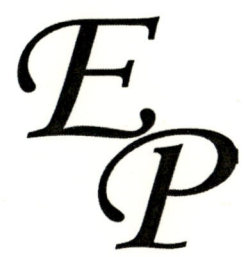

Eternal Press
A division of Damnation Books, LLC.
P.O. Box 3931
Santa Rosa, CA 95402-9998
www.eternalpress.biz

Elysium
by Diane Scott Lewis

Digital ISBN: 978-1-61572-371-3
Print ISBN: 978-1-61572-372-0

Cover art by: Dawné Dominique
Edited by: Carolyn Crow
Copyedited by: Michelle Ganter

Copyright 2011 Diane Scott Lewis

Printed in the United States of America
Worldwide Electronic & Digital Rights
1st North American and UK Print Rights

All rights reserved. No part of this book may be reproduced, scanned or distributed in any form, including digital and electronic or mechanical, including photocopying, recording, or by any information storage and retrieval system, without the prior written consent of the Publisher, except for brief quotes for use in reviews.

This book is a work of fiction. Characters, names, places and incidents either are the product of the author's imagination or are used fictitiously, and any resemblance to any actual persons, living or dead, events, or locales is entirely coincidental.

I wish to dedicate this novel to author and friend Ginger Simpson, who always believed in its value.

Numerous people helped with the development of this novel.

The Colonial Beach critique group: Sherryl Woods, Jim Lemons, Carolyn Carlyle, and Alleyne Dickens.

Vienna, VA critique group: Carol Milligan, Mary Lee Malcolm, and Mary Campbell.

The online Historical Fiction group at Yahoo: Anne Whitfield, Anita Davison, Ginger Simpson, Monika Weikel, and Lois Templin. All these people are gifted writers.

Napoleonic scholar, Victor Blair, for his assistance with the geography of Saint Helena, a place he's visited several times. The Napoleon Series Discussion Forum for answering my questions.

If I may thank an institution, the fantastic Library of Congress where I read books written on Saint Helena during Napoleon's exile.

Chapter One

From the sublime to the ridiculous there is but one step.—Napoleon Bonaparte

"Land ho!"

At the news she'd waited ten weeks to hear, Amélie Perrault pushed through the red-coated soldiers and squeezed past sailors to reach the rail. The wood slimy in her grip, she chewed on the tip of her thumbnail and stared at a sea so long empty. A dark mass shrouded in mist hovered on the horizon.

HMS *Northumberland* scudded closer under billowing sails. The mist faded, lifted like a veil by the ship's prow. More of the French crowded around, jabbing her with elbows as pointed as their words. Whimpers, cries and stale perfume filled the air.

Saint Helena's perimeters were forbidding, a citadel cloaked in splintered cliffs.

"She's a volcanic fist, spewed up from the sea." Amélie rubbed a hand below her bodice to smooth down the churning knot in her stomach. A defiant place to cling to this last drop of ocean, the island was no paradise.

She bit down on her lip. Had she insisted on accompanying her father only to suffer a fate worse than being trapped under her brother's thumb in France?

"*Peste*, we sailed a thousand leagues for that black wart?" Clarice elbowed a path to the rail. The chambermaid's daughter swayed her hips with the motion of the ship. "The English are fiends to have forced us to come."

The smug faces of the nearby English officers proved they were relieved to banish the deposed Emperor of the French and his followers to this desolate spot in the South Atlantic.

"That's only the outer shell. Saint Helena has to be lush farther in, or how could anyone survive here?" Amélie leaned forward and studied the terrain—soaring basalt peaks that stabbed into a whirl of clouds. She suppressed a shiver.

"We'll die here," Clarice snapped. "That's what our captors want."

"At least it *is* land. Fresh fruits and vegetables." Amélie's stomach rumbled at the hard biscuits she'd eaten earlier. Bug-riddled tack was all they had left after a storm chased the flotilla away from the African coast. A gust of wind slapped at her salt-crusted hair. She pressed the teak rail and couldn't allow her resolve to whip away. She'd sought a grand adventure, the chance to be of use to her emperor. "The island is an important port for the East India Company."

"Did you study this wart in one of your precious books?" Clarice puckered her upper lip between plump cheeks. "You try to act smart, but you look like a little girl. It's absurd for the head chef's daughter to be so skinny."

"You take too much pleasure in being rude. There's nothing wrong with me or reading." Amélie touched her bony hip and glared sidelong at Clarice, someone she'd tried to befriend but failed. Two weeks into the voyage, she decided it wasn't worth the trouble. "How tragic some women don't bother to learn anything."

"My mother says reading is wasted on women." Clarice put one hand on her hip and tossed back her head, her favorite pose. Her white cap fluttered in the breeze. She brushed her fingers over her cleavage. "Unless I rot here, or the men are blind, I'll make my way."

"You would throw yourself at strange men?" Amélie gripped the rail again as the ship rolled. Water sloshed over her feet and she curled her toes in sodden shoes.

"One man is the same as another."

"They all seem different to me." Unattainable, never attracted to her, but at the ripe old age of nineteen—the same age as Clarice—Amélie hadn't cared, and nurtured her brain. Like her desires for the island, she'd rely on her interior.

The wind swirled around her and she stuffed unruly tresses her mother once called honey-gold under her straw hat. Her throat tightened at that memory, her mother lost to her too soon, too quickly.

The ship's officers on deck shouted orders. Sailors scrambled up the rigging of the seventy-four-gun man-of-war and began to trim the sails. The Union Jack snapped above their heads. Amélie closed her eyes for a moment and imagined the tricolor of imperial France, but the enemy flag remained.

"Saint Helena looks like the Devil's last shit before he dropped into Hell." Saint-Denis, one of the emperor's valets, pushed up in the crowd behind the two girls. "Oh, sorry if I've offended your delicate ears." His sooty eyes flashed above his usual smirk.

Amélie smiled at his frank humor. "We're at the end of the world, with spring now in October. Everything is flipped upside down." Nothing as it should be might work in her favor. An unusual place for an ill-fitting young woman.

She remembered when the Southern Cross replaced the familiar North Star in the night sky as they sailed south of the equator. That change both intrigued and troubled her, emphasizing the vast distance of their exile.

Saint-Denis swept back his dark hair as he towered over them. "A dismal plop of lava, but let's hope we make these English scoundrels regret their error."

"Where is His Majesty? Isn't he coming up to see the island?" Amélie scanned the sad faces around her, her breath sharp in anticipation.

"The emperor will never escape from here as he did Elba." Clarice turned to Saint-Denis, her eyes half closed. "I've wanted to ask you—does His Majesty mind if his valets marry?" She nestled into his side.

Saint-Denis chuckled, but raised his shoulder as if to fence her out. "Our emperor will handle the situation, *mes jeune filles*. Excuse me, I must go below and attend him." The valet tipped his hat to the girls before he stepped back and strutted off, his legs like rapiers in white silk stockings. Amélie hid a grin when Clarice bristled cat-like at his indifference to her charms.

"Maybe we won't have to stay long. France and England might allow us to return to Europe if political situations change." Amélie sighed, unsure if she wanted that either. The bustle of civilization, back to the ordinary, again shuffled aside. In a quick sniff, she inhaled the scent of earth that drifted over the saline sea. "My emperor has faced adversity many times before." She'd grasp that tenacity for herself.

"Your emperor, is it?" Clarice puckered her lip again, her hazel eyes assessing. "We should worry about our own future. You need to stop drooling over something you'll never have. Try enticing one of his valets."

"I'm not—" Amélie's cheeks burned. She swallowed her anger. She'd devise a way to be important to her sovereign, though not in the manner Clarice insinuated. "A clever woman can have influence that has nothing to do with scandal. Have you no pride?"

"Pride will get you little on the Devil's last shit." Clarice wriggled out from the gaping group of people and sauntered down the deck. Several sailors leered at her buttocks through the clinging sheath of her dress.

Near the main mast Amélie's father motioned for her to join him. She waved, but ignored the summons. He mustn't treat her as a child. She left the rail, and walked in the opposite direction. The planks heaved like a living thing beneath her and she adjusted her gait.

The ship drew nearer, the sea splattering against her hull. A cleft in the rock revealed the port of Jamestown—whitewashed houses with red roofs, a church steeple, and a large building with bastions resembling a castle. To her relief, a few palm trees peeked out near the wharf.

Two towering cliffs topped with cannons crowded in a *V* formation on both sides of the town, as if the island cracked open like a crusty walnut. Watchtowers, sentry boxes, and fluttering Union Jacks bordered the skyline, all symbolizing a fortress on the underbelly of the world.

A loud boom of cannons resounded from one of the peaks, announcing the ship's arrival.

Bumped by a sailor who ran by, Amélie stumbled over a coil of rope and squeezed against the rail. A French officer pulled off his hat and bowed. She whirled about.

The emperor stepped out onto the deck. A few people scattered to give him an unobstructed view. More of the French swept off hats and all chatter ceased. Amélie dropped into a curtsy as her emperor raised his field glasses and stared in silence.

Northumberland's officers kept their hats in place. "Take notice, men. Let's see how General Buonaparte fares in this, his *last* campaign," one lieutenant said in overloud French.

Amélie cringed. Nothing in her sovereign's expression revealed what he might have felt in his heart. His face, rounded in middle age, shone pale as ivory. His jaw was still determined as in the paintings she'd seen of him in the midst of battle. Flanked by his generals in their high-collared blue tunics with gold braid, his attire remained simple. The emperor wore a long gray coat over a plain uniform, yet his signature cocked hat distinguished him anywhere.

Napoleon lowered the glasses and scanned with his piercing gaze over the ship's company. Then, with his officers, he turned and went below.

Amélie rubbed goose bumps from her arms. With no experience, and being a woman, she wondered—would Napoleon appreciate her acumen now that they shared such close quarters or would he scorn her efforts? She must prove herself in some capacity as an integral part of her emperor's staff. Amélie breathed her sigh into the wind.

* * * *

Napoleon entered his cabin below the quarterdeck, passing the cots in the after-cabin where his officers slept crowded together amongst the smell of dirty feet. The two generals who accompanied him bowed and he dismissed them. He dropped his field glasses on top of his trunk. "The island is not a pretty place. I would have done better to stay in Egypt."

"I agree with you, Sire." Saint-Denis, who followed behind, took Napoleon's coat and hung it on a peg. The valet picked up the field glasses and polished the lenses with a cloth. "You taught me well about your glory days in Egypt."

"Yes, yes, and I nicknamed you 'Ali,' to replace that Mameluke." These memories from sixteen years before gave Napoleon a moment of pleasure. In Egypt he'd thrived as the assured young general, intent on broadening French influence in the Orient, though he'd failed in that enterprise. "My glory came later." Warmth trickled through him when he pictured his return to Paris and the coup that thrust him in control of France. Such ascendancy from nowhere had threatened the established monarchs. He stared around the bleak little cabin and grumbled, "Ah, my boy, I brought them to their knees in battle. Now they triumph in their revenge."

Napoleon had tensed on deck when that English officer tried to insult him by lowering his status to a mere army officer, along with the Corsican pronunciation of his name.

He massaged his pinched neck and sighed. The weight that tormented him bore down harder. He'd hoped to be received as an honored guest by the British, but instead they humiliated him into the position of captive and forced him out here. He fought to remain in good humor—yet seeing the object of exile before him, could he rally enough inner strength?

The incessant bilge pumps slogged below, rattling the deck beneath his feet. The brackish stink thickened the air and he wrinkled his sensitive nose. Napoleon pressed on his stomach, thinking of all the seasickness he'd suffered. "I'll be relieved to leave this ship at any rate. Hand me the Saint Helena map."

Saint-Denis retrieved it from atop several papers shoved in a valise. He set out the *bonbonniére* containing licorice, Napoleon's remedy for indigestion. "I thought you might need this as well, Sire."

"No, not yet, you rascal. It's folly to despair...this soon." Napoleon appreciated his second-valet's droll humor. It often soothed his melancholy.

In the light from his cabin's one porthole, he ran his fingers over the sketch, the rough edges of an island that looked like a forgotten blot of ink floating in water.

Napoleon eased into his armchair with a grunt. He brushed his fingers over the Legion of Honor on his breast, the medal he'd created to encourage excellence among his men. Such baubles did him little good now. Would his wife and child care if they ever saw him again? Josephine might have. He sighed at his grief over that good woman's passing—the intense love of his youth.

With the map crumpled in his fingers, Napoleon resisted the urge to rip it in half. He looked up at the gangly young man who attended him. "Well, Ali, you see where miscalculation has landed us? Write this down for posterity: 'We've arrived, October 14, 1815.' Let's hope this isn't my last campaign. I must bestir myself to fresh ideas."

* * * *

The skin on the back of Amélie's neck prickled with the rattle and squeak of the chains as the *Northumberland* dropped anchor. From their wood-framed, canvas cabin, below the ship's gun decks, she heard the final splash into the sea.

"Admiral Cockburn will take over Saint Helena's administration now that we're here," François Perrault said. "The island's governor is being brought on board to confer with him."

"The admiral is too arrogant. The English are cruel to refuse His Majesty's title." She snatched the covers across her bed and folded clothes stiff with salt. The denial of her emperor added to the slipping of *her* importance in these events.

"There's a lot of bitterness toward a man who fought their country all these years." Perrault wrapped up his cookware and placed it in his trunk. Her father glanced over at her and combed a hand through his thatch of gray hair. "Are you sorry you wanted to come with me? You might have been happier staying in Lyon."

"*Mais non*, Papa. I'm pleased to accompany you. I'll manage fine." Amélie kept her voice light, uncomfortable explaining her desires to her father. Selfish enough to use their relationship as an excuse to be here, she didn't think he'd understand her wish to move beyond the dreary life under the Bourbon restoration.

Her father bustled about the tiny space, meticulous in his arranging, and it saddened her that he looked frail, so much older. He might need her after their two years apart. She'd joined the entourage at the last minute at Malmaison, before the chaotic trek to the sea eleven days after the battle of Waterloo.

Their door flap pushed open. "They're saying we can't leave the ship yet. *Je m'inquiéte.*" Philippe Gascon mopped his brow and flabby cheeks with a handkerchief. The pastry chef gave one of his dismal moans. "I barely survived the crossing, and now my poor head is splitting."

"Then we'll just have to wait, my friend." Perrault nodded, sat on his trunk and retrieved his book by Condorcet as if to discourage Chef Gascon from lingering. Amélie had been reading *The Odyssey*, which seemed painfully relevant. She coughed and waved away smoke from the sputtering lantern. The light stretched their shadows along the canvas walls.

Amélie slipped from the flimsy chamber as the two men continued to talk. She climbed the ladder to topside and breathed in the fresh air that washed away the stink of perspiration and tar below decks. Soldiers tramped by her to load into skiffs as the *Northumberland* grunted at her moorings. Nearly a thousand men, spread over several ships, had been deployed to guard the infamous captive. Next, the tall, haughty admiral—England's officer in charge of Napoleon—boated ashore with a man she assumed was the governor.

"The admiral leaves to scout for a suitable residence for us." A voice from behind made Amélie look over her shoulder. Louis Marchand, Napoleon's chief valet, walked up to the rail beside her. His soft-featured face and serious brown eyes wore a gentle expression. "Here's our new home. Sorry it's no enchanted land. You'll have ample time to read."

She wanted more than reading. Like the men, she'd enjoy discussing literature, exploits on battlefields, and exotic places with their emperor. "His Majesty should never have trusted that English captain who insisted he'd be received with kindness if he surrendered to the British."

"You're right, we were fooled by the enemy, but His Majesty didn't want to risk running the blockade." Marchand spoke with a quiet grace.

"He used to take risks. We might be in America by now." Amélie danced her fingers along the dipping and rising rail, then turned her back on the people craning their necks on shore. Numerous inhabitants had swarmed like locusts to the wharf the minute their vessel entered the roadstead. "Does His Majesty anticipate he'll be released from here, or taken someplace...more accessible?"

"I believe he does. The emperor wrote in protest to England's prince, but received no reply. Time will tell what we must do next."

The rigging and ship's fabric creaked around them. Amélie shifted with the slight roll of the deck and appreciated the concern on the valet's face for his master's plight. She coveted his closeness with their emperor.

"This is a terrible fall. Our emperor will have to rely on people he never did before." She ran her ragged thumbnail along her tongue and compared their sovereign, this voyage, to the trials of Odysseus. Was she a rope-thin Calypso? Amélie faced the island with a frown. They'd come to the end of the wine-dark sea. Did opportunities or demons await?

* * * *

At sunset, three days later, Amélie noticed the onshore crowd remained undaunted, holding up lanterns winking in the twilight. The French grumbled and sighed as they crawled down into the skiffs. Oars dipped into water and soldiers rowed the boats ashore. Amélie rocked in her little boat beside her father, fishy-smelling broth sloshing around them, and tried not to stare at the islanders' eager faces.

During their anchorage in Plymouth Sound, hundreds of people in boats had paddled toward their ship to surround it, calling out *Bonaparte*. England's Parliament, however, decided Napoleon's presence weakened Louis XVIII's monarchy and the Prince Regent denied their request for asylum. Now the emperor didn't wish to be gawked at, and they skulked in shadows onto an island that stank as mildewed as the warship they left.

At the slime-covered landing stairs, Amélie grabbed the hand rope to steady herself and a soldier hauled her up. She tottered beside her father along the tiny quay, thankful to be on a surface that didn't jounce. A short street paralleled the wharf, separated from it by a rampart and moat spanned by a drawbridge. Her heartbeat trebling, she entered a fortress to be swallowed up.

A line of armed soldiers held the crowd of onlookers at bay. The Imperial Court passed through first, their progress noted by gasps and whispered comments. Amélie's head reeled as she stared at the soldier's rigid backs, their rifles with bayonets thrust high in the air.

By the flickering light of torches, the colonial town looked shabby, huddled on its main street. Amélie forced her head erect and matched her father's pace, squishing along in shoes that never dried since the voyage began. She clenched her hands on her elbows and mused that freedom might be more important than grand adventures.

Soldiers ushered their solemn group past a church and into a large white building at the beginning of the street. A British officer scrutinized them with a sneer once they assembled inside. "Unpack, make yourselves, *harrumph*, at home. You may be in this boarding house for a few months. The permanent quarters, chosen by the honorable Admiral Cockburn, need extensive renovations. We've only a few people to spare with those skills."

The soldiers started to shuffle baggage and people into various rooms.

"A few months? It's as I feared, nothing will go well for us here." Gascon shook his lumpy head, his cheeks and jowls quivering like an undercooked soufflé.

"It could be worse. They almost made us stay aboard the ship." Perrault clasped his shoulder.

"Only dead at the bottom of the ocean is worse than this." Madame Cloubert, Clarice's mother, rushed past them in a flurry of arms like twigs on a spindly tree. "Where is that loafing husband of mine?"

Amélie and Perrault were shown to one chamber with two narrow beds. She glanced around the dingy room. Far too old to continue sharing with her father, she moved around trying not to fall over him. Her roiling innards might settle in a room that no longer swayed, though her legs wobbled as if she still maneuvered the ship. "Perhaps we can ask for a screen to put between the beds. I hope they've found us something decent for our regular household."

"Let's be confident they did, *ma petite*." Perrault smiled in his fleeting way. His bold features and bronze complexion made him look like he'd weathered years behind a plow instead of a stove. He hefted his trunk into a corner.

Her father's smile used to reassure her, but sadness lingered beneath it. Always sparing with his emotions, he acted more taciturn since her mother's death. Sent from Paris to Lyon after that, Amélie hadn't seen that much of him. Her two older brothers had their own lives and families in France. Here she was all he had left, but he needed to treat her as a woman, not his little girl. Restless inside, she burst out at the seams like a changing creature—a caterpillar rustling in its cocoon.

Amélie opened her small trunk and checked her books for damage, the scent of the leather and paper soothing. She unwrapped and took out the miniature she always carried of her mother: a lovely and sweet presence flattened in paint. Sometimes Amélie wanted to ask her father if *Maman* had always been beautiful, never an awkward moment, but to her regret, neither of them spoke of her anymore.

She ran a finger over her mother's face and tucked the painting back. "What purpose does the East India Company use this island for, besides supplying ships, so far away from anything?"

"Ships traveling to and from the Orient stop here to replenish, yes. They drop off their ill, business like that." Perrault opened his portmanteau near the sagging bed closest to the wall. He pulled out a shirt and smoothed down the wrinkles. At forty-eight her father looked like he'd shrunk below his average height, or had she grown that much taller?

Amélie removed a few items from her trunk. Her bodice chafed under her arms and she turned away to scratch. "It will be a relief to wash our clothes in fresh water and rinse away the itchy salt." Braced against the mattress edge, she slipped off a shoe and rubbed her foot through her damp stocking. "I suppose we have to look for anything to be thankful for."

He stared up, his gray eyes intent. "I didn't expect the island to be like this... for your sake."

"I'm prepared for any hardship." She tried a comforting smile to mask her qualms. Her fears that she'd sink under the privation and fall mired into the background, but if she never tried, how else could she test her strength?

A child screamed in the hallway. Amélie stepped out to see a frantic mother chase after, scolding him. From behind closed doors flowed strident and arguing voices. A woman wept.

Bumping noises on the outside wall drew her to a window. Heads bobbed behind the panes, people shoving one another from the yard to peek in. All the windows had cheeks and noses, mists of hot breath, pressed against the glass.

"*Ecoutez*, we won't stand for it. These fools must be cleared away from the building immediately." The Count de Montholon, one of Napoleon's courtiers, clipped down the hall in his shiny boots. The medium-sized man cut a sleek figure in his tailored blue coat with diagonal bars and gold sash piped in blue. Amélie pictured him as something slippery, gliding off a rock into the sea. "What kind of lawless establishment are they running here?"

Clarice strutted over and waved toward the windows. "Such idiots, gawping out there, spying on us."

"They think we're animals in a zoo," Amélie said. In a crack of wood, someone pried open a nearby window sash. She rushed forward and slammed it back down, then met her reflection. Her large brown eyes stared back, wary and distorted in the uneven pane.

"These excitement-starved natives want a view of His Majesty," Saint-Denis said in amused exasperation when he strolled up pulling one of the imperial trunks. "We've hung cloaks over the curtains to shield the emperor's chamber. Marchand and I will sleep outside his door, to be on guard through the night."

"You're very brave." Clarice flashed him a smile, which he appeared to ignore.

"Too bad the islanders knew we were coming," Amélie said. One of the admiral's flotilla had arrived five days before the *Northumberland*.

"As forever as it takes for news to reach them out here," Saint-Denis snorted, "I'm sure they were quite shocked to learn of His Majesty's leaving Elba, Waterloo, and now..."

The boarding house owner hurried past them with the count talking in his ear and Madame Cloubert fast on their heels. The head chambermaid halted in front of the two girls and valet, her angular face scrunched up like a peach pit. "That island innkeeper insists his place is clean. Check your beds with care tonight. Bugs crawled all over mine. Must we settle for any scrap from the British? Clarice, help me find your father."

"Oh, *Maman*, Papa probably doesn't want to be found," Clarice said in a sullen voice as she traipsed after her mother.

"Madame Cloubert and Clarice always insist on sharing their opinions." Amélie swallowed a laugh. "Neither dares grumble loud enough for the emperor to hear though. Oh—"

Napoleon strode down the passage with his grand marshal, Count Bertrand.

Saint-Denis set down the trunk and gestured for Amélie to move back to the wall. He slipped beside her, bowed, and lowered his eyes. She still managed a peek, one of many.

Her emperor's reddish-brown hair looked silky above his short neck and broad shoulders. He wore his green jacket with scarlet collar and cuffs of a colonel of the Chasseurs of the Guard, his medals glinting in candlelight from the wall sconces. His belly protruding over his breeches altered him from the gaunt young officer who wrested France from the Directors. Napoleon's portrait as First Consul, hanging in their Paris cottage, had shown a hawk-like visage with penetrating eyes.

Amélie glanced down at her shapeless body in the high-waisted Greek-style chemise, popularized by former Empress Josephine. People seldom controlled the packages they came wrapped in.

Her desire to rise in importance possessed her. She stepped forward, intending to catch the emperor's eye. Saint-Denis grabbed her arm and jerked her back. Count Bertrand flicked them a surprised glance as he and Napoleon continued past. The two men disappeared around the corner.

"You can't approach His Majesty like that. You know it's forbidden," the valet whispered with a wry smile. "I told you that on the ship. Now try to behave yourself."

Amélie wriggled from Saint-Denis' grasp. She poked her sharp shoulder blades into the wall behind her and ran her hands along her arms. If she resembled a moth more than a butterfly, a moth could thrust out its wings and soar just as high.

Chapter Two

A person who has lost the room in which he was born, the garden where he played as a child, the house of his forebears, such a person has no fatherland—N.B.

Napoleon glanced around the little pavilion built in the Hindu style and regretted his time had come. After inspecting his future home to the east, the day after they arrived on the island, he'd been escorted past this bucolic setting. He'd requested to stay here on this businessman's country property so he wouldn't have to return to the town's prying eyes. The occupants, William Balcombe and family, had proved most kind and accommodating. They'd treated him with unfailing respect in these last two months at The Briars.

Tropical flowers scented the air. The children played on the lawn past the garden, their laughter so sweet. This respite, almost like a bizarre masked ball—dictating to his chamberlain among the camellias, teasing with the young ones—was over.

Napoleon ran a comb through his hair and groaned at his image in the mirror Marchand held up. An image that once struck fear into his enemies. Now soldiers waited outside for him to emerge, to travel under guard and take up residence surrounded by British soldiers like a prisoner of war. How had he allowed events to progress so badly? After escaping Elba and entering Paris without firing a shot, he'd sent out messengers requesting peace, but the nations allied against him hadn't believed him. The ruling regimes never trusted a *parvenu* who dared to make himself the most powerful man in Europe. Perhaps he'd been a little too belligerent and deceitful in his dealings with them, though he'd hate to admit *that* to anyone.

The most heinous of all was Austria refusing him his wife and sweet, chubby-faced little son, so smart for three. No, the boy was now four. A year since he'd seen him! Napoleon clenched his jaw, then peered out the pavilion window. Admiral Cockburn sat astride his horse several yards away, an impatient look on his long face. Napoleon smiled. He'd kept him waiting on purpose, to show he was still the emperor and no one dictated his actions.

He dipped his fingers in his pocket, pulled out several gold coins sticky with damp, and handed them to Marchand. "Give these to that elderly slave who has tended the garden here so well." Napoleon donned his jacket, his uniform crisp and clean, medals shining, and tried to generate the old gusto into his words. "Let's blind that English buffoon with pomp. I will extend my thanks to these generous people who took me in, and we'll be off to explore new territories."

* * * *

Two red-coated officers blocked Amélie's passage on the front stoop of the boarding house. "Ready for your journey?" one spouted in French. He winked at the other. "These frogs are so proud of their Boney. Proud of his endless wars and battlefield butchery. He trampled France and everyone else, but Wellington showed him."

"*C'est odieux*, you English should be more gracious in victory." Amélie gritted her teeth and nudged past him, the humid air thick in her lungs. She banged her small trunk down each step, refusing their peevish offer of help. Relieved to be out of the crowded dwelling, she was eager for the change that would bring her together again with the emperor.

Soldiers led up oxen pulling carts. Several island inhabitants stared and murmured from across the street. A sailor stood in front of a sleazy café and belched. Jamestown's dilapidated wooden buildings sagged in a heat that leached into her skin.

Amélie found it bizarre that this was the *only* town on Saint Helena, an island so small it stretched a mere seven English miles north to south, and ten east to west.

Count Henri-Gratien Bertrand, a spare man in his early forties, assisted his two children into a cart. He looked wilted in his dark blue tunic, a red silk sash with gold fringe tied around his waist. His tall blond wife stood off to the side, a sulk on her face. When he tried to hand her in, she shook off his grasp.

"Now we'll stagnate here. We could have stayed in England, but you insist on following *him* wherever he goes." The countess flounced herself into the cart. Bertrand mounted a horse, his round shoulders drooping more, and followed his family.

Saint-Denis chuckled as he lifted Amélie's portmanteau into a cart. "Countess Bertrand screamed about coming on this journey. Remember when she tried to throw herself out a porthole?" The young man's slick black hair and thick-lashed eyes gave him an exotic look—someone hiding secrets filled with mischief. "The emperor said she didn't try hard enough."

"I feel no sympathy for the countess." Amélie had watched the woman chase after an official in Plymouth, begging him to tell her husband he needn't go to Saint Helena with Napoleon. "I'm glad Count Bertrand is a loyal officer for His Majesty."

Charles-Tristan de Montholon sauntered out escorting his wife, who brimmed with a smile. The Countess de Montholon waved a fan over her plump chest, prominent in the *décolleté* of her silk gown, as she waited for their cart to be brought around. "Do hurry, Charles, I'm anxious to see His Majesty. He must have been so lonely without my, *our* company." The countess pursed her rouged lips and ignored the small boy fidgeting beside her as if he wasn't her own son.

"I'm surprised the Montholons joined this little troupe of ours," Saint-Denis said after the count's cart rattled off. "It seems odd when more loyal men were sent away."

"Madame Montholon is certainly overly familiar with His Majesty. I don't know how he derives any pleasure listening to her inane chatter." Amélie watched them on the ship, but wished she hadn't revealed her envy. "Couldn't a well-read woman be more to his liking?"

"Don't be naïve." Ali snickered. "Our emperor prefers docile females who please him."

"I'm not naïve." Or was she? She expelled her breath. "He hasn't met the one who may change his mind."

"Attention!" An English lieutenant stood on the boarding house porch and snapped out a long sheet of paper. "This decree is from His Royal Majesty, already read to your betters. You are all prisoners of the British Crown. You will not aid in any way the escape of the prisoner, General Buonaparte, under threat of death."

"Death?" Amélie shoved her portmanteau under the cart seat. The English carried their vindictiveness to extremes, but she'd never thought her life was in danger.

"Foreign ships will be fired upon if they approach the island," the lieutenant read on. "Everyone must obey nightly curfews, and if out beyond it they'll be severely punished."

"*Merde!*" Clarice tramped toward the carts, her face flushed. She swept damp auburn hair from her cheeks. "I told you they want us to die here."

The British soldiers smirked at each other and shook their heads.

"Be silent, girl. Don't upset your father." Madame Cloubert butted up next to her daughter and glowered at the soldiers. "If I'd known this I wouldn't have come."

"Please, Madame. Haven't we all sacrificed our freedom for the emperor?" Amélie's own misgivings prickled inside her, but she strained to sound practical. Her father approached.

"*Ma petite*, it isn't polite to question your elders," he whispered when he handed her into their cart. "Besides, in Madame Cloubert's case, it never does any good."

"We will see how long we're forced to languish here." Madame Cloubert knifed her bony frame into a cart, next to her portly husband who sat dormant like a lump of cheese. "*Allons-y*, what are we waiting for?"

"Isn't just breathing irritating to you?" Gascon climbed into the Perrault's cart. He wiped his brow with a soggy handkerchief. "Your squawking voice grates in my ears."

"Oh, save your whining, Philippe." The head chambermaid snarled her thin lips. "Everyone knows you take more interest in your pretend ills than your cuisine."

Amélie settled herself on the hard bench, anxious to leave, and weary of everyone's complaining. They'd arrived and must find a way to manage.

The caravan of settlers rambled through the town crammed in a fold of this narrow valley. They passed brown women and children in colored rags, sitting on the steps of whitewashed stone houses with shingled roofs or boards covered in dirt. A thick vapor of clouds floated above, forming a gray ceiling impaled on craggy peaks. They turned to the left for Rupert's Hill, one of the steep volcanic slopes pressing in on both sides of Jamestown. A path carved into the black rock zigzagged upward with little room for mistakes. Most of the French groaned in unison when they approached. One of the chambermaids burst into tears.

A waterfall cascading down the extreme south end of the valley caught Amélie's attention with a wisp of cool air. The fall's diverted water flowed into a stone drain and out into reservoirs on the wharf to water incoming ships.

She then stared up at the jagged rock face before her, her pulse thrumming—another challenge.

"They call this Side Path," Perrault said when they began their ascent. Chef Gascon sneezed and groaned. "Which sounds far too gentle for such a route."

"Barbaric, *affreux*! Why didn't we stay on Elba? We could have found other positions." Madame Cloubert poked her husband's shoulder as their cart squeaked along in front of the Perraults. The narrow path had only a small lip of rock to keep them on track.

Amélie gripped the cart seat. Clarice sat stiff in her cart, eyes squeezed shut, clutching her father's arm as they jostled to the top.

Leaving the cliff, they entered a hilly region of aloe and pomegranate. Dwarf jellico and samphire, wild among tree fern thickets, crowded both sides of the road as if battling to reclaim it.

Amélie breathed in the sweet perfume and peppery smell and her spirits lifted. "Saint Helena is nice here. It may not be so unpleasant for us."

Her father patted her hand. "I'm sorry for bringing you. There must be a way for me to send you home to France."

"No, Papa. Don't do that." She shifted and stared at him. How could she make him understand she was capable of deciding? "I insist on staying."

The soldiers stopped at a long drive, shaded by banyan trees, leading to a low white house with a Hindu pavilion several yards to the right. African snowdrops and camellias blossomed in the yard and along the house's walls. A sign on the gatepost read The Briars. Here Napoleon, his chief valet, and his chamberlain awaited them, along with the admiral and several soldiers.

Napoleon walked over and hugged a girl of about fifteen who stood in the yard. A radiant smile transformed his face and Amélie's breath caught in her throat. She felt a twinge of jealousy. He was *her* emperor, this man she'd watched from afar since a small child, bringing grandeur to her country. Until, as many insisted, he'd ruined it all with too much ambition.

She stiffened, aware that an intelligent woman didn't allow emotion to rule her.

The emperor mounted his horse and rode between the admiral and Count Bertrand. People gathered along the road to watch him pass. Napoleon carried his head high, features now stern. Several Chinese laborers, jabbering in their strange tongue, dragged the carts with the emperor's possessions.

The caravan rambled farther east and the terrain turned mountainous, the vegetation disappearing. The road snaked around the island's high narrow backbone of hills and knolls. A gray volcanic powder churned in a rising wind that whipped around their carts. Scattered gum trees with whorled trunks bent over and trembled in its wake, their sparse foliage blown inside out like broken umbrellas.

Amélie sneezed in the dust and snatched her straw hat before it blew off. She tied its ribbon snug over her ears to soften the wind's keening—a Siren's lament.

A colonial dwelling sat at a curve in the road that led over a narrow track between two steep valleys. The house and track were called Hutt's Gate, one of the soldiers said. Their procession circled a gorge then rolled onto a desolate, slightly undulating plain.

"This area is named Deadwood," Perrault said. Amélie didn't care for that ominous description. She said nothing, unwilling to give her father another reason to send her home.

Oxen and carts trundled across the plain and approached a yellow wood and stucco structure with a gray slate roof called Longwood house. Surrounded by a low stone wall, broken in spots like missing teeth, the place looked grim. The entire area appeared ravaged by the elements.

A group of mustered soldiers beat out a drum salute. The emperor's black pony reared back, refusing to enter the gate of their new domicile.

Amélie chewed on her thumbnail, a habit she struggled to break.

Soldiers directed the Perraults to the rear of the dwelling. A wooden outbuilding—beaten gray and scarred by weather—stood in a courtyard directly behind the main house, not three feet from the kitchen. Amélie opened a door that squeaked on rusted hinges and peered in at their new home.

"We are better off here," her father confided from over her shoulder. "Marchand said the other servants will be forced to inhabit an attic in the main house."

She turned from the dim passage, which separated two tiny chambers and a rank privy. A spider busily spun a web from the splintered ceiling. "*Tres fortune*, if we scrub it up." Part of her wished for quarters in the main house, to be at the center, instead of always to the side. She stepped farther in, away from her father in case he sensed her disappointment. "Of course, I'll take the smaller room on the left." This chamber resembled a drab closet, but would be hers alone.

After unpacking, Amélie entered the adjacent kitchen and found her father and Chef Gascon already there.

"There's no space for us to do anything properly." Gascon moaned as he plopped his array of cookware and pastry utensils down on the rough-hewn table. He appraised them with his droopy hound-dog eyes. "How can we prepare His Majesty's cuisine under these conditions?"

The kitchen appeared cramped and primitive for their extensive household. The cupboards sagged and the walls had rotten spots like a bad apple. The stench of mildew clung to every surface. Amélie opened the one window. "Some paint, a vinegar scrub should help."

"We'll just have to learn to create miracles." Perrault inspected a severe crack in the stove. He turned to them, his smile placating, if withered at the edges.

"There's a small pantry here." She opened the door of a cabinet against the kitchen's back wall. She started at seeing the shelves, sticky with remnants of flour and sugar, crawling with hordes of ants. Several crept up her arm and she jerked back. The door she held broke off and fell on the dirt floor with a thump. "A sad, neglected place, it requires our care."

* * * *

Amélie left her outbuilding and the courtyard and walked away from the main house. Past the stables, several hundred yards off, a sentry tower loomed in full view. Closer in on the plain, soldiers attempted to pitch tents that flapped in the gale. The wind pulled at her hair as she looked at the jagged cliffs half encircling the plain. The boundless ocean thrashed to the east, stretching to the sky, blending like a bowl of blue.

This part of the island did have a stark beauty. Then the sunlight vanished as thick clouds carpeted the sky. The air turned chill and Amélie shivered, unable to see any distance in front of her through the sudden mist. She rubbed her arms, and hurried back and across the courtyard.

The banging noise of hammers from the ship's carpenters still working on one of the wings followed her through Longwood's back door. The stink of mold mixed with fresh paint filled her nostrils. She passed from one chamber into a dining room where several servants rushed by carrying boxes, arguing over what went where.

A door to the left in the dining room opened. The chamberlain, the Count de Las Cases, pattered past her. Amélie stretched to peek through the open door just as Napoleon strode out. She stepped back and bumped a sideboard, almost toppling a silver candlestick.

"The English are in such a hurry to surround me with guards, they've rushed us in here. These accommodations are not satisfactory. I can't stomach the smell of paint." Napoleon rubbed his nose. "Then Bertrand's self-seeking wife thinks she's too grand to share my abode. Where did they go? Remind me?"

"Hutt's Gate, Sire. Very disloyal of them both, I must say." The diminutive count straightened the medals on his French fleet captain's uniform. He bobbed his head and pointy nose like a wood-boring bird. "They should be honored to be here with you, as I am."

Napoleon paced the room in quick steps. Anxious to draw attention, Amélie knocked the sideboard with her hip. The candlestick plunked onto the floor. She smiled, but only Las Cases glanced in her direction. He waved her away with fluttering fingers.

"Ah, but we must show the British we are above such petty annoyances." Napoleon slowed, hands clasped behind his back, his expression thoughtful. "Cockburn will find no reason to belittle me for the short time I'll remain here." He reentered his chamber and shut the door.

"Above petty annoyances, yes indeed," the little count mumbled before flitting from the dining room.

Amélie sighed after the emperor's closed door. She might have been a flyspeck on the wall as far as Napoleon was concerned. She picked up the candlestick. How did one get noticed in this hierarchy and still follow protocol?

She squeezed by a scratched table and passed into the drawing room. A black stone chimneypiece gave this chamber a touch of elegance. She entered the front hall, the *salon de reception*, a spacious room painted green.

Amélie's stomach tangled in knots over this decrepit abode and furniture that looked dragged from a trash heap. Longwood's walls resembled withered veneer, a thin protection from the gathering soldiers. The wind shook the house on all sides of her, as if giant hands struggled to twist it from its foundations.

"Enjoying our new palace, are you?" Clarice tramped into the room scowling, her arms full of linens. "How nice you can stand around doing nothing. *Peste*, I'm sure I can find something to busy you."

"You have no authority over me. I will busy myself where I please." Amélie turned and walked through the house and outside to her quarters. To have authority over something in her life, even if just Clarice's demands, gave her a moment of triumph.

She inspected her room once more—a space she could barely turn around in between the bed and scarred chest of drawers. In Lyon she'd shared a room with her young niece. Here she was happy to have her own space like in Paris. Amélie picked up the lace doily from atop the chest and held it to her cheek, remembering her mother's soft kisses there.

Madame Perrault had been a skilled lace maker. Her Italian mother's sought after creations helped to finance the children's schooling. To Amélie's benefit, her father championed education, even for girls. She had excelled in the Paris school, fulfilling her father's confidence in her, but after her mother's sudden death, he'd sent her to live with her brother in Lyon. Between helping with domestic duties and longing to be back in Paris, she'd kept her mind sharp with extensive reading.

She replaced the doily and ran her hands over the books she'd stacked on her bed, caressing the tooled leather. Books opened up the world, something a person like Clarice would never understand.

She picked up the herb book she'd brought. Plants might transform the bare ground around them. Her father had requested some seedlings while still in Jamestown.

A red-spotted insect with multiple legs crawling near one book caught her attention. Amélie snatched up a handkerchief and nudged it off the bed. Her room filled with a foul odor that burned her eyes. She held her nose and hurried back outside and almost into the silk skirt of the Countess de Montholon.

"Oh, Charles, this place is worse than I thought." The countess, on the arm of her husband, brushed past Amélie as if she were a fence post. The woman's frown switched to a smile. With her delicate features marred by over-rouged lips, she looked like a marble bust slathered across the mouth with red paint. "How long do we have to stay here? Not that I mind…too much, but you refuse to tell me how dire your money situation is. Is that why we left France?"

"Be patient, *mon ange*. This is all a political necessity. You wouldn't understand." Montholon stroked her cheek, but his gaze reprimanded. "Our stay depends on how long it takes me to do what I must. Hopefully, no one will get in my way."

Amélie stared after them as they entered the main house. The stench from her room seemed to trail behind these so-called aristocrats.

Chapter Three

Their [women] passion must not be awakened, nor must vanity, the most active passion of the sex, be aroused—N.B.

Napoleon mounted his horse. He couldn't wait to leave the staleness of his cramped quarters where the walls pressed in on him. Cockburn promised he could ride unmolested, without escort, the few miles around the property. Imagine, the once master of Europe having to be subjugated by such a man, and limited to this paltry area. He thought briefly of the crowds who had shouted *"Vive l'Empereur!"* as he traveled from Paris to Rochefort after his final abdication—though such memories lost their power to cheer him. "Las Cases, we will ride as if we are on the fields of France," he said to his companion.

"Of course, Sire. We will enjoy our reconnaissance like good soldiers." The count held tight to the pommel, his feet barely reaching the stirrups. "I'm privileged just to ride in your shadow. Like the Colossus of Rhodes, you cast your shadow over the world. Now you're a spirit on the Elysian Fields."

Napoleon chuckled to himself, for Las Cases reined in his pen far more than a horse. He appreciated the man's culture, but knew he'd joined him just to write of his life. "We will live in the past," Napoleon had said to comfort himself when still at The Briars. The little count also spoke fluent English and struggled to teach him that language, which should prove useful.

The emperor allowed Hope his head and galloped over the marled earth. The bleak plain spread between the sea and craggy mountains that thrust up like prison bars—his new empire.

Slowing his black charger, Napoleon glared up at the colored flags that snapped around a high wire suspended from the observation tower. Each morning the soldiers hoisted a flag from Alarm House to communicate the current "condition" of their prisoner to the admiral on the other side of the island. He couldn't recall what some of the colors meant, except the white flag indicated "He is well" and the blue "He has escaped."

Napoleon raised his head and flexed back his shoulders to shed off these insults.

With Las Cases he rode past the Deadwood Camp, a camp thrown together in full view of their residence the minute the French took possession of Longwood. A group of soldiers scrambled from their tents and ran toward them. Napoleon grimaced. Over what infraction would he be harassed?

The soldiers lined up and saluted him. Napoleon filled with pleasure. He smiled and tipped his hat. "Ah, if I had but a few minutes with these troops, they would know how to treat me. They should respect Europe's greatest soldier."

"They should indeed, Sire." Las Cases preened in the saddle.

Hope stumbled near the ravine that separated the camp from Longwood. Red mud scattered from the stallion's hooves and Napoleon jostled in the saddle. He grabbed the pommel and jammed his feet in the stirrups, nearly losing his balance. He righted himself and hoped none of the soldiers took heed. He'd never sat securely on horseback, that's why on campaign he'd preferred to travel in the coach he designed himself. Now, after gaining so much weight, riding proved more unwieldy.

"The English waste their time on these useless precautions," Napoleon blurted to the little count, aware he had to convince himself as well. "France will soon demand my freedom. That Bourbon *ganache* who came in the baggage of the allies will sour them again. The French are fickle. They need me."

"Sire, if the French, fickle as we are—and there *are* the British to contend with—take too long to appreciate you...perhaps you should consider other options."

Napoleon pressed his thighs against Hope's flanks, a brief warmth. Did the little count broach the impossible? "What are you saying, *mon ami*?"

"In Jamestown I happened to have met an Irish merchant captain." Las Cases twitched his lips. "He might be interested in aiding you, if you pardon me, in leaving the island."

* * * *

Her gardening book propped up, Amélie leafed through the pages. Rain pelted the kitchen window, splattering red slime over the pane. A shutter banged against the wall on a broken hinge. She glanced out at the ooze in the courtyard, rethinking her wish to convert this place into a paradise.

"This damp is killing me." Chef Gascon groaned as he rubbed his shoulder. He tossed his pastry tools into a bowl of water and swished them around. "The Trade Winds never stop."

Amélie massaged her own aching shoulder. They'd been in residence five days. She pulled her moist sleeve from her arm and turned to her father. "When I plant the herbs and spices in the courtyard, it might keep the earth from sliding away."

"It will be a useful effort and keep you occupied." Perrault half smiled and waved aside the smoke from the oven, along with the smell of eggs from breakfast.

"Maintain a close watch on your daughter," Gascon said between coughs. "This won't be a good environment. Too many soldiers. My daughters...my wife refused to come with me here. I won't see them grow up. My wife still blames His Majesty because our son...died at Waterloo."

Amélie closed her book. Was Chef Gascon bitter as well over his loss? She found his other comment ironic. From what others teased, she doubted anyone would take advantage of her skinny charms and her father shouldn't concern himself with such things.

The rain stopped as abruptly as it started. She opened a window and ants crawled in. After the wind snatched out the billowing smoke the air smelled clean. Over at the wall, a soldier trudged by, rife on his shoulder. These patrolling sentries sprouted like crimson weeds at close intervals around Longwood's grounds.

"I'm going to rest my head. I don't know how long I'll last here." Chef Gascon lumbered from the kitchen, squelching across the mud.

"I suppose I'll have to do the baking if Philippe stays abed." Perrault untied his apron and hung it on a wall peg.

"I can bake, Papa. I helped Suzanne in the kitchen many times." Amélie spoke of her sister-in-law in Lyon. Her father looked tired and she intended to be useful to him. Each task might be a step up to something better.

"You should be proficient in cooking. His Majesty must receive the best meals we can offer." Her father always took pride in his position as the emperor's chef. "I'll check the butler's pantry for what provisions we have. The supply shipment is long overdue. We're low on flour."

Perrault left the kitchen. Amélie mixed a solution of vinegar and water, dipped in a cloth, and swiped down the greasy stove. The sharp vinegar masked the stink of mildew.

She wrung out the cloth and draped it over a chair. She picked up her seedlings, provided by the Englishman, Mr. William Balcombe, who managed their household purchases. She carried a tray of basil, chervil, dill, and marjoram into the courtyard.

Fertile soil from the western side of the island, requested by the Count de Montholon, slumped in slimy puddles. Amélie had already placed large rocks around the area to deter the wind from blowing it away. She crouched down, scooped out a hole, and loosened roots and placed in a seedling. According to the book, the dill liked shade, the basil and marjoram full sun. The chervil should thrive in both and substitute for parsley. Even with her kitchen garden experience, she enjoyed taking instructions from a book and putting it into practice. Intrigued by the medicinal uses of some of these herbs, she delighted in the pungent smell of the plants.

Her fingers were soon muddy, her apron splattered. She planted four more seedlings, then began to hum. A line from the opera *The Indian Queen* popped into her head, and she sang softly, "'Such slaves like gods did adore. Condemned and unpitied in chains. I fly from the place where flattery...'" She broke off, thinking of her sovereign—condemned and chained to this island.

"I didn't know you could sing." Saint-Denis stepped out the back door. He carried several silver pieces toward the outbuilding where they were stored. "You sounded...yes, I have to admit it, almost pretty."

"Oh, it's nothing. I used to sing for fun, with my sister-in-law Suzanne." Amélie felt her cheeks burn, embarrassed that anyone heard her. "She taught me a few arias."

The emperor, with the Countess de Montholon, walked through a gap in the outbuildings from the left side of the house. The woman's laughter tinkled like glass shards. She clung to Napoleon's arm, swaying her head, her smile bright. She pressed so close to his green jacket in her fluttering blue dress with leg-o'-mutton sleeves that they moved like a plump iris stalk into the courtyard.

Amélie squeezed a clump of mud in her fist.

"Your Majesty, you shouldn't scold us when we want to attend the colonial soirees given by the governor or Admiral Cockburn," the countess said in her purring voice. "There's so little to do here as it is. I feel cooped up like an animal. Why won't you attend with us?"

"Acknowledge an invitation sent to *General* Bonaparte? I haven't been a general since Egypt." Napoleon didn't look at his companion. "Cockburn insults my officers by not seating them according to their rank. We should keep to ourselves and not endure these insults from the British." They strolled nearer, scattering the rats that gathered like barnyard fowl.

Amélie, aware she wasn't supposed to stare, tried to concentrate on her garden again. The woman and Napoleon now talked in hushed voices. Amélie nearly strangled one of her plants straining to hear.

"Our Amélie sings." Saint-Denis walked back and stood over her. He bowed his long frame toward his master, who gestured for him to carry on. "Can you tell me if your father has any cream left?"

"I'll look for you." She rose, more to get away from Montholon's simpering wife, and bustled into the kitchen with the valet on her heels. After washing her hands, she pulled up the stone slab in the floor where they stored items for cooling. "No, we're out like I thought."

"His Majesty said this morning he'd like some of those rolled waffles filled with cream." Saint-Denis leaned against the stove and fought a yawn. "They are his favorites."

"Ummm, I know." She fit the slab back and straightened. "Along with steaming hot soups, roast chicken, lentils…I don't care for lentils. The emperor especially enjoys fresh almonds and cherries, Papa says. So much is difficult to get here, and the local farmers are slow to fill our request for cream. We hope for a shipment soon. When we do, I'll make His Majesty some waffles."

"You cook as well as sing." Saint-Denis winked and stretched. "The emperor had me up dictating half the night. He prefers my fine hand." He crooked his fingers in writing stance. "My excellent penmanship comes from being educated in a notary's office."

Amélie pictured herself as a scribe, surrounded by ink instead of mud. "Men are encouraged to use their skills. What is the emperor dictating to you?"

"His Majesty likes to refight his battles." Ali picked a piece of lint from his coat sleeve. "His mind is profound, and he's so restless with little here to challenge him."

"He seems challenged by the Countess de Montholon." Amélie tried to smooth the envy from her tone. She turned from him and with a rag, scrubbed at the mud on her apron front.

The valet chuckled. "The countess does as she pleases. Her husband spoils her."

"Ali, what kind of courtier is the Count de Montholon? Did he serve with His Majesty in the wars?" She thought of the count's words to his wife in the courtyard that first day here.

"Well, some say the count's military career isn't very distinguished, and he only earned rank because of his stepfather's influence." Ali rubbed his shoulder as if his muscles ached. "He begged to be included in our entourage."

That sounded like her, pleading with her father to come, but she didn't want any comparison to the count. He didn't strike her as someone to be trusted. Didn't he mind that his wife acted like a courtesan with Napoleon? "His Majesty might find more stimulation if he relaxed the protocol around him." Amélie flicked the rag to chase a gray gecko out the kitchen window, thankful it left behind no stench.

"No protocol? We must behave as if still at the Tuileries." The valet made a sweeping bow, leg extended. "No one sits before the emperor without permission, or speaks unless spoken to. Visitors must get passes from Count Bertrand before seeing him." He grinned at her and wagged a finger. "No one's allowed to approach…"

"I didn't mean all of it, *bien sûr*. Does the emperor need a reader? I'm very good at reading, having studied books on history, the Empire." This man so close to her fingertips when once he dwelled at the highest level in palaces should appreciate her. "I am available."

Saint-Denis shook his head, a wry smile on his lips again. "Amélie, you are smart for a girl, but emperor's readers have to be men. You would never be allowed such access." He patted her cheek. "You shouldn't tie back your hair. Your face is too thin. I must be off to the house."

"Smart *for* a girl? Aren't women entitled to the same intelligence as men?" she said before he exited the kitchen. "Emperors' readers *have* to be men?"

"Don't take offence." Ali gave her another wink. "If you want to be of use to the emperor, sing more often. His Majesty enjoys hearing girls sing."

"Sing for the emperor?" Amélie spoke to Ali's back as he loped out the door. She loosened her hair, then stopped herself and pulled the ribbon tighter. Her thick tresses still managed to spring loose here and there of their own accord.

She opened the pantry door, careful not to jerk it off again in frustration at being branded a lowly female. She checked the sparse food supplies. The household each day consumed over ninety pounds of beef, six chickens, seventy-four pounds of bread, five pounds of butter, nine of sugar, two of coffee, and one pound of cheese. According to her father, monthly they drank 210 bottles of Bordeaux, twenty-six of champagne, twenty-three of Madeira, sixty Graves, and eleven of Constantia, the emperor's special wine. Napoleon's wine was kept separate, in a locked cabinet in the house.

"Oh, Sire, you're scandalous. The things you say." Madame de Montholon giggled louder in the courtyard. "There are 'other' ways to find contentment here, if you look for them."

Amélie stepped to the window.

"Saying isn't necessarily doing." Napoleon flashed the woman an ironic smile and removed her arm from his. "Aren't we all in a play? Arranged badly, to my detriment, by these British scoundrels." With a brittle laugh, the emperor strode toward Longwood's rear door.

Nose pressed to the glass, Amélie knew she'd be wrestled to the ground if she dared approach him giggling like a ninny. She thought of David's painting of the young Napoleon crossing the St. Bernard Pass on a white charger, his right arm thrown up pointing the way. She tried to merge that image with this battered man whose scaling of such heights had banished them all to this forsaken outpost.

An intelligent *person* must think of a way to use that banishment to their advantage.

Cannon boomed from Alarm House, the observation tower atop one of the jagged peaks half encircling their residence. The ground shook and Amélie hurried outside.

"It's the ship!" a sentry near Longwood's enclosure shouted. Amélie rushed to the wall. Cheering rose up from more soldiers, and rifles with bayonets swirled in the air. In the distance people mounted horses and rode toward Jamestown. Soldiers swarmed from the tents at the Deadwood Camp and hitched carts to oxen.

"*Grâce à dieu*." Amélie looked to the ocean at the ballooning sails approaching. The supply ship, their bridge to the outer world, tilted her masts as if saluting the ration starved island.

More soldiers gathered, raising field glasses.

"Saint Helena comes alive again. It's ridiculous how these people rely on everything being shipped in, instead of tending their farms." Napoleon walked up to the wall a few feet away, the countess mincing along behind him. "Now these fools will celebrate for days with their English love of drunkenness."

Amélie smelled his light eau de cologne and quivered at his voice so near. She pretended that he addressed her. "The ship arrives just in time, Your—"

"How dare you speak up so brazenly." The countess swept between them in a swish of silk and jabbed Amélie aside with her elbow.

Amélie tripped, scraped her knuckles on the wall, and choked back an angry response. She held her breath as Napoleon turned and stared down at her, his expression, his blue-gray eyes, concerned.

Chapter Four

I believe that nature has intended me for great reverses—N.B.

"Albine, that isn't kind. Perhaps in anticipation she forgets her place." Napoleon pulled a handkerchief from his waistcoat pocket. He reached past the countess and took the girl's hand. A thin waif, her eyes widened in surprise. Admiring her luxuriant blond hair and fair skin, he wrapped his handkerchief around her knuckles. "Your scrape doesn't look too bad. You must excuse the countess's slip of temper, Mademoiselle." He inspected her hand, delicate and small, with dirt under the fingernails. "Do you work here in this garden?"

"Yes, Your Majesty." The girl kept her gaze on him, her smile wavering. Her hand grew warm in his. "I'm planting herbs and spices for your meals."

Napoleon smiled and released her, slightly irritated because she hadn't curtsied. Had he grown too sensitive because of the English refusal to treat him as emperor? "I commend you for bringing life to this arid land. Now run along."

"Thank you, Sire." The girl nodded and backed away, her large brown eyes like a woodland creature watching him. She did have an interesting face.

"*Pardon*, Your Majesty. I didn't mean to push the servant so hard." Albine pouted, her cobalt gaze sparkling under her chestnut curls. Napoleon looked away, satisfied the woman wanted to be intimate with him. He deserved no less, but was not always easy with her forwardness. He sagged with fatigue—this entire farce was grating on him, but he did his utmost to remain respectable before the British. No word must ever reach his wife over an imprudent affair.

* * * *

Saint-Denis directed Amélie's hand in a swipe at the large rodent that skittered along the dining room wall. "Swat it on the head, don't play with it." He laughed. "Look, there it goes. *Rapidement!*"

She pulled her hand with the cue stick free, and scooted behind the creature, but the rat squeezed under the buffet. "I don't want to hurt it." She stopped and swept her hair out of her face. "I thought we were catching them."

The room's humidity seeped under her clothes. Her senses expected the day before New Year's to be cold, but an austral summer rain splattered on the roof. She slid Napoleon's handkerchief from her pocket and dabbed her forehead. She still felt the softness of his touch from three days past, and lamented that her cleverness melted away when he took her hand. She'd forgotten to curtsy!

"Quick, Jules, it heads for home!" Saint-Denis called to another servant. The two men scrambled for the corner, striking at their quarry with sticks, but they couldn't prevent the rat from scurrying back into a hole. In a scratch of tiny feet its slithery tail whipped from sight.

"*C'est ça*, that puts me ahead." Jules puffed out his lower lip. "I've killed three today alone." A stocky, sandy-haired man in his late twenties, Jules Priour worked as the Count de Montholon's manservant. He glared at Amélie through squinting eyes. "You can't just catch them. They have to be killed."

"There's so many, I won't have any trouble beating you." Saint-Denis thumped his stick on the floor. "I'll have to work on Amélie's ratting skills."

"How can you strike them like that?" She flinched at the thought. "We should round them up and herd them onto a British ship to be transported away. Back to England, to bite their government's toes for mistreating our emperor."

Marchand entered the room and shook his head. "Let's cover up these holes and be done with this. You don't encourage blood sport where the court eats. We need to sprinkle poison in the walls. That's why the arsenic was brought here." At twenty-five, a year younger than Ali, Marchand's responsible attitude exuded authority.

"Ruin our contest?" Jules slapped the table and sneered. "First you say we can't shoot them with pistols, now not even sticks? How else can we occupy our time?"

"Amélie, I'm surprised you aid these two in their mayhem." Marchand smiled as if to soften his scold. "Now stop this commotion. His Majesty is receiving guests in the drawing room." The chief valet, in complete green livery, walked into that room and shut the door.

"He's right. We're finding bizarre amusements to occupy our time." She stared after him.

"We'd have more enjoyment if we were involved in the *outside* island society, instead of corralled up here." Jules stepped to the mouse hole and clicked his stick around the entrance.

"Oh, and you'd be included in the social whirl, such as it is?" Saint-Denis shouldered his stick like a rifle with bayonet. "No one informed me you were so privileged."

"Now you know my true value." Jules snorted. "Ali, we are both too well educated to be mere servants. I don't plan to suffer here much longer."

"We serve the emperor, there is nothing 'mere' about that." Amélie watched the calculating glint in his eye. "Where do you plan to be?"

"None of your business." Jules thrust his cue so she had to jump back.

"Stop that." She batted the cue aside and walked toward the drawing room entrance. "Who is visiting His Majesty tonight?" The emperor had previously received officers from the Fifty-third Regiment at Deadwood, and the Balcombes, whom he'd first stayed with on the island.

"Some officers off a ship that just docked from China." Saint-Denis frowned. "The English can't wait for an audience with the famous conqueror, but won't grant him the dignity of calling him emperor."

"Let's peek in." Amélie cracked the door open, her cheek pressed against the jamb.

Generals Bertrand and Montholon, dressed in blue, gold-braided uniforms, swords at their sides, escorted the visitors from the salon. Marchand greeted them at the drawing room's far door and announced them to His Majesty.

Napoleon stood at the drawing room fireplace, hat tucked under his arm, striking in his full uniform. He asked the visitors questions, with the Count de Las Cases as interpreter. Napoleon displayed his wit, and attempted a few English words in a thick accent. His features came alive, eyes flashing, and he resembled the man she'd observed in Paris. A breathless fervor trembled in her lungs. The visitors, by their wide eyes and growing smiles, seemed to fall under the same spell.

"Amélie, come away." Saint-Denis tugged her back and closed the door again.

"The British despised our emperor, and now he's their prisoner they pay courtesy calls on him. They *should* pay court to His Majesty." She ached to stay and watch. Napoleon hadn't noticed her once since the incident at the wall.

"His Majesty gets his revenge," Ali said, eyes twinkling. "He'll keep his visitors standing in his presence until they're about to faint, like he does with his courtiers. That way he can once again be master and bend people to his wishes. These sycophants only come to see a caged beast. Now they'll inform Europe he is still the emperor no matter his situation."

"She's still innocent, our *petite baton*, yet a strange girl who doesn't screech at seeing rodents." Jules flicked his gaze over Amélie in a way that made her shrivel. "The British will kowtow to their government's dictates, no matter how much the emperor charms them. His enemies fear his ambition, even from this rock."

Amélie glared into Jules's face. How would he like it if she called him "squinty eyes"? "When you say something witty, I might care to hear it. The emperor should never have had to give up everything or make a humiliating peace."

"The continent was tired of war." Jules thrust his stick like a sword when a rat poked his nose from the hole. "The only way to secure peace was by forcing the *parvenu* to abdicate."

"Don't ever call him that." Amélie hated the smirk on Jules's square face. "They never thought of His Majesty as legitimate, after he more than proved himself able. He was a threat to the other monarchs 'divine right' to rule."

"She is full of knowledge. You shouldn't trouble your head with such things." Jules snickered as Amélie gripped her cue. "The Bourbons wanted their throne back."

"Their throne?" Saint-Denis twirled his stick, swiping it close to Jules's nose. "The *emperor* decided it better to abdicate after Waterloo, than incite civil war as his chambers of deputies wouldn't support him, but the army wanted to fight on."

"*Mon Dieu*, France hated the Bourbons. Their greedy, self-indulgent rule sparked the revolution." Amélie hoped Ali would thrust his pole into Jules's Adam's apple. If he didn't, she was tempted. "Then England and Russia forced fat Louis XVIII on us for a second time."

"He was the lesser of two evils, in the eyes of the victors," Jules said. "France had no choice, but not all hated the king. Royalists always worked in the background against the emperor's government."

"You sound in the Royalists' favor." Saint-Denis scrutinized the other man. "England, our benevolent host, is the one who wouldn't rest until the Bourbons stole back the French throne. England broke the Peace of Amiens, something they conveniently forget. Then they poured money into the pockets of Russia, Prussia, even Austria to fight against France."

"Austria." Amélie couldn't help but scoff. "They turned against His Majesty though he married their emperor's worthless daughter, Marie Louise."

"Be careful, Amélie, the emperor insists that no one speak ill of his empress. We must always show our profound respect." Saint-Denis's sardonic grin proved he agreed with her.

"She deserted him. So thrilled to be with him in his glory, but when he fell she ran like a spoiled brat back to papa. His Majesty lost his country and his wife and son."

Jules laughed again, a laugh that never seemed to reach deep inside him. "She knew where her fortunes lay, and now she's in the arms of that Austrian count."

"Worthless, as I said. I remember their marriage celebration." Amélie thought of that cool April six years before when her mother had taken her to a main boulevard in Paris—the city of her birth—to witness the spectacle. Men strutted in plumed hats, swords slapping off their thighs. Women rustled in silk skirts, their perfume sweetening the breeze.

The emperor and his new empress were married at the Louvre's Salon Carre. Carnivals and banquets stretched from the Champs Elysees to the Arc du Carrousel. Standing atop a wall near the riverbank, Amélie held fast to her mother's hand— that once secure warmth of her mother's touch—as the imperial coach rolled by. The Hapsburg archduchess had a prominent jaw, her eyes flat in a broad face. An eighteen-year-old of royal birth, she was given in marriage to a man reviled by her fellow Austrians for devastating their country in war.

"I felt sorry for Empress Josephine. She was far more gracious." Amélie lowered her voice. "Marie Louise never smiled, I heard many people say. France hadn't forgotten they'd put that other Austrian, her aunt Marie Antoinette to death, saying she brought bad luck."

"No room for sentiment in politics." Jules crouched down and pulled the delicate, tiny carriage he'd built from under the sideboard. "Now catch me a rat and we'll have a race."

"A man of the people should have married a commoner to prove he cared nothing for royal trappings. Our emperor threw away everything he'd first stood for." Amélie felt this insult close to the bone, as if she owned Napoleon's actions. His efforts were for the birth of a half-royal son in 1811—a boy he might never see again.

After being sent to live with her oldest brother Théodore, Amélie resented missing the excitement, France in a constant state of war. Her father had remained at the Tuileries to serve their emperor.

"Amélie, you look in a daze." Saint-Denis nudged her.

"I remember the emperor's triumphant march through Lyon on his way to retake Paris from Elba. I rushed into the street with my brothers. The people cheered, welcoming him home. Our tri-color flag flew once more over the city." Amélie heard laughter from the drawing room and again felt excluded. She'd appreciate such conversation, but could she untie her tongue to add intelligent responses? Their revolution tried to eliminate this division of the classes—women during the revolution demanded to be equal to men—though she was a child of the Consulate, the Empire.

"*Qu' importe*? That's all past. Waterloo finished him. Now we have only the British and this boring island." Jules managed to trap a rat and fumbled to hitch it to his carriage. The rodent rattled and banged it around the room as he chuckled. "You are quite the devotee."

"You are disloyal, Jules. How dare you say such things." She glared at him. His arrogance bothered her. She stepped aside as Saint-Denis scrambled to catch the noisy carriage.

"I'm loyal to my master, the Count de Montholon."

"You should keep your ugly opinions to yourself." Saint-Denis released the rat and poked the miniature carriage into Jules's chest. "We have enough malcontents around here. At least Admiral Cockburn won't lord over us much longer. The British government is sending out a new governor to run things. A soldier with a notorious past whom the emperor is anxious to meet."

Amélie feathered the handkerchief under her chin. "Let's hope he is kinder to His Majesty and we can relax our protocol."

"Shoo away, you barbarians." The Count de Las Cases poked his face out the drawing room door. His lips twitched in disdain. "You're making too much noise. Out, out."

Jules shuffled from the room. Ali gathered the cues.

Amélie stared down the little count, refusing to scuttle like a rat back into her hole. "May I listen in, Count?" The door shut in her face.

* * * *

Franceschi Cipriani, the thin, swarthy *maitre d'hotel*, stood in Longwood's drawing room arch. *"Le diner de Sa Majesté est servi,"* he announced in his nasal voice, sweeping into a bow.

Amélie peeked around the corner into the dining room after she set the New Year dessert she'd baked on the table in the preparation room. The Count de Las Cases flanked one side of the doorway, waiting at attention, his feverish fingers constantly straightening his coat and sword.

Napoleon entered. The little count bowed low, his sword tip scraping the floor.

The imperial valets bowed, decked out in palace livery of emerald-green tailcoats with gold-embroidered collars and cuffs, white vests, black silk breeches, white stockings, and buckled shoes—all distinct in their dilapidated royal residence.

The Count de Montholon, crisp in his full uniform, epaulets and stars glittering, strutted in behind the emperor. Napoleon seated himself at the head of the dining room table. Montholon elbowed past Las Cases and swooped into the chair on the emperor's left.

Saint-Denis, passing Amélie, grinned and whispered, "Count de Montholon's victory this time." At communal meals, the Count de Las Cases insisted on that chair of honor for himself.

Amélie stifled a laugh and decided that both Montholons had a penchant for rude elbows.

Las Cases sat down one chair away from Montholon and sniffed into a vermilion silk handkerchief. The little count wiped his nose with much aplomb, lips sucked in, so wounded by the nudge, his eyebrows dancing on his high brow.

The Countess de Montholon entered the room and floated over to Napoleon's right. In her slinky dress she curtsied low, her breasts in danger of spilling out. Amélie cringed at such vulgar behavior right in front of her husband.

"Madame, please sit down," Napoleon said in a torpid voice. The countess fluttered into the chair on his right, scratched the back of her neck and made a girlish titter.

Someone poked Amélie's shoulder. She moved aside, basking in the aroma of roast chicken, to let the footmen and valets carry the first course into the dining room.

"Montholon, have you written to Admiral Cockburn, insisting he enlarge my limits to ride and allow any officer or island inhabitant to visit me here?" Napoleon asked. "I refuse to submit to the admiral's society, but it's always stimulating to talk to soldiers about their careers."

"I did it immediately, as you requested, Sire, but I'm not sure he will bow to your wishes. Isn't Bertrand dining with us?" A faint sneer flitted across Montholon's tiny mouth. "A pity his wife refuses to live near you, along with your grand marshal. Madame Bertrand's socializing around the island is an embarrassment, as I've said before."

"Indeed you have, many times. They are both aware of my displeasure." Napoleon didn't glance up from his plate. Perspiration beaded on his forehead and he looked anxious to get the meal over with. Montholon tugged at the high collar of his uniform. He and Las Cases soon had sweat glistening on their upper lips in the stuffy room.

Near the center of the building, the dining room had no natural light. Dozens of candles burned on the sideboard and table. Patches of green mold dripped from the walls near Amélie, the stench thickening the air in the poorly ventilated house. She opened the sachet of rosemary she carried and sprinkled the fragrant herb about.

"*Ma foi*, I'm glad they don't live here. This place is already too crowded." Countess de Montholon smiled for Napoleon and fondled his arm. "Fanny Bertrand can be such a prig, and she's always late to meals—as you can see, which you hate, Sire. They wouldn't act like this if you were presiding at the Tuileries."

Napoleon glowered at the mention of his once grand palace, a palace now occupied by gouty Louis XVIII. Amélie huffed that both Montholons provoked the emperor's upset.

A second course of *boudin á la Richelieu* was served. Count and Countess Bertrand bustled into the room, Bertrand's sword slapping against his boot.

"I'm sorry we're late, Your Majesty," Bertrand said after Napoleon's grunted greeting. The count crumpled his hat in his hands, but the countess looked aloof, her face still as wax.

"I had some papers to go over with Admiral Cockburn," Bertrand continued. "He didn't care for the strong tone of that last letter, Sire. I wish you had allowed me to write it for you." He glanced at Montholon as he and his wife seated themselves at the table. He then watched Napoleon like a lapdog desperate for a pat on the head.

"If you were closer at hand, I might have. I'm certain you will smooth it over with Cockburn. Besides, he's being replaced. Have you studied the island fortifications as I asked you?" Napoleon stirred the food on his plate. "I heard the English have even put troops on the tiny islands close by."

"Yes, Sire. Ascension Island and Tristan d'Acuna."

"I'm sure you exaggerate about the tone of my letter." Montholon slanted his gaze over Bertrand. "Fanny, do you continue to tell the admiral how well we're being treated here in our cow barn?"

"Longwood house was never a cow barn. What's wrong with trying to find a little gaiety? The island isn't so distasteful if you keep busy." Fanny Bertrand's reply clipped, her cheeks flushed red. Her husband squeezed her hand.

Saint-Denis urged Amélie back toward the preparation area, but she hesitated, concerned about the court's disgruntled behavior so early in their tenancy.

"I must say, Charles, you take too much delight in detailing Fanny's every movement." Las Cases appraised Montholon with heavy-lidded eyes. "I still don't know what prompted *you*, as one who enjoys such stellar associations back in Europe, to voyage all the way out here."

Montholon cast the little count a derisive look, before his "courtier's face" resurfaced. His wife continued to fawn over Napoleon and Montholon smiled in a detached manner. Countess Bertrand thumped down her wine glass and frowned at the other woman. Napoleon ignored both countesses and bolted down his food.

Amélie stepped back into the preparation area. "I'll help serve, Papa. One of the footmen just snuck off with a headache, faint from the dank room."

Her father sliced up her cherry cake and put it on plates with a ladle full of rich yellow butter sauce. Napoleon liked his repast to progress quickly.

"Remember, you do *not* serve His Majesty. His valets wait exclusively on him at meals." Perrault raised a gray brow. "Do it quietly, please. The Count de Las Cases has complained that you've been underfoot too much in the main house."

Underfoot, like a dog? She swallowed her retort.

With Saint-Denis, Amélie carried in the dessert. The Sévres plates and coffee cups, accompanied by gold knives, spoons, and forks, were decorated in emerald and gold borders patterned with swords and laurels around Napoleon's battlefield scenes in Egypt. Again inches from her emperor, she wished he'd look up and recognize her.

The plate she held wavered. She bumped it against Saint-Denis, who served the emperor, and dripped a few dollops of sauce onto Montholon's lap.

"Stupid girl." The count swept out his handkerchief and dabbed at his pants. "I see we've left the more accomplished servants behind in France. Pitiful what we must endure here."

"I'm so sorry, count." Amélie set the plate before him, more amused than embarrassed. She backed off a step, wishing she'd slopped all the sauce over his patrician legs.

"Nothing satisfies you, Charles." Las Cases flipped up his wrist. "Sire, I am perfectly honored to be here beside you, no matter the situation, unlike some. I have received more English newspapers which I'll take pleasure in reading to you later."

"Not if I must hear further bad news of the executions of my officers in France," Napoleon said. "Ney was a brave man. Unfortunately his character never matched his courage, but it's still an ignoble end. What the king is doing is monstrous." He resumed eating with a vengeance. Marshal Ney had been shot by a firing squad for joining Napoleon at Waterloo.

"The cherry cake is prepared especially for you, by my own hands." Amélie spoke to no one in particular. She studied the emperor to see if he approved of the dessert's taste.

"Las Cases, can't we enjoy our meal without you persisting in unpleasant reminders?" Madame de Montholon pursed her lips.

"I have proven my worth, beyond and above what anyone might expect." Las Cases sniffed as if she smelled bad. "They still praise my superb atlas in London, which I published as an émigré during the revolution."

"I wouldn't brag about London, or anything English, here." The Countess de Montholon nibbled a bite of cake. She pushed it aside, her snub nose in the air.

Amélie glared at this woman who had almost knocked her over. The countess's rouged smiles seemed contrived. Her flimsy mauve dress, with gaudy jewelry, clung to her plump white shoulders and bosom, making her look salacious.

"Brag all you wish. How I'd enjoy seeing London. If only we could have stayed." Fanny Bertrand gazed off in the distance as if she glimpsed that city from here. A smile tugged at her lips below a strong nose that gave her an air of dignity. "I wonder what they're wearing in society this year."

"Oh, Fanny dear, don't be so tiresome." Madame Montholon tittered.

Napoleon laid down his fork and stared around the table as if he couldn't believe where he'd ended up. "You are only a little group at the bottom of the world. Why can't you try harder to get along with one another? Such efforts will make our time here more satisfying." He raised his wine glass, his face like stone. "To the New Year, 1816, may we prosper."

"May we prosper," Amélie whispered as she picked up the dessert plates.

"They're a house full of vipers," she said to Saint-Denis when they entered the preparation area with trays of empty dishes. "Why did these people come here with the emperor when they just want to snipe at one another?"

"They each want something from His Majesty: money, or the glory of being near him." The valet winked at her. "I suspect some needed to slip away from disagreeable situations in France."

"His Majesty deserves more respect." Amélie stacked plates together by size. She dipped her finger into the cake platter and tasted the sweet buttery sauce. "Madame de Montholon has little shame."

"Do you enjoy being critical like the rest of them?" Her father turned from his tidying up. "You must have picked up some bad habits in Lyon when I wasn't there to guide you. Now let us finish up here, *ma petite*."

"I see nothing wrong with speaking the truth, Papa."

Perrault motioned her out the back door. Amélie snatched up a tray of dishes and carried them across the courtyard. In the kitchen, she rattled the tray down on the table and wondered when someone stopped being *petite*, and at what point did a father's guidance become unnecessary?

She picked up her discarded book, Mary Wollstonecraft's *A Vindication of the Rights of Woman*. It disappointed her that the author still touted marriage as the ultimate goal. From father to husband seemed a woman's fate.

The book set aside, she snatched up her water can and walked out to the courtyard. A rat nibbled at her plants. She stomped her foot to chase it off. The plants looked wilted, even after she broke up crates and anchored them with rocks to shield them from the elements. The breeze ruffling through their leaves brought a damp, earthy smell that made her smile. What kind of herb potions could she prepare to cure the ills of this household?

At the barrel near the kitchen wall, Amélie dipped her can in the murky water. Chinese laborers hauled their water in used wine casks from a stream a mile off. It smelled foul.

Bent to her garden, she trickled water over the plants. Her fingers working the moist dirt, she rummaged through her memory for a showy opera song. She had attended several operas in Lyon. When living with her brother and his family, she'd discovered her sister-in-law had been a frustrated opera singer before her marriage. Suzanne took Amélie to the cheap seats at the opera matinees and insisted that she had sung far better than the performer on stage, but she begged her not to tell Théo, as it wasn't considered proper in decent society. Suzanne urged her to sing along at home when she played diva, Théo away in his bakery. Amélie never thought her voice added much to the harmony, but Saint-Denis praised her singing.

The emperor enjoyed hearing girls sing? She cleared her throat, intending to practice here in the wind. She'd call to Odysseus with the haunting, determined voice of the Sirens.

Chapter Five

A new Prometheus, I am nailed to a rock to be gnawed by a vulture—N.B.

The gumwoods' narrow leaves rattled above, giving sparse dapples of shade as Amélie strolled through. Comprised mainly of skinny gums, she found it ironic that anyone would call these three acres in front of their residence the Park. The islanders named this entire area Long Wood because of these trees, the only ones left on the plain.

She closed her eyes and tried to remember what it felt like to walk in the beauty of the Tuileries gardens. Footsteps crunching over dead leaves behind her shattered that image. Clarice still followed. Turning, Amélie watched her plod along the dirt path.

"Why are you tagging after me?" Amélie stopped to pluck a white flower with a dark purple center from one of the few blackwood ebony trees. The petals flew from her hand, their scent piquant, and scattered like snowflakes.

"I'm so bored with washing laundry and scrubbing chamber pots. I wondered where you were going." Clarice tugged her spencer jacket around her plump bosom. "I thought a walk would refresh me. I hate this weather. The mornings are freezing, but in the afternoon the heat makes the tar paper in our attic stink."

"I hoped to walk down to the Sane Valley. I'd like to look for the herbs I hear grow near the stream, fennel, Jamaica pepper." Amélie strode on, but allowed Clarice to keep pace beside her. She inhaled the air into her lungs and rubbed a hand across her throat. The thought of the last two months saddened her, since her singing hadn't attracted Napoleon in the least. She stuffed down her disappointment, wondering how else to lure him. He was obviously a sad man who might benefit from her company—someone who didn't whine. To give up wasn't an option she cared for. "The scenery there is supposed to be beautiful."

"Will that fussy new governor permit us to go to the valley? I'd rather he let me attend one of the regimental balls at the Deadwood Camp. *Merde!*" Clarice jumped and Amélie almost tripped over a tree root. She looked up. A huge spider, black with white bars, hung upside down on an orb of web stretched between two trees. The spider drooped low enough for the girls to bump into, and they gave it a wide swath.

"This island is full of amazing life." Amélie stepped backwards for a moment to watch, fascinated by the spider's many legs spinning over the orb like a frantic weaver.

"This island is horrible. I wish I'd never come here." Clarice tossed her head and stomped down the trail. "*Saint* Helena? What's saintly about this putrid rock?"

"Saint Helena was discovered by a Portuguese navigator on the birthday of the Emperor Constantine's mother, Helena." Amélie didn't know why she bothered to enrich Clarice's knowledge, but liked to poke at her superior air.

"You read too much. You get all your experience from books. It doesn't matter to you not being back home. You might've gained a little weight, but you're still too thin." Clarice's smug grin spread out her cheeks even farther. "*I* could attract plenty of beaux."

Amélie slowed, not surprised this rare camaraderie hadn't lasted. "There are other attractions besides appearance. If you found interests of your own you'd have less time to ridicule." She did miss home. The busy streets of Lyon and Paris. The bookshops and bustling markets. The luxury of having everything you needed at your fingertips, even if you couldn't afford most of it. She increased her stride to shake off Clarice. "Living here is for the strong, a challenge to survive."

"I have no time for challenges or interests with all my duties. The courtiers complain about everything we do in the house. As if they act any better." Clarice's strident tone changed to conspiratorial as she kept up. "The Countess de Montholon is wanton with the emperor, and her husband doesn't seem to care."

"It *is* just a flirtation?" Amélie tensed and slowed again, irritated at her curiosity.

"She's the emperor's mistress, everyone knows it. She was married twice before, divorced for cheating, and pregnant with the count's child when they married. Of course, His Majesty has always had affairs. My mother was Empress Josephine's chambermaid, and the poor woman wept from his whoring."

Amélie's heart lurched and she walked faster, stirring up dry leaves, the smell of decay, to be tossed by the wind. Their emperor's liaisons were legendary, but she didn't wish to hear about them. Why couldn't one woman satisfy him? What was this enticement of the flesh besides the vague whispers that naïve girls shared?

"After the empress's death, we joined the emperor on Elba. Even when His Majesty waited for the Austrian there, he wasn't without a woman." Clarice grinned and shifted in her dress as if she knew every carnal secret since birth.

Amélie hid her envy at Clarice's long proximity to Napoleon, but Madame Cloubert might have been the reason Empress Josephine had suffered from migraines.

They neared the Park's end. A flock of gaunt sheep with broad tails bleated from a field in the distance. Diana's Peak, the island's highest mountain, loomed to the west shrouded in fog.

A sheet of paper nailed to one of the last tree trunks flapped in the breeze. Amélie ripped it down, glaring at the English words, but she knew what was written. "It's those directives warning the island inhabitants not to speak to us, nor offer us any kindness. We can't even shop in Jamestown anymore because the shopkeepers are forbidden to sell to us."

"You're in trouble now," Clarice whispered with a snicker.

"Put that back, missy!" A sentry stalked toward them. He snatched the paper from Amélie's hands. "I could arrest you for damaging British property. Get back to your quarters, both of you. No Frenchie is allowed to leave the road without escorts."

Amélie stifled a gasp and stared at her empty fingers; any reply would put her in deeper difficulty. She and Clarice headed toward the road, the sentry glaring after them. Clarice threw him a broad smile and exaggerated the wiggle of her hips.

"Behave yourself," Amélie snapped, then halted at the edge of the road. A group of people approached from the direction of Hutt's Gate. "*Attends*, there's the emperor with the new governor."

Napoleon strode with the Countess de Montholon and the Count de Las Cases. The governor, Sir Hudson Lowe, who'd arrived the previous month, brought up the rear.

"That finicky man is the cause of our problems." Clarice smoothed her hair under her white cap. "He keeps all those soldiers from courting me."

"Shhh. His Majesty looks upset." Amélie studied the emperor's grim expression, his face pale under his cocked hat. "I wonder what else we're being forced to submit to."

* * * *

Napoleon stopped and turned around. He struggled to remain calm. "You invade my privacy, open my letters, treat my retinue with disrespect. I can't receive visitors without your express permission. The soldiers swarm about the house every night. How should I feel under such tyranny?"

"Sir, I must object. I do want to render your situation agreeable as it's within my power." Governor Lowe, a reed-thin man with rusty hair, tightened his lips. "These are my government's instructions, as I have stated before."

"Those were also the instructions of your Admiral Cockburn, but *you* carry them out fifty times as rigorously!" Napoleon lost his composure and blustered into Lowe's face. A face that resembled a hyena caught in a trap. His aggravation pricked like needles along his neck and shoulders. "You bring me this edict stating the Allied sovereigns have officially declared me their prisoner. They have no authority to do this in law or fact. It's cowardice to imprison me in this unhealthy climate. Everything here breathes a mortal boredom and death."

"Give me a list of anything you may require. My government is shipping out material for a grander house to be built for you. You will be more comfortable then." Lowe's left eyelid twitched.

"I want nothing like that. I desire no permanent home." Napoleon threw up his hands. He refused to resign himself to the idea he may never depart this island. Such a notion would drag him into a misery he couldn't afford. He had to remain confident in his supporters in France, keep his name alive, and reiterate England's maltreatment. "I can't even ride as I used to before you arrived. Your Lord Castlereagh sent you here to be my executioner. *Mon bourreau!*"

"Not at all, sir. Cockburn was just too lenient with you. From now on the orderly officer, Captain Poppleton, must escort you if you leave this immediate area."

"Then I won't ride anymore with your spies all over me. Only six miles from here to Jamestown and over fifteen posts of sentries. They're in every hole, behind every rock." Napoleon stepped away. Two young women watched this degrading exchange. Aware he couldn't desert the battlefield, his attention snapped back to Lowe. "I flattered myself that because you were an army officer, who witnessed the struggles on the continent, you would behave with propriety towards me, but there's no talking with you. You don't know how to command men. You suspect everyone and behave like a warden."

"Gentlemen, if I may interject, and I hope I may." Las Cases put his hands together like a supplicating priest. "This might be just a matter of different temperaments, third party errors. You cannot trust minions to handle such matters. If we start over and tried again, I—"

"You held back a book meant for me, simply because it was addressed to the emperor. You British refuse to recognize my title, when I was anointed by the Pope himself!" Napoleon marched back toward Lowe, picturing him as something sticky to scuff from the bottom of his shoe. He needed such images to douse the fury that burned up his throat. "You told Bertrand you think it's insufferable that I wish to be treated as an emperor."

"British Parliament has laid down our terms and…and Lord Bathurst's dictates *will* be followed to the letter." Lowe trembled before him—just the reaction Napoleon hoped for. "I do not abuse my power here, as your General Bertrand had the audacity to charge me with."

"Bah! You're a man who cannot be trusted!" Napoleon glared, intending his fierce gaze to bore through this petty official. "I am not General Bonaparte for you, sir. You have no more right than any other person on Earth to take from me the qualifications that are mine! In a few years your Lord Bathurst, Lord Castlereagh, and *you* will be buried in oblivion, or you'll only be known by the indignities you have committed against me."

"I won't stand here and suffer these rude outbursts and insults, this attack on my character." Lowe's skin stretched tight on angular cheeks, his eyes bulging from their narrow sockets. "Slander is the last resort when other weapons fail. Good day, sir!" He whirled about and strode off toward Hutt's Gate, his red coat slapping in the wind.

"I must never speak with that man again," Napoleon said to Las Cases as they walked toward the house. He massaged the ache from the back of his neck. "He forces me to lose my temper and he makes me forget myself. It isn't a proper show before my jailers." He couldn't allow such public humiliation. All that remained was his tenuous self-respect.

Las Cases flicked his fingers at the two girls still standing close, motioning them away. The countess glowered at them before smiling for Napoleon, but he was in no mood for her coquettishness. To salvage his dignity, he nodded as the girls dropped into curtsies. The blond one looked familiar, and *they* at least thought of him as their emperor.

* * * *

Amélie concentrated on rubbing basil leaves into a bowl on the kitchen table. "Let me prepare a tea with this for His Majesty. Basil tea is supposed to chase away sorrow and make men merry." She placed a pot of water over the fire on the stove, the warmth chasing away the morning's chill, their autumn in March. Her twentieth birthday was only days away.

Marchand looked at her with a kind smile after setting down the emperor's breakfast tray. "I'm sure you have good intentions, but our emperor doesn't take well to doctoring."

"I'm afraid I need the doctoring." Chef Gascon dragged into the kitchen and slumped at the little table. He removed a cloth from a pan of dough and poked at it.

"I pity His Majesty with this new governor. We're all tormented by his restrictions, and verbal weapons are all we have left." Amélie identified with Napoleon about being shoved into an ill-fitting role. Her heart had thumped at his every word during the argument. When he nodded, she'd felt a part of his ordeal and not someone pushed to the side.

"Verbal weapons…that's true, and if it makes you feel better, I think your father is being a little harsh with you." Marchand squeezed her shoulder, pulling her from her thoughts.

"The Count de Las Cases probably complained to him." Amélie filled her spice jars with the dill and marjoram she'd already dried and ground. The sharp smell made her stifle a sneeze.

"I think it might have been the countess." The valet glanced away from her.

"*Vraiment?*" Her resentment toward that woman festered. "Now I'm not to leave this area. Papa said I needed to mind my own business and stay out of the court's. I'm a young woman and shouldn't be treated in this way."

Marchand sighed. "The emperor told me to give away his carriage and horse. He won't ride anymore with an escort. Cockburn allowed him to ride into the Geranium Vale, but Lowe decided, after a previous dispute, that the orderly officer must follow. Then he changed his mind and allowed His Majesty to ride in the valley unescorted. We're confused about what regulation to follow. I worry about him, but it's humiliating for His Majesty to have his freedom taken away. Sadly, his and the governor's personalities clashed on their second meeting."

"The governor's actions have been insulting, but His Majesty can't afford to be indolent." Amélie picked at the spice granules in her cuticles, stained red and brown. "Maybe His Majesty should *pretend* to appease Governor Lowe to make things favorable."

"Would you enjoy being peacemaker, Amélie?" Marchand studied her, but not with the gravity she wished for. "That would be unique, a female ambassador to the court of St. James."

"I could do no worse than you men." Men, she fumed, dictated her life, but a woman had betrayed her to her father. "I know His Majesty suffers. I feel so sorry for him, but sometimes diplomacy has to be forced, even when it's not deserved... yet necessary for survival."

"His Majesty has tried that, but some cuts go too deep. You don't understand the emperor's pride." The valet shook his head as if she spoke the impossible. He rocked on his feet, a habit she'd noticed when he was vexed. "Now the emperor wants to sit in his quarters and read, losing interest in events around him."

"We're all losing interest." Chef Gascon massaged his temples, moving his loose skin about. "This new governor wants to isolate us. As if this island isn't isolating enough."

The chief valet slipped out the minute Madame Cloubert stomped in. "Amélie, you said you had some chamomile to put in my husband's bath? He doesn't sleep well at night. His jerking about keeps me up at all hours." The woman ran a bony hand through her hair, a mixture of auburn and gray like cinders in a dying fire. Her skin smelled like linseed oil in the now warming kitchen. "What can I do with such an oaf?"

Amélie fought a grin and pulled down her chipped jar of chamomile.

"There he goes, that nosy Irishman." Madame glared out the windowpane speckled with sawdust from the still incomplete right wing. "Always spying on us for the British."

"He seems a nice enough man." Amélie joined her at the window. Napoleon's doctor, Barry O'Meara, crossed the courtyard.

"You should worry more about the orderly officer stuck right here on top of us, Madame," Gascon said in a lethargic goad. "He's on guard against evil deeds, with *you* their prime suspect."

"They could never suspect you, Philippe. You can't stay out of bed long enough to be suspicious." The woman scrunched up her face. "Mark my words, O'Meara runs between here and Plantation House, Lowe's fancy estate, with gossip from both ends. Strange how he latched on to His Majesty with his fluent Italian after our doctor refused to come to Saint Helena."

"I wish I had refused to come." Gascon moaned, staring into the mound of dough as if he foresaw his rising doom. "Maybe my wife was right to desert me."

Madame Cloubert made no comment, to Amélie's relief. She handed the woman the herb. After Madame left, Amélie checked the pot heating on the stove. "I'll fix you a cup of basil tea, Chef Gascon." She poured the boiling water over her leaves, inhaling the spicy scent, and set a cup before him, hoping it might make *him* merry. "Complaints about the island seem a waste. That's something we can't change."

She picked up a broom and swept the herb debris from the stone floor they'd put in themselves. Then she stepped outside with her basket and looked to the east between the cliffs where a ship's sails billowed as it made its circle around Saint Helena's coastline, passing another ship circling in the opposite direction.

Amélie didn't understand this escort business with the island situated a thousand leagues from anywhere. Up on the peaks, all pointed down at Longwood, the cannon from High Knoll fortress glittered in the sun. A bugle blared in the distance with a sharp roll of drums; gusts of wind rippled the tents at the Deadwood Camp. The soldiers surrounded them like fire ants in their red coats, with British troops divided between the Fifty-third Regiment here at Deadwood, the Sixty-sixth at Jamestown, and various detachments around the island.

Bending to her garden, she picked dill and rosemary, dropping them in the basket. She'd brew the rosemary in tea to strengthen herself and quicken her mind, or so the herbal book promised. Out of habit she began to sing, the effort calming her mood. Recently, she'd borrowed several books from Ali, who worked as the emperor's librarian. Each book she'd opened with reverence and read the front piece inscribed in his neat hand: *L'Empereur Napoleon*.

One of the new books contained a history of Italian opera, with many of the librettos written out in detail. Having an Italian mother, she knew the language and Suzanne had showed her how to read notes and interpret the librettos.

She'd memorized some of them and today sang the aria "Questa Cosa" from the opera *Il Matrimonio Segreto*. She'd seen this opera in Lyon, about a girl who is secretly married to her father's clerk and must fend off the attentions of a wealthy count. Amélie laughed, as if she would ever face such issues. Was Clarice right—did she glean all her life's experience from books?

The wind increased and she raised her voice to accommodate it. Her restlessness released on the notes. The wind howled and she sang louder. Napoleon must hear her now and be drawn from his lair. Her voice vibrated up her throat. A movement to the right made her glance over. Her father beckoned in an anxious manner from the back door of the house.

"Amélie, please come in here immediately." He sounded irritated.

She rose with reluctance and walked toward him, brushing off her skirt. "What is it, Papa?" She adjusted her straw hat, secured with a ribbon under her chin.

"Come with me. Someone wishes to speak to you."

He steered her inside, mumbling words she didn't catch, the wind's song and her own still vibrating in her ears. She dug the dirt from under her fingernails. When in the prep room, he deposited her in front of someone.

Amélie stared up into the face of the emperor.

"Your Majesty, this is my daughter, Amélie Perrault," her father introduced in a strained voice.

She kept her mouth from gaping but felt the blood drain from her face. The emperor scrutinized her and she wondered what terrible crime she'd committed. Maybe he too would scold her for witnessing his tirade against Governor Lowe. Or had her conniving for his attention finally succeeded? Light-headed, Amélie sucked in her breath and managed a smile. "How do you do, Your Majesty."

She realized too late the emperor was supposed to speak first. Aware she should curtsy, her mind went blank, leaving her at a loss as to which foot went where. She dipped her head.

"Mademoiselle, the little gardener. Is that you I heard singing so spiritedly out in the courtyard?"

"You *did* listen? Oh, I'm sorry if I disturbed you, Your Majesty." She grinned wider and didn't glance at her father who stood rigid near the door—he'd faded into the background.

"No, no, you misunderstand. You haven't disturbed me." Napoleon laughed softly. "I find your voice very interesting. Have you had formal training?"

A rush of awe heated her from the inside out at this praise from the one man their entire world revolved around. Her knees trembled. "Very *informal* training, Sire, and self-study recently…from the books I borrowed from…I—"

"You learned to sing like that from books?" His sweet smile and flashing blue-gray eyes illuminated his pallid features.

"No, I…but I do love to read. You learn so many different things…it opens up the world…" She broke off, ashamed of her babbling, twisting the ribbon under her chin with nervous fingers.

"Quite right, Mademoiselle. Would you mind singing that song again for me, now?"

She blinked at him. "Of course…I wouldn't mind…Sire." The idea of singing directly in front of the emperor with her limited knowledge of music made her toes curl in her muddy shoes. A voice in the wind might not sound so melodious in the confines of a house.

"*Tres bien.* Come into the reception hall. It has the most space." Napoleon strode from the room.

Passing her father, she didn't look at him as she followed the emperor through the house to the front. The green reception salon was Longwood's largest chamber. A mahogany billiard table the British had brought up in the first months of their residence took up a fifth of the space. An old piano stood in the far corner. Two lumpy sofas and several chairs slumped against the walls. Two globes, one of the Heavens, one of Earth, flanked the door from the drawing room. Amélie stood in the realm she'd been eager to explore. The wind rattled the window panes as she felt her nerves rattling beneath her skin.

She hid her dirty hands behind her back and waited for some signal to begin. Napoleon sat and nodded his head.

After a deep breath Amélie anxiously cleared her throat and started to sing.

Elysium

Tentative at first, her voice sputtered and crackled as she grappled for control. Now gathering momentum, she hoped her singing exuded a rich tone. She closed her eyes, trying to regulate her breath, hitting the high drawn-out notes and concentrating on doing her utmost—fearful of making a mistake. When done, her body quivered at the exertion. She took another full breath before meeting the emperor's gaze.

Napoleon rubbed his chin, looking at her thoughtfully. "Your voice is good. A little untamed around the edges, but brimming with possibilities. Do you know any other songs?"

"A few, Sire." She named some of the arias she remembered off-hand.

"You must practice properly, Mademoiselle. You could have the makings of an accomplished singer."

Caught unawares by this attention she'd longed for, pride tangled in with her fluster. "Yes, maybe someday I might think of such things."

"No 'someday.'" Napoleon rose with effort and approached her. "You need to practice now, and I will help you. I was quite the patron of the opera in Paris. Every week I attended the theater, when not on campaign. We can engineer some sort of strategy for you."

Amélie stared at him and longed for a chair edge to cling to. She'd only hoped to spark his interest with such a caprice. Singing wasn't the basis into his company she'd sought. "That's very kind of you, but not necessary. I *would* like to discuss books, battle tactics, and aren't you writing your memoires?"

"Nonsense. You have talent. Why waste it?" he said, his voice confident, his smile warm. "One must grasp the opportunities thrust before them."

Amélie licked her dry lips, her heart throbbing. She quivered with the excitement she always imagined she would in his personal presence. Drawn by the melancholy she sensed beneath that smile, she said, "Yes, Your Majesty. You're right, one must."

Chapter Six

...Nothing is more ill-considered and blameworthy than to make girls stage theatrical performances—N.B.

The same ugly cramped kitchen seemed to glow with a new radiance, the chill of evening ineffective against the warmth simmering inside her. Amélie flicked a piece of rotten wood from the window frame and smiled.

"Amélie, are you listening? What is this singing for the opera? I had no idea you were interested in such things." Her father scrutinized her with the green eyes that had steadied her throughout childhood, but for her, childhood ended when they'd sailed to this island.

"I didn't intend it." She'd broken through the wall, by accident or hidden design it didn't matter. Not just a brief encounter, but the promise of time to come. She wiped grease from the stove in absent-minded strokes. "I just entertained myself, but His Majesty seems to think I have talent."

"I have heard you singing in the garden. I hope you weren't flaunting yourself there in the courtyard." Her father's tone didn't accuse, but she knew he sought reassurance. He bent his gray head to scrub out his favorite iron pot, distrustful of anyone near his cookware.

"Papa!" Amélie stepped again to the window and looked at Longwood's back door. She didn't want her father to see her guilty face.

"I asked you to stay away from the court. Now I suppose...I don't want to displease His Majesty, but you cannot be a nuisance to him." Reflected in the window, he dried the pot with a cloth. The last wisps of smoke from the stove faded, and his hair reeked of it. "Still, I must tell you, don't speak to His Majesty until spoken to, and you are supposed to curtsy when introduced."

"I...if I'm not well versed in court protocol, I can learn." She shrugged this off as she continued to gaze outside, the evening too lingering. She rubbed a nose smudge from the pane and smiled at her reflection.

"Just do your best, *ma petite*. That's what I would expect from you." He removed his apron and hung it on a wall peg. "Remember to always be polite to his courtiers."

"Papa, I think someone my age should no longer be called *petite*." She faced him, stepping forward. "Even though you mean it in the kindest way."

"I didn't know it bothered you." He gave her a rare, indulgent smile, which didn't help either. "I'll try to remember not to." His gaze turned serious. "Maybe I made a mistake, giving you too much education, putting you above your class."

Did her father think her unworthy of the emperor's consideration? The regret in his face made her uncomfortable. Her wish to be independent alienated her too quickly from him. She touched his hand. "No, Papa, it wasn't a mistake. I've always appreciated my studies. You should be happy I'm not a feather-headed female."

That night in her room, she rubbed her hair dry after a bath in the dented metal hip bath crammed between her bed and door. Stored in the privy, the tub smelled slightly of urine and the rosemary she sprinkled in there to diffuse odors. She mulled over the day's events: how to proceed, how should she behave? Napoleon's attention intrigued her. She deserved it, her yearning fulfilled…but as an opera singer?

* * * *

The emperor requested that she come to his study the next day at one o'clock. Amélie put on her nicest gown, a plain gray thing that now shamed her, fussed with her hair—the ribbon too childish? She tore it back out, snatched up her opera book, and entered the house at the appointed time. At awakening this morning, she wondered if the previous day's encounter was all a dream. Napoleon couldn't have spoken to her, or laughed, or listened with interest to her singing.

After her hesitant knock, Marchand came out from the study, smiled, and motioned for her to enter. A loyal servant who must take everything his master did as expected, he registered no surprise at her change in status.

"Welcome, Amélie. His Majesty will be with you shortly." He stationed himself like a sentry inside the door.

"I've never been in here before." Amélie edged in, curiosity overriding her flopping stomach. At last she stood in Napoleon's "interior." The Imperial study, a narrow chamber off the dining room, had a fireplace centered on the side wall between shuttered windows. Two makeshift bookcases stuffed with books sat on either side. She stepped close and scanned Machiavelli's *The Prince*, John Barrow's *History of England*, works of Jean-Jacques Rousseau, Montesquieu, Goethe, and many others. A shabby writing desk, sideboard, old sofa, and green-painted cane chairs filled out the remaining area.

Contemplating dingy yellow wallpaper and the faint odor of musty decay, she lamented her sovereign's downfall. The Perraults' simple cottage in Paris had been grander.

"*Bonjour*, Mademoiselle." Napoleon strode out his bedchamber door dressed in white kerseymere breeches straining at the seams and a waistcoat with gold buttons pulling. Hadn't he realized how corpulent he'd grown? At the same time, without his epaulets, polished military boots, and cocked hat, Napoleon appeared smaller, more vulnerable.

"*Bonjour*, Your Majesty." This time she managed an adequate curtsy. "I brought my opera book, as you requested." She held this out, and her hand remained steady.

"Fine, fine." He took the volume and leafed through it. "You must know how to read notes then, Amélie. May I call you Amélie?"

"Yes…please, Your Majesty." His interest, his remembering her name, delighted her.

Napoleon smiled and asked her to sit on the sofa. Since the emperor rarely let people sit in his presence, he granted her an enormous courtesy, but her legs froze up and she respectfully remained standing.

"What about the reading of notes?" he asked again.

"Yes, I can read notes, but I'm slow at it, and make mistakes." She admitted her shortcomings.

"I noticed you had a little trouble with that aria yesterday, but we can remedy that."

"I have heard…attended several operas. My sister-in-law studied opera and we sang a few." Amélie took a deep breath, wishing her pulse would calm. "She helped me with learning the librettos."

"Taught by your sister-in-law?" Napoleon's expression grew amused. "You seem to have a natural talent. That's excellent. You understand Italian?"

"Yes, Sire. My mother was Italian. She spoke it to me as a child."

"Splendid. Italian is my native tongue, so I can help you there as well." His enunciation still held an Italian flavor, even after his many years in France. "Which operas do you prefer?"

"I…like Mozart's *Le Nozze di Figaro*." She stated the first opera that came to mind.

"Libretto by Lorenzo da Ponte. Yes, and why?" Napoleon sat on the sofa and patted the cushion next to him. "Come, come, don't be shy, sit."

"The Countess Almaviva sings such poignant laments, believing the count no longer loves her." Amélie lowered herself to the cushion. Careful not to sit too close, she didn't want to appear rude.

"Another count lusting after a servant girl, but a comic opera with a happy ending." He said this as if he disapproved of such things. "You enjoy the tragic aspects?"

"I like the comic too." She didn't care to sound maudlin with the stale air pressing around her. His quarters felt like the rest of the house when it should feel different, superior, in here. "Sometimes one needs to sing comedy to lighten the heart."

"I myself always preferred the tragic operas. Tragedy is noble and creates heroes. You seem an intelligent girl. What type of schooling have you had?" He laid down the book, folding his plump hands on his knee in a graceful gesture.

"I attended Madame Vamoulet's in Paris until I was seventeen. I learned history, geography, mathematics. I did well in most." Amélie fingered the cushion beneath her, uncomfortable with bragging. She tried not to stare Napoleon directly in the face, but his large vivid eyes drew her own.

"I am well aware of that Paris school. An excellent establishment, and not inexpensive." His smile encouraged her to continue, while his gaze probed into every corner of her being, making her defenseless and giddy at the same time.

"Oh, yes, Your Majesty, you would be aware…" Amélie winced, sorry to remind him of his lost eminence. "My parents saved for us to attend good schools, my brothers and I. Madame Vamoulet was regarded as progressive, to teach girls in such a manner."

"Paris had many progressive schools. It was I who reorganized France's school system." He spoke with quiet pride before scrutinizing her again. "In what manner do you mean?"

Amélie swallowed, trying to stir up saliva. "To teach them things other than the usual lessons considered appropriate for girls…the math and such."

"That is so, but a woman shouldn't be filled with too much wisdom, making her wiser than the men around her. It isn't becoming." Napoleon said this as a statement of fact. His narrow view of women upset though didn't surprise her. "Did you ever think to study singing?"

"Oh, no, Sire. It isn't a profession that's…considered…it isn't well respected." Her cheeks burned. Just because she came from a lower station, he shouldn't think her lacking in morals.

"*En vérité*, but I see I've embarrassed you. No, I didn't mean for the stage. Singing for small gatherings as entertainment is proper. Now you're on this rock at the end of the ocean where no one will hear you." He seemed to sag and include himself in that remark. "Why did you come to Saint Helena?"

"To be with my father, Your Majesty." Her response sounded inadequate as she looked at the man before her. *To find my grand adventure*, she didn't say.

"Indeed, you are an obedient daughter. How old are you, Amélie?"

She didn't think herself an obedient daughter, but as a woman, her expected definition was as property of another man. Why couldn't she belong to herself? "I will turn twenty in three days, Sire."

"Twenty? You look younger. What else do you do to busy yourself here?"

"I grow the herbs and spices in the courtyard." She resisted a glance down at her attire to see if she did appear too childish. Her drabness again shamed her. "I also read, and—"

"Ah, yes, the little herb gardener." He nodded, his gaze now elsewhere, as if he assessed a distant battlefield. "A noble undertaking, trying to force life onto this desolate plain."

She strived to keep his attention and absorb his experiences. "I've always wanted to ask you, Sire, what was it like in Egypt?"

A shadow fell across them and Napoleon turned toward the door. The Countess de Montholon hovered in the doorway. Marchand, still the quiet sentinel, bowed his head and stepped aside.

"Albine, come in," Napoleon said with a sweep of his hand, though he remained seated.

Amélie's heart sank and she shifted on the sofa, disappointed to share this interview.

"You wanted to see me, Your Majesty?" The countess smiled and curtsied, not bothering to acknowledge Amélie. Her dark blue eyes sparkled for the emperor.

The woman minced farther into the room and hovered near him, bending forward. The countess's dress revealed too much cleavage for afternoon attire. His alleged mistress smeared her rouge too heavily over her cheeks and lips. A woman nearing forty, she must be desperate to disguise her aging.

"Yes. Mademoiselle Perrault is an aspiring opera singer. You can accompany her on the piano." Napoleon rose to his feet. "Let's go into the reception hall."

"I would be happy to play for you, Sire." The countess slinked beside him and relegated Amélie to trail behind. When the woman placed a neat white hand on the emperor's shoulder, Amélie's stomach clenched.

* * * *

Napoleon strode the length of the room. The girl, bright and not overly forward, sang two arias from *Le Nozze di Figaro*: "Porgi amor" and "Dove sono."

He stopped and confronted Amélie in her plain little dress.

"Having a great voice is one thing, but you must learn to conduct yourself with distinction like the women of the Paris Opéra. You have to project your voice from deep inside to give it strength. You must improve your gestures, make them flow. I myself showed the great Talma how he should play Nero in Racine's *Britannicus*." He waved around his hand to demonstrate. "Albine can assist you in clarifying your note reading."

Albine faced him and fluttered her eyelashes, but he ignored her impertinence—the woman could be tiring at times. The countess grimaced at Amélie. He'd reprimand her for that later.

"Your Majesty, I did sing only for fun," Amélie said, sounding unsure of herself, "but...of course, if you insist."

"I do. I won't allow you to disregard your talents. Now I appreciated the finest drama in opera. I rarely suffered these sentimental librettos." Napoleon continued his stride around the room, his mind on something pleasant for the first time in weeks. The great commander in him came alive, again formulating plans. His innards relaxing, blood flowing. He smiled at this invigorated feeling. "The renowned Ferdinando Paer was my Imperial composer. As was Etienne Mehul, who wrote *La prise du Pont de Lodi*, celebrating my victory over the Austrians in 1796. The magnificent Girolamo Crescentini, who dazzled in Zingarelli's *Giulietta e Romeo*, sang exclusively for me in Paris."

"Don't forget Guiseppina Grassini, Sire." The countess gave him a probing smile as she rose from the piano bench and swirled around her skirt. She then fluffed out her curls. Napoleon admired her ample figure, but in public she should behave less like a courtesan. He'd dismissed Montholon years before for disobeying his orders over marrying her. You never married your mistresses.

"Grassini, yes, a ravishing woman. She displayed her brilliant voice at many of my soirees." Napoleon warmed at this memory. Madame Grassini had been his mistress when he was First Consul, before he grew bored with her. Abruptly, his memory soured. Rumor had it this disloyal diva was now the mistress of the Duke of Wellington. He sighed. Salon and theater women, you couldn't trust them. "Amélie, come back to my study. I have something for you."

In the study, he pulled a large book from his bookcase of pine-board shelves painted green—a sad comparison to his immense library at the Tuileries. He doubted King Louis had the intelligence to appreciate it. "Since you have studied history, read this on Alexander the Great, then tell me what you think." He winked at her—a fresh face, eager to please, a new interest in his stagnant existence. "I doubt it will matter if you're wiser than most of the men around here."

"*Merci*, Your Majesty." Amélie clutched the book, her smile wide and sincere. Her thick blond hair waved about her face. "To discuss literature with you is my fondest wish."

Napoleon thought of the evening ahead with the same dreary people. "Tonight, you should come to listen to my little court in our simplified version of going to the theater."

The girl almost stood on tiptoes. "I would be so honored, Sire."

"Fine. Speak with Ali, he will set it up." Her enthusiasm pleased him. The malleability of girl performers. Napoleon thought of the actress Mademoiselle George, his once mistress. How many times had he watched her in his favorite play, *Cinna*? Now he'd grown too jaded for such misalliances with young girls. Again, he studied Amélie. Her attentive brown eyes drew him off the island and back into Paris for a moment.

* * * *

Amélie returned to her quarters and slumped on her bed in a daze. He didn't mind making her wiser than the men? Napoleon always promoted men on merit alone. Women, at least she, should have the same opportunity. She caressed the leather cover of *Alexander the Great*. Personally entrusted with one of the emperor's books and a promise of discussion, *that* relationship she coveted all along, and now he invited her to attend a reading with the court. His valets often spoke of how his court spent evenings reading drama.

After a dinner she barely ate, Amélie climbed up narrow steps and entered the attic. The air smelled like sweaty bodies and soiled clothes, even with the few tiny windows open. Dirty skylights dripped from the recent rain. The ceiling's black exposed beams were cloaked with spider webs as if wrapped in gauze. Wooden partitions divided the area into cramped cells for the servants.

"Ali, are you here?" she called into the shadows that crept up the walls. Loud giggling erupted from the far corner of the room.

Saint-Denis stepped from her right, ducking under a beam. "I always smack my head up here. Perhaps we should go down now."

"How can you breathe? I'll give you some wild thyme to sweep across the floor." Amélie heard more muffled laughter. Floorboards creaked across the room and some area of skin sounded playfully slapped. Curious and embarrassed at the same time, she asked, "Is that one of those prostitutes the servants gossip about?"

"Shhh, don't give our unholy chamber away." Ali's bright grin reflected in the light of his candle, and he steered her back toward the stairs. "Count de Montholon complained so much about them, he ordered twice as many sentries at night. He's scandalized by the activity he hears through his ceiling."

"Shouldn't he worry about his own wife's conduct before anyone else's?" A bed frame squeaked and Amélie flushed. These women provided something wives or mistresses did with men behind closed doors, but now she speculated on the finer details of this "activity."

"His Majesty raged over the increased sentries, since he hates being guarded," Saint-Denis replied as they clattered down the stairs. "He told Montholon this place wasn't a convent. The sailors do call Saint Helena the 'brothel of the Atlantic.'"

"It is strange to ask for *more* guards from your enemies."

"Montholon wants to be in control of the emperor, and does it through wheedling and false words. At least that's how I see it. He makes policy changes and insists it's in His Majesty's best interests." Ali stared her up and down with that glint of mischief. "Our little Amélie has been invited to the theater?"

"Why not? I managed to slip in here before the night patrol marches around the house." She squinted in the dim dining room. "How do these town women get past the sentries?"

"They have their own sleazy bribes. We suffer enough without being deprived of entertainment." Ali's airy tone drained away. "Everything gets harsher, and many already talk about leaving. The British want the emperor abandoned."

A chill crept along her spine, and Ali's candor surprised her. "I'm afraid that's true. I've heard it as well, but you won't abandon him, will you?"

"Me? I'm as loyal as they come. Better for him than his officers, if I may be so brash." He took his taper and lit a few candles on the sideboard. The smell of tallow filled the room.

She laughed. "You're most often brash."

"How can you misjudge me, lovely *demoselle*?" Saint-Denis wrestled his expression from a smirk to playful innocence.

Amélie shrugged off the flattery. She'd gained more weight, but no one ever referred to her as lovely, and she considered Ali a big brother. "I doubt your sincerity, *Monsieur* Saint-Denis. Am I only of value if I might be pleasing to the eye?"

"What do you mean—have I insulted you?"

She wasn't sure if he had or not. "Women are worth more than just their attraction for men. Girls need to be educated and useful too. My father agreed with that. Does the emperor ever...pay attention to those prostitutes?" She tried to sound nonchalant.

"No, no. He said when we arrived on the island that he was already an old man. Women had nothing to fear from him."

"He's not so old. Especially when he's excited about something." Napoleon's warm smile, those vivid eyes, warmed her. "Life here is aging. Are there no females here who appeal to him?" Amélie wanted Saint-Denis to denounce the rumor about their sovereign and the Countess de Montholon as a lie.

"I thought your interests were academic." Saint-Denis winked and set down the candle.

"They *are*." Why did her emperor's alleged dallying with the countess bother her?

"You like empire history. Have I ever told you why the emperor calls me Ali?" The valet thrust his hands in his waistcoat pockets, his long arms flapping.

"Something to do with a military honor?" Amélie threw this off. Voices came from the drawing room. "Oh, they must be gathering now."

"When His Majesty was in Egypt..." Saint-Denis cleared his throat. "He hired foreign young men, Mamelukes, an ancient military caste to work as his bodyguards. They proved troublesome, so the emperor called me Ali and I acted as the new Mameluke."

"What does a Mameluke do, exactly?" Amélie edged toward the drawing room door.

Saint-Denis placed a hand on his heart and raised his dimpled chin. "Decked out in ceremonial garb from the Orient, on the emperor's every campaign I was by his side, bearing the imperial spyglass, dressing-case, and a silver flask of brandy. Since Mameluking isn't needed here, I keep busy rewriting His Majesty's dictation and being his librarian."

"*Ecoute*, I think it's time to join them." She tugged on his sleeve, her anticipation sharp.

Ali stepped ahead of her and poked his face around the door. Then he picked up a stool. "You can sit behind the screen and I'll stand in attendance. Good, the Bertrands have consented to come."

"Behind the screen?" Amélie almost protested at being hidden like a stain, but thought better of it. She should be flattered to have been invited at all.

With the stool placed behind a Chinese silk screen, Amélie sat and peeked around near Ali's thigh, able to see most of the room. Las Cases, along with Counts Bertrand and Montholon and their wives, waited at attention as Napoleon entered.

Countess Bertrand looked elegant in a white conical gown with long, repeated puff sleeves. She stood half a head taller than their emperor, who reached just average height. Her perfume wafted around as she swept into a curtsy and Napoleon wrinkled his nose when he passed. He sat and nodded. The others arranged themselves in chairs. Marchand stood silently behind Napoleon's larger arm chair.

Amélie grinned, elbows on her knees and her chin cupped in her hands.

The emperor gave them a token good evening. Count de Las Cases fluttered into a pose of adoration, sitting on a stool near the emperor's feet. "We are all honored to be here with you, Sire. Me, most especially," the little man said. "I await with suspense over what we shall hear in your august presence."

"*Monsieur* Rapture," Montholon muttered, still keeping his smile between curly sideburns condescending.

"Now, what shall we read tonight, my captive audience?" The emperor reached into a scratched bookcase and pulled out a book. "*Andromaque* or *Phedre* by Racine, Corneille's tragedy, *Horace*. The translations of Homer or Virgil?"

"Homer, the *Odyssey*, we have something in common," Amélie whispered, her pulse quickening. Ali shushed her.

"No, I think Voltaire's *Zaire* is appropriate." Napoleon opened the book on his lap and began to read. He'd obviously made his decision ahead of time.

Fanny Bertrand slumped in her chair. She rolled her black eyes, which contrasted with her fair coloring and made her face lively. Amélie stroked her cheek. Did that combination of dark and light work for her?

"Very good, Sire." Countess de Montholon smiled and fanned herself with her silk fan. The women appeared overdressed in these shabby surroundings with their silks and jewels, their husbands in full uniform, this strict code of dress always maintained before their sovereign.

"Sire, haven't we read *Zaire* too much already?" Countess Bertrand said. Her husband flicked a startled gaze at her.

"Madame?" Napoleon lowered the book and glared at her.

"*Zaire* is...perfect, Your Majesty." Bertrand squeaked this out, his neck growing scarlet. He grasped his wife's hand as if to quiet her.

"Anything you read is ideal, Sire, I must say." Las Cases bobbed his head, his needle nose twitching. "Some people just enjoy complaining and stirring up discontent, unlike myself."

"You need only tell us your wishes, Your Majesty. We are here to serve." Montholon seemed to parody the effusive Las Cases. Amélie pictured them both doubling over into toads.

"*En vérité*, Sire, only to serve you." Countess de Montholon flashed her contrived grin. Both her and her husband's commiseration, their gestures and words, so perfect, so rehearsed, Amélie couldn't believe the emperor didn't see it.

Napoleon resumed reading, his sentences speeding along. He didn't give the words nuance or the correct emphasis. Amélie didn't care. She leaned forward eagerly on her stool, her temple bumping the screen.

Fanny Bertrand yawned, barely concealing the fact.

"You are bored, Madame?" The emperor's words cold, the company squirmed in their chairs. Amélie stiffened on her perch. "Would you like to finish this, since it seems you are?" He bent forward and thrust the book into the woman's hands.

Amélie started to rise from her stool, anxious to be the one chosen to read, but

Ali dug his fingers into her shoulder.

Countess de Montholon gave a taunting titter behind her fan.

Countess Bertrand sighed, her face redder than her husband's throat. She glanced around the room, the book unsteady in her grasp. She began to read in a tentative voice.

Napoleon settled back in his chair, closed his eyes, and it was soon obvious he'd fallen asleep.

Ali gestured for Amélie to get up and he skulked from the room. In the dining room, the valet shook with laughter. "That's as bad as the other evening at dinner, when the emperor told both ladies they looked like washerwomen dressed up in their Sunday finery."

"Both of them?" Amélie relished that Napoleon spoke to the Countess de Montholon with disdain, but didn't he understand that the women arrayed themselves in his honor?

"The emperor upset Madame Bertrand so much, she told her husband she'd never come to Longwood again, but you see he's dragged her back. It's hard to stay aloof in this tiny social circle." Ali snickered. "Count Bertrand's mortified. He regards himself the savior of etiquette. He's been with him since Egypt and is selflessly devoted to the emperor."

"He seems one of few." Amélie sighed and gripped her elbows. "Countess Bertrand shouldn't have yawned. She ruined my evening. I'm sure the emperor is just as bored with their society. Are you certain His Majesty wouldn't have allowed me to sit nearer to him?"

"You still want to abolish all protocol?" Ali leaned against the dining room wall. "His Majesty seldom holds court anymore, but when he discusses his career, his experiences, then his listeners are never drowsy. They all enjoy that."

"I'd adore it. The emperor and I are going to discuss books." Amélie, heavy with disappointment, longed to be more effective than his courtiers. She didn't want to leave the house and walked over to the chamber across from the emperor's, used as the Imperial Library. "Ali, did you ever catalogue those thirteen cases of books requested from the British government?" She opened the door. The soft light from the dining room outlined stacks of books along the walls.

"The majority. His Majesty was so excited when they arrived, he helped unpack them, but the British also sent him the bill, over a thousand in their pounds. Nearly 25,000 francs. The emperor was furious and refused to pay." He chuckled again.

Amélie moved closer and reached out to touch one of the books. "I'll help you sort through them. *C'est ça*, you could appoint me your library assistant."

"A girl assisting in the emperor's library? Don't you have your hands full now?"

"Why can't a girl, rather a *woman*, do such things? You shouldn't discourage me."

"The emperor prefers women in their place, as comforts to their husbands and households. You are too forward at times, but amusing." The valet's smirk exasperated her.

"A progressive man shouldn't feel that way." The countess was fawning and far bolder. Did she bring comfort to someone other than her husband?

Amélie gazed back into the drawing room. Napoleon shifted in his sleep, as if bad dreams pursued him. She had the sudden desire to brush the lock of hair from his pale forehead.

Ali pushed away from the wall. "I'd better make certain His Majesty's fire is roaring hot." He hurried into Napoleon's chambers, leaving Amélie near the library doorway.

The courtiers quietly exited the drawing room into the front salon—his previous sycophants now scurrying away like rats. Both Montholons' expressions looked aloof and dismissive toward their sleeping sovereign. Quite a frigid contrast to their actions under his gaze.

Amélie shuddered. Longwood's walls seemed to close in on her, someplace more unsafe than she realized.

"You should encourage His Majesty to go out riding again," she said when Ali rejoined her. "It isn't healthy for him to stay cooped up inside." She glanced over at the back door, at the glass pane, just in time to see a sentry trudge by shouldering his rifle.

"You don't speak to the emperor about things he doesn't care to discuss." Saint-Denis brushed soot from his sleeves. "No one wants to face His Majesty's temper. Though it's short-lived and he strains for good humor here."

"Even if the subject is for his own welfare?" Amélie rubbed her arms, feeling ice-cold in this cloistered atmosphere. "Hasn't His Majesty written in protest to the British government about his treatment?"

"Do our letters actually make it to their government after being scrutinized by Lowe? Everything we mail has to be sent 'open' through the governor. Then most of the words are scribbled over or cut out." Ali couldn't hide a sly twitch of his lips.

"I know correspondence is smuggled off the island, sending Governor Lowe into more fits." Amélie glanced away, aware she shouldn't say such things aloud. Incoming letters were treated with the same scrutiny. The last letter from her brother had half the words indecipherable. "What does His Majesty do to stay occupied since he won't go out?"

"He goes over his battle errors, reorganizes troops, artillery. His Majesty's generals write different aspects of his career." Ali took a deep breath. "I have firsthand knowledge of some of it. I served with him in Russia, and...Belgium."

"Outside pursuits would be a change of pace for His Majesty. He should ignore any British escort."

"He finds that intolerable, but we're all at a loss to keep occupied. The emperor does in-depth research on various subjects apart from his career. He's fascinated by science and mathematics." The drawing room door opened wider and the valet turned. "Now he has you to sing for him. He changes his habits at will."

Napoleon ambled into the room, rubbing his face. "Ali, bring me a hot lemonade, or that special tea you make. I feel a cough coming on." He looked at Amélie as if, for a moment, he'd forgotten he invited her. "Ah, Amélie, did you enjoy our theatrical display?"

Amélie smiled into his tired expression and curtsied. "I wish it had lasted longer, Sire."

Napoleon nodded and continued toward his study. He moved, shoulders and head slumped, like walking were a burden to him, his ankles swollen in his stockings. Marchand followed behind and closed the study door.

"At once, Your Majesty." Ali straightened from his bow. They heard him coughing behind the door. "The slightest humidity and chill affects the emperor. That's why this house is terrible for his health. To the kitchen, Mademoiselle Perrault."

"*I* make that special tea for him, with orange flower leaves and maidenhair syrup." Amélie grasped credit where it was due. "Marchand said no, but His Majesty might take herbs for his well-being. Maidenhair is a fern."

"The emperor seldom follows any advice on his health. He can be like a child sometimes." Saint-Denis spoke with indulgence. "He doesn't know how to take care of himself."

"If no one has the nerve to advise him what's best." Amélie opened the back door, the wind sweeping in, rustling her hair. Ali asked permission to pass from a sentry. "His Majesty needs someone to attend him who isn't afraid of him. You are all too submissive." She took a deep breath. Here was her chance to be useful, but would she have the nerve to tell her emperor what might be best?

Chapter Seven

You have miscalculated the heights to which misfortune, the injustice and persecution of your government, and your own conduct have raised the Emperor—N.B.

Fire crackled in the study hearth, warming the damp air with a tinge of smoke.

Napoleon flicked a finger across the offensive paper he held. "Now that muddleheaded governor insists that I report to the orderly officer twice a day. Like a lackey? *Grand Dieu!*"

Count Bertrand stood by, hat in hand. "Admiral Cockburn apparently had the same rule, but never enforced it. Lowe is angry because you refuse to receive him anymore, Sire."

"I can't reason with such a man. He wants me to be humbled, resigned." Napoleon tossed the paper on the floor. How much more humiliation did the British expect him to swallow? He felt the chains tremble around his body, squeezing like tentacles until he couldn't breathe. "Insult piled on insult. Bertrand, I also demand you reprimand your wife for her behavior last night. I won't tolerate such disrespect among my own court."

"I understand, Sire, and have spoken to Fanny. What will you do about this? The governor is concerned that you'll...escape. He wants to make certain, for his government, that you're still here." The count's head seemed to shrink into his round shoulders.

How much influence did Napoleon retain over Bertrand since he resided elsewhere with his domineering wife? Bertrand, only four years younger, served as his aide-de-camp and distinguished himself as an army engineer before Napoleon appointed him grand marshal of his palace—the man should be grateful.

So many others deserted him when his power faded, but to relax his guard, reveal a crack in his fortitude, and be grateful himself at Bertrand's loyalty—Napoleon needed to keep these few who remained under his thumb.

"Escape? I *should* think about it." If the only viable option. Louis XVIII stuffed onto his imperial throne—a throne carved from the ashes of the Revolution. Now that fat Bourbon ruined France while he rotted here. Dare he continue to expect another coup that might bring him back to Europe, or did he wish to go elsewhere, unencumbered by prejudice? He'd recently made queries into other plans of action and spoken to that Irish merchant captain—an interesting man—introduced by Las Cases. Napoleon had money available to him, the gold he'd had his valets secure in belts worn on their persons when they boarded the British ship. He stroked a knuckle over his forehead. He couldn't allow this place to devour him. "This enrages me. I won't bow to this petty official's insults. Marchand!" He glared around the shabby chamber wishing he could shatter it with a cannon ball. The chief valet rushed in. Napoleon jabbed a finger at him. "Make sure my pistols are loaded and put them on my night table." The valet ran out.

"Your Majesty, what are you planning?" Bertrand asked, mouth agape, hat crumpled in his grasp.

"I plan to shoot any Englishman who dares invade my private quarters."

* * * *

"The emperor refuses to see anyone but myself and Marchand. He even sent his doctor away, because he might tell Lowe about it," Ali said to Amélie in the kitchen. The two of them mixed together an array of jasmine, orange flower, and other herbs steeped in spirit of wine they used to make the emperor's cologne, since the French type Napoleon preferred was impossible to obtain on the island.

"He can't keep hiding away. It's been three days. What about my lessons?" She regretted sounding like a petulant child, but couldn't believe he forgot her already. The mixture's light, musky smell reminded her of what she might lose.

"His Majesty is stubborn." Ali smiled and shrugged, his sooty eyes giving away little. He recapped the small crystal bottle with its silver gilt lid and left the kitchen.

Amélie stepped into the courtyard, disillusionment roiling inside her. She must request an audience with Napoleon, and strode toward the house. She hesitated at the sound of galloping. Several horsemen raised dust over the Deadwood Plain—soldiers, like red hornets on their steeds. They entered the grounds and careened around the left side of the house. Amélie gasped to see Governor Lowe followed by his henchmen.

Clarice snatched towels off the nearby clothesline and rushed across the courtyard. "Now we'll see some excitement in this godforsaken place, won't we?" She swayed and flashed a grin for the soldiers.

"Ali told me His Majesty keeps loaded pistols with him, intending to shoot." Amélie rushed toward the back door of Longwood, fearing gunplay between Napoleon and the orderly. She almost wished the English hadn't returned their weapons.

Lowe dismounted, his frame as stiff and brittle as a twig. His horse snorted and swished its tail. "Captain Poppleton! Come to me at once!"

The orderly officer sprinted from around the house and saluted Lowe, almost knocking off his own hat.

"Why can't you do your duty? I'll have you replaced for incompetence. Spy in his bedroom window if you must." The governor flailed his fist around as if trying to strike something. "Pound on his door and demand admittance! I won't have this breach of my authority!"

Poppleton, red in the face, slunk under the emperor's bedroom window and put his nose to the pane, but the closed blinds blocked his view.

"Demand entrance!" Lowe pointed at the door leading to the emperor's study from the outside. "I *will* write to my superiors about this. The prisoner must make himself visible." He glowered at the servants who gathered to watch. "You French glean some joy from…from making things difficult for me. I can be a reasonable man…but…"

Poppleton knocked. The door finally opened and Marchand confronted him with an apologetic smile. "The emperor is ill and in bed, and receiving no one," the valet said in a calm voice, blocking the doorway. "You can't disturb a sick man, Captain."

Elysium

The orderly officer turned to his commander in embarrassment and shrugged.

Lowe clenched his fists, his mouth working. "Tell your master, the *general*, I won't have it! Poppleton, if any of these people continue to tear down my directives, arrest them immediately."

Amélie cringed when Lowe seemed to glare toward her. The governor remounted, fidgeted angrily in his saddle, then kicked his horse in the flanks and rode away in a fume of horse sweat.

She hurried over to Marchand. "Will His Majesty speak to me? Is he really ill?" She searched his gentle face for clues.

"I'm sorry. It's best to leave him alone in his present temper." The chief valet's smile was kind yet firm as he shut the door.

Sighing, she walked toward the wall. Lowe's retreating figure crossed the plain. The governor would forbid any ships from sailing from Jamestown until the orderly "saw" their emperor, terrified he might slip away. "Why do the British have to shove everything down our throats?"

* * * *

Amélie worked in her garden not long after the cannon fired from Alarm House to announce the rising sun. She didn't bother to sing, and guessed Ali was right when he said the emperor changed his habits at will, but she wasn't ready to accept his brief focus and her return to a life on the fringe. She had to devise some way back into his company. An egotistical part of her was convinced Napoleon needed her in his life.

"How can you stand to touch dirt with all the creepy things in it? My hands are raw enough from all my duties." Clarice sauntered over, carrying her laundry basket. "I heard you sang for His Majesty. You must not have impressed him."

"Clarice, you always like to insult instead of having a simple conversation." Amélie shifted on her knees in the soil. She tugged at her corset where it rode up under her arms. Her herbs tangled into each other and she started to thin out the plants.

"I don't need conversation. I need a life away from here." Clarice jerked the basket from side to side. "You thought you had it better than me, but here you are back in the mud. Did you think you had a chance with His Majesty?"

"Don't blame me if you're unhappy." A chance? How absurd. Amélie bit down on her lip. "I know you're afraid of spiders, but do you like worms?" She picked up a caterpillar undulating toward her plants. She held it higher in the palm of her hand where it wriggled: a dark brown, smooth-bodied creature with black and yellow lines. With luck, the creature would chase off Clarice. "They damage the plants, but don't you think it has its own natural beauty?"

"*Peste.* There's nothing pretty on this island." Clarice started to step away when Marchand walked from one of the outbuildings. He smiled, greeted the two girls, and entered the house. Clarice sighed, heaving her ample chest. "You prefer worms, but don't you think Marchand has *his* own natural beauty?"

"Yes, I respect Marchand." Amélie liked that he rarely joined into the petty antagonisms of the others. Too bad he hadn't stopped to deliver a message to her from the emperor. She jerked a weed from the earth to redirect her frustration.

"You're getting older and aren't so thin now. You need to pay attention to the men around us. We haven't much to choose from." Clarice prodded Amélie with her foot. "There's more to life than plants."

"You're far too anxious. I'd choose none of them." Toiling with her hands, the earth moist between her fingers, seemed one of the few things Amélie could control. Her outward appearance had taken on more flesh, her clothes tightening around her breasts and waist. Her efforts for the garden to flourish seemed to leach from the earth into her own being. This strangeness fueled a need inside her, the island's backwards rhythms coalescing with her own. "What happened to your attraction to Ali?"

"He has a whore in Jamestown. Now if I acted as brazen as the Countess de Montholon does with our emperor, Marchand might notice me." Clarice bounced her basket against her knees, tendrils of auburn hair sweeping over her fat cheeks. "Did you know the countess is breeding? I wonder whose child it is. His Majesty's?"

"I don't believe it." Amélie ripped at her plants, tasting bile from her churning stomach. She hadn't known, and didn't want to know, about the countess's condition. A jerk on the Double Gee, a tenacious creeping weed, flung dirt in her eye. Blinking at the sting, she wiped her eye with her sleeve. "Why would her husband put up with that from His Majesty?"

"The emperor has had husbands' consent before." Clarice stared longingly at the door Marchand passed through. She wriggled hips that now stretched out her dresses, hiking the hem above her ankles. "Don't think you're alluring enough to attract His Majesty again."

Amélie stood, strode into her chamber, dipped quill in ink and scribbled a note: *Sire, when shall we continue my lessons?* She hurried into the house and handed it to Marchand.

She warmed with a feeling of success when Napoleon replied in turn: *tomorrow*.

* * * *

At the piano, the Countess de Montholon tapped her satin-slippered toe, a sound that pounded into Amélie's head. The woman's gaze raked over her as if she schemed to rip Amélie in half and push her through a window.

Napoleon paged through the opera book and approached. "Amélie, let's try this piece today, a quick run-through."

"Of course, Your Majesty." She smiled and he smiled back. Submissive, yes, but she fluttered at his reaction.

The Count de Montholon pranced into the reception hall.

"What do you want, Montholon? I'm very busy." The emperor didn't look up from the page he marked. His indifference to his courtier had the countess wriggling on the bench, her toe tapping louder.

"*Excusez-moi*, Sire. I'd forgotten this was your school time." The count's tone patronizing, he gave an insipid smile. "May I stay and observe, if it won't bother you in any way?"

"Have you finished organizing my dictation on the battle of Wagram? You have?" The emperor waved his hand and Montholon positioned himself against the wall between two windows, a slender statue with arms crossed—the Imperial Gatekeeper.

"You don't mind if Montholon stays, do you?" Napoleon stood in front of her and over his shoulder the count watched Amélie with slitted eyes—much like his manservant Jules—his slender nostrils flaring. Between the two Montholons she felt as welcome as rotten fish.

"No, of course not, Sire," she said, lying, surprised the emperor consulted her. Montholon was unnerving and the countess revolted her, but back in Napoleon's company she'd strain to be worthy of his attention. Her muscles bunched in knots. "You do like the Bertati libretto?"

"It is what few we have, this comedy of a secret marriage. I prefer Cimarosa's other opera, *Gli Orazi ed i Curiazi*. A tragedy of substance." Napoleon clapped the book shut. "The heroine ends up being stabbed by her brother."

Amélie finished the song, wincing over the slightest mistake.

The countess rose from the bench. "Are we done for the day, Sire? I must find the laundress to scrub the mildew stains from my silk shawl." She rolled her shoulders as she ran her hand around the garment, frothy at her neck.

"Perhaps His Majesty's little friend can find the laundress for you, *mon ange*." Montholon strutted over as Napoleon strode to the other side of the room.

The countess dropped the garment onto Amélie's head. "This damp house has ruined most of my clothes."

"I'll *try* to inform the laundress, if I have time due to my busy schedule." Amélie pulled the silk away from her face—like a cobweb left by a spider. Her irritation bubbling, she suppressed the urge to stare at the countess's waist for evidence of an impending child.

The woman flashed her a quick sneer.

"We don't wish to disturb you with such trivialities, Sire," the count said when Napoleon paced back. Montholon caressed his wife's arm, his manner as smooth and transparent as the shawl. "We are here to please. Shall we play a game of chess, now that school is over?"

"Perhaps later. Yes, we all have many trials to contend with, but me much more so than you, *mes amis*." Napoleon sounded weary. All the enthusiasm Amélie noticed during the lesson had drained away.

"Your Majesty, it's the weather, these damp days and frigid nights. I feel sluggish before I even get out of bed in the morning." Albine's petulant tone changed to a simper. "Oh, do forgive me, I didn't sleep well last night."

"Keep your manner serene, for His Majesty." Montholon spoke in a tranquil voice.

"Listen to your husband. The more we suffer the more bounteous our return." Napoleon spoke sharply, but he sounded as if such thoughts no longer cheered him.

Amélie wrinkled the silk in her hands, then dropped it onto a new marble-topped console behind her. "If you please, Sire, we have fresh lamb and a lentil salad for dinner tonight." Aware he enjoyed these food items, she strived to be a part of the conversation, not just an instrument of entertainment.

Montholon's ice-blue eyes widened, then narrowed on hers as if she'd scuttled out like a cockroach from under the baseboard.

"That's right, you do work in the kitchen as well, Mademoiselle." Napoleon's expression brightened. "Keeping occupied is a virtue." He walked close and tugged Amélie's earlobe. Her heart quivered at this unexpected touch.

"Are we playing cards this evening, Your Majesty? I hope Fanny Bertrand isn't attending. Her haughty demeanor is so disturbing to me." The countess clearly wanted the attention back on her. "All she does is whine about how we have no proper society here."

"You should pay more attention to your court, if I may be so bold, and *not* the servants." Montholon stepped beside Napoleon, angling himself to nudge Amélie aside. He brushed a hand over his left epaulet as if to sweep her beneath him. "You promised me control of the household, Sire. Only I know the correct way to conduct matters, unlike Bertrand, who has a more, let's say, ordinary background. Which he proves with his undignified actions."

"Enough of your bickering. All of you must work out your differences. I'm disgusted at being the moderator among you." Napoleon turned away, hands clasped behind his back.

Amélie bristled as well, tired of being dismissed by these grand elite, but confused about her footing here. A strange dance she needed to learn the steps to.

"How will this little amusement of yours look to the English?" Montholon capered after the emperor like a court jester. His disrespect was shocking. The more time they spent here, the more the layers of etiquette seemed to peel away, though that might be fortunate for her.

Amélie moved over to the windows, out of the line of fire.

"I forbid you to question my behavior or to interrupt me anymore." Napoleon stalked away from the Montholons and up to her. "These people will drive me insane," he muttered under his breath. "To rise above such things they need to forgive one another's weaknesses."

Did he consider himself weak for dallying with a servant?

"They should try harder, Sire, for your sake." Her voice soft, she wanted to erase the tension on his face. "They should seek a compromise or…it's futile. Perhaps a walk in the fresh air, away from these quarrels, might do you—"

"Futility at its worst." Napoleon lowered his voice. "I'm not impressed with Montholon's handling of the finances, but since Bertrand doesn't live here I have little choice." Then his eyes shimmered on hers, his smile returning. "Until tomorrow, for your next lesson, *ma chère*."

"I think I'll take a walk, to clear my head. I always enjoy that, Sire." Amélie warmed all over, his admission pleased her. Her emperor's disdain for the count was surprising. After the way he—and especially the countess—treated her, she liked being the more significant confidant.

She left the salon. Two chambermaids dusted in the dining room. They whispered and cast her derisive looks as she passed. One giggled behind her hand. Lately, several people had behaved this way in her presence.

Despite Napoleon's disinterest to accompany her, she walked around the courtyard and stables, then entered the kitchen and put an iron on the stove to heat. She'd promised her father she would re-iron a shirt badly pressed by Clarice. "The servants seem envious of me," she told him, mentioning the chambermaids. She didn't relay the Montholons' attitude toward her.

"I'm not surprised. The emperor has picked you out for attention. It might be a useful experience…in poise." Her father ran his carving knives over a wet stone, scraping in swift, even strokes. He sounded wary. "I hope you aren't being any trouble to His Majesty or the courtiers."

"Papa, you can't keep thinking I'm a child." She couldn't tell her father she might be the one sweet event in Napoleon's day—and she reveled in that position. She even enjoyed the singing. Her intellectual pursuits pushed to the background, there would be time for that later.

"His Majesty needs the attention. There's so little for him to do here." Amélie smiled as she maneuvered the hot iron over her father's linen, careful not to burn her fingers. What did she care about envious servants or spiteful courtiers? Her importance in the household rose.

"Just remember to always behave with ladylike decorum." Perrault rushed over his words as if it were something uncomfortable, though required to be said.

"I always do, Papa." She'd let him believe—for the moment—that he still dictated her actions. Her father loved her, but without the vibrancy of her mother—he either came off curt or negligent. Amélie sprinkled more water on the shirt. Pulse like a drumbeat call to arms, she'd never allow decorum to spoil her aspirations to stay by the emperor's side.

Chapter Eight

How time drags, what a cross. It takes courage to stay alive in a place like this—N.B.

The May humidity clung to the air, the sun weak behind a haze. Amélie ran her fingers over the wilted plant leaves, more rat nibbles along the edges. Rain drenched down the previous day and her hands turned brown, caked with mud, her apron soaked at her knees.

Governor Lowe slashed their household funds, saying they wasted too much money. Food was scarce, the island plagued with shortages, supplies half-rotten when they arrived. The soldiers consumed most of the provisions and prices soared.

She ran a finger inside her sweaty collar, inhaled the rich smell of the earth, and admired the sprouting evidence of even minor accomplishment. Still, her garden wasn't producing as she'd hoped. She sang some of the aria she'd practiced the previous day.

A shadow loomed up over her herbs.

"His Majesty is right. You have a strong voice, Mademoiselle. *Tres bien!*" the eavesdropper declared. Amélie stared up to see Cipriani.

An older Corsican with sharp, sepia features, the servants considered him a mysterious character. As *maitre d'hotel* he managed the household food, but everyone knew he worked in a shadier capacity for the emperor. Cipriani went into Jamestown on the pretext of purchasing food. Gossip said as Napoleon's spy, he gathered tales of the outside world from sailors at the cafes and coordinated the underground system that smuggled correspondence to Europe despite Lowe's restrictions.

"*Merci, Monsieur* Cipriani."

"You struggle in this garden. The best crop to grow on Saint Helena is yams. Their roots are so bitter the rats won't eat them. That's why the soldiers call the locals Yamstocks." The wiry man stepped around her toward the wall, and then turned about, his long coat flapping. "You have ripened better than your plants, and become very interesting to look at."

"I don't care for yams." Amélie's face seared and she turned away from the swaggering *maitre d'hotel*—a man of almost sixty—to pull more weeds.

Cipriani leaned down toward her. "Maybe you might like to accompany me to Jamestown some afternoon?" he whispered in his nasal voice. "It's so dull to remain around here all the time."

Amélie glared up. "No, I would *not* care to. That's a very forward invitation."

"Such dismay, but, no, I wouldn't try to usurp His Majesty." Cipriani watched her with a crafty smile. "I think you tantalize the emperor with much more than just your singing voice."

"How dare you suggest…" Amélie snatched up her basket with the few basil sprigs and hopped to her feet. She marched into the kitchen and scrubbed her hands to deflect her anger.

"What did that man say to you?" Her father stirred a pot over the stove, one brow raised.

"Not much, we were talking about yams." She glanced out the window to check if Cipriani lingered. Her fingers trailed down her body—a fuller more womanly form? She sighed. Now noticed, as she'd once been teased, for something she had no control over, she was accused of more brazen acts. She'd done nothing wrong. The emperor was her friend, dare she hope. She tore up the herb leaves. "Here is some basil for your veal stew."

Perrault sprinkled it in. The veal simmered, stringy and unappealing. The tangy smell thickened the kitchen air. "Watch this for me. I'm going up to the attic to see if Gascon is feeling better." His tone weary, her father left the kitchen.

Amélie felt a twinge of shame for not helping him more.

The door banged open. Madame Cloubert staggered in with a pot of water. She plunked it on the stove to heat. She sniffed and glared toward the other pot. "I'm not eating any more of that disgusting island meat. We'll starve with that governor's new restrictions. He expects our emperor to eat like a peasant."

"Governor Lowe punishes us since His Majesty refuses to receive him." Amélie stirred the veal; her stomach churned at the prospect. "The emperor won't ride so the orderly has a clear view of him, but he only hurts himself. Doctor O'Meara should insist the emperor stop hiding inside just to irritate the English." Amélie had tried to talk Napoleon into riding again, but so far he'd ignored her. She'd failed in being tantalizing.

The tar paper shingles flapped on the kitchen roof. One blew off and whacked the kitchen window, before sailing like a crow into the courtyard.

"That *mouton*? O'Meara cares more for his gossip than being a true physician, and Lowe has the gall to send two of our footmen and one groom away. O'Meara probably told him we're overstaffed, when I work my fingers to the bone." The woman waved her skeletal hands in the air. "Have you read those new papers Lowe's pushed on us?"

"*Mon dieu.*" Amélie peeled and dropped garlic into the meat, the smell pungent. "The document we must sign swearing to stay until His Majesty's death? The British have no plans to ever release him." She'd signed the papers that arrived that morning, but feared Napoleon's reaction. Just the thought of his death filled her with helplessness.

"Lowe's an evil rogue." The head chambermaid snorted. She opened the pantry door, then slammed it shut. "No wonder His Majesty instructed his departing staff to contact his older brother in America, to hatch some plot of rescue. That's what I heard, anyway."

"Shhh, Madame. You shouldn't speak of such things." Amélie banged down the spoon, feeling excluded from any schemes. "It's unsafe if the soldiers catch you." She waited for the woman to say more, then chided herself for listening to gossip.

Did Napoleon entertain thoughts of escape or rescue? Of course, he must. He couldn't let the English keep him here until his demise.

The kitchen door opened and Ali strode in. A clanging noise rang through the courtyard. "The emperor is having his silver smashed up. He's ordered Cipriani to carry it into Jamestown to sell, to let the islanders know of our foul treatment, to shame the English for cutting back our stipend."

Amélie peered out the kitchen window. A footman swung an ax, pulverizing the imperial serving dishes—a crushing of their former way of life. She turned to Ali. "What does His Majesty think of this newest declaration from the governor?"

"He ordered us not to sign it, but I have. I'm sure you will too." Ali's evaluating look made her uncomfortable, as if he believed the same as Cipriani. "I came to tell you no lesson. The emperor isn't feeling well. He has a severe headache and chills, and his eyes burn even in candlelight. These strange symptoms come and go."

"That's terrible. His doctor should be reprimanded. His Majesty needs to eat more fruits and vegetables and walk out for his health, but I imagine this other has saddened him."

"It's saddened the hell out of me." Madame Cloubert stifled another snort and checked the temperature of the water she heated. She eyed Amélie. "Don't you have any influence over our emperor?"

"Doctor O'Meara seems conscientious, but he can't force himself on his patient." Ali stared into the veal stew, nose wrinkling. "I'll inform His Majesty what tasty treat we're having for supper."

"Wait, take him some chamomile tea." Amélie hurried to prepare it. Escape and death swirled in her head. The selfish idea surfaced that if the English kept him imprisoned here, she'd retain her relationship with Napoleon in such close proximity. A relationship a few seem to have misconstrued. If only her mother had lived long enough to explain every aspect of intimate behavior.

Sudden moisture filled her eyes. Amélie blinked it back, yearning for *Maman's* advice, her presence, in so many matters. Her mother's painful death had punctured an abrupt hole in her life.

* * * *

Napoleon closed his eyes. Her voice was so sweet to his senses. Music had always calmed his nerves, soothed his melancholy, and warmed his heart. The afternoons passed enjoyably now. He had someone to mold to his wishes. The girl blossomed under his tutelage, the waif developing a figure with hips and bosom. Her face rounded, softening the sharp edges, complementing her large brown eyes. She no longer resembled a haunted undernourished creature, though the smell of herbs that surrounded her gave her a woodland aspect—something ethereal and untouchable.

"Your Majesty, I know we've discussed this, but you should take up riding again."

He opened his eyes and sat up straighter in the chair. Amélie smiled at him shyly. She'd sung without accompaniment, Albine pleading a headache. Horses galloped outside. Had he fallen into a dream?

Amélie hurried to the salon's front window. "It looks like Governor Lowe is here, Sire."

Napoleon rose and peered through the holes he'd had his servants cut in the shutters, so he could look out without anyone seeing him. "Yes, our esteemed governor, cowing back from his minions. What could he want?" Governor Lowe had reigned in, allowing a group of soldiers to ride up near the front porch, their hat plumes fluttering in the wind.

Their smug faces annoying him, Napoleon motioned Saint-Denis out to inquire.

"I wish to speak with the Count de Las Cases," the governor's assistant, Sir Thomas Reade, Deputy Adjutant General, announced. His moon-face barely shifted with his sly smile.

Ali returned and Napoleon sent him to fetch the count who sat in the drawing room, having his hair trimmed by the imperial barber. "Go out there and see what that beast wants with you," he said when the little man trotted in.

"I must say, I can't imagine what he might want of my humble person." The chamberlain bowed, twitched his nose, and stepped out the front door.

Napoleon bent again to scrutinize the trespassers; his shoulder muscles tightened. He nodded to Ali, who slipped out the door and followed Las Cases.

"That's a large contingent of soldiers for a conversation." Amélie touched his arm, but he didn't mind, her hand comforting.

Several minutes later, Reade and another soldier escorted Las Cases out the front gate.

Two more soldiers followed, carrying trunks brimming over with papers obviously from the count's quarters in the back wing. Napoleon's blood boiled.

Saint-Denis bounded up the front steps and into the salon. "Your Majesty, the governor has arrested the Count de Las Cases and the soldiers confiscated everything in his rooms."

"Arrested for what reason? They've stolen all my dictation? This is insufferable! Ali, fetch Count Bertrand. Tell him to send Doctor O'Meara to find out what has happened." Napoleon's left leg twinged, something he experienced when overwrought. He resisted the urge to run out and demand an explanation. He could no longer act the impetuous youth who let his temper run wild—snatching up banners and storming bridges on battlefields. He had to preserve his imperial dignity.

"Sire, do the British have a right to seize our people and haul them away like criminals?" Amélie asked, her fawn eyes earnest.

"They will push their arbitrary rights to the limit." Napoleon felt powerless, unable to protect his own people. He couldn't let the girl sense his weakness. He smiled and squeezed her hand. "Don't worry, *ma petite*, Bertrand will see to it, at my direction."

* * * *

Amélie lit candles in the drawing room to push back the late evening dark. "The count's valet confessed to smuggling letters?"

"That's what Doctor O'Meara told His Majesty." Saint-Denis leaned on the black stone mantel. Other servants gathered around. "The mulatto is shipping off in a few days with a new master, but he turned cowardly and told Governor Lowe he had letters written on white satin and sewn into his clothing. He was supposed to smuggle the information to Europe for the little count."

"He was a coward for turning against the Count de Las Cases. It's so hard to know whom to trust here." Amélie pulled down the room's blinds, shutting out the soldiers. She resented their vulnerable existence and her own risk of arrest by tearing down a poster.

"Now Lowe has all the count's papers." Ali spoke in disgust. "Those hundreds of pages dictated by the emperor, his justification of his career."

"That spy O'Meara probably reported Las Cases to that stickler of a governor." Madame Cloubert crossed her skinny arms, nodding her head, almost in imitation of the little count.

"Bertrand, go at once to Plantation House and demand the return of my chamberlain." Napoleon paced through from the salon with Counts Bertrand and Montholon, his features twisted in anger. "That *boja* Lowe has no right to do this."

"Sire…" Amélie wanted to reach out to him, but he slammed into his study.

Bertrand's drooped his round shoulders and glared at Montholon. "Las Cases probably got what he deserved, playing with such intrigues." The two men walked back toward the salon. Montholon seemed to fight a satisfied smile.

"Las Cases is being held in a cottage not far from here, and can't see nor speak to any of us." Ali shook his head. "The little Jesuit snatched from his idol. He's being ordered off the island immediately."

"My duties will be simpler without that persnickety little man." Madame Cloubert sounded a shade regretful, as if now she'd have less reason to grumble.

"His Majesty is distraught to lose the count. He's been so fond of him." Amélie chewed on her lip, then braced herself for Madame Montholon's rushing in to offer Napoleon her inappropriate solace. Thankfully it didn't happen. "Will the governor destroy the papers he found, all that work?"

"He just might. One of the letters was a scathing criticism of Lowe himself. I'm sure that didn't delight him." Ali ran a hand through his slick hair. "From now on anyone who comes near us will be turned inside out before they're allowed to leave the island."

Amélie frowned. "Or we'll be forbidden any visitors."

"His officers aren't sorry to see the little man go. They're so cutthroat for His Majesty's attention." Jules shouldered into their group, slitted eyes glinting. "The Count de Montholon told his wife that Las Cases bungled this himself, so he could leave. His work was done, and he didn't want to be chained here forever."

"The count deserts the emperor on purpose?" Amélie shivered. She didn't want to believe Napoleon's courtiers now betrayed him, and Las Cases, his most effusive champion.

"My master said Las Cases is relieved to escape this reeking hole." Jules's laugh crept under Amélie's skin. He turned and strode off. "As all of us will."

"We should be devoted enough to stay if His Majesty must stay." She pictured all the courtiers making a mad scramble to abandon their emperor, leaving him at the full mercy of the British. To her chagrin, she still stood on the other side of Napoleon's closed door.

Chapter Nine

What do I care how people feel about me, so long as they show me a friendly face—N.B.

Amélie set down the untouched cup of basil tea on the kitchen table. Marchand had sent her out of the main house, the emperor refusing the beverage. Napoleon had cancelled two of her lessons, staying in his rooms, lamenting the loss of his chamberlain. She couldn't comfort him—his valets kept her at bay—and she tried not to consider how much comfort the indiscreet countess provided in her absence. She struggled not to be crushed by this bizarre existence and sorted through her herbs in her baskets, enjoying the fragrances, but her world felt scraped dry.

Chef Gascon removed fresh baked brioches from the oven, the buttery smell mouth-watering. "Amélie, can you take these out to the Count de Montholon? He's having breakfast with Governor Lowe near the Park." Gascon moaned and wiped perspiration from the folds in his neck.

"How silly. The governor refuses to even enter the grounds since the emperor won't grant him an audience." She laughed in irony. Napoleon and Lowe were both mired in stubbornness—more futility. If people didn't speak to each other, how could they reach an understanding? "I'll be happy to, Chef Gascon."

Gascon put his brioches on a plate, covered them with a linen napkin, and gave the plate to her. Amélie walked around the house and out the front gate, the aroma rumbling her hunger. A small table had been set up in the meager shade of the gumwoods, their brittle leaves snapping in the breeze. She placed the plate on the table. The two men didn't bother to glance at her.

"Pour us some more tea," the Count de Montholon ordered. He lifted the linen to inspect the contents. Amélie picked up the ceramic teapot and poured. She didn't look at their faces but watched the count's slender hands with polished oval nails as he caressed the porcelain plate. The governor's bony fingers, with red tufts of hair on the knuckles, twitched near his teacup.

"I've gone into detail about the regulations I'm entrusted with," Lowe said. "After all, our government has never acknowledged your Bonaparte as an emperor in any official sense. It is only proper to refer to him as 'General' here, no matter how much it upsets him, as your General Bertrand is *fond* of telling me."

"Governor, not everyone has been brought up in the realm of diplomacy. I hope you realize I'm the only true *aristos* in His Majesty's court, and I assure you I do understand your constraints." Montholon spoke in a smooth manner. His offered the plate toward his guest with a feline liquidity. "Brioche? Our pastry chef is quite talented when he makes the effort."

"I still think your general misunderstands my intentions. I know he is angered by my sending away the Count de Las Cases, but the count's underhandedness left me little choice." Lowe turned his teacup in his long fingers, the liquid sloshing about.

Amélie placed the cream and sugar close to the cups. If she spoke to ask what each preferred it might break her cloak of being an invisible servant.

"Las Cases deserved what happened. We're better rid of him," Montholon continued with a self-satisfied tone, "and, I myself find it childish to insist on being referred to as emperor, when one no longer has a throne."

Amélie bit her lip, and turned and stalked away, silently daring them to call her back for further orders. She kicked a pebble when she passed the front gate, her hands clenched on her elbows. A deep sadness weighed her down. The count always seemed a slippery character, and now she had proof he only pretended to be a loyal courtier. She dreaded informing Napoleon of the man's treachery so soon after losing the Count de Las Cases.

The heat of anger sent her rushing into the house. "Marchand, please let me see His Majesty. I have something very important to tell him," she said when the valet poked out his head at the study door. "I won't be turned away."

After a quick consultation, Marchand invited her in. Napoleon sat on the sofa in his dressing gown. He hadn't shaved and looked forlorn, a pale ghost, in this shuttered room full of depressing shadows.

"Now what is so important?" he asked with a sad smile.

She gulped a breath, hating to add to his sorrows. "Sire, I was just in the Park. Governor Lowe is there with the Count de Montholon. I overheard the count make a disloyal—"

Napoleon held up his hand. "Amélie, I would dislike you to become a carrier of sordid tales like so many others. Please, I am not in the mood. Be a good girl and stick to your singing."

He rose and lumbered into his bedroom.

"Sire, the man is not who you think he is." Amélie quivered, speaking to a closed door. She felt chastised as well as ineffectual. She couldn't allow the emperor's forceful personality to reduce her to an anxious minion.

* * * *

"No, I don't care for any 'soothing' at this moment." Napoleon stared into the mirror above the gray-painted wood fireplace in his bedroom. He ran his hands along his cheeks: too jowly. At forty-six, however, his face remained unlined, and not a speck of gray in his hair. Albine's reflection smiled at him and he turned. "I'm in no mood to follow the script. I'm long past believing in your farce; let's put an end to the play."

"Don't be so cynical, Sire." Albine pouted, caressed her hand down his waistcoat and fingered one of the gold buttons. "I insist on honoring you. Have I not pleased you in the past?"

"I understand your type of honor. You'd enjoy fondling coins and jewels." He plucked her hand from his button, weary of being surrounded by false fawning. All this close occupancy with minimal distraction made him realize he had no true friends here, yet he'd discouraged friendship as his power rose, insisting on his place at the center of them all. "If I care to partake ever again, I will let you know."

"*Hélas,* if you didn't spend so much time with the little kitchen maid, you wouldn't neglect those dear to you." She purred like a cat, but he saw a wolf instead. A wolf with red rouge, like blood, on its front teeth. "I'm experienced in the ways of pleasure."

"Pleasure is in the mind, my dear Albine." Napoleon thought of Amélie's voice and her eager smile, but she was just a child to amuse him. This woman before him took too many liberties. He'd grown bored by her attractions. Especially now, when her dress started to bulge with child. She had no dignity. Only the lack of selection had prompted him to encourage her in the beginning. A bad habit from his younger days, this perfunctory bedding of women, to confirm his prowess—and hide his insecurity. He sighed and walked from the bedroom and through his study, out to the salon. The countess minced along behind him.

Amélie awaited him, fresh in her plain little dress, that lovely hair over her shoulders like woven gold. Napoleon couldn't help a genuine smile when he looked at her. Here was someone unsullied and selfless.

"Back already, Sire? Is everything satisfactory?" Montholon's unctuous voice broke the spell. He seemed to sprout out of nowhere beside his wife.

"Albine, play the piece we discussed yesterday." Napoleon pointed at the piano bench, hiding his irritation. Had Montholon no pride? He acted far too anxious to force his jaded wife into the imperial bed. He'd taken it as his right, but now suspected the count's motives.

"Your Majesty, I don't know if I can play today. I've broken a nail. These lessons have become a chore. I'd rather we play cards, since I've so missed our time together." Albine made no effort to sit. "My dear husband can't recall the last time you played chess with him. You know how we cherish our moments with you."

"You leave no time for those most devoted to you, Sire." Montholon didn't twitch an eyelash over his wife's refusal. "Now that Las Cases is gone, we desire nothing more than to attend you to our fullest capacity."

A look crossed Amélie's face and she glared at Albine's changing figure. The rumors flying about over the child's paternity at first flattered, now embarrassed him.

"Then attend me as you profess, and sit and play the piece, Albine."

"Sire, have you had time to look over my account books?" Montholon capered before him with his wheedling gestures, an insipid parody.

"I'm prepared to sing unaccompanied, Sire." Amélie turned away from the count with raised brows. Even she saw the buffoonery of his courtiers. This farce loomed all around him, and Napoleon would have laughed if their actions didn't anger him at this moment.

"You may have to," he replied to the girl, then turned his scowl on Montholon. "Your ledgers seem to have some discrepancies in the household accounts that we can discuss later." Napoleon had cut off Amélie's tale on the count's meeting with Governor Lowe, not wanting to know that this man he relied on might betray him. His little court dwindled down and he struggled to retain it. He couldn't allow this community of hardship to diminish his rank. If he had no court, he was no longer an emperor to the world at large, just what the British wanted.

Montholon's wily smile surfaced. "As I've said, it's Bertrand that has—"

"Enough! Am I not supposed to have any enjoyment here? Both of you try my patience." How he missed the witty conversation of Las Cases. His invaluable help. Napoleon left the Montholons and came over to Amélie who had seated herself at the piano and now toyed with the keys. *Her* growing boldness amused him for some reason. "Perhaps you should take lessons."

"If it's necessary, Your Majesty. The countess never helped with perfecting my note reading, and I hate to take up her time. I've studied hard on my own." Amélie's subtle jab at Albine made him chuckle. Her warm gaze cooled his temper and her perceptive smile drew him.

Napoleon smiled back. He sat on the bench beside her. She brushed her fingers over the ivory keys. "You seem more relaxed in this pursuit of opera. Yes, I noticed your discomfort, but with hard work you will come into your own." He put his hand on her arm and felt her tremble beneath it. A sliver of pleasure rose in him that he still affected an innocent like her.

"Such insolence, she sits in His Majesty's presence without being asked," the countess said to Montholon, loud enough for all to hear. Napoleon glared at them, amazed by their own insolence. He pointed to the far door and they shrank back, finally creeping from the room.

"I did not mean to cause offense, but I intend to come into my own, Sire," the girl said with a new maturity that intrigued and unsettled him at the same time.

* * * *

Across from the kitchen, Amélie and Ali gathered up empty wine bottles in the butler's pantry where the majority of servants ate their meals. "I don't care how much the Montholons complain about me. The emperor is in a very unhappy household. Their self-serving rivalry for his attention is disgusting." Her presence must relieve Napoleon from the disgruntled atmosphere for the short time she played pupil.

"Don't *you* enjoy his attention? Now His Majesty spends time with you, that cuts into theirs even further." The valet smirked and took the bottles.

She turned from his assessment, but warmed when she remembered the way Napoleon's touch made her feel, almost ashamed that she desired more. Then she clenched her teeth, thinking of the countess's "condition." What exactly did the woman's *fullest capacity* entail? "I don't know how His Majesty trusts those Montholons. The count...he's underhanded."

"Mr. Blue Blood himself?" Ali shook his head as if to contain his broad grin. "Something he likes to remind us of as often as he can."

"Because his title wasn't 'awarded' to him by the emperor, like Count Bertrand's? That's more deserving than inheriting it whether you're worthy or not."

"Isn't it ironic that Count Bertrand has the aristocratic wife when he's the *parvenu*?" The valet chuckled as they strolled into the courtyard, the bottles clinking in his arms. "Our blue-blooded Count de Montholon's wife has a shady past."

"I tried to tell His Majesty the count made betraying comments at his luncheon with the governor, but he refused to listen." She wiped sticky hands on her apron.

"You intend to arouse his anger? Everyone here makes nasty comments, except for me, of course." Ali winked at her. "The emperor prefers his women sweet and docile."

Amélie heated again under her clothes. "The count spoke right in front of me, as if I'm not the emperor's *friend*." She regretted not insisting that Napoleon hear her out. He remained such an imposing force to her, though her stomach knots since beginning the lessons had disappeared.

"Montholon likes to preen himself up in importance to whoever might be in charge. It's probably nothing." Ali stirred the weeds she'd put in a pile near her garden with his buckle-shoed toe, a challenging spark in his eyes. "Now with Las Cases gone, the Montholons will ooze closer to our emperor. You'll have a battle before you."

"I'm not afraid of battles." Amélie worried that her emperor deluded himself that his courtiers served him the same as when he reigned supreme. People changed with circumstances, and not usually for the better.

A footman hurried up and the valet handed him three of the bottles. "Smash away, my good man," Ali said with a grand wave of his arm as if imitating Napoleon.

"No, please, no more smashing. Wai—" Amélie jumped when the footman cracked the first bottle against the side wall, in full view of the sentries. Glass shards with the smell of wine tinkled over the ground like falling sleet. She grabbed the other two from his hands. "This makes the governor more contentious on us all. We have to stop this." Lowe demanded the return of all wine bottles to be reused since they were scarce on the island. He ranted about the French overconsumption, so out of spite the servants sold bottles to the nearby soldiers and destroyed the empties.

"Amélie, come away from those silly games." Napoleon stood in the back door entrance. "I want to discuss something with you."

She handed Ali the two bottles and whispered, "No more breaking." She walked toward Napoleon as if pulled by a string. "Yes, Sire?"

In the house, Napoleon took her hand and led her to the dining room. "I've decided it's time for you to give your first performance in front of the household. To show everyone how well you're progressing."

"Oh, no, Sire. Perform before people?" She sucked in her breath and held fast to disbelief. "You're teasing me...aren't you?"

"Indeed I'm not. You need the exposure." With his intrigued smile and sparkling eyes, Amélie feared he was serious. "Now I have chosen the songs I'd like you to sing. Have you a finer gown?" He put his arm around her and they walked into his study.

She absorbed the warmth of his embrace, her previous resolve to be strong trampled over by her racing pulse. "I'm afraid I haven't a nicer gown. I don't think I—"

"Too late to do anything this time. Don't worry. I'll take care of it." The emperor patted her arm, then handed her the list of arias in his almost illegible handwriting. "Don't look so shocked. Everything will be fine."

"Sire, really, do you think me good enough to perform in front of an audience?" Like some diva? Playing the pupil was one thing, but this hadn't existed in her wildest imaginings.

"Yes, you will be a delight. Didn't I say that intimate gatherings were perfectly acceptable? I decided to eliminate *Proserpine*, even though Paisiello is one of my favorite composers. He worked for me when I was First Consul, but the play wasn't well received in Paris."

"I hadn't planned to make a career out of a temporary amusement." Amélie licked her dry lips, forced decisiveness into her words, yet anxiously watched his face. "More weeks of practice would be better, don't you think, Your Majesty?"

"Nonsense, time is a wasting." His expression turned pensive. "Please, when we're alone, you may call me Napoleon." He now patted her cheek, almost a caress.

Amélie tried to hide her surprise at this sudden honor, though reveled in the privilege "I...if you insist I be so familiar. Napoleon." She liked the way it sounded on her tongue.

"There, see how easy that is." He nodded and smiled again as if he too enjoyed the intimate way she pronounced his name.

Amélie's head swam and she grasped at something more important than an unwanted recital. She took a deep breath. "Your Majesty...Napoleon, I would like to discuss what I mentioned about the Count de Montholon and Governor Lowe. The count said he thinks it childish to insist on being called emperor when you don't have a throne. How can you—"

"Montholon? Don't worry. I understand him. We will speak no more of it." Napoleon turned his back and walked into his bedroom. She bristled, perturbed that he still didn't take her seriously. He dismissed her concerns as had Ali.

Suspecting her pending feat would be less than delightful, Amélie returned to her quarters to sort it out. She touched her cheek, still feeling the stroke of his fingers, the heat of his arm around her shoulders. Had Napoleon given her a step up in protocol to manipulate her to his desires?

Before the dinner preparation, her father caught her in the narrow hall separating their chambers. "The emperor has asked my permission to have dresses made for you. I told him it wasn't necessary, but he insisted. You're to perform in some recital? An important evolution in your development?" His vexed expression barely penetrated her dilemma. "Are you sure you want to be part of such a pageant?"

"I'm thinking it over. His Majesty shouldn't have asked you about clothing. That should be my decision." Her father doubted her, but the emperor did not. Did she want to sing in front of people who might pick apart her every imperfection? Her voice sounded good. She knew that now. Did she intend to be another courtier displeasing His Majesty in his arduous circumstances? Her stomach jumped, jittery.

She'd probed into opera as something daring. Here lay her chance to be bold before everyone and prove herself to the emperor.

Chapter Ten

I also repent not having talked more with the ladies. I would have learned a great many things from them that men did not dare to tell me—N.B.

Amélie pushed a damp curl from her forehead. The study fire roared and she moved away from it. Her mouth was so dry she coughed and strained to swallow.

"This is your important night. Do you understand what's required, *ma petite Amée*?" The emperor paced back and forth, increasing her fluster. In the past few days he'd ceased calling her Amélie and had shortened it. Napoleon stopped in front of her, appearing ready to do battle, face flushed, eyes glittering, while she struggled to take even breaths.

"Sire, even my father no longer calls me *petite*...at my request." Her voice croaked out and she forgot about using his first name. "May I have something to drink?"

Napoleon handed her a cup of tea, tepid, but she gulped it down.

"Do you think those two arias from *Cosi Fan Tutti* complement each other back to back?" She prayed for the liquid to settle in her roiling stomach.

"Yes, yes, of course they do. They show off your voice, the jumps from top to bottom of the soprano range."

"Fiordiligi is a taxing part." Amélie rubbed her throat, thinking of the length and leaps from high soprano to contralto and back again in "Per pieta, ben mio perdona."

"*Cosi Fan Tutti* was performed at my court in Compiegne...in 1811. Let's see what we can do with it here. Remember to keep your chin up, and project, project. Are we ready? Then let's greet your public." Napoleon extended his arm graciously. She accepted it, hoping he couldn't detect how badly she quivered.

Her "public" sat in a semicircle facing the piano in the capacious hall. The Count and Countess Bertrand were there, with Count de Montholon. In the back, alongside the wall, stood Cipriani, Marchand, and Saint-Denis. Chef Gascon waited next to her father, with various footmen and maids shifting beside them. Even Madame Cloubert appeared enthusiastic as she awaited the event's start. Clarice slouched against the wall, her expression sullen.

Amélie crossed the room stiff on the emperor's arm, and her father gave what seemed a smile of reluctance rather than encouragement.

At Napoleon's request, the seamstress had altered one of the Countess de Montholon's dresses for Amélie to wear this evening—a rich, blue velvet gown with delicate white lace at the collar and sleeves. Scooped low in front, Amélie had pinned the neckline to tighten it. Overheard grumbling to her husband, the countess hated lending it out. Then the woman had the audacity to announce this garment was a discard intended for one of her servants.

Where would a servant wear this on Saint Helena? Amélie fiddled with the gown's lace collar chafing her collarbone. Despite the finery, she felt like a dowdy peasant as she took her place beside the piano.

The emperor sat in his reserved chair directly in front of her, then smiled and nodded. The countess, after making a production of swirling around her skirts on the bench, began to play. Amélie shut her eyes for a moment, inhaling a deep breath, her body trembling with tension.

First she sang from Mozart's *Cosi Fan Tutti*. She sang the part of Dorabella: "Smanie implacibili," then Fiordiligi: "Come scoglio" and "Per pieta, ben mio perdona." Two sisters whose fidelity is wickedly tested by their betrothed after the men trick them to prove all women are fickle. Napoleon barely approved of its comic, though satirical, tone, but they were limited to the available material. Amélie sighed in relief to get through the exhausting sweep with few mistakes.

After this she performed as Alcina from *La Liberazione di Ruggiero dall'isola d'Alcina*, by Francesca Caccini. Amélie had insisted on the piece, as this seventeenth-century woman was hailed as the first female opera composer. She relished the part of Alcina, an alluring sorceress on an enchanted island, though in the end she descends into a fiery inferno.

Everyone applauded at the first break, commenting in surprise over Amélie's wide range of voice. Albine de Montholon smiled and bowed her head, as if they meant the praise for her.

Amélie's finale for the evening was Carolina's aria from *Il Matrimonio Segreto*, "Questa cosa"—the aria that first enticed Napoleon to notice her. All at once, Amélie didn't care for the premise of a girl trying to convince her patrician suitor she's unworthy of him.

She finished, her throat and ears vibrating.

The company applauded, with a few bravos. The emperor jumped to his feet to congratulate her. His courtiers congratulated him. Amélie pressed her fingers to her abdomen, dizzy, but relieved. She tried to swallow past her raw throat.

"You are *magnifique*, my dear." Countess Bertrand squeezed her hand. "What a beautiful voice you have. This was a refreshing change of pace. Where have you been hiding all this time?"

Amélie smiled, frozen in place, thanking the bobbing faces and surge of voices. A confidence in her ability seeped through her like a tonic, filling her up, and steadying her at the same time. Power came with success. This must have been, on a much larger scale, how Napoleon felt when as a young captain he'd chased the British out of Toulon—the first glint of his star.

"You were superb. Didn't I tell you?" Napoleon clasped her by both shoulders. She giggled nervously and he laughed too. "You see, it wasn't so frightening as you thought," he whispered. "Don't deny it, you trembled like those flags hanging on wires from Alarm House." She now trembled with his breath in her ear—Calypso luring Odysseus with her haunting voice.

Napoleon turned to the audience. "I have a special surprise for Amélie, since she has entertained us so well tonight."

To her astonishment he handed her a small white box tied with a pink ribbon.

"*Merci beaucoup*," Amélie murmured, her cheeks growing warm. Everyone stared at her, her father with a brooding expression.

"Open it," Napoleon urged as she continued to clutch the box in her hands.

Amélie fumbled with the bow as everyone leaned forward. Inside the box, nestled in white paper, lay the most exquisite necklace she'd ever seen: a delicate gold chain embellished with three oval pink stones, each framed in tiny pearls and gold filigree. She held it up, and the audience made appreciative noises.

"Here, I'll put it on for you." Napoleon took the necklace and draped it around her neck. Fastening the clasp in back, he whispered, "This was Josephine's. A rare pink topaz. Her daughter gave it to me my last night at Malmaison. I have cherished it dearly."

An important gift, once owned by his beloved Josephine. The emperor proved his deep affection by giving it to Amélie. She rippled with pleasure that Napoleon thought this highly of her. His fingers on her nape sent excited chills along her neck and shoulders.

"Don't you like my gift?" he asked in the face of her silence.

"I adore it, Your Majesty." Catching her breath, she saw every critical eye in the place glued to her, yet they mattered little. Her heart soared above them. She caressed the stones, cool against her throat, and turned to Napoleon and kissed him on the cheek.

The emperor appeared dazed by her forwardness, but smiled with pleasure and touched his cheek. "I too receive a present."

Amélie laughed and it seemed to bounce off the walls. A few in the audience chimed in as others gaped in silence or looked away.

Perrault strode up, his brow furrowed, mouth pinched. "Forgive us, Your Majesty. My daughter has forgotten her place."

"Papa," Amélie whispered, embarrassed by her father's interference. She yearned for a different place. Like the necklace, lifted from her box and caressed.

"Perrault, we are here to enjoy ourselves." Napoleon rescued the moment, his voice theatrical, filling the room. "What finer compliment than to be kissed by a beautiful girl? Now, wine for everyone."

The valets rushed forward and poured wine into glasses and passed them to the audience. Gascon plodded up with a tray of his miniature cream tarts: darioles. His droopy face ashen, he looked in danger of coughing onto the pastries.

Amélie ran her tongue to the corners of her mouth, still tasting Napoleon's musky skin on her lips and couldn't stop grinning. Her emperor's face when enthralled appeared years younger, and his touch made her giddy and simmering inside.

"He'll tire of her soon enough, *mon ange*. His Majesty's 'infatuations' never last long. I'll make certain of that." The Count de Montholon elbowed Amélie as if by accident as he put his arm around his wife's plump shoulders. The couple moved past her. Amélie shoved down her anger at their obvious ploy to ruin her evening. "How embarrassing," Montholon spoke again, "when all of Europe hears that the great Napoleon fancies himself a singing master."

* * * *

The pink cotton frock, gathered at the neck, with lace on puffed sleeves, looked almost too little girlish. Amélie held the garment up in her chamber after the seamstress dropped off her new apparel. Days past her performance, she still reveled in her triumph and this added to her feeling of privilege. The elegant, column-like white gown with its typical low-cut bodice presented the complete opposite.

The material felt featherlight as she traced her fingers along the dotted muslin. The deep-blue dress with square-cut neckline fell somewhere in between, the silk sleek in her hands. All had high waists with ribbons that tied under the breasts.

She twirled the blue dress around. Never in her life had she owned such beautiful clothes. Little wonder the others in the house might question her status and expect the worst, but who cared about their perceptions.

Still, the emperor spent money on her, but previously destroyed his own silver to support his household? No, that had been a ruse to mortify Governor Lowe.

Clothes neatly folded, she hurried into the main house. Amélie walked through the half-open study door, then realized her serious breach. The emperor and Albine de Montholon stared in surprise from the sofa.

Amélie's face burned, but she twinged with jealousy. "*Pardon.*" She dropped a quick curtsy. "Please forgive me, Your Majesty."

"What is it, Amée, what has happened?" Napoleon rose and smiled, not appearing upset, though the countess glowered enough for them both.

"I wanted to thank you for the fine dresses that just arrived, Sire." She straightened and returned the woman's provoking glare.

"*De rien.* You must start to wear them immediately." His expression warmed with pride. "Of course, a Parisian seamstress would have been far superior, but we must make do. Did you finish the Alexander book yet?"

The countess's features glazed over like desolate arctic ice.

"Do you have time to discuss it now?" Those gowns weren't suitable for her regular duties, but glancing at her drab garment, Amélie wished she'd slipped one on. She stepped farther into the room.

"Yes, Albine was just leaving. Come in and we'll review the book." Napoleon waved her over to the sofa.

The countess stood slowly, her manner stiff at this dismissal. Her glare slashed across Amélie. Chosen over the emperor's supposed mistress, Amélie suppressed a grin. She averted her eyes from the woman's growing abdomen as the countess passed from the room.

"I don't know what possessed me, to walk in uninvited." Amélie gave Napoleon a shy smile, though didn't feel bashful now. "I hope you didn't mind."

"No, strangely, I didn't. Your valor was a storming of the ramparts." Napoleon radiated amusement, brightening the chamber as if the sun flowed in. "A little excitement around here won't kill anyone. In fact, we could use it."

"I also want to say, and I'm very grateful, but you needn't have been so generous to me with the clothes. The seamstress said silk is difficult to get here, although we're on the route from China." A rat skittered along the baseboard, almost over her toes, before disappearing into a hole in the wall. Even the rats dared to disturb her emperor.

"Why not be generous? A performer must dress accordingly, even in this dreary land where everything is impossible to get." His amusement faded, then he forced a smile. "So, what is your opinion of Alexander the Great?"

"Alexander was loved and inspired by his men. A brilliant general who moved troops at unheard of speeds." Amélie rehearsed this in her room, determined to sound as intelligent as possible. "His early death kept him from realizing all his plans." Suddenly, she wasn't talking of Alexander. Wasn't an indefinite imprisonment similar to death?

She didn't mention Alexander's growing tyranny, his desire to surpass even the gods as he annexed the world under his sovereignty. Were these parallels as well, these traits whispered by some and shouted by others when the Bourbons held France and Napoleon's enemies exiled him to Elba? Cowards wheedling for favor in the new regime? Still, Amélie's hero worship couldn't blind her to Napoleon's faults.

"*C'est vrais.* Alexander barely outgrew his boyhood when he captured most of the globe. He fought few battles, but arranged his troops well. That was his genius." At his bookcase the emperor pulled out another thick volume. "Here's one on Julius Caesar, a man whose genius and boldness were equally great. The more you read, the more you'll understand events and why things repeat themselves throughout history."

"I do want to learn everything. I have read Shakespeare's play about Julius Caesar..." Caesar's murder by close associates fearing his ambitions mirrored the emperor's betrayal by his allies. Amélie's pulse skittered. Napoleon must know she understood this correlation.

"Next I might give you Plutarch's *The Lives of the Noble Grecians and Romans.* That stimulated me to the exploits of the empire-building of Alexander and Caesar." Napoleon appraised her closely—here stood the great soldier of the past, so proud—and she shivered. "Unless this is all too much for you. They say truth will set you free, but I say it's knowledge. Though much more so for a man than a woman."

"No, of course it isn't too much." Amélie's favored position today emboldened her. "Can't a woman be considered an equal to a man, Napoleon?" She hoped he remembered his permission to use his name.

"A woman should be of a gentler mind and occupation," he said as another statement of fact. "She keeps the household and cares for the children, both important tasks."

"Still, you're giving me all these history books to read—and I'm happy you are." She gushed this out in case he changed his mind. "Many women have intelligence and courage to offer. There have been numerous great women throughout history. Joan of Arc is one."

"In some ways, perhaps, a woman might be equal, but Joan was burned as a heretic—by the evil English, no less." Napoleon walked toward the fireplace and his thoughts seemed to drift elsewhere. He pulled his bell cord. Ali rushed in, stoked the fire, and left quickly.

"Women during our revolution strived for equality with men." She wouldn't drop the subject close to her heart. "Such as Marie Madeline Jodin, and Olympe de Gouges."

"Most were prostitutes or actresses, melodramatic women full of artifice, catching the spirit of madness that prevailed." He leaned on the mantel, flipping up his hand in a grand gesture.

Napoleon hadn't minded actresses when they served as his mistresses.

"Some insisted on lodging and training for poor women, and women's divorce rights—"

"Does your father know you read about such things?" He stared at her wide-eyed, though she suspected he baited her.

"My father doesn't dictate what I read. He encourages my education."

"An overly educated woman can be a domineering, unfeminine shrew. Most learned women are shrill and ugly." Napoleon grimaced and her boundaries crumbled.

"Is a woman worth nothing if she isn't beautiful?" Amélie pressed the book to her chest. Is that how he thought of her?

"There are ways to be beautiful that have nothing to do with physical attraction." He ran his fingers over a music box on the chimneypiece mantel, his eyes now unfocused. "I think we are through discussing this."

"*Bien entendu.* We can discuss other topics." Amélie studied the emperor. His brisk manner had to hide his deep sadness. She'd test the limits of her influence and raise him above his enormous sorrows. A *woman* might tread where a valet wouldn't dare. "I wish you would reconsider and start riding again."

Napoleon turned to her, brows raised. "What do you mean?" he asked gently.

"I know you don't ride your horses anymore." Amélie fingered the book's edges. "You ought to get out of this place once in a while. The fresh air would be good for you."

"Are you aware the governor requires a British soldier to follow me if I leave this area? I refuse to ride under such ridiculous conditions." His voice swelled in pitch, his gaze narrowed.

Amélie regretted his upset, but he scrutinized her with an expectant air. "That shouldn't matter. Isn't it only hurting you to confine yourself here? You...*everyone* needs exercise. If I had such fine horses, I'd ride them every day."

Now he laughed, though it came out harsh. "Are you saying I'm getting too fat?"

"*No,* I didn't say that. I would never—"

"I know that I am. You think I don't have eyes, Amée?" He fixed her with his penetrating stare, and she bit at her lip. "Giving in to the British is out of the question. Remaining out of their sight, I retain my dignity. In here I'm always the emperor and not reminded of this unjust captivity by having the soldiers or Lowe dictating my every move."

"I'd hate to be shut up inside this house day after day. Fresh air is good for a change in outlook. Still, it's none of my affair. I'm sorry to have brought it up." She feigned resignation, a new tact—again testing her sway, and moved toward the study door, clutching the book.

Napoleon looked her up and down, a faint smile playing across his lips. "O'Meara constantly insists I resume riding as well. Harps on it, in his unassuming way."

She flushed under his scrutiny. "If you went out again, you'd be showing the British they have no effect on you. That...what they do is beneath your notice."

"They want me to give up exercise by insulting me—to perish sooner, as if from a natural death and not one they forced upon me by these restrictions." He rubbed his chin and spoke philosophically.

"If that's what they want..." Amélie's conviction strengthened as she twisted the doorknob. "Then take it away from them by defying their wishes, and riding out as you need to."

He studied her as if absorbing her reasoning, assessing his battle plan. "Your point is...tempting. Very well, I might go riding again, if you will go with me?"

She'd succeeded. She almost slumped against the door in relief. "I would be happy to."

"Splendid! Tomorrow I'll have my groom prepare the horses. We can ride after breakfast. Is that satisfactory?" Napoleon spoke louder as if trying to convince himself.

"Yes, quite satisfactory." Amélie opened the door and smiled. She wouldn't admit that she'd never graced the back of a horse before, but how hard could it be?

* * * *

That aristocratic bearing that gave Montholon his superior air struggled against the disapproval in his expression. "You intend to ride out before the British, with your kitchen maid?" He coated his words with a deferential tone, but Napoleon still bristled. "Do you think that is wise, Sire?"

"I don't need you to question my motives." Napoleon pulled his snuffbox from his waistcoat pocket and took a pinch. He ran it beneath his nose, inhaling the acrid smell, and threw the rest in the study fireplace. How much longer must he put up with these people? He'd thought Montholon a useful addition to his entourage: an actual tie to the old aristocracy, to make him legitimate in the eyes of European royalty, even in exile. The prissy man, however, grated on his nerves. "You will accompany us. Now leave me."

"I only wish to protect you from any slander the English might attach to such a display, but, of course, it is your prerogative, Sire." Montholon bowed and strode from the room, leaving behind that prick of chastisement.

"She is just a child. No one will care." Napoleon smiled, dismissing his annoyance with Montholon. That little scamp Amée had talked him into this before he knew what happened. She had more depth than he'd first surmised. She brought him out of his torpor, challenged him, and made him feel alive again. When was the last time a girl had so affected him, beyond the selfish occasional need to have one in his bed? His first months with Marie Louise had brought him pleasure—his dominance over her royal person, but as soon as she'd slipped from his influence... He rubbed his thumb over the antique coins on his snuffbox and refused to allow himself to dwell on that.

Yes, Amée would be a pleasant distraction until his situation changed. Napoleon had to trust that the situation *would* change, that this island was but a stumbling block in his illustrious career. Stuffing the obvious devastations—loss of family, territory, prestige, in a separate compartment in his mind—kept him sane. Like the eagle, he had to stare forward over the horizon. That's how he survived in a world that had punctured him far too many times.

* * * *

Perrault knitted his smoky brow as he rattled his pots onto their hooks. The evening candlelight wavered in the drafty kitchen. "You've never ridden before, to my recollection."

"No, in Paris and Lyon I could walk everywhere." Amélie stepped down off the stool where she hung herbs to dry from the rafters. "It's the only way the emperor will resume his exercise, and he has grown extremely overweight and slow."

"Amélie, I hope you didn't tell him that to his face." Perrault arched both eyebrows, and smoothed back his thick mass of gray hair. "Has your outspokenness made you forget your manners?"

"Papa, allow me more sensitivity than that."

"As long as you don't weary His Majesty." Perrault poked wood into the oven to ready it for the next morning. "You like to be too forward at times. I hope there will be a chaperone?"

"Of course." Amélie barely let his question register. She felt swept up, caught in a wind that might blow her to the edge of the island's cliffs. She had to balance herself carefully.

"Our emperor has always been fond of young people." Perrault bent to brush ashes from the bread oven. "He enjoys playing with Count de Montholon's and Count Bertrand's children."

"*Mon Dieu*, Papa, when will you stop seeing me as a child?" She said it softly, and picked up the broom and brushed herb remnants toward the door. In this tiny community, he had to have heard the insinuating gossip about her. Was this his way of denying it might be possible?

"A mature adult knows when to be humble." Her father removed his apron and shook off the day's debris, his tone brusque. "I hope you don't intend to misbehave the way you did after your recital."

"He didn't mind. You shouldn't scold me now that I *am* a young woman." She smiled and patted her father's shoulder.

"We are now so familiar, we need only say 'he'?" Her father's gaze grew more disconcerting. His haggard face pricked her with guilt.

"Did I? My mistake." Amélie gave her father a peck on his dry cheek, something she hadn't done in far too long, but it didn't improve his expression. "Why don't you go and rest?"

"Just remember, *ma fille*, you come from decent family. I will curtail these... lessons, if I must." He turned and left the kitchen.

Amélie retired to her room, her father's threat unsettling. Now she'd gone from child to woman before his eyes, the transformation might not be to her advantage.

An emperor overruled a chef, and she was through being subservient. She wriggled into her shabby cotton nightgown, threw aside the blanket, and stretched out on her thin mattress. She traced her fingers along her goose-bumped arms when she thought of her deepening tenderness toward Napoleon.

Chapter Eleven

The native earth has invisible charms...the very smell of its soil is so present in my senses...—N.B.

Napoleon shivered in the dank air of his bedroom—he'd always been sensitive to cold—and lamented his impulsiveness. He crawled from his moist sheets and rang for Marchand.

After stoking up the fire, Marchand brought him breakfast then helped him dress. The valet wiped the blue mold off Napoleon's leather boots, a frequent occurrence in this climate. The young man draped the green hunting jacket with green velvet collar and cuffs over Napoleon's shoulders: a garment he insisted his tailor turn rather than replace with English cloth. He rubbed an ache from his shoulder, thrust his arms in the sleeves and fastened the stag and fox-shaped silver buttons over his paunch. He plopped his cocked hat on his head and strode from his interior. Outside the misty air made him grumble. Already July and an austral winter was upon him.

At the stables Amélie waited. A prompt girl, a key virtue. She wore a frayed spencer jacket and a straw hat for her introduction into horsemanship. Yes, he suspected she'd never ridden before. She talked with the stableman, Cloubert, a plump, fat-cheeked man of kind nature. Married to an abrasive woman who worked as head chambermaid, so Ali had told him.

When the girl looked at him, Napoleon increased his gait to appear jaunty. Despite his girth, he would carry himself with a commanding presence.

"Are you ready for this great ride, Amée?" Napoleon smiled and her face lit up as if he were a ray of sun. This idea warmed him in the chilly breeze. He turned to his groom who approached leading three horses. "You found a proper sidesaddle, Archambault?"

"*Bien sûr*, Your Majesty. Mademoiselle, allow me to assist you onto your mount." Archambault, stinking like cheap wine, stooped and cupped his hands.

"I'm more than ready, Sire." Amélie stepped over and the groom hoisted her up onto the horse. She settled herself uneasily in the saddle. Archambault handed her the reins.

Montholon strode into their group as Napoleon mounted. "You're late, Charles. You disrespect me in such behavior."

Amélie frowned at the count.

"Please except my profound apologies, Your Majesty. Albine is feeling a little ill. After all, her delicate condition, and Tristan has the sniffles." Montholon, straight as a saber, sliced his shiny boot toe into the stirrup and mounted.

"Your wife should take your son out more, to enjoy God's good air. Let us begin." Napoleon inhaled the air and urged Hope forward. Amélie's horse followed, and his jolting walk forced her to grip the saddle for balance. She looked uncomfortable with her leg looped over the pommel.

They circled the house and left the grounds, heading out over the Deadwood Plain. Another rider galloped after them.

"Ahh, my English spy." Napoleon's irritation crept up. "The orderly officer who dogs my every step. How does he know I intend to leave the designated area?"

"I...might have informed Captain Poppleton, Sire. As due course." Montholon's words sounded only marginally contrite.

"Sometimes I don't know whose side you're on." Napoleon flashed his courtier an angry glare and urged his horse on faster, his shoulders hunched. Amélie warned him about this man. He must keep a close watch on Montholon.

Napoleon's muscles, unused to riding, soon ached, but it was an ache he didn't mind. He stretched his back and neck and watched the girl grow familiar with her horse's pace, a smile replacing her cautious expression.

Before Hutt's Gate, the trio followed the twisting road around the Devil's Punchbowl, where gorse bushes hung over the edge by their roots. Navigating a steep, muddy track beyond, they rode down into the hollow known as Sane Valley. Napoleon dubbed it Geranium Vale, due to its geranium plants as tall as trees, so his people referred to it as such. A few pines and yellowing oaks clung to the grassy slopes. Napoleon breathed in the sweet, peppery scent from the mango, aloes, and myrtle.

"I've never seen geraniums and begonias so large." Amélie scrutinized the valley with interest. Their nearest water source, a stream shaded by weeping willows, intersected its center. "I wished we lived here, surrounded by such scenery, sheltered from the wind."

The indigenous Wire Birds, resembling ringed plovers, hopped on their wiry green legs and flapped gray wings at the intruders. Amélie laughed when one bird dove for a large black beetle as it skittered over a rock among tangled briar. Napoleon smiled at her spontaneous mirth.

The English soldier maneuvered closer and Napoleon kicked his horse into a canter. Amélie rocked in the saddle when her mount also picked up speed. She yanked on the reins, jamming her foot in the stirrup until her horse fell behind.

"I'd like to lose that English *imbecile*." Napoleon slowed his mount to let her catch up. "Cockburn, at my request, made the 'escorts' wear plain clothes and stay far back, away from me. Often I prevailed with no one. I could reason with Admiral Cockburn, but never that rascal Lowe."

Amélie winced and arranged herself more securely in the saddle, as if her buttocks were already sore from rubbing across hard leather. "Isn't the valley part of the area permitted without an escort?"

"May we gallop over the hill, Sire? Like we used to do," Montholon said as if to drown her out. The haughty *aristo* brimmed with jealousy.

"How fast is a gallop?" Amélie tightened her grip on the reins, her eyes wide.

"You're not afraid are you, Amée?" Napoleon asked with a wry smile.

"This sidesaddle is awkward. I don't know if I can keep my balance." The girl's mouth thinned in determination. "How do women manage to ride in such an odd position?"

"You're used to riding the conventional way? You should have told me." He chuckled when she narrowed her eyes. His suspicion must be obvious, but he appreciated her bravery.

They left the valley and skirted Longwood's grounds again, past the Deadwood Camp, rambling through arid soil dotted with red thistle and loose pebbles. The mist swirled about their horses' hooves. "Such a desolate place. It reminds me of the bleak plains of Russia, burned by her fleeing inhabitants." Napoleon wished he rode in the lush woods at his St. Cloud palace where he'd indulged in hunting—images that still comforted him. "Do you know overzealous tanners ruined a great forest here, by stripping tree barks to boil and tan goat hides? Leaving the trees to fall over and rot. That's why they call this plain Deadwood."

They approached the area known as Great Horse Point. Stunted trees sprouted among scrubwoods emitting a strong aromatic smell. Tangles of herbal boneseed, with hairy stems, crept like worms along the sandy soil.

"Look, Sire. That plant is called 'Old Father Live Forever.' It's a cousin of the geranium. The thick gnarled stems resemble the withered appearance of an old man." Amélie grinned and pointed. "Saint Helena has such unique plants."

"The British want me to become another of them, my roots dying in this soil," Napoleon replied, the bitter words automatic, yet he enjoyed the girl's enthusiasm in her surroundings, making him see the scenery in a new way.

He reined in Hope on a cliff overlooking Prosperous Bay. The perpendicular lava coast was striped in dark blue and reddish-gray. Towards the east naked hills divided ravines, the hill's clay strata a variety of reds and purples. His shoulders slumped—so far from Europe.

Napoleon dismounted and assisted Amélie down. Her body felt delicate in his hands, her scent so clean. "Now, tell me the truth—you've never ridden before, have you?"

"No, I haven't, Sire." She fumbled to adjust her dress, her cheeks flushed. "I didn't do so badly. I think it would be easier to ride as you do than on this silly contraption."

"A woman must ride appropriately, not like a heathen." Napoleon provoked her, amused to see her expression grow stubborn, to test her perseverance. "You want to be a wild island child? Charles, we must find Mademoiselle Perrault a proper saddle, and make certain it isn't silly."

"*Sur l'heure*, I will do my best, Your Majesty." Montholon stood stiff after dismounting. He glanced at Amélie in prim annoyance when he must have thought Napoleon didn't notice.

"Many will think it daring if you ride like a man. Scandalous, in fact. The British will mock you," Napoleon teased. He gripped his hat in the salty breeze. His gray greatcoat flapped about his body.

"I don't care what the British think." Amélie walked to the edge of the cliff. She took a deep breath. "I never thought I'd enjoy the smell of the sea again, or care to hear the slap of waves."

"Come away from there." Napoleon pulled her aside and pointed to a saffron-colored scorpion crawling across a rock. "You don't want to feel his sting."

"Oh! No, Sire." Her startled expression softened as she looked at him. He felt a wave of pleasure that caught him off guard. He let go of her and rubbed his chilled hands together.

Still mounted, the English soldier hovered just out of earshot.

Napoleon glared in distaste. "How does Lowe presume I'll make my escape, by jumping off this sheer cliff? British naval vessels encircle the island. Does he assume I can fly away as a bird? There's a difference between instructions and their execution. Those London Lords who made them would do things differently if they saw this place. On this ugly island, it's enough if the coast is guarded."

"Sire, just think of that soldier as your bodyguard, not a jailer," Amélie said, her eyes steady on his. "If you see him that way, maybe his presence won't be so exasperating."

"The governor says I can't speak to anyone I might pass on this island unless the sentry is with me, listening. I used to visit the islanders, invite them for dinner. I would offer them financial assistance if they were in need. I had to stop, so as not to compromise anyone."

"Remember that pretty young woman you flirted with, Sire?" Montholon slanted his gaze over Amélie.

"Not especially. I'd gallop all the way to Alarm House with Las Cases, cross Woody Ridge into Sinner's Valley. Now, no more!" Napoleon approached his horse, jerked the reins to channel his anger. Hope shied, throwing his head. "Lowe is deranged with punctiliousness. He often makes these insipid regulations, then changes them moments later. I never know over which restriction I'm to be harassed."

"Deranged might be the right word for the governor," Amélie said.

"I heard Lowe has nightmares of my escaping and rides to Longwood in the middle of the night to verify I'm still there. What an irritating fool." Napoleon flung this off, not caring for his slip of temper. He stroked Hope's silky nose. At the girl's anxious face, he lightened his manner and chuckled. "You think *I* am the one being petty?"

"No, Sire, but sometimes you have to make allowances. It's to your advantage to ride again. You should even walk every day. Ignore the English. I'd feel happier if you took care of yourself."

"Then how can I convince them I'm suffering from this climate?" Her concern touched him and Napoleon repeated his usual rationalization to fend it off. "The damp weather and backward seasons. That this island will be the death of me?"

"Do you want it to be the death of you?" Her voice sad, she frowned.

"To what else would you attribute my strange maladies? Headaches, shivering, chills in my legs?" He turned away for an instant from her troubled expression. Pity, a demeaning emotion—he'd never sought it before. "Strange fevers and dysentery are rampant on this island. The British claimed it's healthy, but they lie. Hardly a day goes by without a burial."

"Perhaps inactivity is the cause of your ailments, Your Majesty?" Amélie flashed a beseeching smile. Her straw hat blew back and she pulled it forward and tightened the ribbon.

Montholon sniffed his patrician nose. "Isn't it too cold for you out here, Sire? Perhaps we should go back. Some people have difficulty understanding their places."

"You're a wise girl for one so young." Napoleon ignored his general's remark. "You see you already learn too quickly. If I walk every day, I won't be so fat either." He gazed at her, then reached over and pinched her earlobe. "Perhaps you don't comprehend my tactics against the British government."

Amélie caressed a finger over her ear. "I'm not so young anymore. I'm twenty."

"Twenty, as old as that?" Napoleon smiled. Despite his efforts, her sweet empathy tugged at him more than he should allow. "I was commissioned in the army for four years by then." His smile faded. What was he doing teasing with this girl—no, a burgeoning woman—gawked at by the English? Too impatient to wait for his former country to demand his release, he had another scheme, tactics he shared with no one. That Irish merchant captain seemed willing. Now he was at the Cape with Las Cases. Always have alternate battle plans. "It is time I venture out again, to study the lay of the land. Official channels have done nothing for me." He pulled out his field glasses and scanned the cliff-line. "This will give that British watchdog fits. Climbing down the cliff does look impossible from here."

"Sire, you couldn't possibly...you would injure yourself in such a foolhardy undertaking." Montholon practically stammered, his gaze sharp.

Napoleon resented that his courtier didn't even encourage him in such an endeavor. He questioned more and more the count's reliability. "Pipe dreams, my good man." He shoved his field glasses into Montholon's hands and assisted Amélie up onto her mount. They rode slowly back to Longwood where he gave over the horses to his groom and dismissed the count.

"Not a bad day. It is a trial to keep occupied here," Napoleon told her when the two of them re-entered the house. The gloomy dwelling pressed down on him again, but he needed to keep up his strength. "When do we start this walking business?"

"Tomorrow, I should think, Your Majesty. Right after breakfast?" Amélie sounded pleased that he heeded her advice, the little minx.

Ali rushed out of the duty chamber and took his hat and coat.

"Fine. I'll see you tomorrow. No practice today, take a rest." Napoleon walked toward his study, scooting the girl and her tender compassion from his mind, though the excursion invigorated his spirit. He rubbed his aching thigh and thought of the letters he'd smuggled out, requesting details on what support he had left in Europe, the situation with the king in France. He sighed, but had to keep abreast of such things for his next move.

* * * *

Amélie suspected Napoleon needed the rest. She felt her muscles twisting in opposite directions after straining to keep her posture on the horse. Napoleon walked into his study, and Albine de Montholon sailed into the room like a silk-clad galleon and begged to be received. The study door closed after them.

Amélie tensed, her heart grew heavy. The woman always seemed primed for attack, even in her obvious condition.

"Allow me to help you, Louis." Clarice bustled past her from the preparation room, carrying a tray of food. Marchand stepped behind her, his expression vexed. She set the tray on the new mahogany dining room table. Ten chairs painted black and covered in silk Taboret had also been brought up to replace their shabby furniture.

"I serve His Majesty, if you don't mind." Marchand tried to take the tray, but Clarice leaned over it, her breasts in danger of flopping into his face. The valet averted his eyes, slid the tray from under her, and carried it into the emperor's study.

"If you insist. I'm here if you need me." Clarice tossed her head, then turned and saw Amélie. Her smile quirked into a sneer. "Well, there she is, the emperor's favorite, the little opera singer."

"Clarice." Amélie bit back a grin and walked to the rear door.

"Since you weren't here, I had to help serve. Of course Marchand wanted my aid." Clarice trailed outside after her, and kept pace like a shadow right into her chambers. "The emperor takes you riding now, does he?"

"Yes, and why not? I had a wonderful time." Amélie untied the ribbon from her chin. After sweeping off rat droppings, she placed her hat on the dresser.

"It's wrong to go off riding with two men and no chaperone. Doesn't your father think it unseemly?" Clarice almost shouted as if to penetrate into her father's chamber.

"I make my own decisions where I go." Amélie massaged her bottom, her buttocks and thighs raw and bruised. Her right knee throbbed from gripping the pommel.

"Do you? What secret comforts do you give His Majesty to deserve such attention? He even bought you dresses…and gave you jewelry. Your talent must be vast." Clarice's nasty laugh reverberated around the tiny room.

"Do you envy me my talents?" Amélie snatched her brush from her dresser top, her euphoria over the day tarnished. "I'm tired of your remarks. Please leave."

"Don't be naïve. We're all discussing your growing expertise."

"What I do is none of your business." Amélie concentrated on brushing her hair in the cracked looking glass above her chest of drawers. Perhaps the countess provided "comfort" right now to Napoleon in his study. She raked through the wind-blown knots until her scalp hurt. "You still need hobbies of your own so you have less time to be rude. Take your jealously elsewhere."

"Hobbies? Is that what it's called? How polite. Can you put in a word for me with Marchand? That would keep me busy. I also wouldn't mind a new dress." Instead of leaving, Clarice flounced down on the bed, the scent of lye soap drifting around her. "What have you done so far with His Majesty?"

Amélie flushed hot inside, but smiled at the other woman. "I mind my own affairs, as should you." She resisted a chuckle at her word choice. Many people suspected this relationship, but could Napoleon ever see her in such a way? His hands had lingered when he helped her off her mount.

Clarice lolled back on the mattress, her upper lip puckered. "Once you've lost your maidenhead, you'll be ruined for any good marriage. Of course, it's only when a man sticks far up that it's too late." She spoke in a languid tone, running her hand down her abdomen to between her thighs. "Have you gone that far? Like dogs mating, but face to face."

Amélie fumbled with her brush, repressing a shiver. She'd seen dogs mating and it looked painful. Certainly for humans sex had to be better. Did a book exist that explained the intricacies of sex? Was that her intention with the emperor? She turned to glare at Clarice, though she wouldn't have minded more details. "I would like to be alone, so please go. *Now*."

Clarice rose with an exaggerated sigh and went to the door. "Then you just leave us all to gossip about the outcome. *Quel dommage*." With a shrug of her fat shoulder, she sauntered out, nose in the air.

Amélie plopped down on her bed. Napoleon's touch always left her jittery. Was this a part of pleasure and did she want more? Where could she find information about carnal relations?

* * * *

Every muscle and sinew in her body ached from their equestrian adventure but Amélie kept walking down the same path ridden the day before. Napoleon kept pace though grumbled. They reached the steep slope that led to the valley. Napoleon staggered. Amélie slowed, thankful only a footman accompanied them today, no Count de Montholon.

At the stream, the smell of plants ripe in the soft air, the emperor collapsed on a large rock and groaned. "I'm too tired, too old, and too fat for all this."

"If you walk every day you won't be so tired or...overweight...and you aren't that old." Amélie overstepped her bounds, easier in his presence. Their discourse had slipped into the *"tu"* form of intimates.

Napoleon stared at her, guffawed, and slapped his knee. "I'm not *that* old, am I? You make me laugh, Amée. The others in the house have become ridiculously dull, but you, *mon amie*, amuse me."

"I'm thankful for that." She'd hate to make him angry, having witnessed his famous temper directed toward the others. She beamed with pride he called her a friend, her first desires, but had her wishes changed? She toed the dirt, her thoughts confused.

"I can't, however, totally give in to Lowe's treatment of me, ignore the soldiers and so on. It's the only power I have left, to resist what that scoundrel does." He gripped his hand on his knee. "The English insult me by even assigning that rogue. Lowe commanded a group called the Corsican Rangers, consisting of Royalist émigrés and Corsican traitors against my government."

"There must be better ways to resist that don't harm you." Amélie stepped near the hillside and picked a sprig, dark green with a white felted back, from a crooked tree. "Here's wild rosemary. If you put it in your coffee, it helps fatigue."

"I used to be the most robust of men, until I came here. Lowe offered to build me a barracks to walk in when the weather was foul and I could be unseen. He wants to confine me in a box like a trained tiger. None of them have the authority to keep me prisoner. I came of my own free will to the British captain in the straits." Napoleon grimaced, his hands clenched for a moment. Then he jerked to his feet and they continued their walk. "Indeed, if I'd been born to the throne they would never treat me like this."

"I was there, Sire. They betrayed you horribly." She wanted to hug his arm, absorb his sorrow, and feel his skin warm against her. Instead she bent to inspect some watercress and wild celery alongside the stream and tried to banish the image of amorous canines. "Do you think the allied powers will release you?"

"The Hapsburgs allowed me to marry into their family. Why wouldn't they assist me in my present situation?" He increased his pace, his boots crunching over dead leaves.

Amélie doubted the Austrians would lift a finger to help him now that he had no power to wield over them. Napoleon deluded himself in such hopes. She, on the other hand, wanted to keep him right here. "I guess it depends on the political—"

"The English want me humbled before them." Napoleon raised his head high, his eagle profile under his cocked hat proud. "Lowe thinks he has power over my body, but my soul shall always elude him."

"*Bien sûr.*" Amélie nudged a rock into the stream, where it rippled the surface for an instant, and suddenly had a revelation. "Now you might understand how a woman feels, humbled by the restrictions of men."

"An interesting...if misguided parallel, I have to admit." Napoleon chuckled then stopped, his expression changing to reflective. He pointed up on a slope, to the aromatic shrub myrtle. "That plant is native to Corsica. I grew up smelling that scent. It grows blue-black berries I used to toss down a village girl's dress." He laughed as if once again that mischievous little boy.

He'd found pleasure in something so simple, even if he did sidetrack her remark. Couldn't he trade one island for another?

She picked up a mint sprig and sniffed the piquant bouquet. No matter the season, plants continued to bloom on Saint Helena. "When you were a child, did you dream of becoming a powerful man?"

"Not exactly. I was stubborn, rebellious. After being sent off to school in France, I realized my capacity for learning, my resistance to being ruled. I wanted to command." He walked on farther, coughing into his hand.

"Resistance to being ruled." Amélie smiled at that, a yearning she understood. She caught up with him. "I have a recipe for sage tea you should try—a cure for coughs, colds, and liver complaints. It's sweetened with honey."

"Like the basil tea you tried to give me? I don't believe in medicinals, or magic potions." His voice took on a lighter quality. "Do you aspire to be a sorceress too?"

"I aspire to many things," Amélie half sang out, enjoying the walk, the scenery, and the company. The footman followed unobtrusively behind. She ran her thumb over the white felt leaf she'd first picked. "Rosemary also helps memory. Put rosemary tea in your bath and it invigorates the blood."

"Too much knowledge makes you dangerous." Napoleon winked and squeezed her shoulder, his fingers running briefly down her back.

"Am I shrill and ugly like most learned women?" His caress gave her a shuddering sensation, and she almost laughed out loud to contain it.

"Not at all." He stared off. "Perhaps you're right. I do need to look to my health. New events may present themselves that will require all my strength."

"What events? Can you tell me? Do you ever think of...escape?"

A scuffling of hooves from high up the valley slope startled her. She and Napoleon stared up at the same time. A horseman in a well-appointed red coat wheeled his steed about on the crest of the ridge and galloped off in a scatter of dirt—Governor Lowe, spying on his prisoner!

"*Basta!* My executioner." Napoleon raised his fists, his blue-gray eyes livid.

Amélie stepped back, cowed by this vision of her furious, defeated emperor. His familiar silhouette towered above her. A man that she, as well as the English, had no right to cage.

Chapter Twelve

True character always pierces through in moments of crises—N.B.

Lord Amherst gave what passed for a sympathetic smile on his cadaverous features. "I can fully understand your difficult circumstances, sir. The extreme logistics of the island is problem enough. I will be pleased to mediate with the governor for you."

Napoleon came close to feeling satisfied, but kept his face stern. Never let your opponents know if they've affected you, good or bad. He stifled a cough, the phlegm rumbling in his chest. "Lowe has a demented need to torture me with his petty restrictions." He stepped from the black stone chimneypiece in the drawing room, his hat tight under his arm. Candles flickered around them, giving off the cheap smell of tallow. "Tell your parliament that I await, as a favor, for the executioner's hatchet to put an end to my jailor's outrages."

Amherst flinched, just the reaction Napoleon intended. "I protest such thoughts, sir. I will see what I can do. Our government has much to answer for, but their fear of your power, even in this situation, prompts their actions."

"It can be construed as cowardice on their part." Napoleon stiffened his jaw. "When you reach Europe, give my good Louise my tender regards, and tell her that I stay faithful to her." This remained his set statement to anyone returning to Europe, no matter how much it hurt to say it. He clung to the belief his wife was coerced into deserting him by her perfidious family.

After Bertrand showed Amherst out, Napoleon walked back to his study, coughing into his handkerchief. His cold almost stopped him from granting this interview, but Amée insisted he meet with the man. She'd become a demanding little creature. Still, her compassion pleased him when he had little sincerity from the others.

He sank down on his lumpy sofa and Marchand handed him a cup of broth. He tasted it, inhaling the steam, glad to find the soup hot enough to burn his lips. "Amherst hasn't a kind face. He failed in his China embassy by refusing to submit to the humiliating protocol of the Peking court. I must have faith he'll report the indignities Lowe torments me with to his superiors in London. I gave Lowe a pretty lesson." If this official didn't help him, he'd have to forge ahead with his alternate plans. His elation dampened, a little, at the thought of never seeing Amélie again if he left Saint Helena. She'd begun to invade his senses. So strange, when he strained for his emotions to be bronzed over. He had to ignore such folly.

He slid over a tortoiseshell box on his side table and opened it. Several strands of fine blond hair lay within. "Make certain to thank your mother for this gift, discreetly of course." Napoleon stroked the hair and smiled. His eyes moistened with tears. Marchand's mother, who had gone to Vienna with the empress and Napoleon's son, had sent this hair to Marchand saying it was hers. Napoleon saw right away it belonged to his little boy, the child he hoped someday to see again. The Emperor Francis wanted him to have nothing more to do with his son. Napoleon feared they would teach him to follow the legitimists and feel horror for his own father. This was hardly the destiny he'd planned for his little king at his long-awaited birth.

"I will most assuredly, Your Majesty."

"What do you think of Amélie?" Napoleon pulled his flannel blanket closer around him. Some might think it strange that he'd ask his valet's opinion, but here in these tight quarters he'd grown closer to this young man who tended him like a friend.

"She's a nice girl with a good reputation, Sire." Marchand crouched down and wrapped a warm towel around Napoleon's feet. He placed a heated brick under them.

Napoleon sighed, gratified by the warmth coming through his soles. He heard no condemnation of their relationship in the young man's tone—he always remained deferential. "A nice girl. Yes, indeed. I must find her a good husband."

He would depart this island, by legal or illegal means, it didn't matter. The Irish captain of the East India should return from Cape Town, South Africa soon, but the "extreme logistics" of the island kept measures at a crawl.

* * * *

Amélie muffled a cough, straining to hit the correct notes while struggling to form the guttural words. She rehearsed as Pamina, who seeks her own death in "Achd, ich fuhl's," from Mozart's *The Magic Flute*. The following month the Bertrands would host her next recital at Hutt's Gate.

Napoleon stood at his study fireplace, watching her. She bit her lip, frustrated he insisted she sing this aria in the original German. His having an Austrian wife must prompt this desire. It saddened her to see him pine for a shallow young woman who cuckolded him the minute her situation became difficult.

"Amée, you are so close. *Ecoute*, if you would just pay attention to what I'm saying. You're fighting the entire process." The emperor's scolding compounded her upset. "Now try it again."

Rain beat down against the study's shuttered windows. Amélie perspired around her neck and down her chest, but Napoleon always enjoyed a raging fire.

"This has none of the lilting quality of Italian operas. May I have some water?" she croaked. "I don't think—"

"Water must wait. One more time, you almost have it. Let's not waste a moment!"

He expected her to be flawless, but she feared she disappointed him, something she never wanted to do. Her head throbbed, her throat felt scraped with broken glass. "Let me rest. I can't do this! I know why you want it!"

Napoleon's glare made her tremble with failure and she burst into tears. Humiliated, Amélie fled out the study side door. Blinded by tears and rain, she rushed through the chilling downpour, squelching in mud as she rounded the back of the house to her quarters.

In her room, she flung herself on the bed, mortified by her behavior, but angry with him for pushing so relentlessly.

A frantic knock on her door. She bunched her pillow around her head and hoped it wasn't her father. "Please...go away."

"Amée, let me in."

At Napoleon's voice she hopped up and hurriedly straightened the bedclothes. Wiping her face with a discarded nightgown, she fretted over what to do next. She had no choice, fingers flexing, and pulled open the door.

Napoleon looked so distressed, she took a shuddering breath, amazed he chased after her. He proved himself a mortal man, weakened by her tears.

"It's all my fault." He stepped into her narrow chamber, his hands gentle on her shoulders, water dripping from his hair. "I didn't mean to hurt you, Amée."

She sniffed as more tears escaped. "I should never have behaved so. I'm sorry, but I needed so much to rest."

He pulled a handkerchief from his pocket and dabbed her moist cheeks. "I would never intentionally make you cry, you must believe that. I got carried away. I realize I can be a hard taskmaster. Will you forgive me?"

"Yes, but…I don't like that opera in German. It's harsh, even if that disappoints you."

"A strange language I once tried to learn myself. Worse than the English Las Cases tried to teach me." He stared into her face as if mulling something over. "All right, if you insist, we'll strike that song. Who wants to hear German opera? Italian is far superior, with grace and melody." Napoleon drew her into his arms and kissed her tenderly on the forehead.

Amélie laid her cheek on his shoulder, absorbing the warmth of his embrace even through damp cloth. Content to be held by him, she trembled, then relaxed against his thumping heart. His hands tightened on her back.

Napoleon pulled away as if she'd stung him like a wasp. He patted her face and said quickly, "Are we all right now? Good. Then rest, until tomorrow."

He hurried back out the door. She hugged her empty arms around her tremulous body.

* * * *

Amélie turned from the Countess de Montholon who lounged like a fat cat in the study doorway. "I have no problem singing *a cappella*, Sire."

"Go and soak your hands, Albine." Napoleon waved the woman away, his voice gruff. "We will dispense with your playing for the time being, since it so tires you."

Albine rubbed her hands together, her pout mawkish. "It's only because of my condition." She stroked her protruding belly. "You understand, of course, Your Majesty." The woman grinned.

"I'm certain your husband is very concerned about *his* baby." Amélie smirked back through clenched teeth. The countess loved to flaunt the suspect paternity of her child.

Albine wrinkled her nose and flounced from the room.

"Ignore her. Albine likes to distract me. She's not up to the task, so we don't need her, do we? We'll wait until she has her child." Napoleon's attitude showed no possessiveness toward the impending event.

"We don't need her at all." Amélie smiled for him, but he looked away and walked to his sideboard. She relived his arms around her the previous afternoon, her quivering reaction—she'd never realized an embrace could stir up so many emotions. Now Napoleon seemed distant, ashamed?

"Now, Amée, I want to commend you for your performance improvement on the points we discussed." Napoleon raised a crystal decanter. "As a treat for your perseverance, I will give you a glass of my special wine. It isn't my Chambertin, but the British won't allow me such luxury." He seldom shared this wine, reserving it for his own consumption.

"I'm honored. Ali says you receive this wine from South Africa." She accepted a glass, their fingers almost touching.

"The British import it from near Cape Town, the Constantia vineyard. It's called the Vin de Constance and has an unusual bouquet." He poured his own glass and took a sip.

Amélie sampled the wine, but the acrid flavor disappointed her.

"*Eh bien*, do you approve?" Napoleon asked as if her approval was important.

"Yes...but I think it's...too rich for my tastes."

"I'll admit, many have felt the same." His smile turned thoughtful, sad.

"I'm not much of a connoisseur when it comes to wine." Out of respect she finished her glass, smiling through the bitterness. The beverage left a strange aftertaste in her mouth.

"Have you seen this bust of my son?" Napoleon set down his glass and went over and pulled the item from his mantelpiece. A child's impassive face encased in marble.

"He is a handsome boy." His longing saddened her. Rumors said the bust was a fake, made in London by men hoping to cash in on a father's love, and not commissioned by the empress as Napoleon deceived himself. She, however, wouldn't diminish his parental joy at the gift.

"He looks too much like Marie Louise." He turned the bust in his hands.

Amélie savored his remark, as if that resemblance displeased him. "He has your chin." She moved closer, her shoulder near his.

"Yes, he does have my chin...and forehead." Napoleon ran a finger over the child's cold, noble brow. He stepped away and set the bust back on the mantel. "Lowe refused to forward this gift. The islanders protested and he was forced to release it. Another reason I can't give in to Lowe's edicts and let him refute my title. That will negate my son's inheritance and rights to the throne of France."

"No one dares deny your sovereignty over France. Enlightened people will rally behind your son." She fingered her empty glass and prayed the Austrians wouldn't keep the child prisoner for the rest of his life in their embarrassment over a now inconvenient liaison.

"In the difficult birthing of our boy...I asked the doctor to save the mother. My good Louise was grateful to me for that." Napoleon sounded wistful.

"That was kind of you. What a concerned husband would do." Amélie almost wished the unfaithful empress had died in childbirth. Napoleon should forget about such a vapid creature. He had people close by who cared about him.

"You are a loyal subject, Amée." He patted her cheek, tenderness spreading over his face. His hand lingered for a moment. "Always compassionate. Your sincerity honors me. Not like the empty flattery of so many others."

She tingled inside with a strange heat, but wanted to be more than a sycophant. "Will we walk again soon? I know you're angry at the governor for observing us, but this battle of wills is bad for you both."

"Please don't mention that villain to me. You have no idea of the complexities."

Elysium

Napoleon paced to the other side of the room, hands clasped behind his back.

"A tolerant relationship would have to improve your situation." Amélie softened her tone under his glare. She rubbed a hand over her throat at a slight burning sensation. "You can't understand one another if you never speak."

"If we weren't stuck on this rock, you could practice properly in a theater. This ridiculous island doesn't even boast such amenities." Napoleon's expression brooding, she might have grazed on the truth. "Though nothing compares with Paris and her grand houses: the Théatre-Français, the Opéra. If Saint Helena *did* offer the finer pleasures of humanity, Lowe would wring any drop of joy from it. That's his character."

"I heard they do have a small theater in Jamestown, but you *know* I'd never care to go on the stage." He continued to deflect her concerns. She had to maneuver around his stubbornness. "Couldn't you find a way to be happy on Saint Helena?"

"Never. What is there to be happy about with a man who blindly follows orders? England wants me to be *General* Bonaparte, prisoner of war. Lowe threatens to send my servants to the Cape if they dare violate his rules, the islanders banished, a soldier accused of high treason. Are these the workings of a rational man?" He picked up a discarded newspaper and tossed it into a corner. Then he turned to stare at her, a glint of mischief in his eyes. "Don't tell me you're content here?"

"I am, and I keep busy, which leaves me little time to be otherwise." She flourished in the stimulating company she'd kept these last months. The one person who fed her need to stretch her limits, Napoleon had risen from obscurity to magnificence by his own will. Her stomach started to churn. "Your life here could be enjoy—"

"How could a pretty girl like you be satisfied in this existence? You should be attending balls, riding in the park with young gallants anxious to please you, desperate to ask for your hand in marriage." Napoleon's gaze pierced her as if he'd shot an arrow.

"I'm not looking to wed." Her reply sharp, she pressed a hand to her gurgling stomach. She'd stay on Saint Helena—with him—safe in their cosseted world. "A person can be satisfied anywhere if they put their mind to it."

"That will be all for the day." He scrutinized her with a new wariness she didn't like.

"Very well, Napoleon." Dazed, she left the study. He'd called her pretty, but was that empty flattery? She'd grown poised in his company, enjoying his interest in her talents that had nothing to do with outward appearance. Now pulled in another direction, she craved those touches, warm embraces that sent shivers along her body.

Outside her room, her stomach heaved. Amélie rushed to the privy and vomited into a basin. She coughed and sputtered, the sour taste burning her mouth and nose. She'd *never* drink another glass of the emperor's special wine.

* * * *

After Amélie left, looking a little pale—he had to discourage their closeness, marry her off—Bertrand arrived at the study door. His grand marshal swept off his hat, his neck crimson.

Napoleon sighed. "Over what ridiculous infraction is Lowe to torture me now?"

He yanked on his bell chord. "Marchand! Fill my bath."

"It isn't the governor, Your Majesty." Bertrand stepped in and bowed. His brown hair had thinned on top, his pasty scalp showing through like a goose egg in a nest. "I have a letter, or I should say, a proclamation from the British ministry. Lowe just had it delivered to me."

"Well, what is it?" Napoleon's shoulders stiffened. It wasn't good news, or Bertrand wouldn't be staring at his scuffed boots. He heard splashes as footmen poured buckets of water into his tub in the other room and closed his eyes, anxious to soak away these torments.

"Lord Holland held a debate in Parliament over your harsh treatment here. We had high hopes for this, if you remember, Sire?" Bertrand's head about sunk into his shoulders.

"Of course I remember." Lady Holland had met him as First Consul during the peace of Amiens and admired him. "And? And? Tell me." Napoleon rubbed his hands through his hair. Could you still kill the messenger who brought bad news?

"Unfortunately, Lord Bathurst, the Colonial Secretary, has prevailed, preventing any change in policy toward you, Sire." Bertrand straightened and looked at him with sheepish eyes. He held out the paper, wavering in his fingers.

"They think they've heard the last of me, these men who once negotiated with me as the sovereign of France." Napoleon snatched the paper and read through it. He then flung the letter into the fire, where it curled and blackened like his hopes. "Bertrand, we will write a rebuttal to Bathurst's speech. We must keep matters stirred up at all times!"

Napoleon couldn't wait for Amherst, or any of the British. His strategy, no matter the risk, definitely changed now. He kicked a log in the fireplace and the air in front of him shimmered with sparks.

Chapter Thirteen

He who fears to lose his reputation is sure to lose it—N.B.

Amélie breathed in the crisp morning air as she crossed the courtyard, eager for her walk. Jules cavorted around near her garden, snickering at the large rodent he'd tied to his miniature carriage. The creature wriggled and snapped the item about behind it.

"Watch where you step, you'll crush my plants," she said. His eyes turned flinty on hers.

"This proves how foul this place is. We play with rats instead of dogs." Clarice filled Longwood's rear doorway. She strode out and tripped the tiny vehicle, then laughed at Jules's glower. "Can't you find something better to do, Montholon's toady?" She sauntered, her hips swaying, back into the house and slammed the door.

"She's a shrew, that one." Jules sneered. "Grown too broad in the beam as sailors say. I wouldn't mind a bounce off her, but she'd slice my throat with her tongue." He turned to Amélie, eyes glinting. "Now you've put on flesh. Not too unappealing for my tastes."

"Don't flatter yourself." Amélie rushed past him in disgust. She checked her garden in case he'd trampled her herbs with his big feet.

"We can't all be ex-rulers to tickle your fancy." Jules stomped on the rat's tail to stop it, and bent to unyoke the squealing creature. "Or grace your bed."

"You don't know what you're talking about—and stop abusing the rats." She flushed at the accusation, but with the odd power of people believing her capable of enticing Napoleon.

"Just remember, *mignonne*, even *ex*-emperors have fleeting interest for kitchen maids." His slit-eyed gaze roamed over her. "Especially one who has all of Europe watching, while he pines for a throne he'll never regain. Your, I mean *our* emperor infuriated too many with his ruthlessness."

"I'll report your nasty words. If the English looked into their own past they'd find actions far worse than his." Jules was as disloyal as his employer, the Count de Montholon. The house brimmed with enemies. She shuddered and wanted to scrub her skin just standing near him.

In the dining room, Marchand hurried by her with a water bottle.

"His Majesty is ill again. He's chilled and weak in the legs." The valet's face tightened with concern. "He refuses to eat; he says his stomach is on fire, his head pounding."

"His stomach's on fire?" She laid her hand on the water bottle, hot beneath a towel. "I had the same symptoms yesterday, after drinking the emperor's wine."

"I thought these problems gone since he's riding and walking with you. I sent for Doctor O'Meara, but you know the emperor balks at taking medication."

"Let me bring him the bottle." Amélie tugged it from Marchand's grasp. "He told me his maladies were due to this peculiar climate. I thought it was inactivity, but I must be wrong. I think it's the wine."

"Amélie, please, I don't know if this is a good idea. He's not in a pleasant temper." Marchand pulled on the bottle, but she held fast. He darted his gaze toward the door, then stepped aside.

She entered the gloomy study. Napoleon sat on the sofa, bundled in a blanket. He looked pale and shaken even in the dim light. Her heart sank. "Sire, here is a bottle to warm your legs."

"Amée, I don't wish you to see my like this." He sounded surprised, but not unpleased she was there. "No walk today, any light still splits my head."

She sat beside him and placed the bottle in his hands. She touched his sleeve, but resisted caressing his arm. "Maybe you shouldn't be drinking your wine. It made me sick after only one glass."

"You'll be my little nurse, won't you?" He slid the bottle under his blanket. "It isn't the wine, but this vile place. The British are murdering me by forcing me to remain." His words didn't sound as bitter as before, as if he had hopes she knew nothing about.

"I wish you would stop drinking the wine, just the same." If his accusations about the island were true, why weren't the rest of them stricken with similar symptoms?

* * * *

"Stoutness bespeaks prosperity, Sire." The Count de Montholon assessed him with his prim gaze. "The kitchen maid has you out and about too much. It will only tire you. Now we eat like goats with all her vegetable dishes. French sauces are esteemed everywhere."

"Stop acting like a child." Napoleon buttoned his waistcoat, pleased that it fit him so comfortably, even if he'd never recapture the slenderness of his youth. "Even Socrates advised against overeating. He said, 'One must never leave the table with a feeling of satiety.' You seem to want me to stay fat and listless." He glared at his subordinate. Montholon's cool blue eyes revealed nothing. Napoleon bristled. His time spent with Amélie encouraged the others to act in too familiar a manner, yet *her* barging into his study hadn't upset him. She cared about him, but what would she want in return?

"I heard Governor Lowe convinced Lord Amherst that you exaggerated your trials here." The count sauntered to the study door. "Accept my sincere—"

"Go and finish my report on the battle of Leipzig." Napoleon grimaced, now refusing to rise to this man's obvious manipulation. Bertrand already told him about Amherst weeks ago.

Ali ushered Montholon out. The clock struck one, and Amélie's sweet face appeared at his door.

"Come in, and behold. The tailor has taken in all my clothes. I believe I've lost nearly seven kilos." Napoleon put his hands at his waist and turned for her.

"You have; you look wonderful." She clapped her hands, her grin bright. "Though the Countess de Montholon complained to my father about the food choices."

"Let them all complain, that's what they do best." He chuckled, preening before her. Then he sighed. "*Grand Dieu*, I don't know why I should be happy. If I look too

Elysium

healthy, these British scoundrels will never see how this island is destroying me." Lowe might suspect he had no intention of decaying here.

"Don't let anything destroy you." She stepped close, a mixture of girl and ripe woman in her pink dress. This little bud now a full flower, scenting so many of his moments. "You need to keep up your strength."

"Ah, sometimes I think you're smarter than a man who once ruled most of Europe." Napoleon winked and tugged on her earlobe. Her statement was valid, but for reasons he'd never share. He would need all his vigor for what he hoped lay ahead. "You see, I'm not so obstinate as to deny you your due, even if you are but a woman."

"I could never be as wise as you." Amélie pushed her hair behind her ear, as if inviting another touch. "I try not to be an empty-headed female though."

"Women would have been the charm of my life if I'd had more time for them. My hours were short." He pressed a knuckle to his upper lip, but couldn't conjure up one of his mistresses' faces. Josephine's flitted into his memory. Marie Louise...He blinked it away and looked into Amée's tender expression. "I had so many things to do...back then."

"Can't you appreciate women in a higher role than just adornments for men? Even women in ancient Rome and Pompeii were esteemed for political and civic accomplishments."

"They were also busy behind the scenes poisoning their husbands to gratify their malicious desires." Napoleon smiled when her mouth turned stubborn. He took a pinch of snuff from his snuffbox and passed it under his nose. For some reason, the acrid scent displeased him. He discarded the leftover into the fireplace, leaving snuff sprinkled on his shirt.

"Napoleon, you have an answer for everything." Amélie laughed and brushed off his shirt, then pulled back her hand.

His name sounded like music on her lips. He'd missed such endearments, her gesture forward. He'd relaxed too much with her, and couldn't allow it to go far. He tugged her hair, perhaps too hard. "You like to challenge me. You are growing into the shrill shrew I warned about. A belligerent child."

"That's unfair. I am certainly *not* a child." She stretched to her full height, her bosom pushing out her bodice.

"Remember, your big recital is tomorrow." He suppressed the heat inside him—a long dormant reaction—and strode a few steps away. "Hutt's Gate, a change of venue from this prison."

"How could I forget?" Her gaze probed him. "I heard about Lord Amherst. Do you ever...entertain thoughts of escaping from here, if there's no hope of release?"

"Where do you get such fanciful ideas?" Napoleon chuckled to hide his surprise. Gossip on his half-formed ideas couldn't be circulating. He averted his gaze. She had a disconcerting way of poking into his mind.

"If you ever have such plans, I hope you'll share them with me." Her serious, intimate voice slid along his nerves.

"There is nothing to trouble yourself with." Napoleon turned his back on her. He never allowed women to interfere in things beyond their grasp. He didn't care to be manipulated. He fisted his hand to regain control. "Now run along. We'll forego your lesson so you can rest your throat for tomorrow."

* * * *

Amélie squirmed on the chair, wincing as Madame Cloubert swept up her hair. The deep honey color had lightened in pale streaks in exposure to the sun with her garden duties. Her stomach knotted—her impeding fete an hour away.

"You should keep your hair pinned up; it's easier for a servant. I've wanted to tell you this since you have no mother to guide you." The woman's peach pit reflection scrutinized her from the looking glass nailed to the wall of her attic cell.

"I might cut it off, like the stylish ladies of Paris." Amélie's heart twinged at the mention of her mother. She shifted on the stool, impatient for the woman to finish.

"I don't know how your father allows you to be alone with a man of such reputation with women as our emperor." Madame sliced in another pin.

Amélie winced. "His Majesty always treats me with respect." Napoleon still often dismissed her like a naïve child. She'd encourage him to think of her as a woman. A woman with desires. "My father trusts me." She wasn't sure of that, either, and perhaps he shouldn't. She shrugged her shoulders and smiled, to stir aside the conflicting emotions.

"It's not *you* he should worry about trusting, ha!" The spindly woman stood back, hands on her sharp hips. "We have enough lewd behavior in this house, high and low born. My prude of a husband is scandalized. Has anyone ever cautioned you over nature's facts?"

Heat seeped under Amélie's dress. Did Madame have a better analogy than Clarice's about lovemaking? She did want to know, but how to ask? She tried to envision Madame Cloubert allowing her husband to caress her with his calloused, manure-stained hands. She hopped off the stool. "Thank you for your help, Madame, with my hair."

Back in her chamber, Amélie slipped the white gown over her head and tied the matching silk fichu above her bodice to conceal its low neckline. She admired the way she filled out the garment, the muslin light as gauze against her body.

Waiting for her father under the green trelliswork of Longwood's tiny front veranda, Amélie watched the Countess de Montholon roll by in a cart with her husband. At almost eight months breeding, the woman should have stayed hidden. The countess's silk dress barely covered her chest, which jiggled like two cow udders ready to burst. Amélie stared down at her own prim bodice and pulled off the scarf. Half the match for the countess, she appreciated that her plain cotton corset's two gussets pushed up her bosom to some advantage.

"I hope you aren't making a habit of imitating the Countess de Montholon?" Perrault walked up behind her.

"Papa, many women wear gowns far worse than this. It is the fashion." Amélie swallowed her embarrassment and trotted down the stone steps. She raised her skirt slightly to keep the dust off the hem as they walked from Longwood's grounds. Napoleon had gone ahead to have dinner with the others, which included British officers of the Deadwood regiment, but he hadn't invited her.

"Responsibility comes with growing up. It shows in how you present yourself. I cannot condone this." Perrault studied her again. "Has the emperor seen you, exposed as you are?"

"Napoleon won't disapprove, and I've never behaved irresponsibly." Not yet. She twisted the scarf in her hands. Her father didn't understand she was no longer his to control.

"Napoleon? Your behavior gets brasher. Don't think I haven't noticed." He slowed his stride along the path. "His Majesty derided the women of Paris who flaunted themselves in revealing attire."

Such derision never deterred the countess. Amélie hurried her pace, the scarf draped around her shoulders. She did feel self-conscious as she'd never worn anything *décolleté* before.

"I hope you always conduct yourself appropriately in every situation that occurs." Perrault seemed intent, if reluctant, to drive home his concerns. "Remember what I said about curtailing all of this."

"Please allow me to make my own decisions, Papa." Amélie squeezed his arm. Was her aloof father listening at keyholes to the nasty comments of others? She tensed with guilt and pulled her scarf close around her shoulders.

They approached the colonial structure of Hutt's Gate. Tall willow trees shaded the home's front veranda and buffeted the trade winds. Situated on the edge of the plain, the land sloped from the rear of this place to the Geranium Vale.

Inside the Bertrand's home, numerous voices drifted from beyond the foyer. Countess Bertrand bustled toward them with a welcoming smile. "I'm so glad you've arrived, and what an attractive dress." She clasped Amélie's hand. The countess's burgundy cashmere gown looked withered, like a rose pressed in a book. Her plunging V-necked bodice and split oversleeves showing white lawn beneath seemed a brave attempt to dazzle at the end of the earth. "Chef Perrault, please go on into the parlor."

"How kind of you to invite me, Countess." Amélie traced her forefinger across the pink topaz necklace at her throat, feeling her pulse vibrate at the idea of tonight's exhibition. The woman's friendliness relieved her.

The tall, graceful lady showed her to a tiny boudoir to freshen up. At a vanity with a large oval mirror, the countess helped Amélie rearrange her windblown hair. The countess had her own light hair brushed up with diamond combs and pulled back from her temples in the elegant Parisian fashion.

Amélie admired the fancy toiletries on the vanity top.

"Have you ever tried rouge?" Madame Bertrand opened a pot and stared in. "*Hélas*, everything here puddles, if the ants don't carry it off first. This looks all right still."

"No, I've never tried it, Madame." Amélie should dislike Countess Bertrand after her behavior in Plymouth over deserting the emperor, but the woman displayed none of the other countess's arrogance.

"Sit, let me dab some on." Madame Bertrand carefully applied color to Amélie's face, the woman's finger cool against her skin, lips pursed in concentration. "Don't look in the mirror yet, wait till I'm finished."

Lips and cheeks rouged, Amélie smiled at her reflection. Her sophistication should impress Napoleon.

"You're lovely, Amélie. The men will pound down your door any second, begging for your hand." The countess patted her shoulder and winked.

Amélie blushed beyond the rouge. "I assure you, I'm not seeking a husband."

"You will eventually, my dear. We all do." Countess Bertrand put a dab of her expensive perfume behind Amélie's ears. "Some young British officers are here tonight. You'll definitely draw their attention."

"I'm not interested in any British officers." Amélie smelled lavender in the perfume and stared at the woman, amazed she'd suggest such a thing. "I'm quite happy with things the way they are."

"If not marriage...I see, then it's a career that interests you?" The countess frowned, thoughtful. "With your beautiful voice you could easily return to Europe to study properly, if that's the sort of path you want."

"No, I don't care for professional study," Amélie said, thumping one of the silver boxes on the vanity, her brown eyes wide in the mirror, "or returning to Europe."

Ma foi, why not? There's nothing for you on this rock. Nothing for any of us. Away from here you might have a chance at an actual life." The woman grimaced in the glass.

If Countess Bertrand saw her life ending, Amélie ached to spread her wings, her life beginning. "No, Madame, I don't want to leave Saint Helena." She stood and smoothed her skirt. "I'm completely satisfied here."

"Oh, you're young still. There's plenty of time to decide these things." The countess bent to tighten the ribbons around her ankles that secured her worn satin slippers. "Let's join the others. You can drink a cup of tea before you sing. I'd put honey in it, if we could get any."

The guests milled about in a small parlor with threadbare oriental carpets and two rumpled sofas—the same shabby furniture as in Longwood. Three uniformed young men turned to stare, but only one person interested Amélie.

Napoleon saw her and strode over, his smile brilliant. "You're very captivating tonight, Amée. That dress suits you. Your hair, though, I prefer it loose over your shoulders."

In his finest silk breeches and pressed green jacket, he resembled again an emperor receiving the crowned heads of Europe. His face leaner, complexion healthier, he illuminated the room with his radiance.

"Do I resemble a woman of accomplishment?" Amélie caught her breath and grasped his arm to steady herself.

"Indeed you do." Napoleon escorted her to a handsome woman and a balding man with a plump belly. "This is Mr. and Mrs. William Balcombe. The generous people I stayed with my first two months on Saint Helena. A substantial reprieve from that dismal boarding house."

"Here's the little herbalist." Balcombe was in charge of purchases for the emperor's household as an employee of the East India Company. Amélie had seen him around Longwood many times. "I have another herb you might fancy. Just arrived from India, brought down from China. It's all the rage in the Orient, called ginseng of all things. No gin in it, I hope." He chuckled at his own jest, rubbing his paunch.

"What is it used for, sir?" Amélie asked, intrigued, and eager to humor the emperor's friends. She'd heard this man also smuggled letters for Napoleon.

"It's put in tea. Many drink it to enhance...vitality and stimulation, among other things." Balcombe's plump cheeks reddened. He listed to one side, his right leg swollen with gout.

"That sounds valuable. I'll be happy to try it, sir, thank you," Amélie said. Balcombe promised to send it right up.

She was introduced to two more couples, and their names swam together in her mind. Amélie clutched Napoleon's arm, her unease sharp over singing in front of so many strangers.

Napoleon brought her a cup of tea, and they stood in a corner quietly discussing the songs she was to perform. The others in the room watched them, a few sneers from the officers. She wished everyone would disappear, leaving her to sing for Napoleon alone.

The Countess de Montholon sauntered over in her low-cut Turkey-red gown. "I wish I felt up to playing tonight, Sire." She fingered the black velvet ribbon tied beneath her pendulous breasts. A diamond-studded bandeau wound around her chestnut curls and puffy face.

"I'm surprised you are even here." Napoleon didn't glance at her.

"I still wouldn't mind piano lessons." Amélie blushed for the countess in her offensive display of clinging silk, far too scanty for a woman of her age and bovine figure.

"I just had this dress made. Do you think it attractive on me, Your Majesty?" Albine leaned close to Napoleon's ear, breasts quivering.

Amélie bit at her lip and almost stuck out her own chest, but accomplishment and demeanor should outweigh shallow attractions.

"You might catch a cold in it, Albine." Napoleon gave a dismissive smile. "A woman in your condition should be *at home*, preparing for her blessed event."

Amélie stifled a laugh and clung tighter to his arm.

"I hope this girl Fanny hired to play can match my expertise." The countess glared at Amélie as if she'd made the comment. Then she scanned the room with narrowed eyes. "What have we come to when we invite the help to these fetes? *C'est normal.*"

"The *help* appreciates fine music." Amélie raised her chin as the woman waddled off.

The girl from Jamestown sat at the piano. Fanny Bertrand raised a hand and announced the entertainment was about to commence.

Amélie surveyed the eager faces and slowly stepped to her place beside the piano. After a deep breath, she began—the act of using her muscles for singing calmed her innards. Performing most of her old repertoire, she added a new aria from Zingarelli's opera *Ifigenia in Aulide*, which she'd practiced. A young woman in Greek mythology about to be sacrificed to the gods.

At the finish many were full of praise, but not all of her "outside" audience seemed impressed. With a twitch of a lip or roll of an eye, they might have thought of far better arias they'd heard in London. Were her French enthusiasts desperate for any amusement?

Two very tall, somewhat handsome British officers converged on her and in halting French refused to take no for an answer. She found herself sitting in the best armchair with these gentlemen in attendance, fetching her wine, snacks, and asking questions. Amélie stared about the room. Napoleon talked with the Balcombes, the Countess de Montholon hovering close.

She tried to bask in this, her own attention, especially after two glasses of wine. Part of her encouraged them, jealous of Napoleon with the countess.

Finally catching the eye of the emperor who now stood near the fireplace, Amélie shivered at his grim expression. Did this indicate her singing wasn't as fine as she'd hoped? For a few minutes more she listened to the officers' chatter until impatience flushed through her. When they asked if they might call on her, she rose. "I'm sorry, I'm too busy with my studies, and your governor scorns such fraternization. Now if you'll excuse me, *Messieurs*."

* * * *

Amélie walked toward him, looking so graceful in her sweeping white dress, so youthful, a rare orchid. Napoleon hated his response to her: a young man awed by his first glimpse of beauty. He wasn't a young man anymore.

"Is anything the matter, Sire?" she asked in a low voice, sidling close.

"No, of course not," Napoleon replied, his voice unsteady before he firmed it. He couldn't meet her searching eyes. "Things are progressing well, I can see."

"Was the new aria satisfactory?"

"Satisfactory enough, in light of all these distractions." Napoleon turned to smile at one of the women in the group of visitors and started to move away from Amélie's endearing face, a face that asked so much of him.

"I'm tired. Could someone please take me home, Your Majesty? I'd be extremely grateful. My father has already left. I waited…to speak with you." She put her delicate hand on his arm.

Napoleon studied her now, seeing no guile, only her desire to be near him. He needed to snatch her from this place, away from those groping soldiers, yet keep her at arm's length. "Are you sure you've had enough socializing?"

"Yes, quite sure."

He measured her for too long, their gazes caught in some unnerving trance. Yes, she'd bloomed into an alluring woman, dangerous. "I suppose I can take you back. I've had enough here as well." He called to Marchand to retrieve her wrap and his hat. The valet joined them in the cart back to Longwood.

Napoleon marched through the house and into his study, but Amélie followed behind.

"Are you angry with me about something? Is my singing a disappointment?" she asked as Marchand lit a branch of candles before putting wood in the fireplace and lighting that. The valet waited until he dismissed him.

After he warmed his hands over the crackling flames, Napoleon leaned on the mantel, not looking at her, but smelling her perfume. "Your singing was fine, as always."

"Then what is it?"

"I thought you were tired, Amée. Go to your chambers."

She sat on the sofa instead. "I'm not leaving until you tell me what's wrong."

"Wrong?" He faced her, his temper slipping out. "What could possibly be wrong? You had your glory tonight, with those English idiots staring down your dress all evening."

"They were being kind. I didn't invite it." Her startled look reminded him again of a fawn.

"Kind?" He wrestled with his anger, but with luck it might chase her from the room. "They drooled all over you like hungry dogs."

Her mouth twitched. "If you didn't like it, why didn't you come over? I couldn't find you when I finished."

"You can impress whomever you want, Amée, but to waste time on stupid Englishmen." Napoleon struck his fist on the mantel. A candlestick jostled and fell with a plunk to the floor.

"I cared nothing for them. I was being gracious. Isn't that what you wanted, for me to act polished?" She stood again as her voice level rose.

"It doesn't matter…what I want." Napoleon lost his sharp edge. His confidence at Hutt's Gate evaporated like the smoke from gunfire.

"It does; it matters to *me*." They glared at one another across the room. She walked nearer, closing the distance between them, that dress flowing around her slim figure.

"Amée…" He raised his hands as if to push her back. "I admit, I was jealous of those officers' attentions to you."

"You had no reason. They meant nothing to me."

"I shouldn't be jealous, Amée. You don't belong to me." His words tender, he hadn't disguised his longing. His bravado vanished, opening him to the vulnerability he hated.

Napoleon stiffened when she moved up, her breasts brushing his waistcoat. He breathed slowly, breathing her in, his hands stroking her arms. She laid her cheek on his shoulder. Unable to stop himself, he hugged her body against his and kissed the top of her head, her fragrant hair on his lips. She felt so soft, so natural, as if she did belong with him. He fought the desire to lift her chin and kiss her on the mouth.

He closed his eyes, held her for several minutes, and trailed his fingers down her spine and along her hip. Then he rallied his senses and pulled back, grasping at an excuse. "Did Fanny put that perfume on you? Don't let her do that. You need no false scent." Napoleon stared into her face and summoned his officious manner. "Go on now to bed, it's late. Next time wear the fichu with that dress. You don't want to give men the wrong impression." She looked dazed as she spread her fingers over the top of her bodice. He squeezed her other hand and almost dragged her toward the study door. Who could he find to marry her, and soon? "I'll have Marchand take you to your quarters, and…see you for the races tomorrow. *Bonne nuit.*"

Chapter Fourteen

Cupid's treacherous arrows, are poisoned, it's said—N.B.

Amélie lingered in her bed and watched the sunlight creep through her window. She stroked her hands over her body, reliving Napoleon's embrace, smelling the herbal scent of the cologne on his skin. Again her nerves bundled beneath her flesh, her skin aware of every inch of theirs that had touched. Her emotions trembled, peeling away her former intellectual desires as if stripping away everything and leaving her naked.

Napoleon said she didn't belong to him, but what if she wanted him to belong to her?

She stretched, hopped up, used her chamber pot, and dressed. She took special care with her toilette, donning the blue dress and her best straw hat.

Given his reluctance to display himself before the English officials, Amélie's pulse quickened to see that Napoleon awaited her for their walk to the Deadwood Camp to attend the races.

"Good morning," he said, his smile distracted.

She waited for a special, intimate sparkle in his eyes, a sweet word, but he said nothing more. Disappointed in his brisk demeanor, she fell silent after greeting him. Their intimacy last night distanced him, while she desired more. How best to pull him back?

Count Bertrand joined them and they walked around the small ravine that separated their residence from the camp a half-mile away. Napoleon always balked at showing himself at the races. Before this, he'd watched these events through field glasses from a window at Count Bertrand's house.

In the cold August air the mists crept along the plateau.

They arrived as the Ladies' Race began. The women, riding habits trailing over their horses' flanks, leaned forward, hands anxious on the reins. A shot fired and they rode off down the track, jolting in their sidesaddles.

"Are you betting on any of the races, Sire?" Amélie stood on Napoleon's left, watching him as well as the riders.

Napoleon glanced at the canopies set-up for attending dignitaries. "Lowe looks furious that I'm even here," he said in amusement to Bertrand who stood on his right. "He's afraid one of the *Commissaires*, who wait like vultures for a glimpse, will sneak over and talk with me. That Austrian, Stürmer, hadn't the decency to bring me news of my wife and son."

"This is the perfect opportunity to meet the foreign delegates, Your Majesty." Amélie repeated her argument of the past several days, but winced at his mention of his wife. She huffed. He needed to move beyond his past. A semblance of higher society might make Napoleon less hostile to the island.

Count Balmain and Baron Stürmer, the representatives sent from Russia and Austria to oversee England's custodianship of Napoleon, stood under the tent awnings. Governor Lowe and his wife, Sir Thomas Reade, the Count de Montholon, and various army and navy officers filled out the spectators. The wind rippled the canvas around them and swirled the dust kicked up by the horses' hooves.

"Montholon seems to be enjoying himself...as usual," Bertrand said in his quiet way, as if not wanting to offend too much, "parading about for everyone to appreciate. Fanny says he 'uses all his oily charm on that peahen Lady Lowe,' and I must agree."

"Sire, why not send someone over to the tents to express your compliments to the delegates." She raised her voice, frustrated by his mood, his ignoring her.

"Bertrand, you and Montholon must come to terms. This constant bickering is impossible to bear." Napoleon turned his shoulder to her.

Soldiers trudged by leading horses smelling of sweat and oats. All the participants whispered and gaped at Napoleon as they went about their business.

Another race prepared to start. Archambault, their groom, mounted one of the stable nags. The man weaved in the saddle. When the shot fired, he kicked his horse into action, his arms flailing, head wobbling as if his neck were jelly, obviously drunk. Rounding the first bend in the track, he tumbled from his horse into a heap in the grass. Many of the soldiers laughed.

Napoleon lowered his field glasses. "Go and fetch that idiot. See if he's hurt," he said to the footman standing behind him, who sprinted off toward the crumpled groom.

"Montholon undermines me, Your Majesty. He...happens to stretch the truth to put himself in a better light." Bertrand hunched over. "Some of us wonder why he even came here, when more loyal men were refused. We hadn't seen a trace of him for years, now he's here as your supreme devoted subject?"

"You told me you wanted to talk to Count Balmain, Sire." Amélie struggled to drag the attention back to her. She brushed her fingers near Napoleon's elbow, yet bit her lip to keep from spouting about Montholon's supposed devotion.

"Enough, does any of this matter now?" Napoleon still spoke to his general. "It's just jealousy on your part. Why must we constantly go over the same things?"

"I'm sorry, Sire, but Montholon only tells you to your face what you want to hear." Bertrand's voice now sulky, his subservient manner seemed to blow away with the trade winds. "I think you put up with him because his wife amuses you."

Amélie stifled a gasp at Bertrand's very personal remark. The pregnant sow couldn't still be amusing her emperor. She swept her hair off her shoulder. Had his kiss in her tresses meant nothing?

"Montholon is useful to me. When he is no longer, then I have no need for him. Try to be more like him." Napoleon's face impassive, his fingers clenched on his field glasses. "You have accompanied me here to be my comfort, then behave as such. Look to your own wife's conduct. The eyes of foreigners are on us all. You are dissatisfied here? Think of me, all my humiliations. How much I have to blame myself for."

"The dullness of this island is so hard on Fanny." Bertrand lowered his head. "I've tried to interest the *Commissaires* in visiting, as you wished, so we'd have social contacts. I thought Count Balmain was amenable, but now he avoids me."

"Perhaps Count Bertrand could invite Count Balmain to join you, Sire. He might not refuse with all these people watching." Amélie's heart pounded. She shivered in the cold, acting like the worst of Napoleon's courtiers, scrambling for his attention.

Bertrand flicked her a surprised glance, pushing her farther from the center.

Two footmen dragged Archambault, stinking like cheap wine, stumbling by them, in the direction of Longwood.

"The governor wants me to have little contact with outsiders. Look how Lowe stares over here." Napoleon chuckled, but anger lurked beneath it. "If one of the delegates comes anywhere near Longwood, Lowe interrogates them with petty annoyances. I'm not the only one to swallow his insults."

"I heard that as long as your door is closed to the governor, the delegates won't come into Longwood." Amélie moved closer, her arm brushing his sleeve. That proved Napoleon needed to form a relationship with Lowe, if his stubborn pride would allow it.

"*I* heard that Baron Stürmer declared Lowe wasn't quite sound of mind," Bertrand said.

The delegates stared in Napoleon's direction, but none made a move from the awnings. The governor and Lady Lowe stepped into the dignitaries' line of sight with broad gestures, as if to redirect their focus.

Horses snorted and men shouted as the Deadwood regiment set up another race.

Montholon left the canopy and walked over to his sovereign. Amélie tried not to shrivel under his derisive stare. "Sire, I'm afraid you will have to make the first effort at reconciliation." Montholon dabbed at his cheek with a handkerchief. "Though I realize that is too inferior a position to subject you to. An insult for Lowe to even insist."

"*Vraiment*, it is the governor who should prostrate himself before me and those delegates, their governments have no power over my person." Napoleon's voice hardened at Montholon's words. The count purposely stirred his anger. "I've witnessed enough races today. I must go and see if my groom has survived his fall." She started to follow, anxious to be alone with him. "No, Amée, stay and enjoy yourself."

* * * *

Napoleon returned to the house after checking on Archambault. The fool was only bruised and sore. He'd chided him before about his drinking, making a spectacle of himself before the British.

He entered the study and rubbed his aching neck. A draining sadness wouldn't leave him. He'd spurned Amée, but needed to keep her in her place no matter how he cared for her. Caring for her would do neither of them any good. He'd almost lost his equanimity last night with her in his arms. She sparked the flint inside him that he couldn't allow near the gunpowder. He refused to sully her. He had to do something, send her away from this island, so it would never happen again.

"Your Majesty, the Count de Montholon requests an audience," Marchand said when he walked in and stoked up the study fire.

Napoleon stood in front of the flames, the warmth soothing on his back. "Very well." A distraction might do him good.

Montholon strode in and bowed. "Sire, I have to tell you, when over beneath the awnings, I heard everyone whispering about your little friend. She's become quite an embarrassment. Is it wise, if I may be so bold, to flaunt her under the British noses?" The man brushed at his epaulets, looking as fresh as if he'd stepped from a fashion plate.

Napoleon bristled with irritation. He felt rumpled and wrung out.

"Don't speak to me of these things. They are none of your business." The count's words cut too close. Napoleon dropped into his chair, having second thoughts about this distraction. "Have you prepared those letters for me to sign to give to Count Balmain? I know if Alexander understands the conditions I live under, he will request a more humane treatment." The tsar, once his great friend, the Treaty of Tilsit, when he stood at the apex of his power. If all else failed, he might at least be moved closer to Europe. At someplace like Malta, he could slip away again—perhaps America this time. Napoleon picked up his penknife and gouged at the wood on his chair arms, over his previous scratches.

"Of course I have, Sire. Like all your correspondence, we will be discreet, but I don't know if Balmain will accept anything without the governor's approval."

Napoleon suddenly doubted the veracity of the count's words about the discretion of his letters. He hid many things from Montholon, how else to be in control of everyone? He'd have to consult Cipriani about this—the one man he could trust.

Napoleon dismissed Montholon only to find Bertrand waiting to speak to him.

"Sire, I have just learned that an East Indiaman is in the harbor." Bertrand watched him carefully. "On their way back from the Cape."

"Who's the captain?" Napoleon sucked in his breath and gripped the chair arms.

"That O'Sullivan. The one you—"

"Yes, yes, I met with him before." Napoleon rose and stalked to the window. He grabbed up his field glasses and trained them on a shutter hole. His mind racing, he saw nothing unusual outside. "Go back to your house. I will be expecting a request for an interview from the man. You must grant it immediately, but don't appear too anxious." He calmed down his tone and shrugged at Bertrand's startled expression. "I enjoy this fellow. He amuses me." He prayed the boisterous sailor would agree with all his wishes. How fortunate Las Cases had met this man, a trusted employee of the East India Company who had free access to the island. An Irishman who hated England.

* * * *

Amélie, perturbed at being left behind at the races, knocked on the study door at one o'clock. She refused to let Napoleon treat her in this cavalier manner while her affections grew. Dare she have intimate feelings about her emperor, or contemplate an illicit relationship? Not illicit, romantic. She sighed and pushed these confusing thoughts from her mind.

"Amée, no practice today. I might be having an important visitor," Napoleon said after inviting her into his study. He seemed to force an air of affability, yet his clenching and unclenching hands betrayed anxiety. "However, I do have something important to discuss with you."

"Earlier I felt you were a little indifferent to me, but I might have been mistaken." She kept her voice sweet, knowing that affected him. Now who played the coquette?

"Was I? Well, listen to me now. How would you like to go back to Europe and study for the opera? Milan would be ideal." He gave her his boyish smile that usually disarmed her.

"No, I...don't care to do that." Her heart lurched and she swallowed hard. She stared into his face to find the jest. "I told you I have no interest in going on the stage." Her *faux* serene manner wavered. "I have no more to say about that."

"Ah? Maybe then I should marry you off to Marchand. That would be a good position for you. He's a decent young man, and has been with me since 1811." Napoleon paced to his fireplace, his back to her as if he couldn't meet her eyes.

His words stung deep. The room swayed around her. He had a penchant for marrying off his mistresses when they became too demanding, though she hadn't yet risen to that category. Even the word sounded tawdry.

She tried a flippant laugh. "I don't care to be married off either. A woman should be able to choose her own husband." Napoleon punished her for his own slip of ardor. She recognized the signs. When he got too close, he pulled back. If she intended to fulfill her mounting desires, she had to tread lightly even as her pulse echoed in her ears.

"What greater honor than to be married to one of my staff? I'll give you time to consider." Napoleon strode across the room. He bent down and pulled a large book from his bookcase. "Have I given you this book about the great Emperor of the French, Charlemagne? A man whom I modeled my own Empire after. Like Charlemagne I united the crowns of France and Lombardy and my Empire extended to the Orient." Now he sounded sad, lamenting the loss of that empire.

"Charlemagne was a great man. I'll enjoy reading about him. You don't really wish to send me away?" Amélie tensed against the hurt, stepped forward, and put her hand on Napoleon's shoulder to draw him close again. They each jostled for a different place in these unfolding events.

The study door creaked open wide with a waft of perfume.

"Your Majesty, remember you promised to play cards with us." Albine hovered in the doorway, her rouged lips in a pout. Her small features squeezed into the center of her plump face like raisins in a cream puff. "Don't disappoint me, *us*, again."

"Never barge in on me, it is unacceptable behavior," Napoleon groused. "I don't have time...I might be...on second thought, let us play. A good distraction. *Sur l'heure*."

"May I...join you, Sire?" Now Amélie barged in, refusing to be shuffled aside. She held her breath.

Napoleon raised a brow at her. The countess smirked as if certain he'd say no.

"Very well, we'll make it a household occasion." He threw up a hand and marched from the study.

Amélie strode after him, leaving the lumbering countess to follow.

In the drawing room with its yellow Chinese wallpaper and worn flowered carpet like a trampled garden, Montholon waited with his supercilious smile. Saint-Denis placed the cards on the game table, still warm from the oven where they had to dry them or they'd bend and stick together.

"The new furniture is here at last, Sire." Albine indicated a set of black wooden chairs with bronze gild and green velour cushions. She swished around her skirts before sitting in one of the chairs, then grinned up at Napoleon. "Do forgive my being presumptuous, but I didn't think you would mind." She patted her mound of belly and Amélie choked down a groan.

"The little mademoiselle is playing?" Montholon cast her a withering glare, then caressed his wife's shoulder.

"This lovely furniture is for the new house the governor is building for you, Sire. For your future comfort." Amélie tapped an oak octagon table with brass inlays. She'd love to plan a new household for him...for them?

Napoleon gave a dismissive snort and sat down. "I told the governor I want no permanent home here. He's wasting his time."

Amélie sat beside him. "The carpenters have started building out on the plain. The house looks like it will be much larger, and airier than Longwood." She wanted Napoleon to be interested in the house, to acclimate himself to happiness here.

"Isn't this marvelous, Sire? We haven't played thus in such a long while." Montholon perched himself in a chair and crisply shuffled and divided the cards. "Shall Albine be your partner? I'm certain the mademoiselle is unfamiliar with piquet."

"Learning has never been a problem of mine, Count." Amélie caught Napoleon's eye, and smiled. "I would like to be your partner."

"True. If one never tries new things, one never learns." Napoleon dealt himself and Amélie twelve cards each, leaving eight in the talon.

"Don't deny you have neglected us, Your Majesty. Being so busy with *other* things." Albine shook a finger at him, then stroked his arm. "It's almost your birthday. How would you like to celebrate?"

Napoleon stiffened his shoulders. "I would like *not* to be reminded of such things."

"I'll bake you a cherry cake. I know you're partial to that flavor." Amélie balanced on the edge of her chair, now sorry to sit among these courtiers' glowers.

"When we switch partners, I hope you don't try any of your little tricks with the cards. I'm wise to them." Albine's chair creaked as she moved her bulk about.

"Albine, don't upset His Majesty." Montholon gazed languidly at his wife. "Our emperor only does it to test the intelligence of his adversary, as in the wars."

"*Mais oui*, if he's caught it is such a jest for him. Naughty boy, Sire." Albine scratched her neck with the edge of her cards and tittered.

"Lavender flowers, cinnamon, nutmeg, and cloves, drank with distilled water, helps giddiness." Amélie arranged her cards, chewed on her lip, and resisted kicking the countess under the table.

"Just what do you insinuate?" The countess sat back, her lips pursed.

"Enough of this. Stop acting like children. Let's play," Napoleon said, and they all studied their cards.

Amélie looked indifferently at her hand. She was supposed to discard and replace from the talon. Out of the corner of her eye she watched the countess's fingers creep like snakes along Napoleon's sleeve.

"You have indeed neglected us, Sire. Perhaps you have explored all you can with Mademoiselle's singing." The count looked down his saber thin nose, shadowing a crimp of mouth, at Amélie. "How much more could there be?"

"I'm sure there's plenty more." Amélie strained not to sound like the fearful child who rumbled inside her. "Isn't there, Your Majesty? We could try *Proserpine*, by Paisiello again. You did say he's one of your favorite composers."

"We'll see...we'll see." Napoleon concentrated on the cards in his hand. When he swept Albine's fingers from his sleeve, Amélie grinned.

"You are a forward girl, aren't you?" The count's tone patronizing, he snatched up a card. "Something His Majesty has never liked, too obvious for your own good."

Albine muttered "impudent brat" under her breath. She draped her hand on Napoleon's shoulder and her husband smiled. Amélie cringed. Why did the count sanction such intimacy?

"Albine," Napoleon warned. Whether for her touch or utterance, the woman removed her hand.

"At least I try to keep my self-respect, *Comtesse*." Amélie struggled to remember what sequences she needed to score. The woman's actions on top of Napoleon's urge to send her away or sacrifice her in marriage sliced into her.

"So you say, but what else have you given up?" Albine lowered her cards.

"Are we playing or ridiculing?" Napoleon frowned and laid down his hand. "Montholon, control your wife. A wife's sole duty is to preserve her husband's peace of mind. That should apply to all the men around her. Amée, you should also attend to this advice."

"Your Majesty, Rousseau said that." Amélie's cheeks burned—rebuked in front of the Montholons. Her fingers curled around the cards, her grasp on her emperor slid off. "Rousseau allowed a woman to be unfaithful in marriage as well as a man, but *she* must misbehave in secret to 'preserve the husband's peace of mind.'" She flicked a gaze at the count, who showed little on his deadpan face, except his eyes freezing on hers. "Men have no such obligation. Many women, especially ones in high places, don't bother either."

"This game is over." The emperor rose and tossed down his cards, his glare on Amélie. "Sometimes advice on behavior is better heeded."

Amélie recoiled from his stunned expression. Her chest constricted as if someone squeezed her heart. She'd just thrown his wife's dissolute actions into his face.

Napoleon stalked from the room. Montholon jumped up to follow like a soldier called to action.

"Do you still keep your self-respect?" The countess smiled shrewdly from across the table. "Now you've upset His Majesty, but my husband will comfort him."

Amélie dropped her cards and stood, feeling queasy. "As long as it's *just* the count who comforts him."

"You are quite bold for the kitchen help." The countess studied her fingernails. "You're so far beneath His Majesty's attention—a frivolous pastime. He'll discard you soon and only show devotion to his empress."

"You are shameful in your boldness, Madame." Amélie walked toward the door, pressing on her stomach. Tears gathered in her eyes. Napoleon was trying to discard her. "You should leave the emperor alone and only show devotion to your husband."

Albine scraped back her chair, lumbered to her feet and flung her cards on the floor. "I won't tolerate a servant speaking to me like that! His Majesty will send you packing, back to your scullery!"

Chapter Fifteen

...Marriage is not derived from nature but from society and its mores—N.B.

Napoleon gripped the study mantel, knuckles white, anxious for O'Sullivan's visit. Still grumbling over Amélie's words of yesterday—too close to the truth—he should stay angry with her, yet found it difficult. He hadn't walked with her this morning; neither did she show up to attend him. Napoleon lamented his need to pull away, but couldn't afford to weaken. At the same time he struggled with the urge to keep her close, his own possession, her sweetness soothing. More weakness! The schemes that stormed through his head must come to fruition, and he'd never allowed any woman to thwart his ambitions.

Voices sounded in the dining room. He tipped his ear to the study door.

"Captain O'Sullivan, Your Majesty." Bertrand opened the door after Napoleon's permission. Napoleon stepped to the fireplace again and affected nonchalance. He'd insisted on a private meeting in here, instead of the grand display in the drawing room.

O'Sullivan bounded in, that broad grin on a ruddy face, one tooth missing. He smelled like the sea—of freedom. "'Tis great to be seeing you again, your emperorship," he said, his Irish brogue stronger than O'Meara's, his French stumbling. He stuck out a meaty paw.

"You may go, Bertrand," Napoleon said. Bertrand's throat reddened, but he left, shutting the door.

Napoleon rarely shook hands, but gave the Irishman the honor of his own. "Captain, I would like to expand on what we touched on at your previous visit." He lowered his voice. "My...discreet removal from this island."

"Aye, you want to go through with it?" O'Sullivan bounced his bulky frame with his sailor's wide-stepping gait around the chamber. He didn't seem surprised by this decision. "Been mulling it over meself, to and from Cape Town. I 'spect there is no other way?"

"The recent efforts on my behalf have failed and I'm tired of waiting." Napoleon told him about Lord Holland and Amherst. He scraped a fingernail along his frock coat, heart drumming, but kept his face impassive. "You will be generously compensated for your risk."

"It won't be easy, but you know that, now don't you? Will be many weeks before I return from England." The man gave an impish smile, as if this venture enthralled him. "Your incarceration at the hands of these scoundrels, 'tis not fair. O' course, I will need the money for me family back home."

"I'll arrange everything. Including the arrival of a certain man for my subterfuge." Such relief coursed through Napoleon that he grew weak in the knees. He leaned on his sideboard.

O'Sullivan bowed his head, his hat slapped against his chest. "I do it for me countrymen, your emperorship. The proud Irish who been treated poorly by them English and their insane king. We must show them they're not the lords over everyone."

Napoleon smacked the rickety sideboard. A new strength knotted through him and he couldn't help a thoughtful chuckle. "They forgive their insane king for being born to his sins, but *parvenus* like me are guilty for freely choosing them."

* * * *

"Doctor O'Meara. Wait a moment." Amélie caught the emperor's physician in the courtyard. She'd hurried from the kitchen, leaving her reading of *The Housewife's Herbal Remedies*.

"Aye, Mademoiselle Perrault. What may I do for you?" The doctor smiled, his round face framed in a riot of woolly nut-brown hair, his Italian Irish-tinged. The dreaded spy, according to Madame Cloubert.

"How is His Majesty today? I hear he has a visitor." She stifled a yawn, since she'd slept badly the night before, upset over her quarrel with Napoleon and the countess's threat. She'd injured his pride with her hasty words and must rearrange her footing to remain in step with the court's business.

"Napoleon does have a visitor. A compatriot of mine, Captain O'Sullivan." The doctor used Napoleon's given name, as the British were warned never to address him as emperor.

"A captain of the East India Company..." She angled for more information. Napoleon had acted too excited when he heard this man's ship was in port.

A rat scurried by her.

"That he is." O'Meara averted his eyes. "You're a good lass, Amélie. You did what I couldn't, encouraging Napoleon to exercise again. Sir Hudson is also delighted. It makes the orderly officer's life easier."

"I'm happy to oblige everyone." She gritted her teeth, and hoped her Italian didn't express dismay. She hadn't brought Napoleon out of his hermitage to spend time with others. As with her garden, she'd coaxed his life from the arid soil of Saint Helena. Their relationship had brought her closer to his level, more intimate—the way he'd held her in his study proved his interest. "Tell His Majesty I'm ready to walk when he is."

The doctor bowed his head and entered the house. She breathed in the pungent smells from her garden. She relived Napoleon's sensual embrace, the way her heart had pulsed, her body steaming from the inside out. She longed for more of those sensations. How could he not feel the same? Amélie leaned against the kitchen wall, wrestling with a hedonistic emotion that crept up in her soul. This place was like the Tower of Babel, with everyone trying to communicate in different languages and no one understanding anything.

* * * *

Napoleon strode past the gate guards slumped in their little white lodges. The winter air chilled his face, but he planned to be gone from here before another winter arrived. O'Sullivan promised action. Amélie walked beside him, the footman following. He'd consented to walk, to remain strong, muscles stretching.

"You angered Albine at cards." He coughed, stared around the plateau, anywhere but her earnest face. "She complained, but I calmed her. She's gone into confinement at last."

"I hope I didn't upset you as well with my ill-advised words."

"You have become a sharp-tongued shrew." He'd keep their conversation playful, just a light scolding, his spirits too blissful.

"You shouldn't try to marry me off. I'm capable of deciding on my own husband." She sounded on edge and stumbled to keep up with him. They stepped around an everlasting flower that waved in the wind on its skinny stalk.

"I don't want you marrying someone undeserving of you." Hands clasped behind his back, Napoleon made an effort to relax and enjoy the stroll. His own fears of tarnishing her prompted him to push her into someone else's arms, yet he intended to control whose arms they were.

"When a woman marries, she becomes subordinate to her husband and I don't think I'd fit into such a role."

Three wild peacocks strutted in the distance, flaunting their rainbow tail feathers.

"When a woman becomes too sharp it ruins her femininity." Napoleon's boots crunched over the pebbles, scattering red thistle—boots that once stirred the dirt on the great battlefields of Europe. "That's the one charm she has over a man."

"If she is forced to marry someone cruel she's stuck by law, no matter her desires." Amélie hunched down into her jacket and he fought the desire to put his arm around her.

Instead, he chuckled. This is why he needed to choose her a husband. "There's a poem about unsexed female writers instructing and confusing men and themselves in the labyrinth of politics, or turning them wild with Gallic frenzy." Napoleon threw up a hand, his breath sharp in the wind.

"Gallic frenzy—our revolution. Archaic laws against women still need to be changed." Her sullen tone showed she wasn't really interested in this subject today. They passed over marled earth, dirty white or crimson in color, running like veins through the soil, both so obviously skirting the heart of the matter.

The orderly officer trailed them in the distance on horseback.

"The pounding fists of Poseidon cradles us on this shore," Amélie said when they stopped at the sea cliffs, the surf rushing below.

Napoleon smiled at her whimsical words and pictured himself sailing away over that ocean. "What about Saint-Denis for a husband?"

"Pardon? He's...like a brother. We'd never suit." She hung her head and he prickled with guilt as they both sat on a large rock.

"Opposites are complimentary. What one lacks the other provides. Josephine and I were a perfect example, yet we understood one another." He took a deep breath. "Of course, Marie Louise and I had little in common, but she was very attached to me."

Amélie picked up a boneseed stem at her feet and twisted it until it crackled. Her blond hair blew about her shoulders. "Did you love the Empress Marie Louise?"

He almost reached out, to run his fingers through her locks. Now his heart pinched.

Had he loved her, or just cherished her as the mother of his child? For the Hapsburg blood she carried? Hadn't her sluggish, dull ways annoyed him after a time? A fatal liaison, that marriage, for the Austrians still betrayed him. Her sordid affair with the Austrian count. He never let anyone know how that affected him. He'd made it "policy" to behave as if she remained his devoted wife.

Snatching up a pebble, Napoleon tossed it. "She was a sweet, naïve girl…yes, I cared for her. She seemed to love me, but her family intervened. She was easily dominated. They persuaded my good Louise not to return my son, or join me in exile." He stared off over the ocean. When he glanced back at Amélie he saw a pity there he couldn't stand.

"I'm sor—"

"I suppose we ought to return." Napoleon pressed her hand to stop her words. He held her soft skin for several minutes before remembering himself. He stood, fingers clenched. They strolled back. The orderly officer left them when they entered their grounds. Napoleon sighed with satisfaction. The place didn't look so desolate now that he wouldn't languish here waiting to die.

"Who is this Captain O'Sullivan you seemed so anxious to meet yesterday?"

"No one, only a distraction." Napoleon cringed at her sudden inquiry into forbidden areas. "What about Doctor O'Meara?"

Passing the dismal Park, several Javanese sparrows rustled in the tree limbs. Their ash plumage with white collars made them look like miniature nuns chirping devotions.

"What about him?" Amélie frowned.

Napoleon dismissed the footman at the front veranda. "To marry. He's a physician, and I'll pay him well when he decides to leave this rock."

She glared at him, her eyes startled. "No, thank you. I'll make my own choices. I might never marry."

"Nonsense. A woman's crowning achievement is a good marriage." Napoleon resisted pinching the tip of her nose, to return her to the role of child—which countered with his efforts to interest her in matrimony. Perhaps he shouldn't walk with her anymore.

"You're pushing me onto your valets, but they already have women in Jamestown." She crossed her arms, mouth in a thin line, though the lower lip trembled a little.

"Just mulatto women they use as their mistresses. No one important." He started up the steps.

"The mistresses might think they're important." Her brown eyes scrutinized him, probing where he didn't want to go. "You shouldn't dismiss them as insignificant."

"A mistress doesn't keep a man from making a proper marriage." Napoleon forced himself to sound gruff. If she only realized how significant *she* was, how she tore at him. He slammed into the house.

* * * *

Amélie lit the kitchen candles once the cannon fired to announce sunset—the drumbeat of their lives. Her father sliced turnips at the table. Chef Gascon prepared dough.

"The countess is about to give birth." Aware she shouldn't speak of such things before the men, she didn't care. Whose baby was it? She chopped parsley, tarragon, chervil, and chives for an herb sauce to pour over the tasteless albacore steaks they fixed for dinner. She thrummed inside and couldn't allow the emperor to tire of her, but how far would she go to assure he didn't? A mistress, as she'd contemplated? Amélie now understood her appeal and her desires. Desires for a man who denied his own. "Weren't the Montholons a strange couple to invite to Saint Helena?"

"Very true. His Majesty once dismissed Montholon, and I heard the count had legal problems back in France." Gascon pinched and punched his dough. "The countess, married twice and unfaithful to her husbands. The emperor scorned her…before we came here."

Perrault raised a cleaver and sliced the last turnip in half. "We spend too much energy insulting one another, Philippe, and to what purpose?" Perrault dropped the turnips into a pot of boiling water, and stirred onions sautéing in a skillet. "Hand me more butter, Amélie."

"François, everyone knows this." Gascon frowned, mopping his sweaty brow with his handkerchief. "*Peste*, this flour we get from the Cape is so gritty. They say it's ground with soft stone, which grinds into the flour, making a shambles of my creations."

"Montholon must have followed to hide from his legal problems." Had Albine come to seduce their emperor? Why? How *did* you seduce a man? Amélie lifted the floor slab, swiped aside a trail of ants, and handed her father the butter.

"That needs to rise." Gascon gave his dough a last slap and plodded to the door, his handkerchief fluttering. "I must lie down to soothe my head. How much longer will I last? If His Majesty had stayed on Elba, I'd still have my Pierre, and wouldn't be here."

"The king refused to pay the emperor's pension, that's why he left Elba." Amélie glared after Chef Gascon. His subtle resentment toward Napoleon bothered her.

"Amélie, maybe you should start spending time with people your own age." Her father sounded tense over the sizzling butter. He placed the fish into the mixture. "A footman is not a sufficient chaperone. An older woman should accompany you."

She blinked at her father. He'd be devastated if she became Napoleon's mistress, but she couldn't appease everyone. Amélie stirred lemon juice, salt, pepper, and a little olive oil into the herbs to complete her sauce. "Don't worry, Papa. One of the chambermaids is walking with us next time." A small lie. How many more lies were to come? She stirred faster avoiding his scrutiny.

"You must make certain to introduce me to this chambermaid." His words prickly, he seemed intent tonight to act the overly concerned parent. She chewed on the tip of her lemon-scented thumbnail.

Madame Cloubert barged through the kitchen door like a sand-filled sirocco. "The countess just gave birth to a baby girl. What a fuss in the house. His Majesty is all in a dither." She leveled her sharp gaze on Amélie. "I wonder who the child resembles, the mother…or the father?"

"I'm certain the count is very proud of his daughter." The smell of food suddenly made Amélie's stomach roil. Perhaps the child was Napoleon's.

"Didn't you say you had some lady's mantle tincture, good for slowing bleeding?" the woman asked. "The countess could use some after her travails."

Perrault coughed and stirred the fish. "We don't need to go into any of the details."

"I'll bring it to her maid, Madame." Amélie opened the pantry door and took out the tincture she'd prepared by soaking the herb in brandy for three days. She stepped outside, anxious to leave the kitchen, her thoughts in turmoil. The cold evening air made her shiver after the heat from the stove; she'd cut through Longwood. Entering the dim house, she walked into the dining room. The floors squeaked. Someone came out of the shadows and almost knocked her over. She gasped and clutched the small bottle to her chest.

"Amélie." Jules jerked back from her as if pricked by a thorn. He held a set of keys, which he thrust behind his back with a jingle. "Why do you lurk in these corners?" He glared at her, his annoyance sharp.

"What is the matter with you? I'm not lurking." She crept back a step. "Here, take this to your master. It's for his wife. A spoonful every three hours."

"I have duties elsewhere. Mind your own business." Squinting at her, he snatched the bottle from her hands anyway and stalked from the room toward the front hall. He'd have to exit this portion of the house and walk outside to reach the Montholons' quarters in the right wing, where he slept in a tiny chamber next to theirs.

Amélie recognized the keys as the ones to the wine cabinet, keys the Count de Montholon usually possessed. Was Jules stealing the emperor's wine? She'd tell Napoleon of his suspicious behavior.

* * * *

Amélie watered the gilly flowers she'd planted in front of the house, near the veranda. Their spicy scent tickled her nose. Napoleon stood near the wall, talking to Count Bertrand.

Bertrand finally walked off. She tucked a flower in her bodice and approached Napoleon. She licked her lips and wished for the experience of a courtesan.

"Good morning, Sire." She flashed her best smile.

He stared through his field glasses over the plain. "Good morning."

She waited a few minutes. "Does the Count de Montholon's manservant have access to your wine cabinet?"

"What? He shouldn't. Why?" He spoke in a distracted manner.

"I saw him there yesterday with the count's keys. He acted angry that I'd caught him."

"I'll mention it to Montholon." Napoleon lowered the glasses. "Those fools, building that place on this same windblown, treeless plain. Don't they understand that soon it will drip with mold as our present dwelling?"

The rising structure of Longwood New House, or New Longwood as some called it, loomed a few hundred yards away. The building's foundation was complete and a few walls erected. The breeze shifted and the smell of new wood carried through the air with the plunks of hammering.

Amélie put her hand on his sleeve. "That's because you refused to tell the governor where you wanted the house built." For Napoleon that meant accepting the fact he may never leave Saint Helena. "Will you walk over with me and at least look at it?"

"It's an insult for them even to build it." Napoleon scoffed. "A waste of their time and money."

"Don't you want to live in comfort...even if it might be for a short while?" She threw the last in to placate him. "I've heard it will have a Grecian front with alcoves for statues. They're sending out a marble bathtub for you. We could plant some pine trees for a windbreak."

"Perhaps I should walk over, lull Lowe into thinking I'm settling in here. Ease his fractious mind." Napoleon tapped his upper lip with a knuckle.

"*You* wish to lull the governor?" Amélie didn't like his calculating words.

"Never mind that. I've been thinking, the household needs to go on a picnic. Sandy Bay has striking scenery. Las Cases and I used to ride over there, before Lowe slithered into my life." Napoleon turned to smile at her. "Marchand will accompany us, and we can invite that chubby maid who moons after him all the time."

"Clarice?" At least he wasn't forcing the valet on her. Had he changed his mind about marrying her off? She caressed his arm.

"Let's plan it for next Saturday. I'll invite the Bertrands and their children, if Fanny isn't in one of her tizzies. I presume I can't invite the Montholons, though fresh air would do Albine good."

He goaded her and she relaxed with a laugh. "Please, only the Bertrands."

Napoleon tugged her hair. "Might we try to instigate a little romance between Marchand and this Clarice?"

"As long as you don't try that trick with me. Clarice will be overjoyed." A picnic with her sounded interesting and perilous at the same time. She hugged his arm close, unsure how an aspiring mistress should behave. Albine's blatant actions invaded her thoughts. "How are the countess and her new baby? You seemed very concerned about her."

"She's doing fine. Yes, I'm aware of the talk about the child's paternity." He turned back toward New Longwood and raised his glasses. "Did this rumor upset you?"

"No, of course not." If only she had the sophistication to overlook such things, instead of hoping he'd give an outright denial.

"My concern was just a diligent sovereign in my little empire." He lowered the glasses again. "The woman is desirable to no one but her husband."

"Is her husband so devoted to her?" She swatted away a jade dragonfly that buzzed about her face.

"Amée, don't become like the rest with their pettiness." He squeezed her hand and her heartbeat trebled. When she laid her hand over his, he slid away and walked toward the house. She sighed. How did one discern between the touches of deep affection and the fawning of a courtier? Didn't he feel the sensations when they touched as well as she?

"Please speak to the count about his manservant, Jules," she called before Napoleon disappeared into the house. Jules, a devious man, but was he any less devious than his master? An aristocrat her emperor once dismissed who eagerly joined him in exile?

* * * *

Napoleon tossed his hat onto the sofa in his bedroom. He would have to bring up the study in Milan idea again. He'd only break her heart if things stayed as they were. Amée was too good to make into a mistress. He had to ignore his desires.

Her touches, her smiles today. She needed to be sent off the island—for her own protection. This picnic at Sandy Bay would be their last excursion together, and all in the innocent name of friendship. He could arrange her departure far faster than his own. No one would care if she left Saint Helena...except for him.

Cipriani came in, dissolving his gloomy thoughts. "You sent for me, Your Majesty?"

"Yes. You are certain that letter to my Uncle Fesch made it safely off the island?"

"Of course, Sire. Yesterday, as you commanded me." Cipriani, dressed in his silver-embroidered emerald coat and black silk breeches—the way he served him in Europe—made a respectful bow.

"Yes, yes, I keep asking, don't I?" Napoleon rubbed his face hard. "I'm impatient for a reply. In France I had couriers rushing to and from me constantly. Here the ocean deters us all. This next segment of my plan is vital. We will accomplish this, won't we, Franchesci?"

The older Corsican's face creased into his enigmatic smile. "We will, Sire. As the Count de Las Cases said in his last smuggled in letter, there are many on the outside eager to aid in your departure."

"Numerous people mourn my unfair incarceration here. Even England's Lord Byron wrote an ode to me. Life never turns out as we expect it to. We must be vigilant in so many things." Napoleon walked toward his fireplace. He looked up at the Consular watch positioned above the mantel, hanging from a braid of Marie Louis's hair. Then he thought of Amélie's hair, the clean scent, the silkiness between his fingers. Folly to have such feelings like a love struck boy.

Napoleon strode into his study and snatched a piece of licorice from a tortoise-shell box on the sideboard. He chewed methodically on the sweet in an effort to calm his stomach. Hadn't he sent other women away when they got too close and inconvenienced him? He must be growing muddled in the head to feel such regret at having to do the same to her.

Chapter Sixteen

...It would be the merciful deed of a protective divinity to rid us of love and to liberate the world from it—N.B.

"I don't know if poor Marchand will appreciate your pairing him with Clarice." Amélie smiled at Napoleon as she loaded his calash with the picnic repast her father prepared. The sun shone bright, no mists or rain.

The valet rushed from the house, his expression harried, toting three bottles of wine. Clarice, her plump face as alight as the sun, followed too close on his heels.

"Oh, I have other plans for Marchand, but a bit of distraction won't hurt them," Napoleon said in amused conspiracy.

Amélie dropped the matter, and she'd also pretend he'd never mentioned marriage or study in Europe.

Napoleon boarded the rear seat of the carriage and she slid in beside him, behind Archambault. Montholon's son, six-year-old Tristan, wriggled in excitement beside the groom after the emperor had insisted on including him.

"Will you sit with me, Louis?" Clarice gazed at Marchand. The valet gave a tight smile and shook his head. He helped her up into the front seat, then asked permission to squeeze in beside the emperor and Amélie. Clarice pouted, but continued to gaze fondly. She giggled, her smile returning as she twirled an auburn strand and rolled her shoulder at the beleaguered valet.

Amélie sympathized with Marchand, yet almost wished he returned Clarice's ardor, since it so improved her nature.

Archambault snapped the reins and the calash trundled off the grounds.

The Bertrands joined them at Hutt's Gate, following in a cart with their children, young Napoleon, age nine, and seven-year-old Hortense. Bertrand would normally ride as escort beside the emperor's cart, but Napoleon bade him to stay with his family. The orderly officer galloped in their wake.

To Amélie's delight, Napoleon whistled and hummed as the calash plunged down the serpentine road that wound around the mountains to the southern side of the island. Napoleon took obvious pleasure in their swift movement and urged the groom to more speed.

"Archambault, aren't we too close to the cliff? *Affreux!*" Clarice spoke in anger. A moment later she whimpered and grasped the groom's arm. "Can't you slow down a bit?"

Amélie relished the rumbling beneath her and felt a possessive joy in being pressed against Napoleon. The carriage groaned, careening down the rutted road. Its left wheels—dangerously near the cliff side—sprayed rocks and cinder.

"Are you enjoying this, Amée?" Napoleon smiled and winked at her. "Madame Bertrand usually screams when I take her out for this ride."

"Oh, yes, immensely. I won't scream." She gripped the seat with both hands. When they eventually slowed, she rescued her heart from her throat, the exhilaration akin to fear. Tristan grinned and squealed at the ride but Clarice blanched pale as linen.

On the island for ten months, Amélie had never seen this side of tiny Saint Helena. The coast in the distance, between barren conical rocks, was dun colored with veins of red and purple clay. The ridge they passed around bore a combination of bare conical hills and striking rock pinnacles. Sharp ravines and rises gouged the volcanic landscape. The perforated ridges here resembled arches with gothic fretwork. Wide-eyed children tending goats on the hillsides, near huts with mossy roofs, stared as they rambled by.

Passing Long Range, a mass of rocky mountains two thousand feet high, they entered the region known as Sandy Bay. The cove's remarkable beauty struck Amélie: one of those clefts in this harsh earth lush with vegetation. On the box-wooded slope of Diana's Peak, stretching down to the cove, enormous ferns, red hibiscus, and pink camellias rippled in the breeze. Scarlet splashes of canna and yellow ginger plants bordered the track they followed. Cabbage trees with long, splayed leaves provided sporadic shade.

"This area is so beautiful. I wish we lived here." Amélie craned her neck to observe this verdant contrast to their home on the Deadwood Plain.

"Now, Amée, do you think the British would let me stay anywhere near a bay? I might swim away to Africa," Napoleon said dryly.

To the right of the cove, they slowed before a gradual slope that leveled out to an area overlooking the bay. Enough pine and date palms were present for shade, along with dense thickets of wild mango. Cattle and sheep grazed on the grass farther up. The cool breeze stirred the musky scents.

"This is as good a place as any," the emperor announced. The groom reined in and jumped from the calash.

Marchand spread a large blanket beneath the trees. He and Clarice laid out their baskets of food and wine. Roast chicken, ham, fresh bread, cheese, a cake, and the small local peaches and bananas comprised their repast. Amélie pulled out the basket of imported cherries. She'd included this rare treat, since Napoleon enjoyed the fruit.

"Let's walk down to the beach. I need some relaxation after that awful ride." Clarice adjusted her cap and grinned at Marchand. "It looks so steep, I will need a strong arm."

The valet's shoulders drooped.

"Take us too!" The Bertrand children shouted, clapping anxious hands. "Please."

"Go on, all of you. I'm quite comfortable here." Napoleon sat under the largest tree with a book in his hand and waved them away. A puff of air ruffled the leaves above him.

Marchand hesitated, reluctant to leave his master, or petrified of accompanying Clarice. Napoleon urged him to go, as well as Amélie. "Archambault will remain with me to tend the horses."

Curious about the cove, Amélie joined the others in the trek down the valley. Marchand went first, hobbled by Clarice who'd quickly grabbed his arm. The children skipped along after them, and the Bertrands with Amélie brought up the rear.

Ridges and ravines converged to form this valley, sloping down from trees to shrubs, then thin grass giving way to slag. Dipping toward the sea into a crater-like cove, the surface was in shades of lilac, pale lime, and russet like layers of a cake. Red-legged partridges sat on the rocks near the water. Amélie looked up as a crimson dragonfly buzzed over her head.

This *is* an enchanted land. In their seclusion on the wind-ravaged plain, the French didn't appreciate the island's primeval beauty. Did she see herself as Calypso, who held the sovereign-soldier captive? To Odysseus, even after seven years, her island was nothing but a prison and he wept to go home. Amélie had to muster womanly sophistication, not rely on foolish fantasy.

The three children scrambled to hunt for seashells, their eager voices reverberating off the volcanic slopes. Amélie tasted the salt in the breeze, feeling her lungs cleansed, and picked a batch of blue irises at the edge of the grass.

"Maybe the tide will come in while we're here," Fanny Bertrand said as the woman stood near the slag's edge. "I wouldn't mind being swept away. You promised only a year here, Henri, and that's now come. If we'd stayed in Europe, I could have seen my mother before she died."

"Fanny, again, I'm sorry, but we can discuss this later." Bertrand stroked his hand on the shoulder of his wife's embroidered *canezou* jacket.

"Look at them, watching our every move. It's disgraceful to be treated like this." Countess Bertrand sounded on the verge of tears. "We've rarely been out here, yet that ship is ready to attack...just because *he's* with us."

A British warship, anchored not far from the beach, floated huge and menacing in the water. Flashes of redcoats among artillery spread along the cliffs on both sides of the bay.

"Darling, please." Count Bertrand slid an arm around his wife. "Sandy Bay is the only area at the southern end of the island safely accessed by sea. With Jamestown, Rupert's Bay, and Lemmon Valley in the north. Unfortunately, the navy does guard it with precision, as well as the soldiers."

"*Ma foi*, they're suffocating us and savor every minute." Fanny bent from his embrace and picked up a stone, flinging it into the white-capped waves. "What of the schemes you said His Majesty...The rescue you—?" Bertrand put his fingers to his wife's lips and shook his head. The Bertrands walked off, farther along the cove.

Napoleon *had* kept schemes from her. Amélie distracted her frustration and poked around in the rocks looking at unusual plants—purple amaryllis, pink Venus roses, and moon lilies. Clarice jabbered in Marchand's ear as she urged him to keep walking. In fits of giggles, Tristan and Hortense chased near the lapping surf while young Napoleon scampered over various rocks.

After she'd seen enough, Amélie clambered back up the slope, arriving out of breath at the top. She sat down on the blanket beside Napoleon and asked for a glass of wine as she laid her flowers near his feet.

"Done exploring already?" Napoleon said, after requesting the groom do the honors. "Your cheeks are flushed." He brushed a finger over one of them.

"The cove is beautiful. You ought to go." Amélie leaned in closer, reveling in his touch. "It might give you a different viewpoint of Saint Helena."

Archambault uncorked a bottle of wine and poured two glasses. Handing one to each, he sniffed the cork and sighed before returning to the horses.

"Do I need a better look at that sentry warship on my horizon? Perhaps my shadowing friend on horseback will shoot me, convinced I'm planning to make a break off the island." Napoleon slapped his book shut. "No, that's a little too dangerous for an old prisoner like me."

"Stop that, please. You're not old." Amélie frowned, sipping the tart wine, relieved it wasn't the Constantia. "You've lost weight and said my ginseng tea made you feel more energetic. You must have...had thoughts of escape."

"Why are we on that subject?" He shifted on the blanket, obviously uncomfortable.

"You brought it up, yet it's a subject you won't discuss with me, and that makes me wonder." She was certain she'd grazed a nerve.

"England's evil goal is to keep me here until I die."

"*Mon Dieu*, don't say such awful things." She stared deep into his eyes to discern if he teased, aware of Napoleon's ability to slip in and out of various moods. "Don't think I don't know you're trying to change the subject."

"The English would be ecstatic if I died. Save them the money of maintaining all these guards...for just one man. *Three* regiments with nothing better to do than prevent my escape."

"Who cares about the English? Just ignore them. If you don't plan to escape, then you're safe, aren't you?" She watched him closely and took another sip of wine.

"No plans. I count on a change in the English government and their realizing their mistake in sending me here." He half smiled. "Bertrand and I used to explore this area, these valleys. Then Lowe arrived and put up a cannon and assigned guards to secure me. Seeing these things reminds me of my torture and sickness on this island."

Amélie often worried over what he labeled his "climatic" illness. "I thought we were enjoying a nice outing. Are you feeling ill now?"

"Only a sinking of the spirit. O'Meara informed Lowe I probably suffer from hepatitis." Napoleon stared again toward the ship as if assessing its capability. "Lowe threatened to send him away, insisting I only despair in losing my throne."

"The governor is tactless to say such things, and your doctor for repeating them. It's that sour wine you drink, that would make anyone ill. Thank you for not bringing any today." She cringed at the idea that Montholon was in charge of that beverage. "Did you ever speak to the count about his manservant, Jules, having the keys to the wine cabinet? I thought the count allowed no one to handle his precious keys."

"Did you ask me? I'm sure the servant was there at his behest." Napoleon thumped his fingers on the book. "You refuse to believe the English are assassinating me by dumping me here?"

Amélie saw the teasing glint in his eyes. "I wish you'd try to enjoy today. Perfect weather, scintillating company, delicious food awaits." Staring at the dark liquid in her glass, she'd almost said "loving" company. "You should stop drinking that wine and share what the rest of the household drinks, and please tell the count his servant is behaving oddly."

"Why should I stop drinking the wine? Do you suspect someone is trying to poison me?" He asked this with eyes too wide, mouth agape.

"Don't you need to be cautious of such acts?" Amélie's heart fisted at the mere word. "I wouldn't trust Jules." She didn't trust the count either, but it seemed outrageous to accuse him of poisoning. Napoleon would think so.

"Don't scowl at me like that. All right, I'll be cautious. You win, I surrender, we're having a wonderful outing." Napoleon reached over and lightly pinched her cheek.

A rush of heat simmered through her. "What are you...reading?"

"A book on the *Ossian* ballads, my favorite poetry. Even if that Scotsman Macpherson made up some of his own. These praise the past, and lament the present." Napoleon raised up the book. "Would you care to read it, aloud?"

Amélie took the slim volume and turned her back. He didn't surrender, but wanted to deflect her prying. Facing the sea she began to read out loud the Italian translation.

"I once suggested an opera be performed about Ossian. Jean-François Le Sueur, my court composer, scored, with libretto by Dercy and Deschamps: *Ossian, ou Les Bardes*. It premiered at the Academie Imperiale de Musique in Paris in 1804."

Amélie paused in her reading to listen to him relate this with a dreamy pride. "We could stage it here." The ocean rushed against the cliffs and she resumed.

Less windy on this side of the island, the cloud cover had still abandoned the sky, leaving only wisps of cotton in the distance. Birds chirped above, responding to one another in mellow tones. The gentle breeze, the wine, and the prose Amélie relayed lulled her. It grew so quiet after several minutes, she turned to check on Napoleon.

He smiled from his position, on his side and slightly behind her. Leaning his head on one elbow, Napoleon pulled the basket of cherries over and held one up. "I always appreciate a woman with a soft, lyrical voice. You could perform Rosmala who loves Ossian, if we had the libretto and music. It was a grand opera. Care for a cherry?"

A Siren calling him to shore? "All right."

Instead of handing it to her, he sat up and dangled it by the stem before her lips. She watched the fruit bobbing close to her nose, then giggled and bit it from the stem.

The sweetness filled her mouth. Juice dribbled over her lip, and she attempted a ladylike removal of the pit. She gave up and spit it into her hand, laughing harder. Napoleon chuckled and tossed her his handkerchief.

After plucking a cherry for himself, he held up another for her. Amélie did the same, dampening her lips with more sticky juice, and she sputtered into his handkerchief. She playfully threw a discarded stem at him.

Napoleon retrieved it and flung it back. Amélie tried to duck out of the way.

"It's in your hair...*un moment*, don't move." He leaned forward and raked his fingers into her tresses. "Your hair is so thick, I can't find it." She felt him separate the strands, searching for the lost stalk.

"Don't...worry about it." Amélie again faced the ocean. Her shoulders tingled with his fingertips brushing the back of her neck, and she laughed in silly spurts.

"Hold still, Amée." Napoleon's gentle voice made her shudder as he continued to entwine his fingers in her hair, across her skin. "You have very beautiful hair."

She held her breath. Feeling heavy and fluid at the same time, she closed her eyes.

"*Depechez-vous!* Look what we found!" A high-pitched cry shattered the moment. Hortense poked up her head from the crest of the slope. Amélie sighed when Napoleon withdrew his hand.

The little girl rushed toward them with the boys following. The adults trailed after.

"What is it you found?" the emperor asked the child, his voice sweet.

"A really big shell. Look, Your Majesty." Hortense held out a sandy, whirled limpet shell, cracked at the top.

"That is an extraordinary treasure." Napoleon cradled it in his hands for a moment. He smiled and pinched the little girl's cheek.

Amélie stared away and fingered the back of her neck.

"I'm hungry." Tristan stood on tiptoes and stuck out his lower lip.

"We've run so hard, we're starving," young Napoleon said, his eyes bright. "Papa says later, Sire, we might walk over the ridge and see Lot's Wife's ponds."

"Then by all means, let's eat." The emperor stood and patted his namesake on the head.

Marchand and Clarice started unpacking the baskets. The air vibrated with anxious chatter, extolling the wonders of the cove and the splendor of the day. Plates were passed around, food unwrapped and commented upon.

Amélie smelled the chicken and ham the valet sliced for serving, yet had little app*etite*.

Hortense's interruption had ruined the interlude and her body still felt sensual and yearning.

Clarice shoved a plate at her. She accepted it, picking at the contents. When she'd had her fill, Amélie excused herself, saying she was going for a walk. She wished to be alone with her thoughts.

"*Attends-moi*, I'll come with you." Clarice sprang up and followed her away from the group.

Amélie quickened her pace hoping to discourage her, but Clarice plodded alongside. In silence they passed pale cacti, brittle Saint Helena tea plants, and the black craggy rocks that formed their citadel, cow grass poking from the cracks.

At a patch of white bellflower, their bell-shaped blooms drooping, Amélie stopped. "Clarice, I'd prefer to—"

"Do you think Marchand could be interested in me?"

"I don't know...you mustn't rush things." Amélie tried to be polite but craved solitude.

"You're such good friends with the emperor. Can't you ask him, in a roundabout way, to ask Marchand if he might?" The petulant young woman bloomed with love, her fat cheeks glowing.

"No, I don't think that would be appropriate. What's to happen, will happen, in its own time." Did she speak for Clarice or herself?

The plump laundress sneered and her bloom vanished. Hands on hips, Clarice tossed her head. "Oh, Miss Opera Diva, now don't you just know everything. I ask one tiny favor and you can't be bothered."

"It's nothing to become irate about, but I won't be dragged into any schoolgirl tactics."

"You're no better than the rest of us. Just because the emperor fancies you, though who knows why. That will change...in *time*. His Majesty eventually throws away his play things."

"You're so spiteful, how can you expect Marchand..." Amélie swallowed her retort. "I'd like to continue my walk, alone, so *pardon*." She dashed off, leaving Clarice to stew on her own. Walking around a large jutting rock, Amélie lost sight of them all.

The rock felt warm and a little sharp against her back. She must mean more to

Napoleon than just a casual diversion as Clarice insisted. His actions proved he had feelings for her. Did she still intend to flout the morals of society as the Countess de Montholon? Amélie held no position of authority to protect her. Servants were bustled off in disgrace in such matters. She risked being cast aside, a victim of her first taste of passion. Passion overruling common sense, the one attribute she prided herself in.

What exactly *did* she want? She slapped her palms against the stone. She wanted removal from society, as on this island, Napoleon beside her, content. Could she make him satisfied with something so simple and idyllic as that?'

* * * *

Napoleon rose with a groan and brushed grass from his breeches. He'd noticed Amélie's return and understood her slipping off. He had gotten carried away with his search for the stem—her hair and skin felt so silken in his fingers. No matter what he told himself, he found it hard to resist her, but resist he must.

"Another story, please, Sire!" The children protested, their eager faces staring up.

"That's enough for now. I must take a walk before my old bones seize up." He strode off away from the group. He needed to do this alone. The others knew better than to follow.

"Please, Sire. May I walk with you?" Amélie rushed after him, defying protocol, her pink dress swishing around her slim legs. He stifled another groan. He couldn't allow it, but his heart warmed at her sincere expression. He'd experienced so little affection lately.

Despite his resolve, he waited for her and offered his arm. They strolled on, he careful not to let his thigh brush against her hip.

"This has been a very pleasant day. It is difficult to occupy one's time on this island, though I've tried." He studied the rock formations they passed. "You have played a tremendous role in preventing me from going insane."

"I'm such a talented little diversion."

Napoleon halted and glared at her. Her mockingly blithe comment hurt. He twinged with guilt because his interest had started out that way. "Don't ever presume that. If I just wanted a diversion, I could find plenty of it elsewhere."

"I'm very happy to hear that." Her brown eyes searched into his. She tightened her hand on his arm.

"You're special to me, always remember that." Napoleon used his stern, nononsense voice, and he spoke the truth. He relied on her friendship when the others only took from him. She made him feel alive, rallying his spirit to prepare for these new plans. He cared deeply for her as he intended to leave her pure. He'd let her down gently when the time came.

"As special as the countess?"

"Don't listen to rumors." He patted her arm, the jealous minx. "Fanny Bertrand is telling everyone Albine's child is mine. Every child born near Longwood seems to be mine. I've been accused of the most depraved acts, even with my own sisters."

"*Bien sûr*, I don't believe the gossip." Her cheeks flushed. Doubts lingered in her gaze.

"Ah, but you blush, Amée. As I told Las Cases, it's only the truth that hurts. The rest is lies and not to be troubled with."

"The countess has never been your mistress?"

"Do you imagine I would bother with such a woman?" Napoleon spotted the cluster of rocks he sought, one shaped like a spearhead. He couldn't chase her off, so he led her toward it. Over these jagged pinnacles lay their wavering cobalt prison, stretching to the horizon and beyond, lapping masses of land he hoped to see again, soon.

"You need a good woman, who loves you." Her tender voice made him shiver.

"I'm beyond love. Too blighted by everything that's been snatched away from me, everything I worked so hard for." His angry words pushed her affection aside.

"I know it's devastating." She caressed his sleeve, staring up at him. "Don't think of the island as the end of your life."

He released her and ran a hand over the smooth rock. "My enemies couldn't have selected a better exile…better for them."

"They're terrified of you. That's why you were sent so far away, so removed from Europe." She stood too close in her pretty pink frock. The gown made her look younger, less dangerous, yet heat hummed around her.

"Indeed, they are afraid of me, Amée." Napoleon felt a crack in the rock. How could he distract her?

"You have choices to be happy here or not. I could help you. Doesn't it make sense to seek comfort?" She bent to pluck a pink Venus rose that straggled on this cliff of slag. Her breasts swelled in her bodice. The longing in her voice asked too much of him.

"If I'd made a humiliating peace I might have kept my empire for the second time, but my enemies wanted me disposed of." He traced his finger in the crack. "Ah, I've made many mistakes and now I'm paying for them. I overextended myself in my aspirations."

"Don't lament the present like Ossian. You have a brilliant mind, put it to use." Amélie sniffed the delicate petals, feathering them over her lips.

"Nothing is that simple." Napoleon stared away from her face, toward the coastline. "They should require me in Europe. I'm the natural arbiter between the past and present, between the ancient nobility and the revolutionary ideals."

Amélie frowned. "Could you stand such an intermediary position for long? Why don't you try to mediate here, with Governor Lowe?"

Napoleon laughed. He couldn't help it. "No more books for you. Your intelligence has surpassed mine."

"For enjoyment I rely on simple things. My garden doing well, a day without rain, a pleasant walk with you. I used to think the singing made you happy."

"It does, Amée, but the kindest thing I can do is to repeat my offer to send you to Italy for professional study." Napoleon squeezed her shoulder.

"It's *my* wish not to go. I refuse to be sent away like an insignificant lackey. I'm worth more than that." Amélie dropped the flower and turned her back on him. He pulled her around to face him.

"You are worth more. I'm trying to be noble and think of you, something that's rare for me with women." He shook his head wearily. She stirred up so many clashes inside him—like his fascinating Josephine, when he was young and foolish. "All right, I'll remain selfish." She'd see reason later. He framed her face in his hands and kissed the tip of her nose, treating her like the child he wanted her to be. He leaned back against the spear-shaped rock that hid the orderly officer's view, hopefully hers as well, and slid his left hand down another crack.

    Amélie stared down as he fumbled in the stone's crevice, feeling for the paper supposedly stuffed there. He extracted it. She bent forward, eyes sharp, mouth open. Her lips dusted by petals hovered close to his. His willpower dissolved, Napoleon forgot his purpose, his reason, and pulled her against him. He tasted her breath, sweet like cherry juice, caressing his lips over hers. Her body felt warm and pliant along his and she sighed into their kiss. His foot shifted and dislodged several pebbles, which ricocheted like gunshots down the cliff side.

Chapter Seventeen

It takes time to make oneself loved, and even when I had nothing to do I always felt that I had no time to waste—N.B.

"That scoundrel Lowe has the effrontery to chase the Balcombes away. Saying they're too sympathetic towards me." Simmering with anger, Napoleon paced in his study after Bertrand brought him the news and left. "That fiend of a governor dared to accuse Balcombe of smuggling letters to the mainland on my behalf. He removed him as purveyor, so the man has no choice but to leave Saint Helena."

"They never proved Mr. Balcombe smuggled anything. I'm sorry for you to lose such good friends." Amélie stood near the open door watching his every nuance.

"Lowe can't stand it if I have contact with kind people. When I loaned his daughter Betsy my horse, Mameluke, to ride in the Deadwood races, and she won, the governor threatened him over accepting such a 'gift.'" Napoleon snatched a licorice from his box. The flavor might chase away the taste of cherries that lingered since their picnic the previous day. He wallowed in ire to shore up his bastions against this girl. "He wants me in solitary confinement with no friends. Who do I have left? Bertrand is subjugated by his wife. Only Montholon stays attentive." He wouldn't comment on the "attentiveness" of the countess. Many months had passed since he allowed her in his bed. The idea of Albine's jaded attractions compared to Amélie disgusted him.

"The count isn't the courtier you believe he is. I told you about his disloyal comments to the governor." Amélie spoke in earnest. Napoleon stared at her mouth, the lips he'd kissed and enjoyed. He regretted his amorous slip and had made a tremendous blunder in kissing her. Her innocence charmed him, and he must keep her that way. He'd part from her so much easier. Only there she stood, expecting more.

"You think I'm not aware that Montholon came here for his own glorification?" Napoleon continued to chew and felt the black stickiness collect on his teeth. He loathed dwelling on the idea that Montholon betrayed him, though he knew him to be a sly character.

"Did the Count de Montholon serve with you in battle as Count Bertrand did?" Amélie walked into the room, studying him with a woman's eyes.

"Briefly. Actually, I had to dismiss him for disobeying my orders, but that was long ago." Napoleon flung up a hand to dismiss this topic. Still, Amée seemed to see through his demeanor to reveal the struggling man beneath.

"Don't you think it odd that a man you cast aside volunteered to join you in exile?" She moved closer. Her lithe body taunted him, dragging him back to earth.

"Balcombe can do me some good in Europe." Napoleon turned from her. He always balked when a woman had too much influence over his feelings. He stepped to his new mahogany desk. Lowe tried to appease him with fine furniture, as if such things mattered more than freedom. The paper in the rock lifted his hopes, just as O'Sullivan promised, but what if the escape plan failed? "I'll provide Balcombe with letters. He can tell people how he and his family suffered from this climate, to prove the unhealthiness of my detainment. To arouse sympathy in my favor. Once there, he'll let me know what kind of board we have to play on."

* * * *

When Napoleon spoke no more to her, shuffling papers on his desk, Amélie left. She'd waited in vain for a warm, intimate smile. His kiss at the picnic couldn't have been just to distract her from seeing that paper. She'd felt his ardor, his need, as it matched her own. His pulling away was so familiar. He protected his lofty station by not falling prey to his emotions. Amélie touched her lips. Her first kiss from the man she loved. Her body simmered with provocative changes.

She walked through the dining room and refused to be disappointed by his manner. She'd devise ways to keep him close. Napoleon needed an intelligent woman who loved him for himself—a woman such as she. What books might reveal instructions on seduction?

First, she must find out the significance of the paper hidden in the crevice.

Outside, a bugle blared in the distance. The soldiers marched and drilled.

She swept across the courtyard and hated to see the Balcombes sent away. The more friends who left the more they were surrounded by the enemy, yet who was the enemy anymore? She shivered. Their world grew smaller, more fragile.

* * * *

The last rays of sun faded behind Diana's Peak. Instead of wreathed in mist, her tip stirred the now familiar constellations in the southern sky. Amélie coaxed Napoleon out to the front garden to witness the rose bushes the Chinese workers planted. "The English brought over fertile topsoil. They're trying to improve the grounds. We need the beauty here."

"You want to make everything beautiful, don't you?" Napoleon still seemed in a dismissive mood. "The plants need to be separated better in even rows. Like mustering troops."

"Water will be a problem." The smell of loamy earth comforted her, the air misty in the dwindling light. "The British are constructing a reservoir up on Diana's Peak, however."

"More waste of time and money. You should become involved, occupy yourself."

So she'd leave him alone? "Didn't you once tell me you planted a garden in school?"

"Yes, as a schoolboy in Brienne—we were all required to do so. My hermitage where I concealed myself from the other students who jeered me as the little foreigner." Napoleon gave a careless laugh. "I showed them what I could do."

"I believe you showed everyone." Amélie wished he could be satisfied resting on his laurels. She crouched down and manipulated the rich moist soil through her fingers.

The cannon fired from Alarm House to boorishly announce the setting of the sun.

"*C'est fini*, our night begins. I should return inside."

"No, please, sit with me." She brushed off her hands. "In a year or so, this whole area could be a lush garden." She pressed on his elbow and they sat on a new stone bench.

"In a year or so, you could be a diva on the stage in Milan." His words even, he stared straight ahead. "I suppose it isn't a decent career for a young lady. Marriage is still your best option. You'll be busy having children."

Amélie forced a laugh, wise to his tactics. "I may never marry."

"Why do you say that?" Now he looked at her. The Chinese workers had drifted away.

"I have my reasons." She felt his eyes on her flesh. "I don't care to be married to anyone."

"You must find a good French officer to marry. I can recommend a few in my Imperial Guard. I'll provide you letters of introduction."

Amélie bit at her lip, but kept her tone glib. "You must promise *not* to request that I marry anyone. Please don't match me with any of your old guard, or anyone else."

He sighed, but with a slight chuckle. "You are a stubborn creature. I must write down these promises you insist upon."

"I'll keep a list for you." She pressed her thigh into his, tentative at first. "You're stubborn as well. You resist what might be good for you, for the past."

"A woman should be married. It is the nature of things." He stiffened but didn't shift his leg. "I must stop giving you books. Undo the damage I've done. No, that progressive school in Paris is where you started your anarchy."

"As an enlightened leader, you should be more broad-minded where women's education is concerned."

"Now you insult me. I'll have you know I created schools to provide free education to daughters of Legionnaires killed in action." He thrust up his hand as if pronouncing a proclamation. "The first time women were given direct educational benefits from their fathers' military service."

"I knew about that school, and that was notable. I trust they weren't just educated in feminine pursuits?" The cool breeze stirred her hair. She breathed deeply. "A woman's brain can't be so different than a man's, but men are allowed any amount of learning."

"Rousseau said it's a woman's place to render herself agreeable to her husband: 'Educate women like men and the more they resemble our sex, the less power they have over us.'" He thumped the bench, his tone irritated. "They should develop their charms, for the good of their families and that should be their influence."

She'd made him angry. Not the best way to use her charms for influence, but his reaction proved she wielded some power over his emotions. "Didn't you pursue your career in the army before you had thoughts of marriage?"

"Not exactly. I longed to be married, but hadn't found anyone. I was quite a skinny fellow in those days, poor and gauche. Very shy around women; they intimidated me." His voice softened. "I never knew what to say, so I came off as brusque."

"Then you met Josephine." He might still be intimidated by women—or at least *her* since their kiss.

"When I went to Paris to tell the Directors my plans for an Italian offensive, I became caught up in the salon society popular at the time." His voice grew dreamy. "So many sophisticated women…and yes, I met Josephine. She was kind and gentle, a smoothness to my rough edges."

The pitch-black night descended, like an ebony cape dropped over the island, the twilight here brief. Mist started to gather over the garden.

"At least you admit women can be sophisticated."

"As well as manipulative, deceitful…" Napoleon sighed. "I did love her. For her it took a bit longer."

Amélie rubbed her arms in the growing chill. Their stormy relationship was legendary, and then he'd set Josephine aside for his marriage into royalty. "I'm sure she loved you."

"She married me, *en vérité*, but I bullied her with my persistence. While I was in Egypt, I learned she was living in a compromising situation with a young dandy…" Napoleon broke off as if this memory still plagued him.

"That was awful for you." Amélie closed her eyes and absorbed his despair, the young general betrayed by love, so distant from home. She touched his thigh.

"I was furious, so I started up a romance of my own." His hand covered hers and she quivered. "A lively, pretty girl, but silly and empty-headed."

Amélie exhaled her envy and pictured herself on the exotic, sandy plains of Egypt: seductive at the foot of a pyramid, attracting the general's fancy. "Did you fall in love with this silly girl?"

"No, of course not. I only loved Josephine. The affair was out of revenge. Not the most intelligent reason, but I was young and impulsive."

"You've had many mistresses. They couldn't all have been out of revenge."

"Such bold questions." Napoleon's fingers tightened on hers. "It was the way of things. Expected of men in high places. A good wife looks the other way."

"That's why I'll never marry." She rubbed her fingers against his. A tingle started low in her abdomen. "Did you enjoy the affairs?"

"Why are we on this topic? Enjoy? Yes, why not? Most meant nothing, it's true. I used them, but they used me as well. I was famous and women threw themselves at me. Of course, the ones who *didn't* were far more interesting." He lowered his voice. "Few engaged my heart. I was seduced by power."

"Power is a cold companion. Mistresses can have broken hearts, too, when discarded." She sagged with sadness. How could she contemplate being the mistress of a man who'd plowed through so many? He had said *she* was special. Her pulse throbbed.

"Amée, I insist we change this subject neither of us is enjoying." Napoleon massaged her hand between his. "It's getting too cold out here."

Amélie stared off over the dark garden, calming her rising distress, her skin heating with the contact. The lanterns hanging over the front porch shined a weak light, but they sat in shadow. The wind whistled over the plain. The sentries marched in slow cadence around the wall.

"You are full of contradictions, reading of Greek fables and insisting on being equal to men. One so whimsical, the other…"

"Is that part of my charm?" She'd meant to provoke him, draw him close with emotion.

He laughed. "Indeed, it is."

"I see you as full of contradictions as well." Amélie gentled her voice.

"Europe has paralyzed a force too gigantic for the security of the world," Napoleon said after a short silence. "Branded an outlaw, but the allies broke the Treaty of Fontainebleau."

She leaned her head against his shoulder. "You escaped Elba. You've never told me if you've contemplated escape from Saint Helena," she whispered.

"More bold questions." Napoleon squeezed his arm around her as if to quiet her. "When I have a plot, you'll be the first to know, though the British will try to ring it out of you, since they're merciless with torture." His teasing sounded forced.

"What about...that paper you retrieved from Sandy Bay?"

His arm clenched around her, pressing her against his side. "Some things you are better off not knowing."

"You just said—"

"Shhh, I'm trying to protect you."

"You're treating me like a helpless woman. I don't deserve that." Amélie felt his heart beating and trembled under the heat of his arm. "Honor my intelligence, please."

Rumors trickled in about people on the outside outfitting ships to rescue the ex-Emperor of the French. Tales that sent Lowe into fits of reprisal against his prisoner by tightening restrictions.

"Amée, I..." Napoleon stroked her shoulder. *"Eh bien,* I don't know whom to trust anymore. I'd be a fool not to trust you, but you're young still, and have no experience with the scheming of the world as I do."

"I'm learning fast. Won't you confide in me?" She shifted her body in his arm, nestled into his warmth, a place she belonged. Now he seemed to tremble.

Napoleon put his mouth near her ear. "It was a note to prove the island could be invaded in secret. A dry run if you will, but there's a lot more to be done."

His breath tickled her nerves. "People are coming to rescue you?" Amélie's throat tightened. She gripped his sleeve. He might be taken from her. Swept from the very isolation she'd thrived on to forge this alliance. She no longer desired elevation, only love. Was she egotistic enough to hope these plans would fail? "Who are they? When will they come back?"

"Shhh. I've given up on a more civilized removal. I'd be deluding myself to think the British oligarchy will set me free. France will never demand me back, but men can always be bribed." Napoleon squeezed her head to his cheek.

Amélie reveled in their skin touching. His hot breath fanned her face. She moved her mouth near his, wanting to kiss him, but instead she whispered, "You could never be content enough to stay here?"

"This is too small a territory for me, Amée." Napoleon trailed his fingers through her hair. He kissed her temple, obviously avoiding her lips.

Amélie steamed inside from the touch of his mouth. At the thump of footfalls, she snapped up her head. The dim lantern light outlined several sentries marching through the front gate and into their yard. She shuddered, afraid they'd heard their conversation.

Napoleon jerked away from her. "I'd forgotten. Lowe now demands the sentries surround the house at six-thirty instead of nine." He stood, his words abrupt and angry. "I will have Bertrand contest this abuse of the governor's authority! This constant insult to my person."

Amélie rose and followed him into the house, the defeated general bombarded by foreign troops. In the salon she grabbed his arm and said, "Who was that note from?"

"You must *never* mention these things to anyone." Napoleon clasped her shoulder, hard—his face the mask of a man still in command. "We will speak no more of it. Now please, I insist you forget it all."

"You know I won't tell. Please don't leave me ignorant of your plans." Amélie's firm words coated the fear she'd be abandoned. Even with the English subjugating their every move, Saint Helena provided the freedom she craved to not be hobbled by society's limitations. Did she cling to a relationship that had no future? Every ounce of intelligence warned her not to encourage an *affaire d'amour*.

Chapter Eighteen

So does Fortune frustrate—N.B

Napoleon smiled after O'Sullivan left his study, his final visit. He reread the retrieved paper. One of O'Sullivan's men had rowed his skiff up to Sandy Bay and deposited it, proving Lowe's precautions weren't infallible. The Irishman and his ship sailed off to England tomorrow. They'd been delayed on the island refitting the ship after damage from a storm. Four to five months he'd have to wait for their return, but his other plan should be set in motion soon.

Montholon lingered in the dining room and Napoleon invited him into his study.

"Sire, I don't know how you put up with that buffoonish captain," Montholon said, his cool blue gaze assessing, "and why you dismiss me whenever he visits anymore."

"Don't concern yourself. We speak of things that wouldn't interest you." Napoleon kept Montholon out of any discussions because of Amélie's warnings about him. Too bad he couldn't let her in on his plans; she always had such good advice. The less people who knew, the better for him. He shouldn't have told her as much as he did, always finding her so easy to talk to. His intentions obviously upset her, and he couldn't add that to his list of worries.

"Albine and I have felt much neglected, Sire. I can't help but think you hide things from me." Montholon gave his wheedling smile between curly sideburns, but even this looked jaded.

"Such as? Sully, that's what his friends call him, tells me about his lusty mistress at the Cape. A half-Chinese woman who knows all the ways of the Orient in pleasing him." Napoleon chuckled at his courtier's reddening cheeks. Montholon affected a prissy exterior, yet married Albine with her notorious past, then seemed apathetic about his wife's attentions to him.

"Forgive me, Sire. I don't want to trouble you in any way, but I do have something to discuss." Montholon sauntered about the room with that annoying feline grace and brushed his hand over his left epaulet. "There are rumors going about the island that *you* have a lusty, young mistress. The officers at Deadwood are laughing over the great Emperor of the French, if you'll pardon me, bedding his kitchen maid."

Napoleon glared, about to shout. This hurt more than he should let on. "Don't speak to me of such slander. I don't think of her that way. She's decent..." He almost said she was a child, but he lied. She'd turned into a desirable woman.

"I'm just repeating what is circulating about the island. I only warn you to assist you in preserving your reputation. These rumors will spread to Europe, Your Majesty. You told me when we first arrived that you don't want to give your esteemed wife any reason to seek a divorce. You must honor the union to safeguard your son's future."

"We will discuss this no more. Leave me." Napoleon loathed it when Montholon struck a sore spot. He had to remain infallible, above suspicion, though always susceptible to vulgar gossip. Now Amélie's reputation suffered, when they'd done nothing wrong—another reason to keep her pure. The stirrings he'd felt when he kissed her would only deter him from his mission. He trailed his fingers over his chest, his heart. Love was an emotion he could ill afford.

* * * *

Amélie put silverware into the drawer in the dining room sideboard. Count Bertrand escorted a visitor toward the salon, Captain O'Sullivan, the boisterous Irishman whom Napoleon liked. He piqued her curiosity because the Count de Montholon always grumbled at his presence.

Amélie hurried to the salon, to eavesdrop, but Bertrand and the captain exited the house quickly. She couldn't help but link this visitor to the paper at Sandy Bay, but Napoleon must be delusional to consider escaping from the island.

Ali strutted in the front door with a box. He placed it on the billiard table. "Look, more gifts from Lady Holland. She never forgets us, the one person who gets past Lowe's scrutiny, though she's never sent anything forbidden."

"Ali, what do you know about that Captain O'Sullivan who just left?"

He ripped open the box and pulled out books and candy from the straw. "I don't know anything. Ask His Majesty." Ali winked at her, but he'd never questioned her about the nature of their relationship.

A loud crash in the dining room sent them both running into that chamber to investigate.

Their major-domo, Cipriani, was on his knees, sprawled across an overturned chair. He struggled to rise. "Call Doctor O'Meara, *sur-le-champ*," he gasped out, his other hand clutching his gut. He collapsed onto his side as Amélie fled the room to find the doctor.

By the time she returned with O'Meara, Cipriani groaned and writhed on the floor, with Ali trying to calm him. The two men picked him up and carried him into the library, as more people gathered around.

Napoleon rushed from his study, his expression vexed. "O'Meara, what has happened to him? What ails my Franceschi? Can you do anything?"

"It's so sudden, sir, I haven't any idea. Let me get him settled and examined." The doctor knelt down, pulled out Cipriani's shirt and unbuttoned his breeches. "Someone bring me a cot."

That evening Amélie carried a bowl of soup in to the suffering man. The room already stank of rot. With O'Meara sitting beside him, Cipriani moaned on the bed. Soaked in perspiration, his angular face was pinched in agony.

Her hands shook so violently, she almost dropped the bowl. She jostled the soup onto a little table beside the doctor. "My father says...try to get him to eat. *Affreux*."

"What's the matter, Amélie?" O'Meara stared at her. "You look about to faint. Please, you had better leave. Tell your father I doubt if he can eat anything right now. He's in serious pain. I've seen nothing like it."

Outside the library door, she gulped for breath, pressing her head between her hands. The man was dying. She knew it, because her mother had died in the same way. At least that's how she remembered it. The dreadful memories gushed back as if just unfolding. Her stomach clenched over that irreplaceable loss.

Amélie bolted for the courtyard to breathe in the outside air, her hand over her mouth to keep from gagging. She'd avoid Cipriani's room after that.

* * * *

"An abrupt, mysterious inflammation of the bowels," O'Meara said in the dining room, his round face deflated in exhaustion after two days of tending Cipriani. The doctor swiped tears from his eyes. "Aye, well, he was my friend, and I couldn't save him. I don't know what else I could have done."

Amélie fought her own tears at Napoleon's grief-stricken face. After the consulting British doctor from Deadwood left, the emperor withdrew to his study. She rushed to knock on that door, to offer emotional support.

The Count de Montholon opened the door. His icy gaze sharpened. "The emperor is receiving no one, Mademoiselle. *Not* even you." He veiled a sneer behind his smile and blocked the study entrance.

"I think he will see me, Count, if you please." Amélie tried to edge past him.

Montholon seized her by the arm and steered her toward the prep room. "*Mais non.* He's resting now and doesn't wish to be bothered, so be off. Attend to your, uh, kitchen duties."

She stared resentfully at the smooth-faced nobleman and his jaundiced expression. She swept his insulting hands away and left the main house.

After dinner, Amélie tried again. On entering the dining room she caught a glimpse of the back of Albine de Montholon's head as the woman minced into the emperor's chambers.

Amélie slumped against the wall. Her heart felt like it tumbled to her feet.

She bristled with fury. An unscrupulous mistress—even fresh from childbed—offered more comfort than the cook's daughter. Her risen status crumbled in the wake of rank and privilege. The count manipulated his wife back into Napoleon's arms!

What if Napoleon became ill like Cipriani and she wasn't allowed to see him? Amélie swallowed a sob and returned to her room. She snatched up her hairbrush, about to fling it against her closed door. Then she clumped the scratchy bristles in her palm. She'd devise another way in.

* * * *

"His Majesty paces within his interior, restless, never sits, won't sleep." Marchand's expression sad, he polished a pair of Napoleon's leather shoes—after removing the oval gold buckles—with Dubbin, a combination of wax, oil, and tallow at the dining room table. "Cipriani was also a friend of mine, so I too feel this loss."

"I wish there was something I could do." Amélie hadn't slept well either, fuming over the harlot of a countess and the count's treating her like a servant, plus Napoleon's upset. "The Count de Montholon refused to let me see Napoleon last night."

"The emperor had some of his peculiar symptoms, which worries me." The valet worked a greasy cloth over the leather, the pungent smell stinging Amélie's eyes. He glanced at her with indulgence. "The count and his wife are jealous of the attention His Majesty lavishes on you."

"I don't care. Help me get in to see the emperor. He'd never deny me access. He needs my comfort." Amélie clutched her elbows, staring toward the study door. "I worry when he has those symptoms too." Something more sinister than an arbitrary island disease infected this house, and she struggled to fit it together.

"Both counts are bending over backwards trying to console the emperor." Marchand said nothing about the level of her "comfort," always the diplomat. "All right, come back later tonight. I'll sneak you in."

Amélie returned to her room and plopped on her bed. Cipriani's writhing pain festered in her mind. Suddenly she wanted to write to her brother, Theo, to see what he remembered of their mother's death. Was it as agonizing as she recalled? She couldn't ask her father. Sadly, they'd never once discussed this poignant subject.

She slid out her writing case from under her bed: a scratched hand-me-down from the house. Paper was scarce on the island, so she rooted around for the crumpled piece of brown wrapping paper she'd saved, and dipped her quill in ink. Her query short, her hand faltering a bit, she sprinkled sand, shook it off, and placed the letter on her dresser.

Albine's mincing form trampled away her maternal laments. Napoleon might be right—a woman's charm did seem the one power she wielded over a man. Her ignorance frustrated her. If no information was available for a woman to learn of the bedroom, why couldn't she write it herself? She laughed. Her inexperience would prevent it. She'd have to seek advice—but where?

Before her courage deserted her, she snatched out more paper scraps and wrote down the theory that a woman needed to be prepared to accept or reject intimacy, whether in the confines of marriage or not.

"Amélie?" Her door creaked open after this soft question, and her father stepped in. Near lunch time, he should have been in the kitchen.

She swept the paper behind her. "I'm sorry if I held you up, Papa. I'll wash and fetch my apron."

"Never mind that. I want to have a word with you, if I may?" His uneasy countenance bothered her.

"Won't you be late for preparing the court meal?" She resisted the urge to drop her quilt over her writing, afraid to smear the ink.

"No one feels like eating." He sat in her spindly chair, his hands on his knees, which almost bumped the edge of her bed. "Amélie, it's come to my attention...As I've mentioned before, I do think it's prudent if you saw less of the emperor."

"In the beginning you didn't seem to mind." Her empty stomach bubbled. Amélie could never explain her feelings of illicit love to her father. "I won't desert him. Too many have deserted him already."

"Things have changed." Perrault furrowed his brow, his knuckles white as he gripped his bony kneecaps. "In ways I might have predicted if I'd paid better notice. I duped myself into thinking you were still a little girl who couldn't—"

"Papa, you aren't listening to the servants' gossip, are you?" Amélie averted her gaze for an instant. She lifted her hair from her neck, her nape growing hot.

"No, but the Countess de Montholon came to me...and she believes matters have escalated." He didn't look at her as he said this, fidgeting in the chair.

"You would listen to her? A woman of her sort." Amélie clenched her quilt, unable to hide her disgust. How dare this courtesan continue to interfere.

"Now, *ma fille*, you're condemning the countess with idle gossip. Just as you yourself wish not to be condemned."

She saw his point, but wished she didn't. "What lies has she told you?"

"I intend to know the truth." Perrault twitched his mouth, speaking slowly. "The countess says there's a more intimate side to your relationship, and it also appears that way to me."

"The emperor and I are the greatest of friends." Amélie regretted lying to her father. She didn't know how she'd handle her parent's shame if she and Napoleon developed a relationship. She plucked at a loose thread on her dress. "Everyone is just envious, as you yourself once said. You've always denounced any gossip, and I appreciated you for it."

"Yes, I have, but *if* this has gone further than it should, as your father I must guide you in the proper manner." Glancing away again, he drummed his fingers on his thigh. "I'm only thinking of you."

"Everyone says they're only thinking of me." Amélie threw this out, anger replacing guilt. Napoleon's offer to send her away, off the island, apart from him. She smiled at her father. "*Pardon*, but can't you treat me as a person responsible for myself?"

"Amélie, you're just like your mother. Very stubborn. I know we're far removed here, but society's rules still matter. If you…ever wish to confide about…anything…" Perrault grimaced, the chair creaking with his movement. "I've kept quiet, for the most part, on your 'friendship,' because it made you both happy, but if things alter, as your father I must—"

"Nothing has changed, and it does make us happy." Amélie doubted he really wanted a confession, not that one was forthcoming. How many "rules" did she intend to defy, and would Napoleon wish her to? "I understand your concerns, but they're unfounded."

"Remember, you're a moral young lady from a decent family. I expect you to behave so." He rose, his manner stiff, obviously not convinced of her innocence. She'd counted on her father's natural reserve and profound loyalty to the emperor to allow her to continue, still she didn't relish having to hurt him.

"Please, don't worry, Papa. You gave me a good education. Now trust me to be wise enough to…to manage." Could she manage, without the experience, the information that would give her confidence?

"I've had my word with you." Her father coughed into his hand. His face looked thinner, his cheekbones pronounced.

"You're working too hard." Amélie stared at him with concern. "I'll make you some carrot soup for your cough."

Perrault gave a dismissive wave and left her chamber.

Matters have escalated? She would speak to Napoleon about the countess's meddling, as long as, despite his denial, Albine wasn't weaving him into her own web.

She jerked the paper back onto her lap. Somehow she'd gather the details she needed for this task, even if she had to interview prostitutes in Jamestown—a daring idea that intrigued her. The Countess de Montholon would be a fount of information. Was it proper etiquette for a prospective mistress to ask a former one for advice? With a groan, she'd never ask that harlot anything. Especially details about an alleged intimacy with their emperor.

As she dipped her quill back into the ink, Amélie sighed at her weakness when all she desired was seeing Napoleon. She ran her fingers over her lips, remembering his kiss. A kiss he pretended never happened, as if by accident the island breeze had swept them together on the cliffs. So near the edge, she staggered to maintain her balance.

Chapter Nineteen

The human heart is an abyss that deceives all calculations—N.B.

Amélie re-entered the main house at eight o'clock that evening. The place felt eerily quiet, gloomy, and forbidding—she suppressed a shiver. She found Marchand in the duty chamber.

"You're in luck. The Bertrands have returned to Hutt's Gate." The valet joined her in the dining room with a candle, his curly brown hair in disarray. "The Count de Montholon is still in the emperor's rooms, but I'll ask him a food inventory question, and coax him into the preparation area. Then you sneak in."

"The count took over that function quick enough, Cipriani not even buried. More ways to dominate the household. Napoleon would never bar me from seeing him." Amélie took a deep breath to soften her stridency. "Why does he even put up with those people?"

"After Waterloo...His Majesty appreciated any officer who showed sympathy and devotion."

She pitied her emperor's desperation. "Even if that devotion might not be genuine?"

Marchand indicated that she wait in the shadows near the drawing room arch. He knocked on the study door and was confronted by Montholon's prissy scowl. "Excuse me, Count de Montholon, but I need to ask something concerning some missing food items. I realize it is late, but His Majesty will be upset if this isn't solved."

Amélie watched them walk toward the back of the house. She darted to the study door, then opened and closed it softly behind her.

The study was empty, the fire smoldering in the grate. Light spilled from Napoleon's open bedchamber door.

Amélie tiptoed toward that chamber, where a candelabra burned on the night table, but the narrow camp bed with green taffeta curtains wasn't occupied. A worn sofa, chair, and chest of drawers crowded around the bed. An elaborate silver washstand was one of two items to suggest an emperor resided here. Sparkling in a shadowy corner, the silver ewer perched on golden swans was supported by a tripod stand. A gold dressing case sat nearby.

The door to the adjoining bathroom was ajar, and this room too had a faint light. At that entrance, she stood to the side without looking in and debated whether or not to disturb him. She whispered his name into the humid space.

"Amée? Is that you?"

She leaned against the door frame; her pulse quickened. "Yes."

"Come in, come in at once." At least he sounded in good spirits.

She crept into the narrow room, not sure what to expect. Steam swirled around her, as if the island mists had drifted over flames and seeped in. As she passed an ornate Chinese screen, she caught a glimpse of him in his bathtub. She gasped and turned her back.

"I didn't realize you were—"

"Don't be concerned, *ma chère*," he replied in a sedate tone. "Come and sit down."

Napoleon sometimes received his court while taking a bath and apparently thought nothing of it. Amélie moved behind the screen, behaving like a novice who hadn't the nerve of his rumored mistress. "I probably should wait in the study until you've completed your toilette."

"Nonsense, stay there. Talk to me." Now he sounded lonely and depressed. "Why haven't you been to see me?"

"I've tried to see you since yesterday, but the Count de Montholon refused to let me in." The steam dampened her hair about her cheeks.

"Ah, he is very vigilant, that one. I will have a word with him. My mind has been elsewhere, but if I'd known..." His tone was dreamy, as though he'd been drinking. Napoleon wasn't a heavy imbiber and no one had ever seen him drunk.

"I'm deeply sorry about your friend Cipriani. If there's anything I can do?" Her sympathizing shaded her discomfort. To be treated as mature she must behave as such. She heard him ripple in the water, a movement of hand.

"What could anyone do for the poor man? This island has murdered him."

"I'd have been the first to offer condolences, if not for the Count and Countess de Montholon." She bumped the silk screen with her bottom, and stepped away. "They treat me with scorn."

"The Montholons worry that you take my interests away from them. I'm tired of them, and they fear it. That's why Las Cases left. He wanted my complete attention, and suffered their animosity." Napoleon still spoke in a torpid manner. "None of them understand I have to be at the center, the same as when I was in power."

Now she strived to be his closest confidant. "The Montholons don't have your best interests at heart." She sounded petty, and added, "*Monsieur* Cipriani always did." Even if he did try to lure her to Jamestown once.

"*Bien sûr*. Wait there, I'm coming out." He sloshed from the tub.

Amélie stared at the mildewed wall in front of her. Her back to the screen, she made an effort to relax her shoulders. She closed her eyes for a moment.

"You can open your eyes now, Amée. I'm fairly decent." Napoleon stood beside her clad in his dressing gown, his warm smile melting her. His hair damp, he looked fresh-faced if tired around the eyes.

"I wasn't troubled." She smiled and wiped a moist tendril of hair from her temple. "You should stop taking your baths so hot. It dries and irritates the skin, as I've noticed washing dishes. I'll give Marchand some olive oil to put in your water."

"One physician did warn me that hot baths were 'weakening.' Still, I ignored him, but I'll consider your advice." Clasping her wrist, he walked her into his bedroom.

Amélie waited for him to continue into the study, but instead he left her and went to the gray-painted fireplace beyond the sofa. The wind rattled down through the chimney, a lonely sound Napoleon must listen to every night before he tried to sleep.

"Have you seen this, Amée?" he asked, as if she'd had free access to his bedroom. He fingered a silver alarm clock that hung on one side of the mantel. "This belonged to Frederick the Great, a man I admired. I took it as a souvenir after the battle of Potsdam."

Amélie stepped behind him, pondering her ability to charm over the nervous quivers in her stomach. She touched his shoulder. "Shall we...sit in here? I can stoke up the fire."

"This is my Consular watch." Napoleon pointed to a gold watch, engraved with the letter B, suspended from a chain of plaited hair on the other side of the mantel. Amélie felt a twinge in her chest; the blond plait had to be Marie Louise's.

"Here is my family." He turned and swept out his hand, but didn't smile.

On the chamber's yellow cloth walls hung portraits shrouded in shadow. The elegant Josephine in a miniature; Marie Louise with the infant King of Rome; and the child by himself, a few years older, riding a lamb. Marie Louise had bulbous fish eyes and thick lips. The fair, plump-cheeked child filled Amélie with sadness over Napoleon's loss.

"Is that your mother?" She indicated a portrait of an older woman with vivid eyes and a well-formed mouth that matched his.

"Madame Letezia Buonaparte. A mother is a man's whole education." He smiled, his tone reverent. "She offered to come here, but I forbade it. The long voyage would be too rough on her and I want no one in my family to see my abasement."

Napoleon frowned and stalked into the study. Embarrassed by the relief she felt at leaving his bedchamber—hardly a *femme fatale*—she followed, mulling over ways to wipe Marie Louise or anyone else from his heart.

* * * *

At his sideboard, Napoleon poured two glasses of brandy, and handed her one. One drink and he'd dismiss her. Her hair so attractively...He sipped the strong contents, a burn across his tongue and down his throat. When in power he'd disdained the effects of liquor, intent on a clear head, but tonight he welcomed the insouciant feeling.

"It has been one tragedy after another this year." He stared into the shadowed corners of the room. The wind keened around the building. Raindrops started to plunk on the roof and he pictured the sunny vineyards of France.

"Yes...though not all tragedy." Amélie clicked her teeth on the rim of her glass, taking a sip. The rain slapped down harder, and she looked up. "Have you ever noticed that during the storms here, there's never any lightning or thunder?"

"Just more proof we live in a bizarre place." He occupied the center of this masquerade, the reason they all suffered from it. Now his compatriot's demise threatened his plans. "Cipriani's death doesn't seem like an act of God. He was with me on Elba. I can never replace such a devoted companion. He brought me all the information I needed from France—the news of Josephine's death. No one else had the decency to inform me." His throat tightened.

"He had unswerving loyalty for you." Amélie took another sip of brandy and coughed. "I know he worked as your spy here. Was he involved in the Sandy Bay—"

"No talk of that. You must preserve my peace of mind." He paced over to the study fireplace where the fire smoldered its last, swirling the brandy in his snifter.

"How will his death affect your...escape?" Amélie hurried and placed two logs on the ashes and stirred the sparks until they caught again.

"*Grand Dieu*, you never listen." Napoleon gazed down at her blond head as sizzling wood replaced the smell of smoke. "'But I must not hope to see Paris again. You see, I am ready to go down to my grave.' That's from *Zaire*."

"Voltaire's words, too sad." Amélie stood and squeezed his hand. "If this escape plan doesn't work out, you shouldn't think of it as your only hope for happiness."

Napoleon raised her hand to his lips and kissed it, to quiet her. "You have cheered me." Her skin tasted sweet, her gaze on him tender if probing. He released her and opened the music box on top of the mantel. The jingle of tinny sounds joined the fire's crackling. "This is a Viennese waltz. Don't you think it pretty?"

"No, I prefer French or Italian music." Amélie's face fell and she turned from him. Napoleon purposely hurt her by reminding her of Marie Louise. If he angered her, that kept her at a safe distance. He grappled with the urge to pull her back.

He forced his thoughts elsewhere, swirling like the liquid he finished in his glass. "Ah, if I were in Paris again. I aspired to make her the grandest city in the world."

Amélie's fawn eyes watched him move leisurely to the tune of the waltz. He tried to envision the majestic balls at the palaces he once occupied. The array of dignitaries and visiting royalty, kowtowing to him. The past glittering as he languished in a dismal present.

"Then I'd never have known you, or you me." Her tense words dragged him back into their confined world. Her presence the one beam of light.

He smiled at her earnest face. "Never have known you? *Je ne comprends pas*."

"I meant you and I would never have met, if you were still in Paris."

"Fate has decided otherwise." He put down his glass. The music box fell silent.

"Teach me how to waltz." She finished her drink, spilling a few drops over her bottom lip, which she licked away. The gesture unsettled him. He should send her back to her quarters, but didn't want to. His need for her welled up in him unbidden.

"Dancing isn't one of my strong points." Napoleon took the glass from her and set it aside. He put his arms around her soft body and waltzed slowly around the room. "You should have been born a princess. You're far more regal than most I've met."

"Too much protocol. I'd be married off against my will to some sloppy prince from a forgotten province." She sounded breathless, her breath too warm on his neck. She stumbled in her steps. "I'm happy to be who I am. I don't need royalty to prove my worth."

"Sage words." Napoleon's irritation flared and he held her tighter. "I suppose I need this title the British won't recognize to prove mine?"

"No, not at *all*. You were voted our emperor. You're the only legitimate monarch in Europe." She trembled in his arms, her breasts pressed against his chest.

"You discourage all my suggestions, however. You don't want to be a princess, or return to Europe and marry one of my officers. Tell me, what is your secret desire, Amée?" His skin tingled. He knew the answer. Why did he want her to say it, to assuage his own ego? They stopped dancing. Rain continued to smack the roof.

"To be respected as a vital person…and to stay here with you." Amélie's voice quavered.

"Those two things won't go hand in hand." He kissed her forehead, avoiding her tender expression. "I want more for you. You deserve more. Your father hasn't chosen this sloppy old prince in his forgotten province, nor should you."

"This is what I—"

"Shhh, come and sit." He held her hand and they sat together on the sofa. "I might be destined to perish on this island purgatory. That's no future for you." He must encourage her to leave the island—to rescue her from a licentious relationship.

"We could be happy here. I'd show you how to take better care of yourself." Her words tremulous, she stroked his shoulder. "We'd learn to deal with the English."

"Everything is not that simple." He drew her confession and now must dismiss it. He'd wring her pity, a less dangerous emotion. "My health suffers here. Last night my climactic illness returned. I thought I'd never recover from it, burning stomach, icy legs. I had to hide in the dark with a headache."

"Did you drink the Constantia? Please stop drinking that wine. There's something wrong with it." Her selfless adoration tugged at him. Her eyes glistened with tears.

Her tears moved him. She wasn't attracted by his power or forced into his bed by a political alliance. "I should have listened to you, I see."

"Don't tell anyone about it."

He laughed, but it came out brittle. "You're back to thinking someone is poisoning me."

"Let's...call it an experiment. You remember the wine made me sick after one glass. Can you grant me this favor?"

"Will I have any peace if I don't?" Who here would gain the most from poisoning him? The English, of course. Then he thought of Cipriani's horrible death: so convenient for them, eliminating his agent. Was his compatriot murdered?

"No peace whatsoever. Promise not to tell anyone, not even Doctor O'Meara."

"*Eh bien*, you always manage to have your way. It will be eternally our secret." Napoleon sighed, wanting to chase his suspicions elsewhere to sort through later. He leaned back on the sofa and draped his arm over the back of it, behind her.

"I don't always have my way." He heard the satisfaction in her voice.

"Yes, you bully me terribly." The little scamp tried to manipulate him, but for some reason, that didn't bother him tonight. The brandy softened his resistance. He hugged his arm around her. "What shall we do on Saint Helena, bring order to chaos as I did with my empire, or will history seldom mention me because I was overthrown?"

She nestled into his side. "You once told me that your enemies could suppress and mutilate you, but never obliterate you."

"Ah, yes, and no one can take away my memories. If I could but begin again."

"You could bring order here by telling Governor Lowe to move the new house down in the Geranium Vale. Less windy, and lovely scenery."

"Perhaps." He brushed a hand through her hair. She'd never give up, but his pride wouldn't allow him to bow to the English. He'd once been too powerful for anyone to oppose him. Of course, he'd started to lose his confidence in battle, and that's how he'd made mistakes that led to this exile. If he *had* another chance, he'd change tactics, arrange his generals better, not trust Talleyrand or Fouché.

"I'm not fooled. You'll still be defiant." She stared up at him, caressed a hand over his cheek. The warmth, her tenderness, unraveled him.

"Stop seeing through me, it's..." Her soft body against him clouded that other decision to keep her unsullied. "I have to fight Lowe, but misfortunes do have their glory. If I'd died on my throne, I'd have remained a problem to many people. Here they judge me in my nakedness."

He flinched at her fingers on his dressing gown, acutely aware he was naked within.

"You should go back to your room." He spoke without conviction. He'd give her the chance to run.

"Why? I said I wanted to stay with you."

The fire, the only light in the room, continued to crackle. The orange hues reflected off her features made her look like a mythical being caressed by flame. He shook his head to clear it. "You don't understand the consequences."

"Show me," she whispered. "Don't you have feelings for me?"

"Amée, you've touched my heart in so many ways." Napoleon kissed her cheek, his fingers stroking the back of her neck. "You've soothed me more than you realize."

"You asked me my desires, and then ignored them." She quivered under his touch. "Am I more soothing than the countess? I saw her enter your chambers... late last night."

"Ahh, you're jealous, little Amée?" Napoleon felt a satisfaction he shouldn't have. "You have nothing to worry about. I discourage Albine at every turn. Yes, she is a calculating woman. I don't want you to be like her."

"I'm a woman with desires for only you." She tipped up her endearing face, like a flower.

"Corruptive influences will change you." Did he speak of what happened with Marie Louise, or did he mean himself, here, now? He massaged his hand through her luxuriant hair.

The brandy, the situation, stripped his defenses. He wearied of holding himself back. He traced his fingers along her cheek, her neck and shoulder, so soft and clean. His hand caressed down her arm, and just aside her breast. The melting look in her eyes held a flicker of wariness, like a forest animal unused to such ministrations. He lifted her chin, gazing straight into her eyes.

"What future do you have? This isn't right. Oh, Amée...you try my very soul."

"You possess mine." Amélie returned her hand to his cheek and stroked it.

Napoleon leaned into her and kissed her lips. She responded and moaned when he deepened the kiss. He felt a fullness, like warm honey, ooze through his veins. Amélie slid her arms around his neck.

Napoleon brushed his fingertips against her breast. He unfastened her dress, kissing along her neck. Her succulent flesh. His hand slipped inside, into her chemise, massaging her bare skin. Peeling down her bodice, he kissed the hollow of her throat, one hand moving along her leg. He felt her shudder and the heat of desire swelled up in him. Back on her lips, he kissed her hungrily, tasting the brandy and both their yearnings. He gathered up her skirt, pushing it higher.

A sharp knock at the door. Amélie started. Napoleon ignored it, and kissed along her breast, her sweet bud of a nipple—how he ached for her. She shuddered again. The knocking grew louder. Now she struggled to pull away from him.

"Who is it?" Napoleon demanded. He sat back from her with an angry groan.

Amélie bunched together her bodice and pulled down her skirt with trembling hands.

The door opened. "I am sorry, Your Majesty. I know you didn't care to be disturbed, but Mademoiselle Perrault evaded me." Montholon leered down at them.

"I had to attend to a few things, then I came back to check on you."

"*You* are disturbing me, Montholon!" Napoleon shouted his fury, his thwarted lust. "I told you never to prevent Amée from seeing me, and you purposely disobeyed!"

"*Mon erreur.* Forgive my intru—"

"Remove yourself from me at once!"

Chapter Twenty

What is happiness?...ruling passions dominates [men] in turn and causes them to prostitute the name of happiness to the fulfillment of that passion—N.B.

In those shadows last night, Napoleon resembled the man on his white charger as in David's painting. Amélie sat up in bed. She'd behaved the wanton coquette, but those sensations, the burning trail to her lowest region. She sighed with pleasure. He'd harbored the same desires. How far would they have gone if the count hadn't interrupted?

She dressed, pulled on clammy stockings and fastened her garters. Her feet jammed into shoes, she almost tripped over her father as she bustled out of her chamber.

"Amélie, I will have a word with you." He sounded perturbed, but she was too full of sensual emotion to dwell on her father's moods. "Where are you going in such a hurry?"

"For my walk. Excuse me, Papa. I really must meet His Majesty." She squeezed around him, avoiding his face.

"I'm thinking of returning to France."

She halted in her tracks, uncertain if she heard correctly. "Return to France... you are?"

"It's evident it would be best for you if we left Saint Helena as soon as it can be arranged."

"Best for me? No, I'm not leaving. You can go if you like, but I'm staying." She struggled for calmness in her confusion, gripping the doorknob of the hall door.

"*Ma fille*, when I leave you'll definitely come with me." Perrault spoke in a harsh timbre she'd never heard from him before. "I'm requesting that the emperor release both of us."

"*Mais non*, Napoleon will insist I stay." She sucked in her breath and turned to face him. The doorknob prodded into her spine. "What's the matter? Why are you so angry?"

"Amélie, you've been lying to me. The Count de Montholon informed me early this morning that he caught you and His Majesty alone, in the dark, in the emperor's study last night. His Majesty was in his dressing gown and your clothing was in disarray." His brow a mass of wrinkles, her father shook like a wind-battered gum tree.

Amélie gulped her fury. The count still plotted to be rid of her. "We were only talking. The count resents me. He'd say anything to pull me from the emperor's company." Perspiration gathered between her breasts, where Napoleon had kissed her so ardently. The scent of him still lingered. "Don't you see that the count is trying to manipulate you?"

"Aren't you trying to manipulate me? I'm not completely blind. I've seen the way you look at the emperor, and the way he looks at you. Do you want to end up... disgraced? Is that the future you have planned?" He choked out the words past his gaunt cheeks.

"Papa, everything can be explained." Amélie bit at her lip. Her defense was more lies. She'd hurt her father, but she had no choice. "Why can't you trust me rather than the count?" She turned from his castigating scowl. She didn't deserve his trust. "Please excuse me. His Majesty is waiting. I'm taking my walk now."

"I want to discuss it right this minute, Amélie. *C'est urgent.* Don't walk away from me!" Perrault shouted—something her dignified father never did.

Amélie opened the door and hurried into the courtyard. She had to warn Napoleon before her father carried out his threat. The emperor would keep her beside him, especially after last night. When she told him how much she loved him, he'd admit his own feelings.

Napoleon stood out front talking with two Chinese laborers. Her breath shivered up her throat. She sat on a bench not far from him. After nine o'clock, the mists had already cleared.

Napoleon finally noticed her and came over. "Aren't we having our walk? I'm fit to tackle it today."

"I need to speak to you first." Amélie grew bashful under his radiant smile. She knotted her fingers together, waiting for a special touch, a look.

Napoleon sat and gazed at her with a thoughtful expression. *"Eh bien,* I must apologize for Montholon's behavior last night, but I've soundly chastised him."

Amélie touched a finger to her bodice. What about their behavior? "Napoleon, I was just talking with my father. He says he wants me to leave Saint Helena with him. Of course I can't go, and I told him that."

Napoleon's smile dissolved. He stared at her with wary eyes. "Why does your father wish to leave?" he asked in a gentle voice.

"He believes that you and I…" Amélie gripped her fingers tighter and fumbled to verbalize their intensifying relationship. "The Count de Montholon told him we were intimate in your chamber last night."

Napoleon stood abruptly and strode a short distance away, hands clasped behind his back. He turned to face her, his manner rigid. "Amée…I know this will sound callous, but someday…" He cleared his throat, his knuckle pressing his upper lip. "The mature resolution…perhaps it is wiser for us both if you did leave Saint Helena."

"No, don't *say* that. I refuse to listen." Amélie's head swam, her heart like a fist, pummeling. "You have some misguided notion that you're being noble by denying you care for me." She fidgeted on the bench, certain he'd declare his devotion now. "We can make a life together. We just need to discuss how…how dear we are to one another."

"Amée, please. It's wrong for us, but especially for you. Of course your father is trying to protect you." Napoleon looked tormented, his eyes moist with emotion. "You are too young to understand…only a child."

"Please don't call me that, and don't send me away." She slid to the edge of the bench, snagging her dress, her fingers scraping the stone edge. She couldn't be this mistaken about his depth of feeling toward her. "You can't mean any of this, you're just—"

"Trust me, Amélie. Someday you'll understand this was far better for you." He didn't come any closer, already distancing himself. "You should go with your father. I must preserve my reputation for the empress. My devotion proves to her and Europe my worth."

Bile churned in her empty belly. The one thing she agonized over was happening, his outright rejection! She felt stripped bare and he offered no sanctuary. Napoleon desired to rid himself of her temptation, to preserve his pretense of fidelity to his Hapsburg wife!

"What a fool I am to think you'd lower yourself to love me. I see I'm worth nothing to you." Amélie lurched to her feet and willed herself to stagger away. He called after her, but she didn't look back.

She dared not return to her quarters. Her body raging with tension, she had to keep moving, somewhere, anywhere. Amélie hurried toward the front gate. Her eyes blurred with tears, she stumbled past the gate guard and strode down the dusty road.

She struggled for a normal breath, her feet scuffing up dust and pebbles, her world crashed in like a pile of stones on top of her. When she drew near to Hutt's Gate, she slowed, unsure what to do now.

A group of soldiers marched down the road from the other direction. Amélie tripped up onto the Bertrands' creaking veranda. The front door opened and a servant peered out at her.

"Have you come to see Madame?"

Amélie flushed, wiped tears from her cheeks, and stepped inside the foyer.

"Amélie, what an unexpected pleasure." Countess Bertrand came out and escorted her to the parlor. "We were just talking the other day about how much we'd like to hear you sing again, but...your eyes are so red."

"Only the wind." Amélie gave a quick smile, a painful crack. They sat together on one of the lumpy sofas. "I am sorry to intrude, Countess. I was taking a walk, and the soldiers were on the road."

"*C'est normal.* Aren't they everywhere, following us?" the woman groused.

"I needed to...get away from Longwood." Amélie tightened her muscles to stop shaking but her heart banged against her breastbone. Her stomach growled, with nausea or hunger, she wasn't sure.

"Is something else wrong, dear?" The countess then turned her head. She picked up a blue velvet-covered stick near the sofa, stood, and swiped it at the wall. "Ugh, one of those lizard creatures." She sat back down, cradling the stick decorated with gold-embroidered eagles, the ends closed in silver-gilt ferrules. "My husband's marshal's baton." She shrugged and caressed the velvet. "Here it's only useful to chase vermin. Forgive me." The woman stared closer. "You do look quite upset. I'll ring for coffee."

"I have...had a difficult morning, that's all." Amélie almost reached over to touch one of the gold eagles. "Nothing to be concerned about, Countess."

"Please, call me Fanny," she said as her plump maid brought in the coffee service. The countess poured a serving for each of them into delicate cups. "I apologize for my chipped porcelain. If I'd known how impossible it is to replace good dishware, I wouldn't have tossed several at Henri's head." Fanny picked up her cup. "I hear Albine de Montholon has requested to leave the island. Is that true?"

"Has she?" Amélie latched on to this surprising topic. Her rival wanted to leave Saint Helena just as Amélie was cast aside? "No, I didn't know." Now she'd never know what transpired in the court, but only the man at its center had mattered. "Cream and sugar, *merci*." Sipping the tasteless coffee, she barely steadied the fragile cup in her hand.

"It takes forever to obtain permission from the governor. Lowe demands total authority over who leaves, tortures us with bureaucratic garbage, then threatens to deport people, as if that were a punishment." The countess's brittle laugh cut like shards through the dreary chamber.

"Everything's a cruel game to the English, it seems..." Amélie fought fresh tears, turning briefly from the countess.

"Cipriani managed to escape, poor man. What a dreadful death. Now a funeral to attend."

"A savage death." Amélie swallowed. "That seemed unnatural."

"Lowe refused to allow the man to be buried at Longwood as Napoleon requested. The governor and his wife don't seem like bad people, but Napoleon's battling with him over every regulation has made Lowe contentious. The governor is high-strung and so inconsistent. One day he says the islanders can visit Napoleon, then the next he posts signs forbidding the inhabitants from communicating with us." Fanny tapped the baton on her knees. "*Ma foi*, it's nerve racking."

"His Majesty and the governor are too stubborn." Amélie coughed, her throat raw. Napoleon's denunciation echoed in her ears: *only a child,* and she'd just acted like a baby by running away from him.

"I begged the emperor to release us for a year. We need a break, the children should be in school, and I haven't felt at all well lately." The woman's shoulders slumped. Her features looked haggard, her blond hair limp as straw. "I've already endured Elba. It's unjust to be tormented here."

Amélie rattled her cup in its saucer. She'd hate to see the Bertrands desert Napoleon. "It's very hard on the emperor...knowing he can't leave, and the rest of us can." Could he leave? Her anger circled around her open wound, yet her compassion for him hadn't diminished. A slight whimper escaped, as neither had her love.

Fanny's gaze softened. She touched her hand lightly. "Amélie, I see you are upset. I want you to know if you ever need anyone to talk with. You have only your father here, and men are notoriously useless on certain...subjects."

The woman no doubt referred to the sordid rumors about Amélie and Napoleon. All of England was probably aware and debated the pros and cons in their Parliament. She gripped the sofa cushion. None of it mattered anymore. Her illusions had shriveled in the open air.

"I'll remember that, thank you, Madame." Amélie might need a confidant in the upper echelon—her last toehold in the court?—if she ever decided to confide, but the shred of strength she clutched in her fists might collapse if she revealed her shattered core.

* * * *

In Napoleon's bedroom, Marchand handed him his late morning coffee, steaming hot the way he liked it, but the liquid tasted like mud to his dissatisfied mouth. Napoleon had promised himself to let Amélie down gently, but instead he'd crushed her with a few words. Her face, her tortured face ripped him inside. Last night he'd given in to his desire, his need for her. Dare he admit it, his love? Love weakened men. He'd fallen prey to it with Josephine. He couldn't let this girl deter him from his plans. She would complicate everything. What if he had taken her? His body still felt the sensual pull. He sighed. Let her believe in his selfishness.

"This coffee tastes like swill. If you spent less time with your mistress, and more time tending me, you rascal, you might learn how to make a palatable brew." He teased the young man to dispel his anxiety.

Marchand smiled, always accepting his jibes with good humor, and took the cup he thrust out. "I will try to improve my cooking skills, Sire."

Napoleon sank back into his thoughts. He could do something for Amélie. A foolish action, he knew. He still held on to her by a thread. There had to be a kinder way to ease her departure from him. Napoleon clenched his hand on the chair arm and glared into the bedroom fireplace. "Marchand. Tell Chef Perrault I wish to speak with him."

* * * *

Amélie picked at her lunch, sitting at the splintered table in the kitchen. The table rocked on uneven legs, and she frequently stuffed wads of material or paper under the short leg, but they kept disappearing.

Her father entered when she was halfway through mashing the contents on her plate, and sat down across from her. They hadn't spoken since their morning's disagreement.

Amélie resisted meeting his gaze and watched a red spotted millipede crawl from the pantry toward the stove. She knew better than to disturb it because of the foul odor it would emit. Some things were better left undisturbed.

"Aren't you hungry?" Perrault asked in a low voice.

"Not really." She pushed the plate of mackerel aside. The fish tasted like damp grass that gurgled inside her, her bowels twisted in knots. "I apologize for my behavior earlier."

"You've been crying?" he asked. Her attempt to sooth her red eyes with cold compresses was obviously a failure.

"I'm all right, don't worry." She'd spent most of the time since returning from Hutt's Gate soaking tears into her pillow, trying to breathe with a piece of her hacked out and missing. Now she slumped in her chair, exhausted with misery and swollen with resentment.

"You have grown into a lovely woman, as much as I'm reluctant to admit it." Perrault tapped a finger on the table and sighed. "You've been one all along."

Amélie stared over at him. How severely he'd aged since they'd come to St Helena. The lines around his mouth and brow were deep gouges; his cheeks sagged under pouched eyes. A normally bronze complexion had turned sallow.

"Not as womanly as I might wish." She chewed on the tip of her thumbnail. She'd failed as a courtesan. "Do you need me to iron anything for you to wear to Cipriani's burial?"

Her father studied her, leaning back in the chair. "The emperor called me into his study an hour ago. He asked, no, he implored me to stay. He said he couldn't do without my services. His Majesty insisted we both stay."

Her heart skipped a beat, and she hated that it still cared. "You told him?"

"I asked him if this was at your behest. He assured me it was his personal wish. I'm weary of battling with you. I'm not a man who welcomes hostility. His Majesty swore that the Count de Montholon acted out of spite, as well as his wife. *Alors*, I consented to stay for the time-being." Perrault's face sagged in uneasy defeat and she almost pitied him. "What I said before…about you being from a decent family and what I expect. I hope you understand?"

"Yes, Papa, I do." Her voice sounded stagnant. She felt dazed by this turn of events, incapable of a coherent thought.

"I realize things would be simpler if your mother were alive. I do insist you spend no more time alone with His Majesty." He reached over and squeezed her arm. "That is very important."

This was his second mention of her mother in just a few days, after being so silent on that subject. Amélie rubbed her temples. "You don't need to be concerned about that."

Perrault stood, eyeing her carefully. "If you ever need to discuss things, as I said before, I want you to…feel you can come to me."

Amélie nodded, anxious to end both their discomforts. "I will, thank you." Though he no longer had reason to worry. She would remain celibate, untouched, virginal, perhaps join a convent. Maybe God would be easier to understand.

"I'm going to rest in my room for a moment before the funeral. I've felt a little tired lately. As everyone says, it's probably the weather." He dragged out the door, leaving her to her brooding.

Amélie pressed her hands to her head. She'd tried to blot out her conversation with Napoleon—too much anguish. She had to face the cruel revelation of not possessing enough appeal to secure her position. Now she was totally baffled. What bizarre game did the emperor play and neglect to inform her of the rules?

Her eyes misted again and she wiped them with her handkerchief. The same handkerchief Napoleon gave her months ago. She wadded it up and stuffed the cloth under the table's short leg. She refused to be manipulated by his whims. How stupid to preach of strong women, then prostrate herself before a man.

Chapter Twenty-One

Death is nothing; but to live defeated and without glory is to die every day—N.B.

Out of a restless slumber, Amélie awoke with a jerk midway through the night. A cold sweat soaked her and she wheezed for air, her hands clutching the sheets. A strange, brooding dream swam in her memory. In the suffocating dark room she tried to recall the details.

She'd stood again at Cipriani's funeral—a funeral the emperor hadn't attended because he refused to show himself anywhere near Lowe or his minions. Alone under a murky sky, utterly abandoned, she'd leaned forward over the burial mound. Instead of the pathetic wooden cross, a headstone loomed and she squinted to read the blurry inscription. Her father wept across from her. The only time she'd seen him weep was when her mother died. Now she stared at the stone and distinctly read the name.

That triggered her leap back to consciousness. The dream was an alarming mixture of her mother's funeral and what took place yesterday for Cipriani.

"Your mother is very ill. We mustn't stay too long. It will only tire her," her father had said before her mother's death. "You understand we have to be brave, Amélie."

Amélie recalled that fearful girl, hovering in the bedchamber doorway of their humble Parisian cottage. She'd watched the figure on the rumpled sheets toss her once graceful head and moan with inhuman shrillness. With so little time, she needed to stay beside her.

I was brave, Papa. She relived the horror of her family's bedside vigil as Madame Perrault gasped her last. Her adored mother would never again spend cherished moments with her. The day before she fell ill, her mother held Amélie's face in a tight grip and told her to grow to be a strong woman and *never* let her heart weaken her.

"I did let my heart weaken me, *Maman*." Amélie sobbed in her own bleak room.

She lay stiff in the sheets until the cannon fired for sunrise, rattling her high narrow window. A heavy rain beat down. She crawled from her bed and lit a candle. She pulled her mother's miniature from her dresser drawer and ran a finger over what existed no more. A tear dropped on her mother's face, distorting it. "Fate has decided otherwise, Napoleon says, but fate can be a hard taskmaster."

* * * *

Rain made a good excuse to stay inside. Napoleon stared out the hole in his study shutters. The deluge soaked the red earth. The dampness ached in his bones. Two people dear to him snatched away. One by a curious death; he should have demanded an autopsy. The other by his own hand. Yet he clung to Amée, asking Perrault to remain. Clung to her from a distance—safer that way. He still had control over her. He would devise a wiser plan.

Napoleon plodded into his bedroom, jerked aside the taffeta curtains, and stretched out on his camp bed. This bed once stood on the field of Austerlitz, his greatest victory, when he thought he gripped the world. He fisted his empty hand. He must put his mind to this new skirmish, battle weary though he was. Always a war to reclaim his life. Captain O'Sullivan, his Uncle Fesch, they both promised results. Still, Cipriani's death hampered so many intricacies they'd set up on the island, almost as if he was purposely swept out of the way. Dare he ponder again if the man was murdered? Did the English suspect his plot?

Napoleon laid a hand on his chest. His heart felt dead, barely beating. Most of his life he'd filed his thoughts in little compartments in his brain. Then he could open a drawer and only concentrate on what was there. Amée had seeped into so many of these boxes. He couldn't lose himself in her pervasive, naïve love, after years of perfecting a cold cynicism where women were concerned. Without her, though, he felt a deep loneliness as if he stood up to his throat in mire and no one would care if he were sucked under.

* * * *

"His Majesty still won't dress or shave," Saint-Denis said after ten days passed with Napoleon never leaving his quarters. The valet sipped his coffee in the kitchen. "Our emperor is unpredictable, restless one moment, then he sits for hours staring at nothing. I told him a hilarious story about a drunken soldier falling into a camp cesspit, and he didn't even smile."

"Here, give His Majesty some Saint-John's-wort tonic. It helps sadness." Amélie pulled down a bottle from the cupboard—she'd sipped the concoction herself—avoiding the valet's probing gaze. She struggled not to care, determined to never fall under Napoleon's spell again. The fact he'd asked them to stay only added to her confusion, her torment over a man who denied his feelings about so many things. "Don't tell the emperor what it's for...and insist that Doctor O'Meara visit him."

"There's Captain Blakeney sneaking around the house." Madame Cloubert stirred the last of the sugar into her coffee and stared out the window. "He'll choke if he doesn't get a glimpse of the emperor soon. This new orderly officer is such a drunk, he makes my flesh crawl." Her glare darted to Amélie who now busied herself at the table making a leek tart. "No more walks with His Majesty anymore, Amélie?" The woman nudged her.

"My reasons are private and I haven't the time." Amélie lined the tart pan with dough. Active work with her hands kept her mind from dripping down into sorrow, that nagging sense of betrayal.

"The orderly officer walks a thin line. Poppleton became too friendly with His Majesty. Lowe couldn't abide that." Saint-Denis threw up his hands in exaggerated affront. "The emperor gave him a snuffbox with the imperial monogram when he left, to show his esteem, and Poppleton had to sneak it off the island. Lowe will be up any day, shouting orders, demanding Blakeney arrange some way to spot His Majesty, even if he has to tunnel under the house."

"*Peste,* Blakeney insists on rummaging through our laundry, as if we'd smuggle correspondence there. He loves to handle the women's underthings, and no one can tell me different." Madame Cloubert patted down her bodice as if fearing an immediate invasion.

Saint-Denis laughed. "He does seem to take pleasure in that, the filthy rogue."

Amélie beat two eggs in a bowl until they foamed.

"Amélie, why haven't you tried to bring His Majesty back to the living?" Ali crossed his long arms, smirking at her. "Certain people in the house relish this change of situation. Why *don't* you encourage the emperor to come out and take walks with you? What happened to cause this falling out?"

"*Monsieur* Saint-Denis, you valets should encourage our emperor to exercise again, but please keep your prying to yourself." Amélie's pain went far deeper for the Montholons' sneers to matter. She spooned leeks sautéed in butter into the tart pan, working in tense precision. Adding milk, salt, pepper, and nutmeg to the egg mixture, she poured this sauce over the leeks, then shoved the pan into the oven. "I'm certain His Majesty is still despondent over his good friend Cipriani's death."

"The English forced us to suffer through that loud-mouthed island chaplain, instead of providing us with a priest for our funerals. There's no one to hear our confessions." Madame Cloubert stroked her pointed chin. "My husband could do with some spiritual guidance."

Amélie pitied any priest who'd have to bear this woman's indiscretions, and had no doubt of her husband's need. Squeezing past Madame and Ali, and their stares, she went out to her herb garden. She kneeled on the ground and idly picked at weeds, glancing at the back of Longwood as she watched a caterpillar crawl toward her plants. She'd forgotten to sprinkle berries about the garden to attract the birds that would eat these worms and other insects.

Captain Blakeney slunk around the walls of the house, trying to peer into the windows of the Imperial bedroom and study—a frustrated soldier anxious to appear vigilant in a distasteful assignment.

Amélie's empathy stayed with Napoleon, a man who couldn't even sneeze without someone writing it down. Even with his rebuff, she had the persistent ache inside that she was the one person who stood between her emperor and disaster.

* * * *

"Countess, thank you for inviting me in." Amélie sat again in the Hutt's Gate parlor. Two weeks had passed with the recluse refusing to see anyone but his valets. If this woman's offer of friendship was genuine—she was probably desperate for any society—Amélie needed advice. "His Majesty won't even see his doctor. The valets say he won't leave his bed. I'm so worried about him."

"He's very moody, our emperor." Fanny raked her fingers through her limp hair. "He gets worse as time goes by, but who wouldn't here? My husband and the Montholons have tried to coax him out. Surely you can get in to see him."

"To be honest, I haven't tried. We had a...difference of opinion, shortly before he went into seclusion." She sighed past the lump in her throat. Fanny emphasized the *you*, thinking Amélie a special being in the eyes of the emperor when this wasn't true.

"Oh, that's the problem." Fanny narrowed her dark eyes. Then her features softened, though still measuring her. "Do you care to talk about it?"

"No, you're mistaken, Madame. I'm not the cause of this." How could she be when she meant nothing to him? She grimaced as if a knife scraped along her stomach lining. "Our difference of opinion went to his satisfaction. He's probably still disturbed over Cipriani's death."

"*Peut-etre*. He did request an autopsy of the man, and the body couldn't be found. That was so odd. Did Napoleon think there was foul play?"

Amélie wished she could share his sorrow, but must stay away from him. "I don't know. Cipriani died so suddenly. Now His Majesty might be ill—"

"Amélie, may I be candid with you? There's something else, isn't there?" Fanny patted her hand, her smile indulgent. "I mean, between you and Napoleon."

"Not anymore." Amélie hunched her shoulders, glanced around the room, and swallowed. "Rather, not what everyone seems to believe…to the *extent* everyone believes."

"Calm yourself, please. You can tell me in strictest confidence, I promise." Fanny rose and poured them both a glass of wine from the chipped crystal decanter on her sideboard. "Are you, by any chance, in love with him?"

Amélie quivered with emotion at the blunt question. "Things are so awful, for both Napoleon and me, and there's nothing I can do." She met the countess's eyes, her warm gaze inviting honesty. "Yes, I love him, but it's over. We were never…that intimate, even if the world says the opposite. He's made it plain he has no deep feelings for me."

"I believe he cares quite sincerely for you, and for Napoleon, that's saying a lot."

"Not enough to abandon his ties with Marie Louise. That would mean giving up his idea of being emperor." Amélie took a sip of wine to wash down the bitter words.

"You're right. He would want to preserve that connection, but maybe just for his son." The countess sat beside her again on the sofa. "Such concerns never stopped his other affairs."

"I was never an affair." Amélie flushed, feeling suddenly inadequate as a woman. Again, her ignorance on sexual matters rankled her.

"No, maybe that's his dilemma. Napoleon might care too much for you." Fanny's eyes widened as if amazed by her own statement.

"He cares nothing for me. I just wish he'd come out of his seclusion." Amélie's tears gathered damp behind her eyes.

"I know he harbors dreams of someday returning to power. We all hoped we wouldn't be here long." Fanny groaned. "Napoleon likes to think the Emperor Francis, being his father-in-law, will come to his rescue. Those are remote possibilities. He's delusional. He can't fathom his own wife's family would betray him."

"The other monarchs only feigned friendship to keep His Majesty from overpowering them." Amélie rambled out words to shore up her fragile composure. "Marie Louise only pretended to be the adoring wife while he was in power."

"Marie Louise was a haughty, self-indulgent person." Fanny took a sip of wine. "She seemed jealous of Napoleon's attentions to their own child. I never cared for her."

Hortense Bertrand ran into the room with Montholon's son, Tristan. "*Maman*, can we have more lemonade and cookies for my tea party? Tristan took bites out of all my cookies, spilled my drinks, and I hate it."

"Of course, go and ask cook. I have company, *ma petite*, go on." Fanny stood and caressed Hortense on the head, her smile tired. The children scampered out. "The Emperor Francis had no intention of letting his daughter disappear into exile, even if she'd wanted to go, and I think at first she did. I'm afraid our emperor doesn't realize how happy the European monarchs are to have him tied to this rock, far away from them. He can no longer threaten their countries, or their very thrones."

"It's a hopeless situation, unless…" Amélie choked down the word "escape." Impossible! She blinked back tears and took a generous sip of wine. "His own ambition has made it so."

"Then you see him for what he is. At least I hope you do." Fanny half finished her drink. "How old are you, Amélie…nineteen?"

"I'm twenty. I know I have my whole life ahead of me." Amélie rubbed her throat, touching the hollow where his lips…"I'm thinking of becoming a nun."

"Don't be that drastic. How about returning to Europe to study singing? You do have a talent." Fanny emptied her glass.

"*He* nurtured my singing. I should start fresh. Maybe in Paris there's a Napoleonic mistresses' society I can commiserate with. As long as the Countess de Montholon isn't a member." Amélie forced a sharp laugh, then finished her own glass. "That doesn't sound very fresh, does it? I don't even officially belong in that group."

"Don't get me started on the dissolute Albine. Then it's true, she was his mistress?" Fanny poured Amélie more wine.

"Perhaps she still is. Not that it matters to me, anymore." Amélie bristled at the idea of Albine warming his bed. She drank her wine. The alcohol blurred the razor sharp edges of her pain. "Did Napoleon never worry over *that* liaison getting back to his cheating wife? A man who can't be faithful shouldn't expect fidelity from anyone else. One woman was never enough."

Fanny refilled her own glass and took a gulp. "Napoleon did everything his way, and all who challenged him paid for it. He cared nothing for anyone else's rights if they interfered with his own desires, and that included his wives."

"I'm certain he loved *only* Josephine in the beginning. Until she betrayed him." Amélie half drained her second glass, trying to give Napoleon a trace of redemption. The wine bubbled around in her stomach.

"He's a man who ruined any chances for lasting happiness to fulfill his ambition. I'm afraid power was his only love, and now that's been taken away." Fanny sat once more and ran a fingernail over the rim of her wineglass. "I just want you to understand this, unkind as it sounds."

"I'm…still glad your husband is devoted to the emperor. He needs friends." Amélie finished her wine and wished she no longer cared.

"Henri is too devoted. I only came here to stay with my husband, and keep my family together." Fanny sighed, swirling the wine in her glass. "Once I believed His Majesty to be an inspired leader, a gifted administrator. Until his own ego got in the way."

"I see your point, Madame. I'm also a little drunk. It does loosen the tongue." She set her wine glass aside. "I'll always love him. I can't turn off my feelings, even if he can."

"You'll find an appropriate beau." Fanny pressed her shoulder. "You're fortunate to get out unscathed, dear. Our emperor has illegitimate children all over Europe."

"I refuse to be a casual amusement for anyone." Amélie hugged her arms around herself. "There's no place for me in his scheme of things. I'll return to the background and stay out of his way, until I decide what I want to do."

The house vibrated with the rumble of hoofbeats. The two women rose and walked out onto the front veranda. Governor Lowe and several men galloped toward Flagstaff Hill—a slim peak with a ruined watchtower atop—in a swirl of dust.

Count Bertrand, standing near the road, hurried up to join them, his expression vexed. "The governor heard about a revolution in South America, a place called Pernambuco, and a fleet coming from the United States, all contrived to free our emperor from the English."

"Is it true, or a silly rumor?" Fanny's jaded eyes brightened.

"I have severe doubts, but Lowe is setting up more batteries and fortifications, and they're doubling the sentries at Longwood." Bertrand shrugged his shoulders. "More problems for us all when His Majesty hears." The count entered the house, closing the door softly.

Fanny turned to Amélie, her mouth drooping. "Napoleon should come out of seclusion just to fight these absurdities." She gripped her shoulder again. "For you, avoiding him is probably wise. Do you think you'll return to Europe?"

Amélie watched the riders' fading dust. Saint Helena under siege. Were these the rescuers Napoleon awaited, involving the Sandy Bay note? "I'm not ready to leave yet." She wasn't ready to let go of this island or Napoleon.

Chapter Twenty-Two

...When, scanning the future, [a man] sees nothing but dreadful monotony...then, in my opinion, he is the most wretched—N.B.

Napoleon left his bath and ordered Marchand to bring him his clothes to dress. "Today I will stroll in the front garden to see what the English have done to improve the grounds." He made it sound as important as reviewing his troops before battle. He'd languished long enough and must keep himself fit for the coming event. Marchand and Ali had suffered from the orderly officer's complaints. Napoleon put on the wide planter's hat and strutted out to the front of the house.

Four orange trees were planted on the patch outside his bedroom window. Their flowers perfumed the spring September air. Immortelles of red, golden, and violet, the seeds sent by Lady Holland, lined the wall. The Chinese constructed a high turf wall along the eastern side to shield the garden from the trade winds. Napoleon would be shielded from the sentries' prying eyes. He smiled. Let Lowe think him resigned to this exile. By next winter, summer here, he'd no longer be on Saint Helena.

Napoleon walked toward the wall and stared at the mountain that loomed at the sea cliffs called the Barn. Many thought it bore an eerie resemblance to his profile wearing his cocked hat. An image frozen in place, staring out to sea. King Odysseus—as Amée liked reading about—tormenting himself with sighs and heartache, gazing out across a barren sea with streaming eyes, desperate for deliverance from this island, her Calypso.

Napoleon stiffened his shoulders. The girl's startled fawn's eyes haunted his dreams.

* * * *

Amélie filled with relief to see Napoleon on the front grounds. She hurried back to her own little garden. She knelt and stroked her plants. Part of her wished she had given herself to him in that weak moment of abandon—to know him better as a man. Then how much sharper his rejection.

The charm of a female, the one influence she held over men? She'd acted as sleazy as the countess yet floundered in her desires. Women needed education, to decide their future from a position of strength.

The velvety rosemary leaves, the sensuousness of her own body when he'd caressed her. She blew out her breath. She'd started to scribble more notes on intimacy, the importance of women's awareness before marriage—or affairs—of sexual matters. Before she chased down whores in Jamestown, perhaps Countess Bertrand could impart these details. This sounded more exciting than pious decay in a convent, something she'd no serious intention of doing in the first place.

Amélie pinched away the flowers on her newly planted basil to make the plants leafier. She set chervil roots aside for boiling, to use in salad.

"Amélie, His Majesty has finally cast you off as I warned, hasn't he?" Clarice plodded up and hovered over her, balancing her laundry basket against her knee. "No woman holds his attention for long. Now you know how *I* feel since Marchand avoids me." Her nasty tone slipped to regret, but only for an instant. "When will we see your protruding belly like the Countess de Montholon's in the past?" Clarice bent down to stare at her abdomen as if expecting something to sprout at any moment.

"Jealous? I'll make certain to send you an announcement." Amélie dug her fingers into the dirt and ripped at weeds, her sorrow at the truth of her castoff sharp. "With all your important duties, how *do* you find time to worry about me? I'm so flattered."

"I'll give you some of my duties. Now you have the time." Clarice snickered.

"Ooooops!" Amélie jerked a Double Gee and splattered dirt into Clarice's basket. "I'm so sorry."

"*Merde!* How dare you!" Clarice swung the basket around, her fat cheeks wobbling. Then she huffed and sauntered away, undulating her bulging hips in her shabby Greek-style chemise. "Welcome back to the wasteland, Miss Opera Diva." Her spiteful laughter echoed through the courtyard.

Amélie pushed damp curls from her forehead and touched the blue-green rue she'd planted to repel caterpillars from her plants. She'd have to devise a potion for Clarice, since this smelly herb was also supposed to repel witches.

Amélie wiped her hands on a cloth and went into the kitchen to hang nettles from the rafters to keep away flies. She forced herself to hum a tune as she worked. The chair she stood on wiggled and she gasped and turned around. "Oh. What do you want?"

Jules's square face sneered up at her, his shins bumping the edge of the seat. "Can your father prepare the Countess de Montholon something mild for supper tonight?" He plucked at her soiled apron. "She's feeling ill. Probably caught His Majesty's cold after their *tête à tête* last night." He snorted. "You, Amélie, finally committed the foul deed of becoming too familiar, didn't you? Too stupid with hero worship to see that a girl can't improve her status. Only a clever man can."

"Don't ever touch me." Amélie swiped his hand aside and rattled down off the chair. "I'll give my father your request, now leave." She rinsed her hands in a bucket. From the pantry, she took out a bottle of olive oil, poured some in her palm, and rubbed the oil into her skin. Albine, sharing sensual kisses with Napoleon.

"Are you still going to ignore me, now that you're in disfavor with the emperor?" Jules moved close, smelling of sweaty linen, his squat nose in the air like a sniffing rat.

She cringed with the creepy feeling he gave her, like ants crawled up her back.

"I'm sure you have people to bother elsewhere." Amélie walked around him, continuing to massage her hands, the skin turning supple.

Jules stuck out his arm, stopping her. "Don't be so aloof. One man is the same as another, *non*? Show me what you learned in the imperial bed."

"You're the last man I'd show." Amélie pinched his arm, leaving oily fingerprints on his sleeve, and he yelped. "Get out of here. I've already told His Majesty about your disloyal comments and strange actions."

"I suggest you keep your tales to yourself." Jules snarled and strode to the kitchen door, rubbing his arm. "My master is quite pleased now that you're out of the way. The court is much better without your interference. You only hindered everyone's position." He pointed at her. "If you change your mind, feel lonely and in need of a man, I'll be around."

Amélie shivered when he slammed the door. His eyes blazed with fury at her mention of his actions. The emperor had too many ominous influences surrounding him, and now she wasn't there to shield him. She must stay near Napoleon to keep an eye on events.

* * * *

"His Majesty must feel better to entertain tonight." Amélie scrubbed her brush over the turnips that would replace the rotten potato shipment. Turnips and cabbage didn't mind the harsh soil of Saint Helena. Ali, her father, and Chef Gascon also crowded out the kitchen.

"An admiral and his wife, and an American diplomat His Majesty hopes to find favor with." Ali pressed an iron over Napoleon's uniform jacket. "The governor unbent to allow them to come to Longwood."

"Does the American have anything to do with the attempted rescue the governor is worried about?" To her selfish relief, no North or South Americans had stormed the island to rescue Napoleon. Another week had passed and she and the emperor managed to avoid one another. Without her company he took minimal exercise. She missed their vibrant talks and morning strolls.

"I have no idea." Ali shrugged.

"It has been far too long since I took the trouble to create my sugar spun palace for dessert." Gascon, his droopy eyes a little brighter, cut butter into a cup of sugar.

"We should always take the trouble for His Majesty." Perrault boiled beef in a huge pot bubbling on the stove. He slid a small fowl into the water. He prepared his rump steak *à la Napoléon Ier*. The fowl would be garnished with rice "alla Milanese," the rump steak with the mashed turnips seasoned in thyme.

Fragrant smells filled the air. Constantly involved in food, she ate little herself. Not much could squeeze past the granite lump in her throat or her stomach's clenched muscles. Her clothes felt loose, swallowing her up.

"I will leave that to simmer." Perrault stepped out with a slow nod to his daughter as the people shifted around. Her father hadn't said a word about her distance from their emperor and his lethargic manner worried her.

"We do need a diversion. It's been far too quiet around here." Saint-Denis held up the green jacket with scarlet cuffs and collar, inspecting it. "Too bad you won't be singing for them." His sooty gaze looked half challenging, half sympathetic.

"I have no interest in singing. The notes became…too complicated to interpret." Amélie dropped the turnips into another pot of boiling water. She glanced at the jacket as Ali pinned on the iron crown and graduations of the Legion of Honor. She bit at her lip and turned away.

Life at court moved on without her, yet she must have meant more to Napoleon than merely a distraction to pass the time. He'd interceded with her father, as if he still wanted to hold on to her, but for what purpose?

* * * *

At sunset Amélie strolled alone out in the recultivated front garden. She hadn't spent an evening outdoors in over three weeks. Maybe the warming air would soothe her fractured mind.

A flock of white terns with black-ringed eyes flapped overhead. They squabbled in their strange grunts. Their mass of wings beat the air, forked tails fluttering. The birds soared and dipped, and faded into the mist around Diana's Peak.

She sat on a bench near the garden's center. Laughter drifted from inside the house—the emperor busy with his guests. Despite her wish to be his protector, she mused about returning to Paris, blurring her sorrows in the bustle of civilization. Could she continue her interest in herbs and sexual enlightenment, while pursuing a career in opera, and dismiss the man who instigated it? That had been the entire allure. Who would pay for her lessons, the one man she should forget?

Amélie closed her eyes and imagined herself at the opulent Paris Opéra, singing her lungs out. She basked in the satisfying roar of applause, long-stemmed roses thrown at her feet...and *he* would be there (how, she didn't know) jealous of the attention paid to her...

Someone came up beside the bench and she startled from her reverie.

"Good evening, Amélie." Marchand smiled down at her.

"Louis. How are you this evening?" Amélie forced a smile and pulled her shawl around her shoulders, now feeling a thief in the emperor's garden.

"Well enough. With the emperor's dinner party tonight, it reminded me of when you used to sing for guests. It has been a long time." He rocked back and forth on his feet as he stood there.

The shadows stretched along the ground, swallowing up their world in darkness. In the cool night's air she smelled freshly turned over earth and the pungent scent of new plantings. "I don't know if I'll sing anymore."

"Why? Your voice is so pretty."

She looked up at his face shrouded in shadow. Why was he here? Had the emperor demanded he court her? *Marchand, grand Dieu, relieve me of this nuisance of a girl...*She almost burst into caustic laughter, but instead replied tonelessly, "merci."

"Amélie, often certain men don't always know what's best for them. It might be their nature to react in a way...in conflict with their true feelings."

His hesitant spiel made her squirm, though she foolishly wanted to hear it. "Yes, many people do that. How very sad."

Voices drifted closer to Longwood's front door and the valet sighed.

"The party must be breaking up. I'll be needed. If you'll excuse me." Marchand touched her shoulder, turned, and headed back to the house.

Amélie sighed as well and forced her thoughts to another subject: her mother. That dark-haired, dark-eyed beauty her father had married so young. Madame Perrault had been a spirited woman, always accessible and sweet. How Amélie missed her. She yearned for her female wisdom at this moment. She'd have to wait months for a reply from Theo to her letter, speculating on the nature of her death.

People exited the house. She stood and hastened toward the perimeter of the yard, sliding into the shadows to remain unseen. The emperor walked out with a medium-tall man in British naval uniform. They were engaged in a lively conversation judging by their voices. Another man and two women followed behind.

Nothing changed for Napoleon. He'd vanquished her and marched on like a true soldier. Amélie clenched her hands, determined to stay strong, vigilant.

As the voices faded out the gate, she went back to the bench and resumed her thoughts about her mother. If her mother were here to speak to, she'd have soothed, but perhaps advised her that she'd fallen in over her head. From the beginning Amélie swam out of her depth. The great Napoleon would never stoop to love a servant. Hadn't she gotten out unscathed, as Fanny Bertrand said? Pushed out might be more apt, but safe just the same. She should feel proud of her resilience.

At a noise to her right, Amélie tensed, sitting perfectly still. Total darkness now engulfed the landscape. The night patrol couldn't be starting yet. Napoleon had managed to compel Lowe to rescind that order, sending the troops swarming around the house back to nine o'clock.

She'd assumed the emperor and his guests had strolled on to Hutt's Gate, but she detected a presence and a chill crept down her spine. "Is...anyone there?"

"Marchand told me you were out here."

Amélie gripped the edge of the bench until the stone hurt her flesh. "I'm...enjoying the fresh night air, Sire." She prayed her voice held steady. "I didn't think anyone would mind."

"*Bien sûr*, you may go anywhere you like." Napoleon's voice soft, he sat beside her.

She didn't move, nor look in his direction, though all she saw were vague outlines.

The wind whistled around the wall, pulling at her hair tendrils.

"I know you're very upset, and have a right to be, but I'm looking out for your best interests by agreeing on your return to Europe. Regardless of what...ahhh." He took a slow, deep breath. "You're aware I intervened with your father, as you first requested?"

"Yes, Sire, but why? I don't understand." His presence, his voice so near, fluttered her senses. She fought the reaction.

"Amée, someday you'll leave this place and make a life for yourself in the real world. An honorable life, one you and your family can be proud of. Within the mores of society, as it should be. If you just stop and consider and see the inevitable outcome."

"No, I do see. I'm not that naïve." She cared nothing for future predictions, only the here and now had mattered. She bunched her shawl around her neck. "Trouble no more, Sire. I will find my own way." For a dazed moment she wanted to prove their connection. "As far as my honor, everyone believes the worst of me, with you, already."

"Servants? Courtiers? They all know full well it's lies, as I've told them more than once." Napoleon groaned. "I owe it to you to be honest. I have feelings for you I shouldn't have—that I've no right to have. The kindest thing I can do is let you go." He reached over and clasped her hand.

The raw emotion in his voice confused her further. He'd founder to the dregs of sorrow before relinquishing his feeble ties with his empress.

"Don't you mean it might be the kindest thing for you?" A mosquito landed on her elbow and she allowed it to nip her flesh. Her hand trembled in his. Nerves shot like pinpricks up her arm and across her chest.

"I'm far too old for you. My time for such things is past." Napoleon sounded desolate. He ran his thumb over her knuckles. "You must consider your future, and soon. It may seem harsh now, but I'd like to offer again to send you to Europe, to any study you prefer…or a respectable marriage."

Amélie eased back her hand, her courage wavering. Wasn't his despair another act to suit his purpose? "I would like to decide my own future, Sire." Her pulse vibrated behind her eyes. "You may preserve your integrity. Just be aware of those in your court who don't serve you well, and remember the one who did. I hope you still do not drink that wine." Her voice thickened. "Good night, Your Majesty." She stood and hurried into the darkness—her eyes fogged with tears—scratching at the bite.

Amélie rushed into her quarters, drying her damp cheeks on her arm. Lighting a candle, she pulled more paper scraps from her drawer. Adding to her notes, she tried to conjure up the concise words to describe that warm, saturated feeling that made you throb inside, and explain the power of kisses that weakened resolve. She had to swallow her embarrassment and ask Fanny Bertrand for details of the ultimate act.

At a flapping noise, she looked up. A moth batted itself against the wall where the candlelight crept along, then flitted around the flickering taper. When first on the island she'd vowed to soar as high as a butterfly. A pity the moth she believed herself to be had singed its wings on the imperial flame.

Chapter Twenty-Three

It is literally true that you can succeed best and quickest by helping others to succeed—N.B.

Napoleon Bertrand, his grand marshal's eldest at nine, recited his multiplication tables earnestly in the salon. Napoleon enjoyed the honest innocence of children, their enthusiasm, such eagerness to please. He smiled at his namesake. How old would his son be now? He dashed that thought away before it pierced him. He'd suffered enough with the public humiliation of his wife cuckolding him in Italy.

Where was that letter of confirmation of the actions put in motion by his Uncle Fesch?

"Sire, I'm finished. I knew them all."

"Indeed you did, and I have a present for you." Napoleon fished a gold watch out of his waistcoat pocket. The boy rushed forward, his grin stretching out his cheeks, to receive the gift. Napoleon pinched his namesake on the tip of his nose.

Fanny Bertrand smiled proudly. Albine fought a grimace since her son, Tristan, stumbled over his figures. Bertrand and Montholon looked on impassively near the open windows where an early October breeze stirred the muslin curtains.

Amélie's lilting voice once filled this chamber. How strange she still occupied his heart.

Napoleon rubbed his face and bent down to Montholon's son. "Tristan, have you been studying your lessons? You must work hard every day. You do eat every day, don't you? One mustn't eat if one doesn't work."

"Yes, Sire," the six-year-old replied, his eyes bright. "I will work hard every day."

"Albine, has our illustrious governor granted your permission to return to Europe?" Napoleon's sharp question made her simper. He wouldn't miss her, but disliked being deserted.

"I have decided not to go, Sire. Now that, uh, matters have changed, I don't mind staying." Albine's coquettish air seemed more contrived than usual. Her nurse stood by, the infant Helene-Napoleone in her arms, but Albine rarely looked in the baby's direction.

Napoleon deflected his irritation over changing matters by taking little Helene into his arms. He tickled her and made funny faces and the baby gurgled in delight.

"What a darling little girl." Fanny glanced at the child, then at Napoleon. "Who do you think she resembles, Albine? You…or her father?"

"Fanny, impertinence ill becomes a lady." Napoleon shot her a warning glare, putting sarcasm into the last word. She needed to be knocked down several pegs. Her zeal for scandal shone in her eyes.

"I don't know what you insinuate, Fanny. Some women just have the advantage of being 'admired' by numerous men." Albine thrust out her ample bosom and smirked. Her figure, ruined from her recent pregnancy, burst like dough from her silk dress.

"Admiration is your 'earned' right, my dear." Montholon masked any feelings behind his courtier's lassitude.

Napoleon pushed down his disgust at this comedy.

"I want a gift like my brother." Hortense Bertrand skipped up and made a pretty pout.

"Aren't you dressed rather badly today, little Hortense?" Napoleon inspected her ugly yellow dress made of shabby material. He handed Helene back to her nurse, who offered the child to her mother, but Albine waved her away like spoiled cheese.

"Your Majesty, the dress was bought in Jamestown, where we haven't many choices," Bertrand replied in apology, his neck red under his collar, as his daughter pouted again.

In their colonial backwater, his courtier's blue tunics were faded, the gold braid shabby, unraveling, the color like unpolished brass. The women's silks looked stained and threadbare in places.

"I can solve that. Marchand, bring me my Consulate coat, quickly." At Napoleon's request, the valet rushed to do his bidding. A devoted young man, maybe Napoleon could still persuade Amélie to marry him. Then he cringed at the idea of her in another man's arms—more weakness he must ignore.

Napoleon held up the striking red coat with gold silk lining the valet handed him. He ran his fingers along the velvet. "Now, Hortense, you can have a pretty jacket made from this. It was given to me in 1800 when I was First Consul. I signed the Concordant in this coat. Come here." Hortense ran over and he draped the item across her shoulders. Her little face lit up. He had the growing need to unburden himself of material things.

Napoleon walked to the salon's front door and peered out the holes in the shutters. Near the steps a footman wielded an ax, breaking apart a bed frame while the sentries stared from the gate. The chopping noise grated in his head. He hated resorting to such tactics.

Albine flounced up beside him, her perfume overwhelming. "Do you think this activity will embarrass the governor enough, Your Majesty?" She stroked the air near his shoulder with her talons, her smile too saccharine.

"Lowe knows I hate the smell of coal for my fires, but refuses to send up any wood. When news of this reaches him, his prickly personality won't allow the soldiers to think I'm so deprived I have to burn my furniture." Napoleon stepped back to his dreary courtiers. "The weather is warmer, however. Amée insists I open my windows for fresh air."

At his spontaneous saying of her name, both Montholons wrinkled their noses. Napoleon's innards groaned. He pressed on his stomach, his digestion terrible.

"Speaking of Amélie, I hope we'll be having another opera recital soon. We could use the entertainment," Fanny said. Napoleon didn't care for the speculative look she gave him.

"That's all *passé*. The girl had a limited talent," Albine said. "His Majesty needs to spend time with his courtiers. We don't need just anyone mixing with their betters."

"Albine, that's enough, your fangs are showing." Napoleon gritted his teeth and felt perspiration seep under his collar.

"You should send the girl off the island, Sire," Montholon harped again.

"In His Majesty's regime, people were qualified by their achievements, not luck of birth." Fanny glared at Albine, speaking in so brittle a manner, her face might crack.

Albine swished around her skirts and sniffed.

Montholon caressed her arm as he pulled at the high collar of his uniform jacket. "You're right, *mon ange*, such 'lowering' would never have happened in Paris."

Saint-Denis walked in to clear up the plates on the table.

Napoleon scrutinized his second-valet. "Ali, where are your shoe buckles? Don't ever attend me unless you're fully dressed." Everyone went too far in their disrespect. He had to retain the upper hand. They must never know how his grasp faltered.

Hortense strutted about the room like a princess, the beautiful jacket flapping around her thin frame. She sang a silly song as she pirouetted past the globes. Napoleon Bertrand opened and shut the gold watch, laughing at the click of the mechanism, inspecting every inch of it. He then snapped it in his sister's face and she squealed in anger.

"Some people don't know how to teach their children manners." Albine snorted.

"Don't tell me how to raise my children," Fanny snapped. "When you ignore yours."

"The children are fine." Sweat beaded on Napoleon's forehead. They all wearied of each other, this farce winding to the finale he hoped for each and every night. He offered a dariole from the sweets set out to Tristan. "The rest of you should stop acting like them."

Tristan stuffed the tart in his mouth, cream dribbling over his chin.

Little Helene, still in her nurse's embrace, burst into tears at the quarrelsome voices.

"*Ma foi*, you're setting a poor example for all of us with your complaints, dear Fanny." Albine trailed one finger across the top of her cleavage.

"Put an end to this bickering, both of you. Albine, see to your daughter. She's upset." Napoleon clenched his fists. Amélie's sweet, selfless face swam before him, but he needed no one. He'd always been his own master.

"Take the child to my quarters," Albine ordered the nurse, who rushed the infant out.

"You dare accuse me of poor examples! A woman of your low birth and reputation?" Fanny jerked from her husband's restraining hand and advanced on Albine. Montholon stepped in front of his wife, who cowered behind his shoulder.

"Stop this now! All of you, you're dismissed. Leave me." Napoleon turned and strode toward the drawing room.

"This place is intolerable. When does it end? What are those people in Europe and America doing?" Fanny sputtered, her eyes moist. Bertrand closed his eyes and groaned.

Napoleon stopped and glared at her in shock, then composed his face to register nothing. He'd dared to let Bertrand in on his plans, and the fool told his wife? *Grand Dieu!*

"What exactly do you refer to?" Montholon slanted his prissy stare over the Bertrands, his right hand fingering his left epaulet.

"*Enough!*" Napoleon lunged forward and slammed his fist down on the table, rattling the remaining dishes. Tristan stifled a sob. Napoleon Bertrand cast his father a nervous glance. Hortense grinned at her emperor, still brimming with pride at her new acquisition.

"Montholon, this doesn't concern you. Bertrand, have you no control over your wife's silly rantings?" Napoleon's stomach clumped like a cannon ball. He'd reprimand Bertrand more fully in private. "I won't tolerate any more of your rude behavior. I am very badly attended by all of you. Children, accept my apology for these proceedings." Tramping into his study, he shut the door. He leaned back against it and the dark, musty room leached into his muscles.

* * * *

Amélie hurried to her father's bedchamber. "Chef Gascon says you felt heavy in your chest. Shall I fetch the doctor?" Filled with guilt, she'd ignored his waning health, too caught up in her own problems.

Her father's face ashen, he lay on his bed fully dressed. "It's nothing, *ma fille*. I'll be myself in a while." His depleted voice did nothing to calm her. "This place drains us all."

She planted a kiss on his forehead. "Then rest. You never take time for yourself. I'll make you some chamomile tea."

"Amélie, the strangest thing happened." He pushed himself up on his elbows in the bed. "The Count de Montholon asked me earlier when we'd be leaving for Europe. Have you discussed this matter with anyone…the emperor?"

"No. You told me the emperor requested we stay. I've spoken to no one about leaving." Amélie swallowed hard. If leaving edged closer as an option, no one would order it, least of all Montholon. "The count just wishes I wasn't here. Don't worry about it."

"The man hasn't been very kind when it comes to you. Jealous, I suppose, of your time with…I know you no longer see His Majesty." Perrault watched her with tired eyes. "In fact, you avoid him."

"Everything's fine. Please, try to rest." Amélie left his room more agitated. Both Montholons were ecstatic she no longer consumed Napoleon's attentions. They insinuated this with bold sneers and sly whispers. Still, why would the count anticipate her removal from the island? Perhaps Napoleon was now determined to send her back to Europe. That thought weighed her down.

After preparing the chamomile tea and taking a cup in to her father, Amélie remembered she'd promised to give some of the herb to Countess Bertrand. She must stop stalling, ask the secrets of the marriage bed, and hope the woman didn't shoo her away in revulsion. A walk would do her good. Amélie snatched her herb jar and strolled down the road to Hutt's Gate.

The maid directed her behind the dwelling, where the countess stood watching her children romp on the grassy slope that led down to the stream. The wind ruffled camellias, sweet alice, and periwinkle on the slope's borders.

"Amélie, thank you for bringing this. I hope it helps me relax," Fanny said with a genuine smile. The woman held a crumpled letter in her hand. "Look at this missive from my cousin, so many words crossed out. She tried to write me of the unrest in France. Of course, Lowe doesn't want us to know how the Bourbons are ruining our homeland. Wouldn't a political upheaval free us all? Children, don't trample the flowers I just planted!"

"Do I want to be freed?" Amélie took a deep breath, unnerved by the woman's mood, and what she came to ask. "Countess, there is something personal I'd like to discuss with you."

"I do hope you're feeling better. I wish you would give another recital." Fanny sounded splintery. Her body looked so thin she might snap in two. "You can't have given that up just because our emperor is his usual hard-hearted self? Now, I'm not his favorite."

"I behaved no better. I encouraged his attentions." Amélie's throat tightened. She wanted to cling in private to her distress. "I think women fall prey to men due to their ignorance. I've been...writing details about intimacy."

Countess Bertrand twitched a shoulder and gaped. "I thought that...you and Napoleon...never...?"

"We didn't." Amélie tensed. "Women are taught to be submissive, and if they had the knowledge, in writing, they wouldn't be afraid or stupid...the way I feel."

"That would be a brave undertaking. *Ma foi.*" Fanny walked off a few steps fingering the jar, stuffing the letter into her bodice. "Are you serious, my dear? It seems a—"

"I'm very serious." Amélie shoved aside her doubts. "I just need to—"

"What a scandal that would cause. You couldn't write under your own name. It would bring shame to your family." Fanny's eyes perked up with a mischievous sparkle. "How delicious that might be to do. Well, not the shame, the writing."

Amélie almost laughed. "I would need help, with the ultimate details, of course."

The countess stepped back to her. "Yes, you would indeed. How will you go about it?"

"I'm hoping..." Amélie inhaled. "That you will agree to provide this information."

"Me?" The woman's black eyes widened above her aquiline nose, making her look like a startled bird. "You're asking me to help?"

"If you would be so kind. I know nothing of the...uh, consummation." Amélie knew her cheeks flamed hot.

"I don't know. The scandal...though I did just say..." Fanny acted caught between intrigue and caution. She glanced toward her children. "You could never use my name. Henri would be outraged." She didn't sound altogether displeased by that idea.

"Of course, I wouldn't. I won't use any names, only information." Amélie's heart raced at the woman's subtle agreement.

Hortense Bertrand scampered up with a handful of wildflowers, smelling like fresh grass. "Mademoiselle Amélie, when are you singing for us again? *Maman* keeps asking."

"Oh, you should sing again. It would break up the monotony of our lives." The countess measured her with her dark gaze. "So will this other, no doubt."

Singing was the last thing on Amélie's mind. She patted the little girl's head. "I suppose I've missed it a little. I think, sometimes, of returning to Europe to study singing, but I haven't mentioned this to anyone." Amélie tried to ignore her feelings of deserting the emperor. She could act as selfish as Napoleon and think only of her future, as he said.

"You should go if you have the chance, my dear. Please agree to a small recital.

I'd be thrilled to host it here at Hutt's Gate, and do anything to help." Fanny gave her a tremulous smile. "If you return to Paris, I'll be so envious."

"If I do decide to perform...here is fine." Amélie couldn't put much enthusiasm into her words. Also, as one of the emperor's followers she wouldn't be welcomed back to Paris. The Count de Las Cases still languished in Germany, awaiting permission to return to France. "You *are* willing with the other topic, Madame?"

A kid goat loped up over the grass.

"I am, but discreetly, remember. How soon can you be ready for the recital?" Fanny stared over her shoulder. "Napoleon, make certain the goats stay out of the flower beds!"

Amélie winced at the mention of the elder Bertrand boy's name. As if *he* stood there, watching her. "Please give me another week. I'm very out of practice."

Chapter Twenty-Four

They [battles] lead in turn to new measures and bring about the crises—N.B.

Napoleon closed his study door and glared at his grand marshal—a man he raised up after the death of one of his most faithful, Duroc. "First of all, write a letter to the governor and inform him 'we' want no more of his chiding over Longwood's expenditures. His constant letters are the result of a too agitated, unstable mind. England brought me here. Do they expect me to live as a pauper as well as a prisoner?" He'd have Bertrand sign this—Napoleon never let Lowe think he communicated directly with him. He clenched his jaw. "Now, about the other day. When I tell you something, I expect it to be kept in strictest confidence. What kind of soldier are you, to tell your wife of my secret plans?"

"Forgive me, Sire. Fanny was weeping…it slipped out in a moment of desperation." Bertrand crumpled his hat in his hands—an imprudent act, since he wouldn't be able to replace it. "I've chastised her for her public behavior."

"A woman weeping! Bah, it's weakness to fall for such manipulations." Napoleon rubbed his stomach where his lunch sat like a stone. "You've chastised her in the past, and it never did any of us any good."

"I understand, but without Cipriani, can we be sure your plans are carried through?" Bertrand rushed this out, his courtier obviously anxious for a change in subject.

"Dare I tell you anything? Can I trust you?" Who else did Napoleon have? "Men can always be bribed. O'Meara and Balcombe proved quite devoted once I paid them." Despite Cipriani's untimely demise, Napoleon had found sympathetic soldiers to help him in smuggling letters. He grew sad thinking of his compatriot, his suspicions over his death.

"It's October. Perhaps by Christmas I will hear from my Uncle Fesch if he's found my double, the one man able to take my place. If your letter to the British ministry was convincing enough on our need for a priest, by that time they have hopefully set sail. O'Sullivan should be close behind on his regular route." Napoleon jerked around and jabbed a finger into his subordinate's face. "Bertrand, don't fall prey to a woman's trickery. Show the fortitude of a man! Keep these details to yourself."

Women, they only distracted you from important issues.

* * * *

After finally hitting the high note on key, Amélie sipped her warm lemon tea. For three days she compelled herself to practice in her room and tried not to recall Napoleon's smiles and encouragement at such times.

The previous day at Hutt's Gate, Fanny gave her information about bodily parts, and the "where they fit" of it. The act sounded painful and messy, not romantic, and did seem as bad as dogs mating. Fanny assured her it usually went better than her words conveyed, especially with someone you loved. Amélie had returned and stared at her notes. How would she describe lovemaking without scaring every virgin into joining a convent?

Amélie traced a finger across her bodice. Could she put down on paper the heat, that sensual pull you felt when your lover kissed your breast? She sighed as her body tingled with loss.

Fanny Bertrand arranged for the recital that Saturday and Amélie continued to practice until her throat was raw. Her empty stomach swished with tea.

On Friday, when she left the kitchen, Napoleon stood outside as if waiting for her.

She started, then winced, lingering so close to him.

"You are going to sing again, Amée?" His even tone disguised any feelings he may have harbored. Napoleon wore the wide planter's hat. He seemed older, a man given up and deteriorating.

"Yes, Your Majesty. I thought it time for another fete." Her voice deferential, she lowered her eyes, every nerve in her body thrumming.

"That's fine. I think you should. One of your many worthy talents, you mustn't ignore it."

"*Merci*, Sire. I trust you and everyone will enjoy the recital." Worthy, he said, yet she wasn't worthy enough for him?

Napoleon nodded with an officious smile, though his gaze had a strange mixture of melancholy and warmth, before he continued into the main house.

Strung as taut as the veins in Madame Cloubert's neck when she ranted, she'd have ruptured all over the courtyard if anyone had breathed on her. Amélie hurried to her room and threw herself into practicing her favorite arias until late into the night.

* * * *

Several British officers milled about in the Bertrands' parlor when Amélie walked in.

"I wish the countess hadn't invited them," she whispered to Marchand who had escorted her over at her request. The footman carrying her father's hors d'oeuvres took them into the kitchen. Perrault stayed behind, feeling ill, and this also concerned her.

"You're trembling," the valet said as she clutched his arm. "Don't worry. You'll be wonderful as always."

"I hope so. His Majesty isn't here yet." She released Marchand and fingered the gauzy dress she'd purchased in Jamestown. A superficial attempt to boost her spirits, the garment was of comfortable cotton in pale lavender. Tense with anticipation, she wondered if it was too transparent, leaving her naked and adrift.

"You look...island-like." Fanny hurried over and handed her a glass of wine. "Definitely not the latest Parisian fashion, but then how *would* we know out here? Let me introduce you to Captain Hargrove and Lieutenant Pinecoffin."

Amélie sipped the wine and grinned at one of them, but found she had no interest or talent for desultory flirting. She pulled Fanny to the side. "I'm really nervous."

"You'll be fine, dear." Fanny squeezed her arm. "I can't believe Albine is attending. *I* didn't invite her. I engaged that girl from Jamestown to accompany you. I can't stand Albine's flaunting of their importance to my husband's detriment."

"You know I didn't invite her." Amélie glared over at the scantily dressed, bejeweled woman. Madame de Montholon preened her plump figure like a queen as she gaily chatted with one of the handsomer British officers, her fingers fluffing her chestnut curls.

A few of the British smoked pipes and Amélie squinted in the smoke, concerned how it might affect her voice. She took another gulp of Madeira.

"Where is her husband, our dear Charles? She needs someone to rein her in." Fanny scanned the small room. "I don't see him here."

"The count is a poor candidate for *that* duty. He's never stopped any of his wife's…'flirtations'". Amélie's retort was bitter, but Fanny laughed.

"Montholon's been telling the governor that our emperor is too soft, and Europe has forgotten him." Fanny snickered. "He connives to ingratiate himself with Napoleon and Lowe at the same time. I never trusted Charles. He hopes for monetary gains in Napoleon's will."

"He's waiting for the emperor's death? I hope you told your husband." Amélie's heart throbbed. She fought the urge to flee the room. "Count Bertrand needs to inform His Majesty of such disloyal actions."

Minutes ticked by and Napoleon still didn't make an appearance. The people muttered and moved around impatiently.

"You should begin. Even though my husband says we must wait for the emperor." Fanny pressed Amélie's shoulder. "I wouldn't if I were you."

"*Au contraire,* I wait for no one. Let's start." Amélie drained the glass of wine, took her place, and plunged into three of her favorite arias. Her words sounded flat, the emotion forced. The girl from Jamestown plunked out the accompaniment with amateur gusto.

For the finale she sang from *Don Giovanni*. In Anna's furious aria, "Or *sai chi l'onore,*" she's realized the man she sought help from to avenge her father is Giovanni in disguise—the same scoundrel who forced himself upon her and murdered her father. Amélie spewed Anna's anger, releasing some of her own.

Afterwards, when many complimented her on her fine voice, she agreed with the ones who stayed silent. She sipped more wine and made polite conversation, but the night hadn't given her any sense of accomplishment.

Albine slithered over, clinging to the arm of another officer. "You were just so… adequate. Still, it's wise you've taken a renewed interest in this, since other things didn't pan out. *C'est la vie.*" With a smug look, she dragged the Englishman away with her.

Count Bertrand stepped up, his balding brown head lowered, not giving Amélie time to react.

"Mademoiselle. The emperor was feeling tired. He sends his regrets over by messenger." Bertrand gave an apologetic smile. Behind him, Fanny rolled her eyes.

Amélie nodded, still glaring at Albine. "I understand, Count Bertrand, thank you." Just as well, since her performance was nothing to boast about and she didn't need Napoleon's company any more than he desired hers.

* * * *

Amélie scuffed alongside Marchand a few yards down the dark road between Hutt's Gate and Longwood. She felt warmed with wine, yet numb from disillusionment, saying little to the valet's compliments on her performance.

"Marchand! Wait. Please come here, I need you." A woman's shrill voice called from behind them.

Amélie turned. Albine stood on the Hutt's Gate veranda, one arm waving vigorously.

"I'm afraid we must return, Amélie," Marchand said with barely suppressed annoyance. They both trailed back, Amélie keeping behind the valet to block out the countess.

"Oh, Amélie, why don't you go on ahead? I'll only keep him a few minutes. I wish to discuss my—our Napoleon." The woman's arrogant expression intensified Amélie's feelings of being cut away from the center, as jagged and forsaken as this island.

"I can walk on, if you give me the lantern." Amélie moved beside him, anxious to be away from the insufferable countess.

"Don't be silly, I won't hear of it," Marchand said. "Come in with me."

"Marchand, attend me now. I have important needs." Albine huffed in irritation, tapping her toe on the boards. "His Majesty won't like you ignoring me."

"Just hand me the lantern and go with her. I'll be all right," Amélie whispered as she clutched the handle.

"*Mais non,* this is out—"

"Please. I need time alone…to think." Amélie tugged the lantern from his grasp.

"I still wish you would wait. I'll be quick and join you down the road." He sighed and tramped up onto the veranda.

Amélie heard the door shut, hefted up the lantern, and continued in the direction of Longwood. The black night swathed around her. She did crave this solitude, a moment to evaluate her next move. She'd leave the island. No more feelings of having to remain to protect her deposed monarch. How naïve to imagine she had any power to do so. Napoleon ceased needing her long ago. He had Albine, who offered more capable comfort. Count de Montholon was free to manipulate Napoleon without interference, while encouraging his wife to cuckold him: all precisely the way the court preferred it, the sinister undertones no longer Amélie's problem.

"I wish now His Majesty *would* escape," she muttered into the air, yet still found it hard to fathom he could.

The moon slid behind a cloud, making the darkness complete. Amélie shivered, wishing she had her shawl. Padding along the rocky dirt lane, she labored to keep the heavy lantern from bumping and bruising her legs. A small circle of light bobbed along with her, feebly penetrating the surrounding shadows. She tripped over Club-rushes, the low, thready plant that sprouted on the Deadwood Plain.

Amélie set down the lantern and rubbed her sore fingers, before squaring her shoulders and trudging on. In the morning she'd tell her father she desired to leave. She would return to Europe to study opera. This talent would finance her growing interest in herbs, and her writing.

In her new existence she'd be her own woman and never speak of Saint Helena or allow herself to fall in love. No man would take up such a portion of her life again.

Stage women already had scandalous reputations. If her undeserved status as

Napoleon's mistress followed her, she'd have little left to lose in writing about sex. She only felt sorry for her father to share her ignominy.

A noise from behind startled her. Amélie turned but saw only blackness. Probably a goat or sheep. These creatures wandered wherever they pleased on the island, crashing through garden fences to risk being shot by both English and French.

Resuming her stroll, she listened to the crickets chirping, the frogs clacking a lonely lament. Wind rustled her skirts and hair. Now she distinctly heard footsteps in the background.

"Marchand?" She paused and turned again toward the sound, the wind feathering her curls across her cheek.

Something swept up and hands grabbed her. Amélie gasped then cried out. She swung the lantern, but it was snatched and tossed aside. She shrieked as thick arms wrapped around her torso, trying to force her to the ground.

"Help! *Secours!*" Staggering on her feet, she slapped her attacker's face and felt a macabre cloth-covered head over a meaty throat. She punched at the cloth and heard a man's curse. She wriggled from the arms, stumbled off the road, and tripped through underbrush. Footsteps instantly pursued. Her assailant jumped on her, knocked her down, and pinned her hard to the earth.

"*No! No! Help me, somebody help me!*" Amélie writhed and wailed, rocks cutting into her back, and struck at unknown features through the material.

Slapped back, she felt warm blood trickle down her chin. Struck again and again in the face by a gloved hand, she threw up her arms to fend off the painful blows. Fingers tightened around her throat. She gurgled and clawed at them in desperation. She feared losing consciousness, wheezing air up through her windpipe.

The sound of running feet and shouting pierced her panic. The weight lifted suddenly. Her attacker swished through the rushes in the opposite direction. Moments later, Amélie heard English voices above her. Rolling over, she sobbed and coughed, gasping for breath into the gritty earth.

"Are you injured, Miss?"

"She's bleeding—someone's attacked her!" A lantern bobbed hazily in front of her, their English babble hard to discern.

"Are you from Longwood, Miss?"

"'Course she is. You know bloody well she is. Let's take her there. They have a doctor."

A soldier reached for her. Amélie jerked around, her instinct to scramble away, but she slipped and couldn't get to her feet. She cried and covered her face, her fingers smeared in dirt and warm liquid. The soldier gathered her up and she went rigid in his arms.

When she next opened her eyes, she was being carried up the steps and into the reception hall of Longwood.

"What is the meaning of this?" Madame Cloubert demanded rather than asked. "*Merde*, what have you done to her?"

"The girl's hurt. Fetch the doctor, Ma'am. An' we had nothing to do with it, far as that goes." This soldier spoke in half English, half French.

"Why are the soldiers here?" Saint-Denis's voice. "Amélie? What's happened?"

Everyone began to jabber, their words crashing around in her mind. Snippets of French and English muddled together. Amélie hated their gaping faces and struggled to be free of her escort.

"If you can stand, Miss. There you go." The soldier set her on her feet. She staggered away from him, up against the wall for balance, smearing red from her fingers on its surface.

"Find O'Meara, *sur-le-champ!*" Madame Cloubert commanded. "The blood... her face."

"I sent a footman to fetch him," Ali said. "Amélie, let me get you—"

"Leave me alone, all of you!" Amélie gasped for breath, pushing the concerned faces away, ashamed and trembling. She tried to squeeze past them, to flee to her chamber. "Let me by."

"Calm down, Amélie." Doctor O'Meara rushed in. His footsteps cut into her brain. "Hold still. What's happened to you, lass? Who did this?"

The doctor reached for her, but she recoiled like a wild thing, frightened to be touched. She tasted blood in her mouth, coughing. "I'm fine. Leave me be. Please!"

A clamp of firm hands restrained her. Amélie struggled but her arms felt like ribbons and she slumped to the floor. "Why can't you...let me go to my room? *Je voudrais aller...*"

"Amée? What is...? Who has done such a reprehensible thing?" Napoleon's furious shout. "Ali, clear out the soldiers, this isn't a spectacle to be gawked at. If they're at fault, I'll have them shot...*someone* will have them shot. O'Meara, bring her in here."

Dragged against her will through the other rooms, Amélie flailed arms and legs, grunting with the effort. They placed her on the emperor's bed—the last place she wanted to be.

"Amée, who did this to you, tell me who it was?" Napoleon leaned over her, caressing her forehead, his eyes bright with worry.

His distressed voice triggered the opposite. He'd poison her with his false affection. She swiped his hand away. "Don't touch me, don't...never again." All their piteous looks repulsed her.

"Everyone, please, she's hysterical. Let me alone with her," O'Meara said.

"I'm staying with her," Napoleon insisted.

"I am *not* hysterical." Amélie jerked to a sitting position, head pounding. She glowered at Napoleon. "I...I never want to see nor speak to you again. Don't you understand?"

"Hush, lass, don't be saying such things," O'Meara cooed, trying to ease her down.

The anguish on Napoleon's face indisputable, in her fevered mind, she relished being the instrument of rejection. He left the room and she fell back and sobbed into his sheets.

"Now, now, you didn't mean any of it." The doctor probed her face. Amélie flung up her arms, groaning and sputtering.

"Bring me warm water and a cloth," O'Meara whispered to someone. "Also a glass of water for a draught."

"Don't give me anything. I want to go to my quarters." Her cheeks and jaw throbbed. She dropped her arms, which now felt like granite pressing grooves into the mattress.

"Ali, go and fetch Fanny Bertrand. She trusts her, *rapidement.*" Napoleon spoke from the doorway.

"Can't you go away? I don't need you." Amélie moaned into his pillow, on his bed.

"Easy now, lass." O'Meara attempted to wipe the blood from her face, but she flipped her head away, aggravating the pain. "You must let me have a look at you."

"I don't need you...because you don't know how...to love me." After this whispered lament, Amélie turned her face to the wall. She bunched the blanket up over her head, and tried to smother the screaming in her brain.

Chapter Twenty-Five

...We dread the horrible solitude of the heart, the emptiness of feeling—N.B.

In a semi-stupor, Amélie remembered Fanny Bertrand giving her a sour liquid to sip and Count Bertrand's anxious questions in the background—the emperor demanded to know who had attacked her—before she drifted away into billows of soft sheets.

Hands reached through curtains and clutched for her throat. She jerked awake and tried to scream, but no sound rolled from her lips. She bolted up and lashed out with her fists, swatting at material. The fingers groped. She hovered on a ledge and lost her balance. Tumbling down, she smacked against a hard surface.

Amélie whimpered and crouched in a heap on the cold floor. She groaned in an effort to raise herself and felt she still tumbled.

Someone rushed into the dim room. "Amée, are you all right?" Napoleon's anxious voice cut through her fog. He knelt beside her, caressing her shoulders.

"No, no...don't." Amélie sucked breath through her raw throat and pushed at him, unsure why he was there. One candle flickered on a table.

"Please, you're frightened. Don't shove me away. You must have been dreaming—you fell out of bed." Napoleon embraced her, but she stiffened and jerked back, sitting on her bent legs.

"Leave me alone...please. You've done enough," she rasped out and coughed. Then she touched her fingers along her aching jaw and neck. "I blew off the cliff."

"The cliff? What do you mean?" The light of the fire from the adjoining room illuminated Napoleon's profile. "Would you like me to bring you a drink?"

"This isn't my room." Amélie's head swam, her limp hair drooping about her face. Her temples throbbed like pestles pounding into her flesh. Her mind began to clear—she now recognized where she was. "Why am I in here?"

"Don't move." Napoleon rose and fetched a glass. He crouched down beside her and held it until she finally sipped the water. "That's better. Everything will be all right."

"No more, thank you." Her thirst quenched, lips stinging, she scooted toward the bed and braced herself against the mattress edge. She looked down at her torn lavender dress, the cold from the floor seeping through.

"Let me help you back into bed." He set down the glass and gently guided her up to sit on the mattress. "How do you feel? I can rouse O'Meara."

"No, it's all right." She felt brittle like a cracked goblet beyond mend, and shivered. "Can someone walk me to my quarters? I'm dizzy."

He sat beside her and put his hand on her shoulder. "You shouldn't move around until O'Meara examines you again."

She rested her damp forehead on the palm of her hand, the acrid taste of blood in her mouth, and wished she didn't take comfort from his touch. "I want to leave the island. I'm not safe here."

"You...You will be safe from now on, I promise." Napoleon squeezed her shoulder, then pulled back the bedcovers. "Lie back down, *s'il vous plaît*."

Slowly she crawled in and stretched out, every move painful. He draped the sheet and blanket over her.

"Amée. Even if it's no longer important to you, I..." He caressed his hand through her hair, his voice distant and sad. "It's something I've rarely said in my life, or rarely meant, but I do love you."

Amélie sighed. She'd longed to hear those words, but didn't believe him. Her heart quivered. "You can't just decide...I don't want to talk anymore." If he sought absolution, she was in no mood to give it. She settled into the warm place so recently abandoned but gleaned no comfort.

"You should sleep now, rest." Napoleon tucked the blanket snug around her. "There's much to discuss in the morning."

She stared up into his face. How could she believe in anything anymore, after the trauma of the night? After her past experiences with him? She felt too trampled on to play games. Her world twisted with sharp memories like a trail tangled in thorns.

Amélie turned toward the wall. He finally rose and stepped out. She tried to relax, but again that person chased her, struck her, and dragged her to the ground. On top of that, Napoleon's words wormed inside her. She trembled beneath the covers, shaking this iron bed that had sat on so many fields of battle.

* * * *

Amélie opened her eyes to green taffeta curtains bathed in weak morning light.

Napoleon rose from a nearby chair. He came and hovered over the bed. "Oh, Amée...who did this to you? Your face is so bruised and cut. I'll kill whoever did this."

Amélie touched her puffy jaw and cheeks, wincing at the soreness. Her throat felt like fingers still squeezed it. Each move thumped through her muscles and bones. Her sleep hadn't been restful and everything confused her. "I don't know who. It happened so fast." She coughed.

"Here, please." Napoleon handed her a glass. "Drink slowly."

Amélie sipped the sweet orange water, cooling her throat. "The person wore a cloth mask. I was jumped on, knocked down."

"A mask?" Napoleon paced the small chamber, his clothes rumpled as if he'd sat up all night in them. "You should have stayed with Marchand. Why were you so rash to go off alone?"

"I had no idea something like this could happen." His rage alarmed and satisfied her. She reeled in her conflicted feelings. "Is Doctor O'Meara coming soon?"

"I've sent Ali to bring him." Napoleon stopped and rubbed his unshaven chin. "No one dared take any...liberty with you, did they?" He glanced away as he asked this.

"Liberty? *Mais non*, nothing like that." She flushed inside. He didn't understand she was already ruined for any other man. She pulled the covers under her chin. His scent floated up. "I think I mentioned leaving the island last night. I still intend to do that."

Napoleon grimaced. "Please don't make that decision yet."

Amélie sat up. Gripping the covers close, she smoothed down her hair with shaking fingers, then looked at the blood stains on them. "It's what you wanted, my leaving."

"Not anymore. We'll find who did this." He stepped nearer, his gaze searching on hers. "I won't let anyone harm you again."

"I'll go to Milan and study, as you once offered." She sipped more orange water, her emotions roiling.

"I deserve nothing less than for you to desert me." Napoleon's eyes glistened with tears. "I let you down at your most vulnerable moment and deeply regret it."

"You manipulated me to suit your desires." Her bitter words masked her shock at his tears. "Then pushed me aside."

Napoleon flinched. "I know I've made you feel this way. Yes, I'm guilty of so many things, and have done just as you said, but I swear I never used you."

Amélie cradled her aching head in her hands. Her own tears welled up and she fought them down.

"I hardly deserve your forgiveness, but…" He spoke in the lingering silence. Close again, he rubbed his fingers along her back. "Give me the chance to prove I love you."

Amélie quivered at his touch. She half thought she'd imagined his declaration of love. His repeating it baffled her more. "I don't think…you know how to love."

"I tried to act noble since I can't offer you an honorable arrangement, but you're right, my capacity for love has always been flawed." His eyes vivid, weary lines were etched in his face. "I hope to change that."

Amélie felt his words prick into her. She tightened her muscles to fend them off, like the previous night's blows. She swept aside the covers to crawl out of his bed.

Napoleon sat on the mattress, preventing her escape. "Amée, can you forgive me for being a fool?"

He was too close, the warmth of him. Her pulse thumped. "I don't know."

A sharp knock. Napoleon stood and gave permission for Saint-Denis to bring O'Meara into the bedroom. She tried not to sigh with relief.

The doctor smiled. "How is our patient this morning? Better, I hope."

Perrault barged in on the doctor's heels. "Your Majesty, I demand to see my daughter. Amélie?"

Amélie cringed. Ali moved out of the chef's way, his dark eyes curious, and departed.

"Please, gentlemen, everyone come in." Napoleon stepped farther from the bed, waving them graciously into the small chamber.

"I have to hear from a valet about an assault on my own daughter?" Perrault nudged O'Meara aside. He grasped Amélie's hand, his face withered like the "Old Father Live Forever" on the plain. "Who would do such a thing? Why wasn't I informed last night?"

"I'm not so bad, Papa." Amélie squeezed his hand and wished they would all leave her in peace. She had so much to consider.

"*Affreux*, someone should have told me." Perrault glared from her to Napoleon. "Why weren't you brought to your own quarters?"

"She was too upset to move around, Perrault." Napoleon pressed the chef's shoulder. "Fanny Bertrand was with her until she fell asleep, and I spent the night sitting up in a chair in my study."

"There was so much confusion. I'm sorry no one told you." Amélie sagged with fatigue. Selfishly, she didn't care to assuage anyone else's feelings but her own.

O'Meara broke in, taking her pulse and probing her facial bones and along her neck. She bit back the pain. He lifted her eyelids and stared into her eyes. "Just contusions and abrasions. Cold compresses will be best for your swelling. A honey-laced tea for your throat. I've something for the cuts." The doctor rummaged in his little black bag. "Lass, I caution you to no more solitary late night walks."

"Have you the slightest notion who might have done this?" Her father's words were tense, his jaw stretched like old leather.

"No…I don't." Two people resented her presence, but Amélie couldn't put her mind around that. "It might have been a random attack."

"Could it have been the soldiers?" Napoleon's anger simmered beneath that question. "I'll have Bertrand insist their commander rigidly questions every one of them."

"The man cursed in French. The soldiers rescued me," Amélie said as O'Meara applied his salve to her cuts. She winced at the ointment's stink and sting.

"Cursed in French? It might be a trick. Bertrand will investigate immediately." Napoleon eyed her, then marched from the room. O'Meara soon followed.

Perrault glared at her, reducing her to a small child again. "Imprudent behavior, Amélie. What were you thinking walking off without an escort last night?"

"Please, Papa. I had no reason to believe I was in any danger." She took another sip of orange water and waved away the lingering smell of the ointment.

"I have to ask, as your father…" Perrault cleared his throat, his hands clasping and unclasping. "Did anything else happen, did…you weren't violated, were you?"

"*Mon Dieu.*" Amélie drew up her knees under the blanket and rested her arms on them, her virtue always in doubt. "I'm still as pure as the day I was born."

"Flippant words. I want to believe that. I can see we need to leave Saint Helena as soon as there's a ship for Europe, and don't argue with me about this. It's for your own good."

Amélie groaned, everyone pulling her in different directions. "Forgive me, but don't I have a say in what I want to do?" She crawled from the bed, ignoring the aches in her body. Napoleon's dressing gown hung on a hook behind the door. She grabbed the garment, wrapped it around her, and limped into the study. She had to escape from the emperor's bed. "Papa, you could bring me a clean dress to put on."

Perrault followed her, scowling at the gown she'd donned. "Again I ask you, do you and the emperor have an inappropriate relationship?"

"Papa, you're overreacting." She stroked the side of her head, a brain swirling with promises she knew she shouldn't trust. "I haven't been violated in any way by *any* one." She staggered to a chair before the study fireplace. "Though if we had a consensual relationship, that would be my private business." She rubbed her temples, trying to decide what was best for her.

"Oh, I think not, *ma fille*. You have strange ideas about what is expected behavior, even after my talks with you. I admit I let it go too far." Her father's complexion mottled gray, he sighed. "This island, this bizarre island has altered all our characters, and not for the better. There are other things happening here that you don't see."

* * * *

Napoleon listened to their argument from the dining room. He admitted his roguish character when it came to romance. He'd walked away from women just as quickly as he bedded them. After seeing Amée's hurt, he didn't want to lose her, or deny his emotions. He allowed his barriers to crumble—who else ever loved him so completely? The impulsiveness of his youth soared through his body. Even at age forty-seven, why not embrace happiness after so much sorrow? Was it transitory? That he didn't know yet. He decided, in a mad whim, to integrate her into his plans. The situation remained delicate. His heart swelled at the challenge and he pushed open the study door.

"Your Majesty, I must leave Saint Helena without delay, and take Amélie with me. It's no good for her here." Perrault confronted him. His chef looked terrible, wrung out.

Amélie sat before the hearth. When Napoleon looked over at her, her eyes held sadness and confusion. He had to manage her upset, her understandable anger at his request to forgive his rejection. He longed to take her in his arms, but couldn't.

"I don't want Amée to leave, and I've told her why. I need her here, very much. Leaving won't solve anything. François, how can I do without you? Don't you know how I depend on you, my chef? And Amée, who means so much to me. She's the only one who forces me to exercise. You're both irreplaceable." Napoleon smiled. Amélie looked away to stare into the cold grate of dying ashes.

Perrault shook a little—the words effective. "That aside, there is one thing more important, Sire, and I have a perfect right to know." His chef's words grew uneasy and he stared at his feet, then back at Napoleon. "Can you assure me there's nothing…improper in your friendship with my daughter?"

"Are you listening to the lowest gossip from this house full of malcontents? I thought you, of all people, above such slander." Napoleon put on his affronted expression, as if such actions never occurred to him. Did Amée understand his tactics? He fought the urge to walk close to her.

"I'm not proud of it." Perrault crossed his arms and faced the other direction. "When my daughter's welfare is at stake, I have to be certain. Can you give me such assurance, Your Majesty?"

"I hold Amélie in the highest esteem. You may be certain of that. I'll take care of everything, don't worry, Perrault." Napoleon would envelop her in his love—imperfect as he knew it to be. He faced a difficult time ahead on many fronts, but he was never one to cower. "You have my word no harm will come to your daughter. You, now, you're one of my most loyal subjects. I can't lose you. I beg you to reconsider."

* * * *

Amélie leaned back and soaked in the tiny tub in her chamber. The water turned pink with the blood she scrubbed off, but the warmth soothed her muscles. She closed her eyes. Who had won the battle of wills? The horror of the night edged into her mind and she swept it away. Napoleon loved her—was it possible?

Once the water cooled, she climbed out and rubbed her body with a towel.

At a knock, she threw on her dressing gown and opened the door to her father.

"You see how His Majesty holds on to you. Do you insist *that* is innocent? Stop lying to me. We need to hurry from this place." He stumbled over his words, sounding less sure of himself.

"There are issues…better not discussed yet, Papa. I know you wish to guide me, but I'm a woman, in my heart, *not* my experience." She patted the towel through her damp hair. "You can say whatever you wish, but I'll decide if I leave the island or not."

"If your relationship isn't inappropriate, I still don't understand it." Her father quaked with restrained fury. "You're in danger. Don't you understand, being close to His Majesty?"

"Papa, I don't know if my attack was personal because I'm close to Napoleon. I wasn't at the time." She narrowed her eyes. "Do you know something I don't?"

"I should have…I don't want you wandering anywhere alone. What happened last night proves it. Promise me you won't." He thumped a fist on his thigh, his forehead crinkled.

"I won't, but what exactly do you mean?" She reached out to touch his hand, but he backed off, entered his room, and shut the door. Pinpricks crept across her skin. Was he trying to scare her into leaving?

After she dressed, Marchand brought her a message from the emperor. "His Majesty has requested General Bingham to meet with you in the imperial study at three to discuss your attack." The valet's brown eyes brimmed with sadness. "I should never have let you continue on alone." He squeezed her elbow. "I feel terrible. I wish you would have waited for me."

"I'm all right. Don't blame yourself." Amélie tried to smile though it hurt her face. The assault had forced an unexpected result. "What *did* the countess want from you when she called you back?"

"A trivial request." He sighed in disgust. "She wanted me to copy a recipe from the Bertrand's chef. I couldn't understand her insistence."

"The countess lied when she said she wished to speak about Napoleon." Amélie shivered. Had the woman known someone waited out on the plain to attack her? Her fears, knotted with anger, rose up again.

* * * *

An hour later, Bingham, who was in charge of the island troops, left. Amélie found the general unsympathetic. She remained in the study at Napoleon's behest.

"He claims his men are innocent, bah." Napoleon handed her a cup of tea laced with honey, prepared by O'Meara. "What scoundrel could have assaulted you like this?"

"He wasn't very tall and had a thick build, from what I could tell." Amélie sipped her tea, the sweetness soothing, and watched Napoleon move around the chamber. She sat in the chair by the fireplace, and warmed herself before the crackling fire.

"I'll make sure the English investigate this to the fullest. To think what almost happened to you." Napoleon walked over and clasped her shoulder, his gaze heated like the flames. "I won't rest until they find the culprit, no matter how blameless they pretend to be."

"*Merci.*" Amélie felt drained and battered, both inside and out, yet trembled under his fingers.

"Bingham says we should be grateful his men intervened when they did, saving you. Then did they bother to chase after this scoundrel? We're supposedly under the protection of their hallowed government, surrounded day and night by their army and navy." His words were sharp, yet he stroked her shoulder blades. "I demand they give us justice."

"What grudge could anyone have against me?" Amélie wanted to relax into the warmth of his touch, but her pulse picked up for another reason. Again, one person schemed to remove her from Longwood. Could *he* stoop to such base physical violence? Somehow she couldn't believe it. His manservant was more the type.

Napoleon dipped down on one knee like a knight-errant before her. "What motive could anyone have for attacking you specifically?"

"Whoever it was waited to attack someone." She strained to wipe the image of Albine waving on the veranda from her mind. Her resentment toward the woman increased.

Napoleon clasped her hand, hot between his. "Amée, I wanted to tell your father earlier that I loved you, but we need to let his father's ethics cool down. I didn't want to put undue pressure on you. I hope I deterred his wish to leave. I hope… you will stay."

His attention overwhelmed her, after struggling to bury her love for him. She swallowed past her racing heart. "I need time to sort out my feelings."

"I know you don't trust my sincerity." His expressive eyes glowed more gray than blue. "I need you beside me."

"Why have you changed your mind about…all this? About me?" She still punished him, and withdrew her hand from his.

Napoleon curled up his fingers like shriveled leaves. He stood once more. "I wanted to save you from being my mistress. Yes, and at first, preserve my past. The allies took everything away from me." He snatched a piece of licorice from his *bonbonniére*. "I suppose I was also afraid to give myself up to the passion Josephine destroyed with her infidelities. I wanted my heart bronzed over, but you melted it. This emptiness inside, you're the one who fills it, and without guile." He smiled, slow and sad. "Can we begin again, Amée?"

She turned from his poignant smile. "With the dismissive way you spoke to me that morning in the garden, I felt beneath you, except as a frivolous relationship. I don't want to ever feel like that again."

"Beneath me? *Grand Dieu*, you're far above me. You, who never let outside influences govern your behavior, steer you from your deepest desires." Napoleon shoved at the music box on the mantel above her head. It tinkled in protest. "I was never a master of women as with men. Josephine didn't love me at first. Marie Louise was seduced away so easily. It hardly inspired my confidence. I felt unworthy of true love, but I need that now, with you."

"You can't change your mind later…as if my feelings don't matter." She inhaled the aroma of the tea to calm her breathing. Her fingers tightened on the china.

"Of course not." He ran a hand through his hair and sighed. "I'll give you time. I treated you badly, when you never deserved anything but the best." He stepped closer.

"I need to rest…now." Amélie set down her cup and rose, unsteady. The room felt too small, too intimate, for the two of them. She walked toward the door, straining her sore body, suppressing the urge to hurry.

"Shall I escort you back? Will you have dinner with me, tomorrow night, after you've rested?" A hopeful smile curved his lips.

She hesitated, a hand on the now open door. His earnest look dug deep inside her. "I can manage my way back. Dinner? Tomorrow, yes." Amélie's heart reverberated in her throat, her chest. She left the main house rubbing a hand over her bodice as if to soften the effect.

* * * *

In her room the following evening, Amélie carefully applied the powder Fanny Bertrand sent over. She winced at each stroke, but was glad to see the burgeoning purple fade under the white mixture. She tightened the pins in her upswept hair, not wanting to appear to please Napoleon, aware he liked her hair down. She tied a fichu around her throat to hide the ugly finger marks, and trembled again at the memory.

Albine waving so persistently sliced like a knife into her thoughts. The countess and her husband working together? The man in the cloth mask, the size and build of Jules. So many troubling images. If true, how could she prove any of it?

Amélie stepped out into the cool evening air and crossed the courtyard. The private dinner with Napoleon. A business arrangement swirled in her mind, something practical to push her limits. She'd made up her mind about her love for him, but he had to accept more responsibility in their relationship.

Clarice's bulging figure stalked from the clothesline and fell in behind her.

"Back in the emperor's good graces now, are you?" Clarice threw several towels smelling like the trade winds over her shoulder. "How you managed to get out of them in the first place, though, I can only guess."

"I'm relieved you're in your typical sweet mood. My health *is* improving, thank you for asking." Amélie smiled into Clarice's sneering face as the two entered the house.

"*De rien.*" Clarice snickered. "The Count de Montholon is irritated as the devil over your intimate rendezvous, the entire change of events. That's what Jules just told me."

Amélie walked away from her and knocked on the study door. A chill crept through her at the count's alleged irritation. *Had* Bertrand warned Napoleon about this man's latest caprice?

Napoleon opened the door, smiled anxiously, and coaxed her inside. "Amée, punctual as always. Everything is ready." His radiant smile cheered her.

The round mahogany pillar table near the sofa was draped with a white linen tablecloth set with Sévres porcelain and crystal goblets. Two candelabra burned on the sideboard, illuminating the room in a mellow glow. Napoleon pulled out a chair for her, then poured the wine. Amélie felt off balance with none of his valets present to do the serving.

The covered dishes held filet of beef, sliced fried potatoes, broad beans, and banana fritters steeped in rum. Napoleon gallantly did the honors, filling her plate to capacity.

"Thank you, but I can't eat all of this." She laughed when he handed it to her.

"I'm not well versed in food portion etiquette." He gave a self-deprecating chuckle. "Eat what you can. I'm afraid the beef isn't tender. More of the gristly island meat. I suspect the English give us goat rather than beef. They have to get rid of the beasts in some way." His attempt to relax her with teasing delighted her.

He appeared nervous and awkward in her company, and that smoothed the edge of her own concerns. "Everything looks delicious."

"I hope your father has calmed down. More important, how are you?" Napoleon filled his own plate and sat down across from her.

"I'm better. I tried to sleep most of today. I told my father it was my choice if I left the island or not." Amélie sipped the wine, savoring the flavor. "You have stopped drinking the Constantia, as I asked before?"

"Indeed I have. With all this other upheaval, I haven't noticed any change." Napoleon took a forkful of food, but didn't bring it to his mouth. "If your father remains upset, we could send him back to Europe and elect you head chef. I'll be the majordomo. How is that for an arrangement—then you would be in charge of me?"

"Very tempting." Amélie's tension drained away at Napoleon's disarming manner. He could be seductive when he grappled for his way. "I'm sure Papa will be all right, but he must voice his parental obligations. He has to realize I'm my own person, and so do you." She tasted a bite of salty potatoes. They stung her sore lips.

"Amée, you are obviously your own person. I've usually ended up alienating those most devoted to me, if it served my ambitions." He laid his hand over hers. "Though if I hadn't cared about you, it wouldn't have mattered if I disgraced you."

"I understand that now." Amélie turned her palm over and clasped his fingers. "We could go back and forth with me acting petulant. I *will* stay with you if—"

"*Grâce à dieu.*" His eyes luminous, Napoleon raised her hand to his lips and kissed her skin. "Who would have known that out of disaster I'd be given a second chance?"

Amélie's flesh tingled. She breathed deeply. "I don't want a causal affair, but something lasting. I realize we can't marry, but I've supported you in your thoughts and feelings. I expect the same from you."

"I will cherish you above myself." He ran his thumb down her hand, her wrist. "Admittedly, it will be an onerous task, discarding my egotism. I'll count on you to assist me."

She quivered down to her toes. "I…I do have terms. I insist on complete devotion and fidelity. You can't turn away from me if the situation here ever changes."

"Of course, it goes without saying." He kissed her wrist, his food untouched.

She sighed. Had she given in too easily? She craved his attentions, her body yearning, but she must keep a clear head. She eased her hand away from him. "I also want a written agreement between us." She stabbed her fork into a piece of beef. "That if anything happens to you, I'll have a small stipend."

"Plus support for any children—that I hope we may have." Napoleon smiled, stood, and kissed her on the forehead.

"We must go slow…for my father's sake." She pulled back, instead of melting into him as she wished. She used her father as an excuse, though his haggard face pricked her guilt. How did a woman manage in these situations, desire over common sense? What could she jot down in her treatise on sex?

Chapter Twenty-Six

Love should be a pleasure, not a torment—N.B.

"Where is Jules? I haven't noticed him around lately." At the kitchen table, Amélie inspected the potatoes brought up from a ship arriving yesterday. A few were squishy and black with rot. She hadn't seen the Montholons either since her assault. More suspicion niggled at her.

"He's been hiding away. Says he has a toothache." Ali poured heated water into a shaving mug. He stirred the soap for the emperor's morning shave, the scent aromatic. "Purple does suit you. How are you? We were all worried."

"A toothache?" At the window she tossed a stinky potato out to dispose of later. A rat scurried up to sniff it. She rubbed the rot between her fingertips. She'd struck her assailant in the face. "I'm much better. Have you seen Jules?"

"Briefly. Now His Majesty has revealed his intense feelings for you, congratulations." The valet winked his long-lashed eye. "You both deserve tenderness."

The kisses she craved...did Ali see her blush? "You can heat up your water in Napoleon's study. Do you come in here just to plague me?" She dropped the good potatoes into a basket.

"How can you say that? I've come to check on you." His sooty gaze held a flash of sympathy. "You'll be looked after, no matter what might change."

She glared at him. "I know there are escape plans." She said it casually, fishing for information. All she had was Napoleon's teasing...the paper at Sandy Bay. "Tell me what you're insinuating."

"How much has His Majesty said?" Ali studied her. He plopped the shaving brush into the mug. "You realize that when Lowe sent people off the island to 'lessen expenses' last year, some were entrusted on a mission from the emperor?"

"*Bien sûr.*" Amélie shoved away the basket, and wedged the pantry door closed. She wiped her hands on her apron and massaged the lingering ache in her jaw. "They were sent to Napoleon's brother, King Joseph." Madame Cloubert told her this, but she hadn't believed her.

"One footman had the *Remonstrance*, the emperor's grievances, written in his coat lining. He also took a detailed map of Saint Helena to pass to His Majesty's brother." Ali continued to stir the soap, foam rising at the sides of the mug. "A pamphlet was put out in England and France regarding the emperor's treatment here, and other things continue in the background."

Amélie snatched up her cup, sloshing the lemon tea. The plans sounded too definite. She sipped the now cold brew. The ginger to lessen swelling tasted bitter. "Has King Joseph set up anything, a rescue?"

"I thought His Majesty told you these things. I've said enough." Ali winked again and strutted to the door with the mug.

"Wait." Her thoughts slid away from Napoleon deserting her—he *couldn't*—and back to Jules. "Does Jules need any cloves for his...toothache?"

Ali laughed. "Perhaps. He's wearing a red scarf wrapped around his jaw and moaning, playing the clown. He won't let the doctor examine him."

"I'll look for cloves." Amélie's muscles tensed. Jules hiding behind a scarf? Hiding bruises from her fists? He was a cruel self-serving rogue, yet a complete toady to his master. Was Montholon that desperate to be rid of her influence over Napoleon?

* * * *

Heavy rain splattered down on the salon roof. Marchand set out billiard balls and cues.

In the past two days of rain, Amélie had welcomed the seclusion. Her facial bruises faded, but her inner bruises were more difficult to mend. She'd tried to help her father who seemed to move slower and slower, though shrugged off any concerns about his health.

"Are we ready for this entertaining game?" Napoleon walked up and put his arm around her.

"Has Count Bertrand written up the agreement between us?" She clasped his hand. She warmed at the idea that this man, who she'd tried so hard to be close to, now sought out her company.

"Yes, to give you spousal rights. We'll both sign it." He squeezed her close.

"I don't want to seem...greedy." Her warmth increased at their contact. "I know I've preached about independent women..." Sadly, women usually depended on men in financial situations. Without the legal protection of a marriage, Napoleon must be bound to his promises.

"You aren't greedy." He kissed her cheek. "Bertrand harps on Bingham and Lowe over your assault, at my demand, but they've learned nothing so far."

"Has anyone questioned all the servants here at Longwood? Perhaps they noticed something?" She leaned against Napoleon, wanting more kisses, but her suspicions remained sharp. Drag Jules out and inspect his face.

Marchand removed the books, maps, and various papers from the billiard table.

"Bertrand will question everyone. Why don't you move into the main house?" Napoleon asked. "After that vicious attack, it worries me where you are at night. The library can be arranged into a nice room."

"I'll think about it." Amélie worried about her father's reaction—the child rustled inside the woman. The woman needed to prevail.

"We'll need to make a decision, where you will sleep...soon," Napoleon whispered, as if reading her thoughts. He then kissed her earlobe.

Marchand set out wine and glasses. He smiled and was dismissed.

Her senses fluttered. Napoleon had far more than sleep on his mind. Such a public show of affection proved how much he cared for her.

"I know. You're right." Her feminine wiles at a loss, she stepped toward the table as her blue silk dress whispered around her legs.

"May I join you, Your Majesty?" The Count de Montholon glided through the front door. His wife followed. Albine slumped on the sofa with a morose expression.

Amélie filled with disappointment. She turned and set up for a game.

Elysium

"Let's see if I remember the intricacies of this amusement." Napoleon picked up a cue, waving it about like a sword.

"Do you recall the rousing game you had here with young Betsy Balcombe, Sire?" Montholon glanced at Amélie with a sly grin. He fingered a cue stick with slender hands. "You two had such a close, playful relationship."

"The table is ready for battle." Amélie tapped her cue on the table edge to tamp down her jealousy. Betsy, the daughter of their former household purveyor, had ingratiated herself with Napoleon when he stayed in their pavilion his first two months on Saint Helena.

"Ahh, yes, I remember that game. Mademoiselle 'Betsee' spent most of her time shooting balls at my fingers, and laughed when I cried out in pain." Napoleon chuckled. "She was a handful."

"A lovely little maid." Montholon leered. "She *was* quite enamored of you, Sire. Of course a girl like that is too young to take seriously."

Napoleon lined up his cue and smacked a ball across the table.

"Are you taking your shot next, Count? At the ball, I mean." Amélie smiled through stiff lips. She shouldered her cue like a rifle with bayonet. These people should crawl back in their holes like rats.

"The child was a hoyden, as I recall, Sire. She followed you around like a smitten puppy." Albine twirled the ribbon on her bodice, her breasts plump as melons above. She idly scratched the back of her neck with a long nail.

Amélie cringed. Both Montholons had a way of chiseling under her skin. Had Napoleon once kissed those breasts? Moisture gathered at her neck. "Shall I go next?"

"You're so right, *mon ange*." Montholon gazed at his wife with affection, as if his former detachment over her attentions to Napoleon wore thin. "Naïve young maidens are always drawn to men of fame and power. Didn't you once say, Your Majesty, that power was a...how did you put it, an aphrodisiac to women?"

"Montholon, I've warned you about insinuations and minding your own affairs. You as well, Albine." Napoleon scowled. "I won't tolerate any of it. Now are we playing or sniping?" He stepped beside Amélie, touching his shoulder to hers.

She smiled and relaxed a little.

"Accept my deepest apologies, Sire, on behalf of both of us." The count bowed low as if to hide a scoff.

"How is your manservant's toothache, Count?" Amélie leaned over the table, studying a shot, fingers tight on the cue.

"Oh, Charles, I have such a headache. I'm retiring to our quarters." The countess stood, then lowered her head. "If His Majesty will allow me."

"Perhaps...Albine and I will retire now, with your permission. Please excuse us, Sire." The count clicked down his cue and held out his arm for his wife to take. Napoleon nodded. The couple bowed and strolled from the room. Both Montholons seemed to sag with the effort it took to patronize their sovereign.

Amélie sagged with relief they were gone. "Didn't the countess ask to leave the island?"

"She changed her mind. You let the Montholons annoy you. They sense this." Napoleon screwed chalk over his cue tip, his fingers soon blue. "What was that about his valet's toothache?"

"Jules is hiding his face behind a scarf, according to Ali. He claims a toothache."

The Montholons had hurried out at her question. She'd ask Ali to look closer at Jules.

"Why does this bother you?"

"I hate to jump to conclusions, but I'll tell you later." Amélie forced her attention to the game. She lined up a shot, struck with her cue, and snagged the table felt.

"Take care, Amée. You aren't plowing a field." Napoleon laughed.

She retrieved her glass of wine from a nearby table and took a gulp. "Then you try again, or have you given up?"

Napoleon wiped blue chalk onto the tip of her nose. "Bah, I'll show you how to master this stupid game." He picked up his cue with a flourish. Snapping at every ball on the table, he sent them haphazardly into one another, but not one found its way into a pocket.

Amélie laughed despite her upset, rubbing her nose.

"A useless English game. *C'est ridicule.*" Amusement in his tone, he shot another ball, which avoided the hole.

She missed her next shot. "Oh, well, we did something different tonight." She sipped more wine, tart in her throat. "It's not an English game. I think a Frenchman invented it."

"I can think of more entertaining occupations." Napoleon laid down his cue and squeezed an arm around her. "Come into my study. Sit awhile."

"All right. I do have matters to discuss." She walked with him through the drawing room. He swiped more chalk on her cheek, and she slapped away his hand, laughing.

Amélie plopped down on the lumpy sofa. Napoleon sat beside her after ringing for his duty valet.

Marchand rushed in and lit two candles, stoked up the fire, then bowed out.

"Napoleon, if Count Bertrand hasn't warned you…" Before he stopped her, Amélie repeated the conversation she overheard between Montholon and Lowe, along with what Fanny told her. "As I said, I don't trust his servant either. He's threatened me before."

"You think this Jules attacked you?" Napoleon grimaced. "I'll have him brought before me immediately."

"I only have suspicions, but yes, you should question him." She pictured Jules's angry eyes when he'd warned her to silence, and shivered.

"Montholon, I realize, came here for his own gain. His words to Lowe are disturbing. Bertrand and Las Cases both warned me about him." He rose, poured two glasses of wine, and handed her one.

She sipped the fruitier beverage. "Then why keep him with you? Send him and his wife back to Europe."

He sat, took one sip of wine, and placed the glass on a table. "He's been useful to me here, to a point. That's all that matters."

"Please be alert in your dealings with him. I'm concerned for you." She touched his thigh. Was Napoleon clinging to his last "blue blood"?

He clasped her hand between both of his. "I'll investigate this manservant. I've also discouraged both Montholons, don't worry." He kissed her fingers, each knuckle. "Enough talk of them, they bore me."

Heat spread through her. She drank more wine, another form of heat. A courtesan would have thrown her arms around his neck.

Napoleon took her wineglass and placed it on the little table. "I promise you my devotion. You have all my ardor, *mon amour.*" He stroked her cheek, his face solemn. "There are few people I bare my soul to. I've kept up my bravado, but I've spoken to you of things I've hidden inside."

"I'm delighted you do." She grew supple under his touch. Had he told her all, or was the note at Sandy Bay a game he played with her? Napoleon might be delusional about escape, not facing facts, as with his Austrian ties, yet Ali knew something was afoot. "I hope you will always confide in me and respect my intelligence."

"Ahhh, I see your distrust." He gave her his most ingratiating smile. "Never doubt me, and don't forget that a woman can have passion as well as intelligence."

"I'm aware of that." Her jittery heart was about to wipe away her acumen.

Napoleon slipped his hand beneath her chin and leaned close. He kissed the tip of her nose.

She fumbled her fingers over the gold buttons of his waistcoat. An experienced woman would unbutton the garment.

He kissed her lips, slow and lingering. She moaned, their breaths mingled, and she trailed her fingers through his hair, light and silky.

Someone coughed from the dining room. Her father? She gasped.

Napoleon pulled back. "What is it?"

"I'm sorry." She flushed with embarrassment at her girlish reaction.

"I see you're not ready yet." He caressed her cheek, his words gentle.

If he'd take her back in his arms, kiss away her nervousness. "I..."

"It's all right, we can wait. I don't wish to frighten you." He stood, pulling her with him. "Remember, I'm but yours to command."

Amélie didn't know what to say to bring the moment back. Her body shuddered with desire, but should she fall so easily into the arms of a seasoned lover? She wielded a little power in his catering to her whims. "I'll say goodnight then."

* * * *

Napoleon climbed into his cold camp bed. He'd lied to her. He hadn't spoken to her of everything he hid inside. He didn't tell her of the escape. Doubts stopped him. What if it were all for naught? What if back in England, O'Sullivan thought better of such a dangerous endeavor, or his Uncle Fesch couldn't locate his double?

Amée would try to deter him from his plans. That's another reason why he didn't tell her. She wanted him to stay here, be an island farmer. She didn't understand that a life under scrutiny was no life at all. What about Montholon? True, she urged his discharge, but he couldn't afford any undue scrutiny from Lowe on Longwood. The dismissal of such a, on the surface, useful courtier would lead to just that. Besides, watching this dandy *aristo* struggle to manipulate him was an interesting game of cat and mouse.

Napoleon rolled over on the thin mattress and sighed. Enough of his wanting the world to mourn his unfair captivity. He and Amée would make a new life somewhere, a fresh beginning.

Soon they would consummate their relationship, but he didn't want to rush her. Her body felt so soft next to his, her skin tender, the clean smell of her. Her luscious lips on his. He smiled against his pillow, stroked the sheets, and imagined her golden hair tumbled over them.

Most of his life, when he made up his mind about something, Napoleon expected immediate action. This island taught him patience. When he had more details, he'd bring her in on the preparation.

* * * *

Amélie awoke, her body quivering from dreams of Napoleon's kisses and caresses. She splashed water on her face from her ewer.

After dressing, she entered the kitchen, surprised to discover no one there. She hurried to her father's room and found him sitting fully clothed in a chair, holding a letter.

"Papa? Are you all right?" She walked closer and pressed his shoulder. Then she kissed his sunken cheek, dry against her lips.

"I'll be fine in a moment." He squinted at her, his sallow color worse than before. "I'm just a little dizzy. I was reading this last letter from Jacques. Théodore, now he hardly writes, but I suppose the children and Suzanne keep him busy."

"I'm happy Jacques has decided to partner Théo in his bakery. After all his luckless schemes for earning money." Amélie sat down on her father's bed, curious as to his mood. "He's been a difficult one to settle down. Are you sure you're feeling well?"

"Bullheaded. Some say he takes after his father, though your mother's nature was determined. I suspect he and his sister are much alike." Perrault smiled in tired amusement from the scratched cane chair. "I still believe it's wiser for us to leave… don't frown at me. I won't argue with you anymore. You're almost twenty-one."

"I don't know the future, but I have to follow my heart." She wrestled with insecurities over how to keep such a man as Napoleon by her side. Was she woman enough? Last night, she should have insisted on staying with him.

Perrault made a deep sigh. "Amélie, I don't want us to be at odds."

"No, neither do I. I know I've been a trial for you, and I'm sorry." A childish part of her sought exoneration. Her father's vulnerability stirred the guilt inside her.

"You have to mature and make your own choices, and live with them. Of course, I would prefer a different situation for you." He fixed her with a weary paternal gaze. "I won't lecture. His Majesty promised me no harm will come to you. I must hold him to that, but I still caution you to be vigilant, close to the emperor."

"Papa, what specifically do you mean, anything, anyone? You've hinted at this before." She gripped his fingers. Would he indict the persons she suspected?

"I don't know who. Just be careful…" Perrault coughed. "I have something for you I'm working on. No, it can wait. I'm not finished."

"Doctor O'Meara should have a look at you. No arguing over this either." She used action to chase off her fears and left the room to find the emperor's physician.

Afterwards, insisting her father lie down and rest, Amélie walked with the doctor in the courtyard.

"It seems to be his heart, lass. I'm sure this climate has a little to do with it. He should take it easier. I advised him to give more responsibility to the pastry chef." O'Meara nodded his round face with its halo of wooly hair.

"Chef Gascon rarely shows up for his own duties." Amélie scuffed at the dirt with her toe. Her father had a weak heart? "If…if my father left the island, would that be to his benefit?"

"No, that long voyage would do more harm than good." O'Meara squeezed her arm, as if he understood her torn loyalties. "Just convince him to delegate his duties."

"I will do my best. He's a stubborn man." Amélie felt responsible for her father, but the doctor's words about the voyage softened her twinge of regret. If her parent had to leave Saint Helena, he would go alone. Her life belonged here.

Chapter Twenty-Seven

The Fates are spinning the lives of men—N.B.

Amélie lit the kitchen candles when the brief twilight crept over the wall beyond the courtyard. She scraped a penknife over her quill tip and dipped the quill into the ink. "You must use caution when just his touch flutters your heart and warms your soul. Don't be fooled by false tales of affection." No second thoughts, but she wanted other females to be alert when they dealt with the opposite sex. "Make certain he is the one you wish to give up something so precious as your..."

The door banged open and Madame Cloubert barged in. "Where is that polish you promised me?" she asked, scratching under her arm. "The rashes in this humid weather! With the house mold, my cleaning is never ending. What are you writing?"

"A letter to my brother." Amélie slid the scrap of paper away from the woman's prying eyes. She'd disregarded her own caution by writing in the airy kitchen, instead of the clamminess of her room. "Here is the polish, Madame." She handed her a crock bowl with the beeswax she'd softened in linseed oil.

"That Jules is certainly an idiot. I went into the dining room a few minutes ago to search for my best polishing cloth and there he was, putting a wine bottle into the emperor's wine cabinet. When he saw me he practically dropped it and had the nerve to scold me for sneaking up on him." Madame Cloubert stuck her bony finger in the waxy concoction and twirled it around. Her rusty hair drooped out from her white cap. "As if I'd bother."

"He was putting a wine bottle *back* in the cabinet?" Amélie's suspicions about Jules angered her again. Why had he kept himself hidden from her all this time? Napoleon had questioned him yesterday, but Jules no longer wore the scarf and he had no bruises on his face. They'd have faded by now. He swore he was in his quarters at the time of her attack. She snatched an onion from the pantry, sliced off the crinkly skin, and started to chop it. Her eyes watered as she minced it up.

"He's a sly one, like his employer. They both slime around like worms. Jules ogles too much at the women." Madame sniffed loudly. "Why are you cutting onion now?"

The cannon fired at that moment and Amélie jolted despite this sound being the serenade of their nights. She scraped the knife tip over the table. "The onion is for my father. Raw onion is good for the heart."

"It won't do much for his breath. I heard he's feeling ill. Give him my regards for a quick recovery, no matter the stink of the cure." The scrawny woman hurried out the door, the summer evening breeze sweeping the onion smell away for a moment.

Amélie needed to speak to Marchand about Jules. She washed her hands of the sharp scent, then stashed her writing in the safety of her room. Her father wrinkled his nose at the plate of onion she handed him, but she smiled and went into the main house.

Marchand wasn't in the attic and Ali had the duty tonight. At a candle lit in the library, she peeked inside and saw Marchand putting final touches to three sketches he'd made of Longwood.

"You're very good." Amélie looked over his shoulder at the stark renditions of their residence and grounds. She'd seen his attractive watercolors in Napoleon's study.

"It keeps me occupied." Marchand smiled at her, stretching his arm as if to relieve a cramp. "Between caring for His Majesty and working on his dictation of the *Summary of Julius Caesar's Wars*. Now what can I do for you? How are you?"

"I'm upset." Amélie gripped the back of his chair. "I have some concerns about Jules. I think he's tampering with the emperor's wine." She related the two incidents involving Jules.

"The emperor's sour Constantia wine? I don't know why he'd want to steal it. We're provided sufficient *vin ordinaire* that isn't locked away. I'll question him about it." Marchand tapped his pencil on the table, his liquid brown eyes serious. "Madame Cloubert saw him putting the wine *back*? That does seem odd."

"The Count de Montholon is in charge of the wine, but Jules had the keys when I saw him, and the count boasts he lets no one touch them." She studied the valet's expression when he turned to look at her. "You don't think someone could slip something in the emperor's wine that doesn't belong there?" Amélie whispered.

The young man's gaze sharpened, and his pencil tip broke off. "I would hope *not*. That was one of the purposes of locking it up in the first place. I'll question Jules first thing tomorrow."

* * * *

"Be careful with those dishes. They're impossible to replace." Amélie swept the kitchen floor as Clarice bustled in and dropped a tray of dirty lunch platters on the table. The force of her entrance scattered the flour, crumbs, and orange peels back across the stones.

"If people don't stop dumping more chores on me. *Merde!*" Clarice brushed a strand of hair from her forehead. "It's not as if I don't have my own private life to attend to."

"We are all expected to pitch in with Chef Gascon down ill again. I'm baking, so someone needs to clean up dishes." Amélie knew the futility of that the instant it left her lips.

"Superior, are you?" Clarice's fat cheeks, dappled with sweat, puffed out with her words. "Selfish is more the truth. You refuse to leave the island when it's bad for your father's health. He's in the house now, looking like death."

"Doctor O'Meara advised him not to leave. I had nothing to do with it. My father hardly listens to my entreaties." She tugged at her moist bodice. "Why are we always at each other's throats? How much pleasure can you take in behaving as you do?" Amélie dragged the broom toward the door, re-sweeping. She glanced out, anxious to see Marchand and discover what he learned from Jules.

"You dare question my behavior?" Clarice jerked off her white cap and fanned herself with it in the growing afternoon humidity. "I know why you won't leave. We *all* do. Back in the emperor's bed."

Amélie swished the remnants over the threshold and hid a smile. "I'm looking to my own happiness now. I hope you find yours."

"Jules told me I'm the prettiest woman on the island," Clarice said, as if daring anyone to contradict, "and I'd have to say he has excellent taste."

"Are you so close to him?" Amélie scrutinized her in surprise.

"We've shared kisses." Clarice heaved her plump chest. "He wants to do far more."

Amélie couldn't imagine Jules putting up with Clarice's temper. Those two together made her uncomfortable.

Out of the corner of her eye she saw Marchand walk into the courtyard and wave to her.

"You're dallying with His Majesty *and* his valet…I didn't think you had it in you." Clarice snickered, yet eyed her with a trace of admiration. "No wonder Marchand avoided me."

"Not everyone has the morals of a dog. I have business to attend to." Amélie shoved the broom at her. She might need it to fly around and cast evil spells. She left the kitchen and strolled with Marchand toward the stables.

"Jules acted quite agitated when I asked him about the wine," Marchand said as the scent of hay and manure drifted over the breeze. "He denied any misconduct, and said he only did what the Count de Montholon asked him to."

Amélie's stomach tightened. "The count knows of this, since Jules only does what he's asked to do?"

"He did act haughty when I said I'd inform his master. I couldn't get anything else from him. Since the Count de Montholon is in charge of the wine, there isn't much I can do. We should tell His Majesty to let the count know of his servant's behavior."

"I did. I'd have thought little of the incident, except for Jules's aggravated manner when Madame Cloubert and I happened to catch him near the wine cabinet. Is it possible that the British are…poisoning the wine?"

"*Poison?* What makes you suspect such a thing?" Marchand's soft features hardened, making him look older. "Do you think Jules is working for the British?"

"I don't know, but the only time I drank that wine it made me sick with the identical symptoms as the emperor's climactic illness. That tells me the wine is tainted, and wouldn't England profit the most from an act like that? Then what about Montholon, if the count tells Jules what to do…?"

"Britain's allies in Europe or any of the Royalists would benefit from such an act." He touched her sleeve. "Amélie, if you're right we have to stop the emperor from drinking the wine immediately."

"I've taken care of that. I don't want to say anymore now." Amélie rubbed her hand through her hair. "I hate to get Napoleon in an uproar until I have more proof, so don't repeat this. Please try to squeeze more out of Jules."

* * * *

Napoleon squinted and aimed the pistol. The goat that foraged through the front garden slipped off beyond the turf wall. He dropped his arm. "I thought I wanted to remain here, a world figure, surrounded and persecuted, while mankind guesses my next move."

"Sire, I know whatever you do will be brilliant," Ali replied.

"Indeed, my boy, indeed. Now I have the delicate matter of making sure Amée follows in good time. You will see to that, of course." He stepped out farther among the rose bushes.

"I will, Your Majesty."

The goat poked out his head from the turf and began to munch on the new strawberry plants. Napoleon grimaced and raised the pistol again. He wouldn't admit to his nearsightedness, and saw only a brown blur. He squeezed the trigger. The shot rang out, snapping open the previous silence. The blur loped off out the front gate.

"Did I miss?"

"I'm afraid so, Sire, but the sentry enjoyed the bullet whizzing by his ear."

Several sentries ran into the yard, rifles in the air. Napoleon laughed at their anxiety as Ali waved them back. Do them good to rile them up, though it countermanded his wish to keep matters sedate around Longwood.

"I used to be quite the shot. I'm out of practice." Napoleon inhaled the familiar scent of gunpowder, then turned to catch the amusement in his valet's eyes. He handed Ali the pistol and heard the sentries commenting on his actions. Napoleon kept his tone officious to minimize his concern: "I want her to remain *safe*. Is that clear? I know she'll have the courage for what lies ahead."

"I have every confidence that Amélie will be brave. Have you...spoken to her of these covert, and extremely clever, plans of yours yet, Your Majesty?"

"No, but I intend to. Keep your own mocking mouth quiet, Ali." Napoleon pinched his valet's ear until the young man cried out. He still marveled that he'd fallen for this girl. Was it lasting, or the misguided lust of an aging soldier? He hoped the former. He blamed all his casual affairs on his youth and impulsive nature. Amée expected him to be faithful, and he'd try his utmost. "I'm certain everything will soon fall into place," he said with a forced assurance.

Chapter Twenty-Eight

It is true that I hate scheming women worse than anything—N.B.

"We haven't yet consummated our relationship." Amélie laid down her cards. Fanny Bertrand sat across from her in the drawing room. They'd just finished Christmas dinner, topped off with the *Bûche de Noël*, prepared by Chef Gascon. Ashamed of her virginal status, she almost laughed. In polite society it would have been the other way around.

Napoleon and Count Bertrand stood near the fireplace having a low conversation. They argued over the lack of progress in Amélie's assault.

"I'm surprised Napoleon has been so patient. You'll have plenty to write about in your treatise after you do." Fanny laughed and winked. "You'll understand better with firsthand experience."

"*Mais oui.*" I have pen and ink ready." Amélie ran a card tip along her lower lip, anxious for the sensual details, that heavy warmth inside her. How much longer would she allow her worries over her father to keep her "pure"? "I don't know how much writing I'll do, if Napoleon finds out."

"That could be the end of your career." Fanny tugged at her gown's neckline. "I'll never get used to celebrating Christmas in hot weather." Her smile faded. "Where are the Montholons? They couldn't join us for another exciting Saint Helena holiday repast?" She scanned the room as if they nestled like vermin in the corners.

"They've been hiding away, not that I mind." Amélie leaned across the little table. "You've known them for a while. What was the count's character back in France?"

"Well...I've always found it odd that in all those years of warfare Montholon never distinguished himself, but was still promoted." She glanced toward the men. "He seemed to be in constant debt and even embezzled money from an army payroll. His stepfather, the Count de Semonville, was rumored to be a Royalist spy during the Empire."

"A spy? I wish Napoleon would send him away. He disregards my concerns." Amélie snapped the cards on the table, more leery toward the count.

"Why did Montholon even insist on coming here? He would have been accepted back into Louis XVIII's regime. Why vanish into exile? He joined the Bourbons when Napoleon was exiled to Elba." Fanny's shoulders sagged. She dog-eared the already fragile cards. "Now I'd take that island over this one. How *much* longer?"

"Is your husband requesting to be released?" Amélie studied the woman's expression. Did Fanny know about schemes that she didn't?

"What is all this whispering over here?" Napoleon strode to the table. "Are we playing cards? Bertrand, we must listen in on our lovely ladies, who seem to be hatching some evil plot." He stroked the back of Amélie's neck.

"We are solving the world's problems." She basked in his attention, the heat on her skin, but she couldn't dispel her anxiety over Montholon. He appeared a man deep in debt and ripe for a lucrative mission.

* * * *

Seen through the lenses of Napoleon's field glasses, Count Balmain stared toward Longwood, shook his head at Bertrand, turned his horse about, and galloped off. Bertrand, his upper torso drooped, strode back to where Napoleon waited in the park of gumwoods. He lowered his glasses. A tree rat scratched on a nearby trunk and Napoleon sighed. Only on this strange island would they have rats that lived in trees.

When Bertrand approached, he saw by his grand marshal's glum expression that the meeting hadn't gone as he wished. Napoleon suppressed any aggravation from his features. "The very proper Balmain still refuses to meet me without Lowe's introduction?"

"Yes, Sire. Pardon me for having to say...again, but it seems you will need to make amends with Governor Lowe before—"

"Bah! I won't lower myself to England's petty official. Lowe discourages any of the delegates from approaching me, except as some creature in a cage to be stared at." He'd hoped to persuade a meeting with the Russian *commissaire* on casual terms, a friendly drink over the New Year tomorrow, but would it have mattered? He'd learned Balmain's master—Tsar Alexander—had insisted on the harshest terms toward the deposed Emperor of the French at the Congress of Vienna. "Destroying me is that villain's sole purpose and Lowe wants the delegates under his thumb as well."

"It would be beneficial, Sire, to have the *commissaires* in your corner. To open up communication with Europe. I could, with your approval, set up a meeting with the governor and yourself, with Count Balmain, for reconciliation."

"No, on this I remain steadfast." Napoleon strode down the path, ducking under a sticky orb of web that dangled between two trees. He'd have to put all his faith in O'Sullivan's return. "I'd like to keep a shred of dignity. Lord Bathurst wrote Lowe that no delegate is to be presented to me except in their official capacity, and introduced by Lowe himself. They knew I'd never agree. I've compromised enough riding and walking again with the degradation of surveillance." He swiped at a branch and wouldn't admit that these actions benefited him. "Before Sully arrives, I'll return to my reclusive ways, pretend I'm ill, and show Lowe for the barbarian he is."

"You shouldn't rely on one source of relief. This is a risky venture, Your Majesty," Bertrand whispered, following on his heels through the front gate of Longwood.

"If Lowe brought news he was taking me back to my throne, somehow he'd make even that disagreeable." Napoleon resented Bertrand's warning, prying open his own fears. He hesitated at the front steps of the house. "I've heard the Duke of Wellington, a man I have reason to dislike, called Lowe a damned fool. As for risks, in my early career during the revolution, I learned that your associations can be helpful at one moment, and lethal the next. This taught me to be pragmatic, as well as an opportunist. I've always taken risks. Why stop now?"

* * * *

Amélie set a potpourri of herbs in the dining room to freshen the musty space. She entered the salon where Napoleon had spread out his maps on the billiard table. With red and white pins representing soldiers, he explained his battle plan of Rivoli to Count Bertrand, Marchand, and Saint-Denis. He flipped through the few numbers of *Le Moniteur,* and the atlas he kept nearby, to accentuate his points.

Amélie watched, intrigued by Napoleon's details and gestures, the dynamic commander in the field.

He looked up and smiled. "Excuse me, *Messieurs,* I have sweeter plans to attend to."

Napoleon offered his arm to her and they walked out the front door, past the trellis where red, white, and purple passion flowers intertwined. An early dinner had been set out for them on a tiny table in the garden. "Amée, this morning I insisted your father relinquish some of his duties to Chef Gascon. I hope his health is improving."

"It's hard to tell with Papa. Thank you for talking to him." She sat in the chair he pulled out, and they ate a light meal of salad, chicken, and lentils. Once finished, she gazed around at the breeze-ruffled bushes. "We need a line of strong pines to block the wind, to protect the plants. If you request that the new house be rebuilt in the sheltered vale…"

"Ah, if I could stroll with you in the gardens of the Elysée Palace." He leaned both elbows on the table, his hands under his chin. "The Tuileries was magnificent, but open to the public. Though I wouldn't mind seeing that public now: French men and women, excited to catch me at the windows." Napoleon stared off, a satisfied smile on his face.

"The English are always excited to see you. What about the house in the vale—do you think Lowe would agree?" She grinned when he flicked her an irritated glance. "Don't you want to be more comfortable?"

Napoleon refilled her wine glass. "This isn't what I care to discuss with you this evening. You're behaving in a facetious manner." He gave a sly wink. "I must be rubbing off on you, but not in the way I'd prefer."

Amélie shifted in her chair and drank from the glass. "What all is kept in that wine cabinet the Count de Montholon holds the keys to?"

"Just my Constantia wine, nothing else, why? I stopped drinking it to please you, and I request a bottle now and then to imply consumption, as you asked."

"Have you had any of your strange symptoms?" Amélie draped her shawl around her shoulders in the cooling air. She smelled the fragrant roses.

"No, I must admit. I also feel less bloated and appear to be losing more weight."

"I have noticed that. Doesn't this change in your condition prove the wine must be tainted? I hope you followed my other advice, about not telling anyone?"

"To the letter, my sweet." He reached over and clasped her hand. "Why these questions?"

"If the wine's been tampered with, who would have access to it? It comes in casks, then it's bottled."

"The British of course." He said this matter-of-factly, more interested in caressing her skin.

"When it's presented to you, are the bottles already opened?" She returned the pressure of his fingers, enjoying their mutual touch.

"I've paid little attention to such things. I suppose so. My symptoms may again flare. Who can predict?" He shrugged, looking disgruntled in the fading light. "It may have nothing to do with the wine, but be the fault of this climate."

"Perhaps you should pay more attention to such things." Amélie stifled a groan. Sometimes Napoleon left too much to fate. "How can you be so cavalier about something so important as your own life?"

"Shhh, we aren't here to discuss murder, are we?" Napoleon raised her hand to his lips and kissed each finger. "Let's drink a toast to New Year 1817—may it bring many surprises."

Amélie clicked her glass with his. The word murder jolted her. "The idea of a poisoner frightens me, and it should frighten you." She gripped his hand. The touch of his lips stirred her yearning.

"Many have betrayed me. Men I heaped honors and riches on couldn't wait to betray me once my power slipped. The British have the most contempt, and now the best opportunity." He released her and swept out his hand as if to encompass the island. "Nothing along those lines would shock me. I've lived surrounded by hazards most of my life."

Amélie scooted to the edge of her chair and leaned her elbow on the table. "Would anyone *besides* the British or their allies have reason to harm you?"

"Why not? I upset the entire world. I did things no one dared to do before." He looked reflective, a quiet pride.

She traced a finger over his hand. "You know I love you. That's why I worry."

Saint-Denis hurried out, cleared away the dishes, lit two candles, and left.

"Let us speak of love then." Napoleon ran his finger along her lips. "As impossible as I've behaved, how long have you loved me?"

She kissed his fingertip. "Since that night you accused those British officers of drooling down my dress, and you admitted jealousy."

"Since then?" Napoleon's gaze mesmerized her. He leaned over the small table and kissed her lips. He stroked along her cheek and trailed his fingers through the curls that cascaded down her shoulders.

Amélie shivered in pleasure. Her desire rose like warm bread. She had a difficult road ahead of her to keep him satisfied on this island, safe from the outside world's influences.

"I hope we will always make each other happy." Amélie stroked his cheek. His lips, his breath sent quivers down her body.

Night had fallen, the sun disappearing behind the ridge of mountains that radiated in spurts of red tufa stone from Diana's Peak toward the coast.

Napoleon kissed the side of her neck. "Not many women have manipulated me for long, but you...you are my compassion. I never cared to admit any weakness in my life."

"Admitting such a sentiment is a sign of strength." She smiled. His expressive eyes mirrored his hunger, and hers must show. "You need to be loved the way I love you."

"Then clarify it for me." Napoleon's voice seductive, he pushed his chair beside hers.

She hunched her shoulders as another shiver traveled up her spine. "You can hardly hope to seduce me out in the garden while everyone watches."

"Let them all watch. I don't care." Napoleon kissed her on the mouth again, drawing the breath from her lungs. His lips massaged over hers, until she wanted to puddle into liquid and flow and eddy around his body. He stroked one hand across her rib cage and over her breasts, his other caressing her knee.

Amélie felt that heaviness low in her body and imagined her and Napoleon sweeping the chairs aside and surrendering to passion under the rose bushes while the British sentries gaped over the wall. She laughed.

"You're not supposed to laugh when I kiss you." Napoleon eased back, his face intense, eyes clouded. The candlelight sparkled over his features. "Now that you've conquered me, my love, what are you going to do with me?"

"I want to...be alone with you. In your bedroom." She pulled him to her and kissed his mouth. Napoleon's once reluctant ardor thrilled her. The sensual sizzle heated her blood. He deepened the kiss and caressed his thumb over her nipple. She groaned.

"Amélie!" Marchand appeared on the front porch. He bowed low. "I'm sorry to interrupt, Sire, but her father has collapsed in the kitchen."

Chapter Twenty-Nine

There are many paths to Paradise, and decent men have always been able to find theirs—N.B.

Amélie reached out to steady her father, but he moved aside with a jerk, returning to his mixing of a tomato paste as if he hadn't stumbled. She maneuvered about the kitchen, trying to anticipate his needs without incurring his anger. He'd recovered quickly from his collapse the previous day, but she still worried.

"I don't need any more help," he finally grumbled. Though he denied it, her reuniting with Napoleon added to his upset, and this increased her guilt.

Amélie left the kitchen, fetched water, and moistened her garden. The smell of damp earth and pungent plants cleared her head. When Chef Gascon entered the kitchen she felt easier, and went into the main house to find her emperor.

"There you are, Amée." Napoleon stepped from his study with a ledger. He tossed it onto the dining room table. "Montholon never does balance his expenditures to my satisfaction." His gaze turned sympathetic and he put his hands on her shoulders. "You look tired. I can assign more help for you in the kitchen. I hate to see you exhaust yourself watching out for your father."

Napoleon's touch warmed her, yet the mention of the Count de Montholon almost ruined the moment. "*Mais non.* Papa resents the help he receives now. He throws me out when I persist." Amélie smiled up at him. "Men are such stubborn creatures, and always want everything their way."

Napoleon kissed her on the forehead, his gaze distant over her shoulder. "I know you're troubled, still I hope we can spend time alone together, soon."

"As do I, but I think his illness is more serious than I wanted to believe." Sadness dragged her down. Any private rendezvous with Napoleon sent her to her empty bed throbbing with an ache that needed to be assuaged. With her father so ill though, she dreaded adding to his concerns.

"The entire atmosphere has changed." Napoleon sighed, his fingers tightening on her flesh. "You frantic in the kitchen. Montholon's constant complaints about my interfering servants."

"I think it is *his* servant who is interfering. What else is upsetting you?" Amélie asked when he released her and turned away.

Napoleon faced her, his expression grim. "Lowe is threatening to have O'Meara removed again, the one man I trust to be my physician. This time it looks like the villain will succeed."

"Because of the doctor's outspokenness on your behalf?" She encircled her arm with his.

"Lowe was furious when O'Meara told him he promised *me* he'd never repeat our conversations, unless they involved escape. Lowe demands to know every word I utter, every thought I think. O'Meara is forbidden to lend me any newspapers, unless Lowe approves their content." He rubbed his chin, eyes flashing. "When I asked O'Meara to present a snuffbox to the island reverend for officiating at Cipriani's funeral, Lowe threw a tantrum and ordered O'Meara from Jamestown."

Amélie feared this would be a bitter blow for Napoleon. "Maybe it's all bluster and nothing will happen. What would you do for a doctor without O'Meara?"

"I rarely took his advice anyway. You've been more of a doctor to me. I like the man. He's a friend. Friends are hard to come by here." Napoleon squeezed her hand, then kissed it. "I must go and speak with O'Meara." He walked off toward the salon.

The sound of arguing streamed through the open back window and Amélie returned to the courtyard. Perrault pushed out through the kitchen door and stalked for his quarters. She hurried into the kitchen and found Chef Gascon, slumped in a chair, staring at the floor.

"Amélie...I...I've tried to assist your father, as His Majesty wishes, but he's so obstinate." Gascon shook his lumpy head, groaning a long sigh. "It's the strain of this island. Often I wish I could go back home. Maybe patch it up with my wife and daughters. She's angry because...our son was killed at Waterloo."

"I'm sorry, Chef Gascon. I will speak to him." Amélie left and entered their quarters, torn by the two men she loved in far different ways.

Perrault sat on his bed, cheeks sunken in ashy skin. His rigid posture looked as brittle as a withered twig. His still-full head of gray hair resembled dried thistle.

She choked back a sob, aware of how much he meant to her. She strained for a serene tone. "Papa, are you all right? Should I bring the doctor?"

"No. Sit here beside me, *ma fille*." His reedy voice, once the steadying force in her life, scared her. She sat on the edge of the bed and took his hand.

"Amélie, I know I can be a difficult man, but no matter how I'd like to ignore it, I feel the time has come—"

"Please don't say such things." She squeezed his hand but it felt like frail chicken bones. "Let me call Doctor O'Meara."

He raised his other hand to silence her. "I have a failing heart. I'm beyond the doctor's skill. Please, just listen to me."

Tears moistened the corners of her eyes as she stared at him and nodded.

"When you leave Saint Helena, and you will someday, please take my body back to France. In the meantime, the cemetery near Plantation House will have to do." Perrault's words were so calm she barely had time to absorb them.

"Papa, we don't need to discuss this now." Her breath quickened and her hand moved around in his dry one, searching for strength. "You've had these bouts before and were fine."

"I wish to be buried in Lyon. Near St. Nizier's...next to your mother. You must see to that." His voice sounded firmer as he ticked this off. "Amélie, will you?"

"Yes, *bien sûr*." Tears dripped from her eyes, the finality unbearable. She sniffed and wiped her face on her sleeve. "I'm finding the doctor now, enough of this talk."

Amélie located O'Meara in Napoleon's study. The doctor rushed to fetch his bag. Napoleon held her in his arms and she gleaned comfort from his embrace, her cheek against his soft shirt.

"I'm sorry for my rant earlier, when you have your own heavy burden." He caressed her hair.

They hurried across to await the doctor's verdict outside Perrault's door.

O'Meara, somber-faced, urged them into the courtyard after his examination. "Your father's heart is extremely weak. There's really nothing more I can do. Lass, I'm afraid he might not have much longer."

She expected this diagnosis. Her own heart lurched. Just when she appreciated her father's love, he faded away from her. "I'm thankful for your efforts, doctor."

"I'm here if you need anything, Amée." Napoleon hugged her, kissing her on the lips. He wiped her tears away with his thumb.

"I...I need to be alone with him. Thank you, both of you." She walked in a haze into her father's room and closed the door. Perrault, now lying on the bed, smiled at her, wan and fleeting. She sat again on the edge of his mattress.

"You have to be strong, Amélie. Strong, as when your mother died." He patted her hand as if she were the invalid.

"Yes, yes, strong for everything...oh, Papa." She blinked back fresh tears. "Maybe you should have returned to Europe. Even if I wouldn't go with you."

"This isn't your fault. My heart would be just as weak there as here."

"I suppose I blame myself." She trembled with regret, but was selfish enough to be glad she didn't follow his wishes.

"I gave you education. I will trust you to manage, no matter the bizarre situation." His intake of breath rattled across his tongue. "I must admit, a father looks on a daughter as someone to...marry off to a good man. Not for what she might achieve."

"Marriage doesn't matter to me. I'm happy to be here, loving you and Napoleon." Amélie ran a finger over her father's veined hand. "No greater love could I have found. Both of you. Please don't upset yourself."

"A father just likes to protect his child." Perrault groaned, his parchment skin wrinkling around his eyes, the dark circles beneath them pronounced. He fingered his leather shaving kit beside him. "Now, Amélie, listen closely. I have something for you, but I want to discuss it when I'm not so tired."

She smoothed down his pillow. "Yes, we'll talk of all this later, rest."

"It's...important that you know." He drew another ragged breath and coughed, but waived away her concern. "In my shaving kit, a letter for you. I finished it a few nights ago."

"Papa, a letter?" She tried to smile, to indulge him, to ease her fears.

"Oh, just remember." Perrault tucked the kit under his arm and shook his head. "I'm so sleepy, but don't want to be. O'Meara gave me a powder..." His eyelids fluttered, then closed.

Amélie sat quietly beside him, watching him sleep, trying not to think of the immediate consequences. She wanted to tug away the kit and open it, to peek inside, but her father looked so peaceful. They would discuss it later. Instead, she fetched a book and read, staying by him now as she'd once pulled away, aware of each change in his breathing pattern.

* * * *

The afternoon drifted to evening, the content of the book barely absorbed. Amélie massaged her aching head. She'd be needed for the dinner preparation.

Chef Gascon wasn't in the kitchen when she entered. He'd probably given up and gone to bed. She waived flies away from the raw chicken breasts laid out on the table.

The door opened, and Marchand popped his head around it. "His Majesty wants to know how your father is faring."

"He's resting now—"

Clarice squeezed in past Marchand, her bosoms rubbing along his arm.

"My mother said to give this chamomile back." Clarice held out a jar, smirked for Amélie, and gave Marchand a rigid shoulder. She swayed her hips as if she couldn't help herself. "*Maman* put it in Papa's bath, but he still can't sleep at night."

"I'll tell His Majesty your father is resting." Marchand backed out quickly.

Clarice glared after him and huffed.

"I thought you were interested in Jules." Amélie accepted the jar, but watched the other, curious how deep her interest went.

"All men are scoundrels." Clarice tossed back her head, upper lip puckered. "Liars to get their own way. You'll see." She nudged Amélie. "I hope I didn't interrupt you two."

"I'm faithful to Napoleon." Amélie placed the jar in the cupboard. How much did Clarice know about the sneaky manservant? "What does Jules lie about?"

The kitchen door squeaked open again. Perrault dragged in like a struggling wraith.

Amélie gasped. "Papa?"

"I must prepare my special Chicken Marengo today. The dish is the emperor's favorite." Her father snatched up his discarded apron and knotted it around his waist. The skin on his face stretched against his cheek and jawbones, his eyes unnaturally bright.

"Papa, you must go back to bed this instant, please," Amélie said, stunned by his abrupt stamina. Clarice stumbled back and watched him with narrowed eyes.

"Why? I'm no better off there than here. At least here I'm busy. Let me attend to my duties. Chop two onions." He snatched these from a basket and handed them to Amélie. Spreading out the five chicken breasts, he lit the fire and put on a large skillet. "Clarice, I need flour, white wine, and three tablespoons of that tomato paste I made earlier. Oh, and mushrooms." He heated olive oil then browned the breasts, adding the onions as Amélie chopped.

Clarice gaped at him, looking about to flee. Then she slowly moved to the pantry to rummage around. "I can't find any mushrooms, Chef Perrault."

"Then we do without mushrooms," he said, sautéing the onions in the oil.

"I'm capable of preparing this. You should rest." Amélie coughed at the sharp smell of raw onions, eyes stinging, then handed her father salt, pepper, thyme, and a crushed garlic clove.

Perrault added these other ingredients with a half cup of water and brought it to a boil. He lowered the heat to a simmer and covered the skillet. "One of you cook the rice."

"Papa, that has to simmer for thirty minutes. I can manage it from here. Please go back to bed." Amélie tugged on his arm.

Perrault grasped her wrist, a little tighter than she thought necessary. "*Ecoutez*, I'm still the parent here, and I deserve the proper respect."

Amélie backed off. Could O'Meara be mistaken in his diagnosis? Her heart lifted.

To her surprise, Clarice rushed to prepare the rice.

When they finished, Saint-Denis and a footman carried platters across the courtyard, fragrant with Perrault's Chicken Marengo over rice.

Amélie followed, to remove herself from her father's barbed stare, and helped to dish this feast onto plates to be presented to the Montholons in their quarters, and the emperor and O'Meara in the study.

Napoleon strode into the prep room, his gaze concerned. "How is your father?"

"I'm amazed, but he's up. He seems to have rallied, and insisted on cooking the meal," she replied with a quick laugh. "Nothing I said would stop him."

"That is excellent news. I had hoped—"

A high-pitched scream echoed from the direction of the kitchen.

They both rushed into the courtyard. Clarice burst out the kitchen door.

"Chef Perrault collapsed on the floor!" Her eyes wild, her cap half off, Clarice ran for the main house. "I didn't know what to do. Doctor O'Meara!"

Amélie bit back a cry and ran for the kitchen, Napoleon behind her. Several servants scrambled into the courtyard, O'Meara with them.

Her father sprawled facedown on the floor. Napoleon went to him and gently turned him over. Doctor O'Meara knelt, feeling for Perrault's pulse. At her father's chalk-white face and blue lips, Amélie flinched and bumped the wall behind her. His glassy, staring eyes sank her muscles and every drop of blood seemed to puddle at her feet.

Ali wriggled in. He and O'Meara picked up their chef and carried him out of the kitchen. Napoleon slid his arm around Amélie, assisting her out the door. She stumbled beside him. Her head dizzy, she felt like she slogged through mud.

They laid Perrault out on his bed. Ali covered the chef with a blanket. Amélie stifled a sob and rushed forward to grasp her father's shoulder. He *couldn't* be gone, not yet.

Napoleon eased her back to sit on a chair near the door. O'Meara unbuttoned Perrault's shirt, pressing a long hollow tube that flared at the end to his pale chest.

"What...what are you doing?" Amélie trembled, her hands knotted together, staring at the man lying limp on the bed.

"It's a new instrument, a stethoscope," Napoleon whispered. He stood beside her, his hand firm on her shoulder. "To listen for the heartbeat."

Murmured conversation seeped in from the closed door behind them. Seconds that seemed like hours ticked by.

"Is he...how is he, tell me?" Her voice croaked out. She feared the answer but prayed for a miracle. Napoleon squeezed her shoulder.

"In a moment, lass." O'Meara no longer concentrated on his patient. Head down, he slipped his instrument back into his bag.

Nausea bubbled in her throat. Amélie might be sick if someone didn't tell her what she already knew.

"I'm very sorry, Amélie." O'Meara straightened up, heaving a breath. "His heart just gave out. He probably passed instantly. He was a good man, one of the best."

"Of course, Doctor." Her words hollow, she staggered to her feet. The room wavered.

"I'm so sorry, *mon amour*." Napoleon embraced her. She leaned into his chest, her cheek against his heartbeat.

"I need to be alone, please." She swallowed, thoughts tumbling. She had to sort through this forever alteration in her life.

"I understand." Napoleon kissed her forehead and opened the door. The servants congregated in the narrow hall scattered. "Let me know if you need anything."

Amélie slid into her bedchamber. The same rumpled bed, scarred dresser, and spindly chair. Her shabby clothes press painted a garish yellow, her mother's doily. She fingered the doily—but nothing was the same.

She sank to the moist sheets on her mattress, and hugged her knees to her chest. The only sound was her strained, shaky breathing. The thick heavy loss as when her mother died flooded into her. Darkness filled her chamber and Amélie muffled sobs into her pillow. Her body trembled over the death of a man she might have undervalued.

* * * *

Amélie woke stiff and sore. Her high narrow window rattled in the wind. A gray morning light seeped in. Her tongue felt huge in her parched mouth. She unlocked her door and opened it to a deserted hallway. She stared at her father's closed chamber, fear trickling into her bones.

She was left alone to handle the rest of her life, no real security for her future. The man she loved might leave her to follow his ambitions elsewhere. She straightened her spine and crept into her father's room. Someone had washed and dressed him, laying him out for burial. Soon the one secure link to her past would be shrouded.

"Forgive me, Papa, for becoming a woman." She touched his forehead. "I always loved you, though it was hard to tell." She kissed his cold brow. He looked as if he were napping, attired in his best brown waistcoat and linen shirt, yet the air already smelled of decomposition. She glanced at the moldy walls, the books piled on scruffy furniture: a shabby end to a worthy man.

In the kitchen she brewed herself a cup of basil tea. No food smells. Chef Gascon must have forgotten to rise early, now *he* had to prepare breakfast. She slumped at the table, digging at the sugar cone to sweeten her tea, flicking away ants. Her head ached like a dry husk sucked of tears.

The kitchen door opened. "Amée, you're up. I've had Marchand checking. I've asked everyone to leave you alone. How are you feeling?" Napoleon stepped in, his eyes tired as if he'd had little sleep.

"I'm finding it hard to believe in a world where my father won't walk in...and take over the kitchen." Her throat thickened. "He said he'd create miracles in here...and he did."

"Under the worst of circumstances, your father was a supreme chef." Napoleon crouched in front of her chair, his hands caressing down her arms. "He worked for me at the Tuileries. I too mourn his loss. Can I—"

"May we talk later? I have so much to consider." Her desire for him improper at this moment, his hands hot on her flesh, she needed to remove herself. The earth quaked beneath her.

"Of course. Whatever you need, please ask. I want to share everything with you." Napoleon stood, kissed her cheek, and left.

She heated water for a bath in her room, and lolled in the tub until her fingertips puckered. Her hair curled in the humid space like Medusa's snakes, her thoughts just as twisting.

* * * *

Napoleon asked Chef Gascon to cook a light lunch. He instructed Marchand to set up a tray, but he carried it himself to the outbuilding. Amélie invited him into her room, her pale little face so wan. His tenderness increased.

"Amée, I insist that you eat." He squeezed into the small space. He'd have to insist that she move into the main house. "I had Gascon prepare a hot chicken soup."

She sat back on the bed, her expression surprised. He placed the tray on her knees, unfolded the napkin, and handed the cloth to her. "My stomach is a little queasy." She tasted the soup as he stood over her. She ate a few spoonfuls.

Napoleon poured a glass of wine from the carafe. "Now sip this slowly." He sat beside her on the bed and stroked her hair. "I took the liberty of detailing Count Bertrand to make the...necessary arrangements."

"I appreciate that." Her gaze met his, her fawn eyes so sad. "I know they've taken my father down to St. Paul's church." She rubbed her puffy cheeks.

Napoleon waited for her to finish the soup. He set aside the tray and hugged his arm around her. "Let me comfort you as you have comforted me. I lost my father at sixteen, and had to take over as head of the family. It is a powerful tragedy to lose a parent."

"I pushed him away in my rush to mature. I suppose all children do that." Amélie gave him a timorous smile. He eased her head to his shoulder, squeezing both arms around her and felt her relax in his embrace. "I need to...find my own footing."

"Allow me to hold you up." He kissed the top of her head, inhaling the fragrance of her hair.

"If one day for some reason you can't be beside me, if things change, I need to be self-reliant." She sighed. "I realize I asked you for money..."

"Oh, Amée, you've always been strong." Napoleon massaged along her back. Her qualms disturbed him. Did they reflect an inevitable truth? No, he'd strive to believe again in the sanctity of love. "You're all that's good, sweet, and honest... something I regret I've rarely encountered."

"I can't help protecting myself." She nestled against his shoulder. "I'll try not to doubt you."

"You are precious to me, never forget that." Could he dismiss all his selfish ways, grabbing whatever he desired? His fingers in her golden hair, Napoleon caressed the back of her head. How supple and warm her body felt pressed into his. "I have numerous faults, however, you will have to suffer with."

"I realize the difficulties." She gazed up at him with a woman's eyes, the child dissolved in the cruelty of death. She cuddled back in his arms. "I love you. That's what matters."

He'd have to manage this maturing woman. Would she turn from him someday, to a younger man?

Napoleon kissed her scalp again, the luscious taste of her, to wipe aside his insecurity. "I wish I could obliterate your heartache." He stroked his thumb along her lower lip, lifted her chin and kissed her mouth. Their idyll would be disrupted by outside events, and he regretted not having more time with her. She'd need to be pragmatic for the future.

Napoleon stopped kissing her, before he couldn't stop—his flesh all too willing and weak. "We'll forge a new beginning, you and I." He hoped fate would move quickly with Sully's return, but not separate them forever. He didn't want this pleasure they'd soon share destroyed.

Chapter Thirty

Man has moral as well as physical needs...the chain of events brings him pleasures and pains—N.B.

Amélie stiffened like a wooden doll as Madame Cloubert fitted the bonnet on her head in her attic room. The whole day seemed like a rehearsal for a distasteful play.

Madame primped at the black material she'd sown over the hat. "I have no black gloves. This bonnet will have to do."

"With the gray dress, I should be fine." Amélie avoided the woman's sharp eyes in the looking glass. Her muscles ached, her spirit sagged.

"Your father was a respectable man. You should remember that." Madame jabbed in a hat pin and Amélie winced. "Some of us would do well to follow his decent actions. *Comprenez-vous?*"

"People find love in difficult places," Amélie replied, teeth on edge. "My father understood that." Her serious reflection stared back from the pitted mirror. "Are we through?"

"Such a place as *this*." Madame rearranged Amélie's hair under the hat. "I wanted to apprentice Clarice to a milliner in Paris. The Empress Josephine promised to help, then that admirable woman died. My daughter would have had a future there."

Amélie pictured Clarice jamming hat pins into customers' heads.

"You know I revered your father." Chef Gascon kissed her cheek an hour later as they prepared to leave for the funeral. His face drooped more in grief. He dabbed at his brow with his handkerchief. "I regret our argument. What will we do? He cannot be replaced, *je m'inquiéte*."

"It means you'll have to remain out of bed and manage the cooking, Philippe." Madame Cloubert rustled by in black, resembling an irate spider. "I'm certain that *will* be a chore for you."

"I'll manage quite well, as long as you stay out of my kitchen, harridan." Gascon blew his nose loudly in her direction. His cheeks wobbled. "Oh, forgive me, Amélie."

"The emperor will secure more kitchen help." Amélie glanced around, but didn't see Napoleon. He offered to accompany her, but since his animosity toward Lowe made it a humiliating sacrifice, she asked him not to. She yearned to have his arms around her.

Marchand helped Amélie into the waiting cart. "Your father was one of the finest men I've ever met. All of us respected him. It's a great loss for the household as well as for you." The chief valet clasped her hand for a moment.

She nodded, trying to numb herself for the ceremony ahead. The others crowded in where they could. Doctor O'Meara accompanied them.

At Hutt's Gate, Fanny urged her to ride in their cart down to St. Paul's church, adjacent to Plantation House.

Most of the household was in attendance. However, the Montholons and Jules were conspicuously absent.

Amélie felt blighted as they stood in the modest little cemetery shaded by cypress trees. The churchyard adjoined the garden of the governor's residence, the small gothic church on a hill behind the estate.

She watched her father lowered into the ground and gripped Fanny Bertrand's hand. The countess hugged her.

Governor Lowe's assistant, the short, plump Sir Thomas Reade, represented the island officials. A few bored clerks stood with him.

"Their governor apparently thinks a cook's death beneath *his* august attention," Madame Cloubert grumbled loud enough for the English to hear. "We're still plagued with a Protestant clergyman, with no Catholic priest on this island."

Count Bertrand said a few words, praising their loyal and diligent chef. He also read a testament prepared by Napoleon to honor François Perrault. Amélie listened through the swirling fog of her own turmoil.

The reverend finished, closed his Bible, and stalked off, followed by the English.

Fanny touched Amélie's arm, pointing up on High Knoll. Napoleon sat astride his horse, on that looming hill of pumice stone, watching from afar through his field glasses. Her eyes filled with tears for her father's death, as well as for the proud man hampered from maneuvering freely about his current habitat.

* * * *

"Amée, you look exhausted. I'm so sorry you had to go through this." Napoleon kissed her cheek and hugged her when she stepped in Longwood's front door.

"I am tired." Amélie rubbed her temples, her mind floating in a haze. She leaned into him for a minute. "I think I'll rest in my room for—"

"I want to make you comfortable, so I'd prefer that you move into the main house. You can occupy the library." He kissed her forehead. "I insist on this."

"I won't argue, though it will seem hasty." She said the last to honor her father. Amélie had few qualms about deserting her room for the larger library. The Montholons, then Las Cases had used the room until the back wing was finished.

"I don't care how it seems. You'll be safer in here." Napoleon's soft voice and the touch of his lips calmed her.

Her things were transferred to the library that afternoon. Saint-Denis and a footman assisted with the larger items. Amélie ignored the pointed stares from the chambermaids. Her father not cold in his grave and his wanton daughter scurries for the main house to be closer to her lover.

She surveyed her new domain. At the library entrance sat a table covered in green cloth; above hung a large map of Italy made by Baron d'Albe, the emperor's topographer in France. Beside the table, three mahogany bookcases with gilt grillwork and green curtains—sent from England—were filled with most of the emperor's books. She ran a finger over the literature she once coveted, but books took a poor second to the man.

"You once wanted to be my assistant. Now you're here, you can help me with the mildew, a never-ending chore." Ali winked and picked up a leather-bound volume with a fine dusting of blue mold. "Unless that might be beneath our esteemed new princess."

"Thank you for your labors. I'd rather be alone now." She straightened the items in her clothes press. She felt like a wrung-out rag, but made an effort to sally back. "I'd prefer empress to princess, if you don't mind."

"I'm only trying to make you smile." Ali patted her cheek. "We'll certainly miss your father. Chef Gascon has huge shoes to fill. Let's hope he stands upright long enough to do so."

He rechecked the bed legs he'd just reattached, bowed in exaggerated deference, and departed the chamber.

Amélie, emotionally drained, stretched out on the bed and promptly fell into a deep slumber. When she awoke, she blinked at the unfamiliar surroundings, the airier room that smelled like leather instead of clammy clothing. She sat up, her head pounding.

She went out into the dining room. Napoleon's and O'Meara's voices drifted from the study. How unusual to now live in the middle of everything, and feel solace here. She entered the prep room where Marchand arranged coffee, cream, and sugar on a tray.

"At last, you're up. I hope you rested well. The emperor has me checking on you constantly." He smiled, his gaze solicitous. "Do you want some dinner?"

"Not really, but I'll have a cup of the coffee."

"My pleasure. You should have seen the Countess de Montholon's face when His Majesty informed her you were moving into the library." Marchand's grin unusually wry, he prepared her cup.

"Now we've turned you into a gossip. I can only guess at the countess's joy." She took the steaming cup he handed her, inhaled the aroma. "With my father's last illness and…I've neglected…have you found out anything more on Jules and the wine cabinet?"

"The count scolded me for interfering and says Jules was there at his behest. His Majesty's health has been good." He clinked spoons onto the tray. "Perhaps we're mistaken in any suspicions."

"I hope so." She wasn't convinced. Why had Jules reacted like a thief when discovered? She took a sip of coffee, and scooped in more sugar. "Marchand, can I ask you something? Was the countess…ever the emperor's mistress?"

Marchand's brotherly expression didn't waver. "I don't think that at all certain," he replied with the flare of a diplomat. "I'd forget about sordid rumors. Together with you, maybe the emperor will find the Elysian Fields he yearned for."

"The *Champs Elysees*. The plain at the world's end where no snow falls, no rain or strong wind. A tuneful breeze refreshes."

Amélie stirred her coffee, trying to untangle her mind. Saint Helena's brutal trade winds might be a poor substitute, and she didn't add the other aspect of the myth: *where the gods are sent to die.*

"Elysium…a delightful paradise. The Count de Las Cases said, when we were at The Briars, that His Majesty spoke as a spirit in the Elysian Fields." Marchand's voice turned wistful. "As if his past were centuries behind him, but it's all around him, a part of all of us."

"So true." Amélie admired the extreme loyalty the valet possessed for his once powerful master.

"Sit and try to eat something." Marchand handed her a small plate of biscuits. "I must tell His Majesty you're awake. He's instructed me to do so." He pressed her shoulder and left.

Why she let the countess aggravate her she didn't know. Napoleon professed the woman was out of favor and she'd promised not to doubt him. Then what about Albine calling to Marchand, urging her down the road alone?

Amélie slumped into a chair at the dining room table and tried to shake that image.

She picked at a biscuit as her gaze wandered around this mildewed, windowless chamber where no one cared to eat anymore. Napoleon's little court had once dined together here nearly every evening on the emperor's fine Sévres porcelain designed with his past victories. That was before she became a part of his life. Before Las Cases left, before Cipriani and her father—strange to resign herself to that—had died. Now she faced the heart-wrenching task of writing her brothers back in France about their father. The thick sorrow moved again inside her.

* * * *

After Marchand brought him the information, Napoleon rose from his study table, ending his discussion with O'Meara. "I regret your inopportune return to Europe, Doctor, but we'll use it to our advantage. We'll find ways to keep in touch. I'll provide you letters for Las Cases and a few more of my faithful." This tactic deflected his anger at the jovial Irishman's impending dismissal. He needed people back in Europe to work in his favor.

Napoleon walked into the dining room. Amélie sat at the table, looking frail and overwhelmed. He sat beside her. "Amée, do you feel better after your sleep? Have you eaten?"

"I'm not hungry. I feel sad, still tired." Her face lit up at seeing him, softening some of the disturbance on her features. Napoleon smiled and she dropped her gaze into her coffee cup.

"Are you settled in? If there's anything you need in your new accommodations, don't hesitate to ask." He put his hand over hers and felt her shiver. It pleased him that he had this effect on her. "I want to see to your every comfort."

"I've just wondered, now with Papa gone..." She stumbled out the words. "What is my official role here at Longwood?"

This question surprised him. How could he define her? A pampered mistress didn't fit with Amée's personality. "That depends on what you want to do. Is it your wish to continue with your gardening duties? I'd rather you no longer assisted in the kitchen. I'm also aware that being on this island with no useful occupation can be tortuous. Though I'm certain I could find...pleasant activities to fill up your time."

Her cheeks flushed, but her bright eyes revealed she was flattered. He'd try his best not to rush her into anything, to take advantage of her vulnerability with her father gone.

"I suppose Chef Gascon will be the official chef now. His pastries aren't much in demand. I do want to keep cultivating my garden." Amélie bashfully met his gaze.

"Nothing has to be decided this instant." Napoleon stood and assisted her to her feet, taking her in his arms. He massaged his hand between her shoulder blades and wished he could sweep her up and bundle her away from earthly concerns, but he had to make certain she understood. "Amée, you deserve to be a beloved wife, and I cannot offer you marriage, just this dishonorable arrangement."

She eased back and frowned. "I know we can't marry. I'll stay with you, and love you, as long as you respect me and treat me as a beloved wife."

"I only want you to be aware of what's ahead for us." Napoleon was unable to resist testing people, even her. "In this society, if we have illegitimate children, you will be the one to carry the shame."

"Another inequity that must be changed." Amélie stared up at him, her mouth stubborn. "I'll love having 'our' children. You promised me devotion. You can't back away now."

"You have it, as I said." Napoleon ran his fingers along her waist, over her hips, his desire for her strong. She was still innocent in many ways, but he was soothed that she loved him when he no longer had power.

When younger, he'd dreamed of a woman who would love him for himself. He struggled not to be too jaded for such pureness of heart. Napoleon squeezed her close, his face in her hair, her breasts plush against him. He kissed her forehead, then forced himself to release her and step back. "Now isn't the proper time to discuss this. You should go to bed, get some more sleep."

"All right," she whispered, but didn't move apart from him. The longing on her face almost prevented him from turning away.

"Good night, my sweet." Napoleon denied his ardor. When he took her to his bed, he wanted her ready for passion, not weak with loss.

* * * *

Crawling from bed to the new sounds and smells of the main house, Amélie stretched and wished Napoleon had kept her in his arms last evening—then she brushed aside her misplaced hunger. She'd jot down more notes about women falling prey to their desires. She must proceed with wisdom. Hadn't she already written that? Confusion clouded in on her.

The murky sadness that her father wasn't in the kitchen, preparing breakfast, returned.

She washed and slipped on her clothes, intending to speak further to Marchand about the night of her final recital. She found him in the duty chamber. "Louis, please come in my room for a minute. I need to talk with you."

"How are you today, Amélie? Is this room satisfactory?" Marchand followed her back to the library and stood in the doorway. "His Majesty has decided to put Clarice in the kitchen to replace you." His face looked so dismal she almost laughed.

"Oh, dear. Poor Chef Gascon." Amélie folded her arms and paced around the cluttered chamber. "I should have mentioned this before, but with everything that's happened...Remember when the countess called you back that night at Hutt's Gate? You said she wanted you to copy a recipe?"

"How could I forget after that awful incident?" He shook his curly brown head, his serious brown eyes brimming with sadness. "A recipe she was dying to have prepared at Longwood. A waste of my time, and dangerous to yours as it turned out."

"The countess encouraged me to go on ahead, remember?"

"I...yes, she did, didn't she?" His unhappy expression changed to quizzical.

Amélie wiped dust from one of the gilt-fronted bookcases, trying to steady her thoughts. "Do you see any relation to that and my attack?"

"What are you implying? That the countess knew someone awaited you out there in the night? You couldn't think..." Marchand rocked on the balls of his feet. "She is a frivolous, rather loose woman, but not capable of such nastiness, even in her jealousy of you."

Amélie motioned for him to step farther in, and whispered, "What about her husband, do you think him capable?"

"Of what? Physical violence? I doubt he'd soil his polished nails."

"What if he had someone else carry out the attack?"

"You believe he's that desperate to be rid of you?" Marchand's whisper tense, he glanced over his shoulder. "Yes, he's petty and envious, and I'm sure out for monetary gain. Still, Amélie, the count—"

"What about Jules and the wine? He acted too sneaky, and I'm positive the wine made Napoleon sick."

"No, you might be wrong. A few others have had those symptoms. Not as severe, it's true." Marchand sucked in his breath. "His Majesty already spoke to Jules. Now you're connecting the wine incident with your assault? *Je ne comprends pas.*"

"Someone wants to take me from the emperor's side." Amélie gripped her elbows and sank down on the edge of her bed. "To snatch everyone away and do him harm, I'm certain."

"That would be the British. Lowe's doing, not someone in our own house. You asked me not to say anything, but have you told His Majesty about these grave allegations?"

"Not every detail." She couldn't get past Napoleon's reluctance to take this seriously. Why was Marchand averse to believing her as well? "Please, keep a close watch on Jules if he's in the house."

Marchand left and Amélie sat back on the bed, uninterested in breakfast. She stared up at a water-stained ceiling, then around the room. Items were in disarray, as if her residence here was obviously temporary. Her gaze fell on the crate that contained her father's belongings.

"*Mon Dieu!*" She straightened with a gasp, remembering what he'd said about a letter in his shaving kit. How could she have neglected this? Did a letter actually await her there?

Amélie debated for a minute, then pried open the crate's lid with a knife from the dining room. The kit was at the bottom, a worn, well-used leather case that held many memories. Warm and friendly moments of watching her father shave when she was a little girl.

She opened the kit and emotion swept over her. It smelled of her father's shaving soap, the clean, spicy smell that was his essence. Her eyes blurred with tears, her throat tightened.

Under his brush was an envelope with one word written across it in her father's concise script: *Amélie*. She tore it open and read:

> *My dear Amélie:*
> *I never wanted to divulge this, but circumstances force me.*
> *First, you are entitled to the truth. Second, which will become*

clearer, something has happened that demands this. Your mother, that beautiful woman you resemble, she our marriage was not what it seemed. In the beginning we were happy, but as years went by and you children grew, she became dissatisfied. For all her strength, she hid a delicate soul. She needed a nurturing I could not provide. Because of this, she sought comfort with another man. When I found out, she was devastated, as was I. She became melancholy, but swore to never see this man again. I thought things settled, and we would learn to love each other once more. Sadly, she suffered deeper than I realized. She was so unhappy despairing she took her own life. She did this by drinking poison. Arsenic! She confessed this, right before her horrid death, but begged me never to tell you children. I was furious and distraught, but shouldered my responsibilities. For your sake, I sent you to Théo's so you wouldn't see my anger.

Now you know this awful secret. I tell you this because I believe Cipriani died from the same poison, his symptoms so similar to your mother's—but his wasn't self-inflicted. The man was murdered. I can only speculate why. Perhaps because he was so close to the Emperor, his "eyes" and "ears" in Jamestown. Whoever did this is undoubtedly trying to get to the Emperor himself. That's why I warned you to be on guard. Your intimacy with His Majesty makes me fear for your life as well.

I should have expressed my concerns of poisoning to Doctor O'Meara, but I denied them. I also wasn't sure who could be trusted. O'Meara works for the British. Be vigilant, Amélie. Warn the Emperor, he will listen to you much more so than anyone else.

My deepest love to you always. Despite what she did, your mother adored you children. When you think of her, let that be your first thought.

Papa

Bile rose up in her throat, threatening to gag her. She reread the letter to make sure of her comprehension. She crumpled the paper to her chest. A scream stirred inside her.

Her sweet, cherished mother, capable of such a vile act? A woman so full of life, so loved, how was it possible!

She too had seen the similarity between her mother's death and Cipriani's. "Oh, Papa," she spewed angrily and clumped her bedding in her fist. "You should have told me about *Maman*...before it was too late. Who will I ask questions of?" Amélie wheezed a sharp breath. "Why didn't I confide to you that I felt the same danger?"

Chapter Thirty-One

When is life an evil? When it offers nothing but suffering and pain—N.B.

"I'm so ashamed and find it impossible to believe. If you had known her you wouldn't believe it either." Amélie sniffed back tears in Countess Bertrand's Hutt's Gate parlor. "Not that I...want to doubt my father's words."

"This is incredible. You poor child. *Ma foi*." Fanny shook her head as she held the letter in her lap. "You haven't told Napoleon?"

"Not yet. Of course he must be told. He'll be outraged about Cipriani. He won't want to accept it. I needed to talk to you first...about my mother." Amélie's voice quavered, on the verge of breaking. "This must be what she meant when she told me her heart was weak, shortly before she died. Somehow I knew...she meant love and not illness. How could she have been that miserable?"

"No one can understand what's really in someone else's heart. Don't torture yourself trying." Fanny clasped her arm, her black eyes sympathetic. "We can only guess at the gloomy place she must have been in, inside."

"My poor father, living with such crippling knowledge." Amélie gripped the sofa cushion. "*Maman* loved another better than he...at least at the end. Their marriage was a charade. My mother went through each day as if we were still the most important people in her life." She shuddered. "What a lie."

"You were important. She loved you, as your father emphasized in the letter. She may not have stopped loving him, but was caught up in a passion that grew out of control. Your father hadn't the...sensitivity...to fully bring her back. He hinted as much here." Fanny sighed, rustling the paper. "Parents aren't infallible or immune to heartache."

"How wretched Papa must have been, and to never let anyone know, not even me." Amélie rubbed the lump in her throat, tasting phlegm. "I disappointed him as well, not that I'm ashamed of what I feel...or want." She thumped the chair arm. "That's different from concealing the truth, though, something I had a right to know...Oh, I suppose it was his male pride."

"Yes, they do have that. You know your father's manner didn't allow him to be very open about his private life." Fanny raised the letter and narrowed her eyes. "About this other, someone out to harm the emperor. Who could it be? How is it since you moved into the house? Have you noticed any strange behavior? Albine must be spitting fire at being replaced."

"The Countess de Montholon has stayed to herself lately..." Amélie met the older woman's probing gaze. "I think you misunderstand. I am sleeping in the library."

"Still a virgin. That won't help you with your treatise." Fanny smiled indulgently. "I might have guessed, knowing you as I think I do. Napoleon must think highly of you to let this go on. He was never so patient with his amours in Europe."

"I've heard all the sordid stories. Circumstances are different here." Amélie chewed at her thumbnail, determined to believe this herself. Soon, she'd remedy her virginal status to satisfy her own needs.

"I have noticed a change in our emperor since you've happened along. You have been wonderful for him, though is being a mistress the life you want?"

"I'd rather be his wife, but I won't desert him. I'm extremely concerned about these accusations my father brought up." Amélie glanced around the Bertrands' parlor. "Countess, the truth is, I feared something underhanded was taking place. My father's letter confirms it."

"You knew there was a poisoner?" Fanny's jaw dropped and she hunched forward.

"It involved Napoleon's special wine, which I asked him to stop drinking. The wine made me ill once...and now he admits to feeling better. It's frightening to think someone at Longwood could be committing this traitorous act. Didn't Mr. Balcombe suspect something and, before he left, insist the governor exhume Cipriani's body?"

"True, and they couldn't find it, *very* peculiar. The headstone Napoleon bought for him had even disappeared. How can you be sure the wrongdoer isn't someone from the outside, most likely one of the British?"

"I haven't ruled out anyone." Amélie took a sip of the coffee Fanny had served, her drink now cold and bitter. The liquid sloshed in her empty stomach. "The British are the obvious choice, but it's more difficult for them. They have limited access to him. Certainly they have access to our food, yet that would risk poisoning all of us."

Fanny nodded, staring at her wide-eyed. "Good point. Now who at Longwood? What about the orderly officer stuck right under your noses?"

"He too has limited access." Amélie took back the letter, folding it between nervous fingers. "Jules *has* to be involved. He was always making disloyal comments about Napoleon."

"Jules who? What's this?"

"The Count de Montholon's manservant." Amélie told Fanny of the two incidents. "Napoleon questioned the count about it. His Majesty has to see the threat. The longer we wait, the more dangerous it is."

"The manservant sounds suspicious." Fanny poured more coffee, then traced a finger over her chipped Sévres pot. "Your father didn't trust O'Meara enough to vent his concerns, but it's a shame an autopsy wasn't done on Cipriani. Being a servant, no one bothered. I suppose the villain bargained on that."

Amélie watched the cream she added congeal in her cup. "I imagine my father didn't trust O'Meara because of his rumored spying for the governor. Lowe is sending him back to England soon anyway."

"I heard. That's a pity for Napoleon. He's quite fond of the man. Amélie, is there a chance O'Meara is involved?" Fanny spoke softly, leaning even closer.

"If O'Meara is an agent for the British, why would Governor Lowe have him recalled? I think the doctor was telling trivial tales to the governor to appease him. I can't imagine he'd harm Napoleon. He's too vocal in Napoleon's defense. That's why he's being removed."

"If we're looking for someone with little ethics or conscience, I can drum up a few people who fit that description." Fanny stood, smoothing her faded gown as she walked across the worn oriental carpet. "Could...Montholon be a part of this? I have always wondered why dear Charles rushed to Napoleon's side after Waterloo. Why join a man who once fired him for disobedience? A man now banished from France…along with me."

"*En vérité*, I've never liked the count." Amélie's prejudice always rumbled beneath the surface. "We can't be vindictive. It is still speculation. His servant could be the guilty one."

"This seems to be related to your attack that night." Fanny sat on the arm of the sofa. "Your father expressed his concerns about you in the letter, saying he'd warned you before?"

"The warnings were always vague. Papa would never tell me why he felt that way. I suppose he'd have had to reveal…my mother's actions," she said, swallowing down her sorrow, "and couldn't face it."

Amélie speculated on Montholon. A man mired in debt, waiting for the promised legacy from the emperor's will, or a paid Royalist assassin? She hopped to her feet. "Please don't mention this to your husband. Let me go now and speak with Napoleon."

* * * *

Napoleon instructed Marchand to set out luncheon for him and Amélie at the small table in his study. How much calmer his digestion was now that he'd allowed himself to open up to her—as much as he dared. He looked up and smiled when she walked in, but her anxious face dissolved his contentment. "What has happened?"

"I have something important you need to read." She held up a letter.

"Your Majesty, I apologize, but there are two British soldiers here with Count Bertrand." Saint-Denis barged into the room. He bowed low, as if to make up for his breach of etiquette.

"Then have my grand marshal deal with them." Napoleon bristled with impatience.

Bertrand entered behind his valet, his expression harried. "Pardon me, Your Majesty, Governor Lowe has requested to see Mademoiselle Perrault."

"He dares again to interfere with my household?" Napoleon clenched one hand into a fist and gripped Amélie's shoulder with the other. "Why?"

"I am…not certain, Sire." Bertrand kneaded the hat he'd swept from his head upon entering. "There are two officers here to escort her to Plantation House."

"I won't have these insults!" Napoleon stalked around the table, bumping a chair. After years of his threatening them in war, his dominance in Europe, the English relished this constant disruption of his life. "That *sbirro Siciliano* has no right with his arbitrary edicts. She won't be going. You tell him I refuse to permit it."

"Please, Sire. I'm sure it can be easily handled. It's probably nothing." Bertrand's head sank into the shoulders of his threadbare blue tunic.

"Nothing? He sends two officers for nothing? I hardly think so." Napoleon strode to the fireplace, hands clamped behind his back, hating his slip of temper. "Where is the warrant for her arrest? Is this the perfidious way he plans to treat us now?"

"Arrest? What have I done?" Amélie's voice quivered a little.

Napoleon hurried back and clasped her hand. "Bertrand, I want a written request as to the nature of this action."

"May I suggest myself accompanying her, with your permission, Sire?" Bertrand looked hopefully at his sovereign.

Napoleon, muscles rigid with fury, filled with frustration that he couldn't protect his own people from his jailor's injustices. "Amée, I don't want to subject you to this man."

"No...I'll go. I don't want to be the cause of any more discord between you two." She spoke bravely, but he saw the trepidation in her eyes.

"I disapprove of this. Bertrand, don't leave her side for an instant." Napoleon hugged her to his chest and kissed her cheek. "Amée, if I could only keep such insults from you." To hide further emotion, his helplessness, he strode into his bedchamber. A man should be in control of his own destiny, and the people he cares about. That's why he must flee this island.

* * * *

The solemn group of four rode across the windswept plain, skirting the Devil's Punchbowl, following the twisted road from Longwood to the governor's residence. Amélie sat stiff in the sidesaddle, hair pinned up under her straw hat, staring at the soldiers' backs.

She tightened her fingers on her horse's reins when they entered a drive shaded by mimosa, bamboo, and lemon trees. A path, edged on both sides with blue agapanthus, led to an expanse of cultivated lawn and a terrace fronting a white stucco colonial structure with light gray shutters. The Union Jack flapped—like her pulse—from a flagstaff in front of the Georgian porch.

The air in this lush tropical foliage moistened her cheeks. A complete opposite world from Longwood, Plantation House was geographically sheltered from the constant trade winds that battered their side of the island. Cocoa trees and baobab provided ample shade.

Amélie swiped loose curls from her eyes and tried to swallow with no saliva. Although she'd attended her father's funeral nearby, she hadn't paid any attention to the verdant grounds and handsome house. She steamed with contempt for the man who lived in this splendor, while they dwelled in comparative squalor. When they first arrived on Saint Helena, Plantation House had been the dwelling suggested for Napoleon, until Admiral Cockburn deemed it too good for him.

As she and Count Bertrand were escorted into the building, Amélie's stomach rolled over. Whatever Governor Lowe wanted, it wasn't likely to be in her favor.

A jug-eared aide took them down polished, dark wood floors, through a long hall dominated by British royal portraits. They entered an antechamber filled with unscratched, elegant rosewood furniture with brass inlays. A blatant disparity to the furnishings provided for her emperor.

Minutes later the clerk bade them to enter another room. From behind a massive desk, a skinny man rose like a ramrod ready to plunge down a gun barrel.

Amélie squared her shoulders, her nerves bundled like knots in a string.

"Good afternoon." Governor Lowe glared at them with small cold eyes. His curly red hair peppered with gray framed a bony face with a high forehead. His narrow lips made no effort to smile. He wore the scarlet uniform with gold braid and epaulets of a lieutenant general in the British army. The room smelled of linseed oil and not a trace of mildew.

"Governor Lowe, this is Mademoiselle Perrault." Bertrand removed his hat and tucked it under his arm.

The governor nodded and sat down. "I will speak with her alone."

"I've been instructed not to leave her side," Bertrand informed him dryly.

The governor cast him a distasteful look, his left eyelid twitching for a moment. "By whose authority?"

"The emperor's."

"I'm not aware of any emperor on this island. Your general is no longer in power. He has no authority here." Lowe's voice was abruptly callous.

Amélie plucked at her hat ribbon, growing tenser by the minute. "If you please, Governor Lowe, I'd prefer for Count Bertrand to stay with me." She scrutinized the man before her, straining to keep her voice steady. "May we have a seat?"

The governor now glared at her. He put his long fingers together and leaned forward. "If you must."

She sat in a chair facing his desk, but Bertrand remained standing.

"Your father passed away quite recently, is that correct?" Lowe ruffled through a stack of papers on his shiny desk, yet his gaze darted across them both.

"Yes, that's correct." She squeezed any sadness out of her response.

"Then I presume you'll be returning to Europe as soon as it can be arranged?"

"I am to remain here, in the employ of Longwood." Amélie forced a smile, to appear confident. He wouldn't dare send her off the island.

"In what function?" Lowe's sharp eyes flitted over hers, his eyebrows a thick mesh above.

"Mademoiselle Perrault is an experienced cook. She was her father's most able assistant," Bertrand cut in, stiff beside her chair.

"You have another cook up there," Lowe said in an officious monotone. "In the interest of frugality, we must lessen your household expenses. I think it prudent to return you to the mainland."

"Most of our kitchen staff was left behind in England." Amélie bit at her lip. "If anything, we're understaffed. I perform other duties, such as management of the spice garden, and—"

"...And General Bonaparte's intimate, how shall I put it, companion?" Lowe punctuated his accusation with a thin-lipped smile. He thrust up a hand as Bertrand moved to speak. "No, General, let Miss Perrault answer for herself."

Amélie squirmed in the chair, but expected this. Lowe wanted her expunged, not because of her father's death, or any need to decrease Longwood's staff, but because she might be providing feminine comfort to the prisoner. Why else ask to see the cook's daughter? She glared back. "Those are false rumors. The emperor and I are good friends, nothing more."

"You intend for me to believe that?" Lowe's freckled face looked ready to break into laughter, if that was possible. He brushed a finger over his twitching eyelid. "You French rarely tell me the truth."

"Governor Lowe, that's uncalled for. As well as your previous slander." Count Bertrand squished his hat under his elbow.

"You expect Napoleon to not have *any* friends." Anger bubbled up inside her.

"Even Count de Montholon, a genuine member of the aristocracy, has informed me that this young lady is no longer needed at Longwood. Now you, General

Bertrand, are trying to convince me she is?" Lowe directed a pointed insult at Bertrand's rank as a promoted count during the Empire.

Lowe's words chilled Amélie. Montholon was out slithering again! She gripped the seat of the wooden chair. "Why take the Count de Montholon's word, sir, over ours? His luck of birth should not be a determining factor."

Lowe grimaced at her. "Because many sources have confirmed my suspicions. The regiment of soldiers keeps a close watch on the house activities, as does the orderly officer during his 'escort' of you and the general. Essential are you? No doubt, but not in the way you'd have me believe. You've done me a service in bringing the general out again, to be seen by my officer, improving him with exercise so I'm not bombarded with letters on his failing health." He darted a sharp eye at Bertrand. "Now your usefulness is at an end."

"I don't understand this merciless treatment." Amélie's composure shattered at Lowe having the nerve to thank her for performing his dirty work. "Why do you insist on humiliating us? Does civilized Europe condone the way you British imprison the emperor? Does Europe even know the dreadful conditions we're forced to live in, while you reside here like a king?"

"*Amélie*. Stay quiet," Bertrand sputtered, grabbing her shoulder, but she knew she'd gone too far. "I'm certain we can—"

"You dare to threaten me, to question my authority, Miss Perrault?" Lowe stood in one jerk, his fingers crumpling a paper on the desktop.

"Please, let's calm down." Bertrand tugged at the shoulder of Amélie's dress. "Governor, we should keep our discussion civil. We can't do without Mademoiselle Perrault. She's invaluable. She handles the food management now that Cipriani is dead. As for those other accusations, they are groundless."

"I was informed that Montholon is the one handling the—"

"*Mais non*, it's me." Amélie stared into Lowe's ruddy face devoid of sympathy. Tears pressed behind her eyes. "Show some compassion, Governor. We no longer face off on a battlefield. Must you torture an already overthrown man?"

"Amélie, we've said enough." Count Bertrand bunched her dress collar in his anxious fingers. "Montholon erred in what he told you, Governor. Mademoiselle Perrault is indispensable in the running of Longwood. If that's all, then our business here is done. Excuse us." He dragged Amélie out of the chair and toward the door.

Lowe's expression flashed livid for a moment. Then he vibrated, as if restraining himself, his mouth a timorous slash. "I do my best for you people, but *he* never makes it easy. Return to Longwood. I'll inform you of my decision at a later time."

Coldly but thankfully dismissed, Bertrand hustled Amélie back outside.

"I'm sorry, Count." In the shade of a mimosa tree, Amélie leaned a hand on its trunk for balance. She couldn't remember the last time she ate. A huge tortoise lumbered by over the sweet-smelling grass. "I saw this place, how he lives, and I couldn't help it. He's contemptible. No wonder Napoleon can't stand to speak with him."

"I pray you did no damage. It matters little that…most of what you said is true." Bertrand slapped on his hat. "We're at a great disadvantage here and always will be. Lowe isn't above enforcing anything. He could send you off quite easily."

"I know, and I let him goad me right into it. *Quel faux pas.*" Amélie fought tears, pushing the flood back again. Had she ruined everything? "If Governor

Lowe showed us—more important, Napoleon—some kindness, understanding, and most of all, respect, all this wouldn't be happening."

"Unfortunately, Lowe is a man unsuited to this position. He's overwhelmed by responsibility beyond his skill." Bertrand cupped her arm. "He's terrified of losing a highly lucrative post if anything goes wrong."

"You seem to know a lot about him, Count." She pressed on her stomach as they walked toward their horses.

"I spoke with his personal physician once, shortly after he arrived on the island. Quite without my asking, the doctor said Lowe was too agitated a person for this post. He's constantly afraid of what will happen if his prisoner escapes. I've had plenty of differences with Lowe." Bertrand helped her onto her mount. "Still, in the beginning, the emperor would have done better to…perhaps…"

"…Stay on good terms with the governor?" Amélie appreciated Bertrand's candor. He'd never be brash enough to advise Napoleon along these lines. "Your sentiments are similar to what mine were, but I'm not certain anymore." She blew out a breath. "How much of your dignity can you sacrifice, day in and day out?"

* * * *

In Longwood's salon, Amélie removed her hat, her hair damp beneath. Napoleon's field glasses lay next to the front shutter, where he'd probably been on the lookout for her return. "Count Bertrand, please wait outside the study for a minute. I need you to hear the news I'm about to tell Napoleon concerning a letter my father left me."

"If I can be of any assistance to His Majesty." Bertrand followed her to the dining room.

Amélie smoothed her humid tresses and walked into the study, closing the door.

"I should have gone with you." Napoleon swept her into his arms, his expression more worried than irate. "I have never been a coward, but that man brings out the worst in me. I felt that twinge in my left leg that happens when I've lost control. What did the villainous wretch want?"

Amélie's nerves ragged, she ran her hand up and down his fraying-at-the-cuffs shirt. "Lowe wants to send me home." She suppressed a shudder, explaining her interview.

"You say Montholon told the governor you were no longer needed? That's absurd."

"I'm afraid there's more. My father left a letter for me. I'll ask Count Bertrand to join us. He should hear this too." Amélie fetched the traumatic missive she'd stashed back in her chamber.

When she finished reading, her hands so unsteady the writing seemed to tremble on the page, the two men stared in shock. She explained to Count Bertrand about Jules and the wine.

"This is reprehensible," Napoleon said. "This is the letter you wanted me to see earlier?"

"Yes. I had just found it, or remembered to look, this morning." She turned to Bertrand. "I thought the Constantia wine tainted because I became ill after drinking it, and Napoleon's illness. Now this other...Cipriani..."

She shivered, and despite Bertrand's presence, Napoleon embraced her once more.

"Amée, I questioned Montholon about his servant. He said he was only helping him inventory the wine, which was still a breach of his authority."

Montholon *did* know of Jules's forays at the cabinet. Amélie cringed. "Then why did he act as if he wasn't supposed to be there? Marchand promised to handle it, but got nowhere."

"Marchand was in on this little misadventure as well?" After a chastising look, Napoleon kissed her on the mouth, holding her so close she felt his heart race in rhythm with her own.

"Then Jules hiding behind that scarf, his toothache..." She tried to calm her breathing. "He might have hidden bruises."

Bertrand, who'd turned away in embarrassment, now faced them.

"I spoke to this Jules about where he was the night of your attack. I saw no bruises." Napoleon grimaced. "He is a toady character. I didn't like him at all."

"They would have faded by then." Amélie swallowed. "I told you of his threats."

"I'll have him removed from Longwood immediately." Napoleon looked to Bertrand. "Arrange the matter."

"First we have to find out who he's working for with his insidious deeds." She averted her gaze for an instant. "Is it...Montholon?"

Napoleon's eyes widened. He tightened his fingers on her upper arms. "You think Montholon is involved in your attack? Prissy Montholon?"

"He could have put his manservant up to it. The count hates me unreasonably. You would think he'd be glad I bring you happiness here, but..." She fumbled to strengthen her position. "His contempt grows stronger."

"All right, we're connecting your assault with the wine and Cipriani's death?" Napoleon released her and raked a hand through his hair.

"The attack was to scare me away from the island. I'm too close to you. So was Cipriani. The wine was to harm you so you never return to power." She touched his sleeve. "The concerns brought up in my father's letter."

"This Jules sounds like the guilty one. If he's laid a finger on you, I'll have his head!"

"You said the count made excuses for why Jules was into the wine cabinet. If he's tampering with the wine, wouldn't it be at his master's behest?"

"I...too thought Cipriani poisoned." Napoleon moved away from her, rubbing his chin. "Jules could be acting on his own, or with the British—you can't rule that out." He paced the narrow room in deep contemplation. Bertrand watched him, his eyes wary.

Amélie walked to the fireplace and tossed a log on the grate, stirring the flames even though sweat already dampened her collar. She turned to face them. "I realize you appreciated the count's support when you first arrived, but please don't forget his disloyal words to Governor Lowe."

Napoleon stepped close to her again. "Indeed, the suspicions are there, yet let's not assign any guilt until we've thought it through and assembled the facts." His manner steadier, he pulled her to him and kissed her firmly on the lips. "Never keep such things from me again."

Amélie didn't rehash his stubbornness to discuss it. She leaned into him. "The countess urged me down the road...without Marchand. What are you going to do?"

"You don't think Albine is in on any of this?" He sounded too incredulous.

"Ask Marchand about her involvement." She bit down on her lip. He'd have to prove his love by believing her, not his alleged mistress.

"More things you kept from me?" Napoleon gazed at her with sadness. "I will call Montholon in to explain at once. No, he's in Jamestown today. Bertrand, mention this to no one until I take care of it. *Bien sûr*, I depend on your discretion."

"Without reserve, Your Majesty." Bertrand bowed. He gave no indication of what he thought of these accusations. "With your permission, I'll take my leave now, Sire?"

Once Bertrand departed, Amélie voiced another fear. "What if Governor Lowe insists I leave, forces me? I wasn't very cooperative."

"Not as long as I'm alive." Napoleon stared deep into her eyes. "He won't send you away. You're the one who brought me out of seclusion, he said so himself. Lowe wants to keep me well so he can maintain his importance here." He sighed. "I need time to mull over this information."

Amélie slipped her arms around him, kissing him below the curve of his jaw. His love for her excited her, even in the midst of turmoil.

"Oh, my sweet Amée. I want to take you away from all this. A place where we'd both be free..." He gazed at her with a mixture of sympathy and desire. "I don't know what to believe anymore. My world is as reversed as this island. I will interrogate Montholon and this manservant first thing in the morning."

"*Hélas*, I'm still grappling with my mother's..." Amélie winced at the mere conception of the word. She pictured her mother's kind eyes and enveloping smile. In Amélie's whirl of school and friends—the excitement of Paris—had she ignored the tension on *Maman's* face those last weeks? She sniffed. "To learn that what you depended on for security as a child was a farce...a lie."

"I'm so sorry. That *was* devastating for you." Napoleon framed her face gently. He caressed his fingers over her cheeks. "We've both had far too many sorrows, and there's more to come."

"We'll manage together." Amélie closed her eyes and pressed her face into his hands.

Chapter Thirty-Two

*...Men almost never act in natural conformity to their characters
but from a momentary secret passion—N.B.*

Napoleon paced slowly in front of Montholon and his servant, enjoying their discomfort as they stood at attention in his study. The manservant, Jules, looked like a conniving rascal.

"There are several disturbing events I demand answers to." Napoleon stopped in front of the count, watching his every inflection. Montholon's face remained smooth as glass.

"Sire, I think we could discuss this better without my valet here."

"No, I want you both here." Napoleon smiled, knowing he increased his subordinate's distress by upbraiding him before a servant. He'd had Ali roar up the fire and perspiration already beaded on their foreheads. He glared at Jules. "I asked you this before, where were you the night of Mademoiselle Perrault's attack? Did anyone see you here at the house?"

"Sire, he was with me, in my quarters." Montholon spoke up, too quickly; a flicker of distress in his eyes? "Why do you wish to know?"

"I will know everything that happens in my household." Napoleon studied the servant's face, his skin tone. "What happened with your toothache? Did O'Meara look at it?"

"It...went away, Your Majesty." The young man lowered his eyes, his voice barely audible.

"I see. Toothaches seldom just disappear." Napoleon loomed closer. "What were you doing at my wine cabinet?"

The valet shriveled under his glare.

"I explained to you before," Montholon sputtered. "He was there at my behest, Sire."

"Am I speaking to you? Did I give you permission to have a servant handling my wine?" Napoleon whipped around to scrutinize the count. Montholon twitched, though tried to hide it.

He jabbed a finger under the count's slender nose. "If I find out that anything is amiss, that you're lying to me...Did anyone see you both at the house the night of the assault?"

Montholon seemed to hold his breath. "I don't remember. If we could just—"

"Come, come, soldiers and other servants are everywhere on these grounds. You spoke to no one that evening, *either* of you?" Napoleon walked to the fireplace and kicked a log, scattering sparks.

Jules's face dampened with even more sweat.

"*Certainement*, Sire, I...we must have spoken with someone. Why do you ask?"

"Don't question my authority here." Napoleon glared at Montholon, the supercilious *aristo*. He'd never seen action in war and yet he was a general. Why had he come here to join a man branded an outlaw by the allied powers? "I want names."

"May we please talk in private, Your Majesty?" Montholon pulled at his high collar, now moist at the top. "With your permission, of course."

Napoleon rubbed his chin and again stared at the valet. A square-faced, slit-eyed coward. If he'd dared touch Amée. Back in France, the servant would be banished—here, it wasn't that easy. "Very well, but you stay away from Mademoiselle Perrault, young man. *I'm* in charge of this household, never forget that. Leave us!"

Jules jumped. "Excellent idea, Your Majesty." He gulped and slunk out, head down.

Napoleon leaned on the mantel, mimicking a casual pose. "How can you be sure your valet was in his quarters the entire time? He might have slipped out without your knowledge."

"Because I insist he stays close, in case I need him." Montholon shifted in his shiny boots. "As I recall, Sire, the foolish girl was walking back alone. The soldiers probably saw an opportunity to amuse themselves."

"Montholon!" Napoleon strode back and unleashed his temper, a strategy he used to throw his opponents off balance—but this truly infuriated him. "How *dare* you spout such slander. You consistently defy my wishes concerning Mademoiselle Perrault!"

"I apologize, but—"

"Stay out of my personal business! Not another word about her." Napoleon bristled with anger that he hadn't intimidated the count enough. This subordinate would have groveled before him at the Tuileries. "What about these comments to Governor Lowe overheard by others?"

"A misunderstanding, I assure you, Sire." His courtier's smile between curly sideburns appeared not so confident. "I would never talk ill of you."

"What of Albine? Marchand says she insisted Mademoiselle Perrault walk down the road alone." Napoleon regretted that this woman he once shared intimacy with might act so vicious.

"Sire, you can hardly think my dear wife knew someone waited to attack the young lady in the night." The count's small mouth twitched. Did he react with sufficient astonishment?

"Her behavior warrants scrutiny." Napoleon picked up his snuffbox from his sideboard and flipped it open. He took a quick pinch, the acrid smell filling his nostrils.

"Perhaps Albine is only jealous of your relationship with…Mademoiselle Perrault." Montholon watched him with his cool blue eyes.

Napoleon suspected the count encouraged his wife to steam up his sheets to lull him into submission. He cringed to think that this man, who tended him so well in the beginning, harbored malicious intentions. Jules might be working entirely on his own. "I demand you keep your valet away from my wine."

"I will, of course. Has the wine not been to your satisfaction? If not, it is the British you should be careful about, Sire. The orderly officer, the governor. I have been your most devoted servant." Montholon bowed. "Heedful to your every wish."

"More exaggerations from you!" Napoleon scraped his thumbnail across the snuffbox. Cipriani, his loyal Cipriani. Could the British have had him murdered, or agents for the Royalists in France? Their faction several times attempted to assassinate him when he was First Consul and Emperor. He calmed himself, to keep to the business at hand. "How is your stepfather, the Count de Semonville?"

"He…is well, Your Majesty." Montholon quickly masked the surprise on his face.

"Are the rumors about him true? He was a Royalist spy during the Revolution?"

"An unfounded tale," the count said through stiff lips. "If I could only—"

"I'm keeping a sharp eye on you, Charles. *Dieu le sait*, I've always been surrounded by betrayal. It's the chance you take when you're in a position of importance." Napoleon slapped the snuffbox onto the sideboard, intent on Montholon squirming. The Royalists could be shrewd enough to send this blue blood with him into exile to make certain he never regained power.

"I would never betray you. I deeply apologize for any ill-conceived comments I might have made…"

"Enough of your self-serving prattle." Why indeed had this man joined him after he escaped Elba, insisting he be a chamberlain of his court? A man he'd dismissed years ago for disobeying orders. Where, however, was the unequivocal proof? He disliked refuting her, but did Amée try much too hard to find guilt in everything the count had done? "Return to your quarters and await my decision on what your future role will be here."

After the count bowed out, Napoleon snatched up the box and took another pinch of snuff. Bertrand and Las Cases as well as Amée warned him not to trust the count, but he had an inborn aversion to being advised. He grumbled. His generals in battle would agree with that. They'd said as much after his abdications. Still, doubts remained.

Napoleon sagged against his sideboard. He'd wanted the British to be the villains.

* * * *

Amélie squeezed a cloth and wiped up crumbs and spills from the dinner mess Chef Gascon left. The kitchen remained her haven—a world separate from court intrigues. Her father's apron still hung from a peg near the door and she trailed her fingers over the stiff, stained material.

She'd fretted throughout the day with the troubles clouding her mind, but had encouraged Napoleon to spend time with his soon to depart doctor.

She scrubbed the table, then the window with vinegar and water.

In the courtyard, Clarice snatched clothing from the clothesline in the setting sun. Amélie heard her arguing earlier with her mother about why laundry was still her duty when now she was forced to be the kitchen maid.

About to turn away, Amélie saw Jules walk up behind Clarice and pinch her fat buttocks. Clarice laughed, faced him, and snaked her arms around his neck. Jules ran his hands across her hips in the fast fading light and the two strolled off together out of the courtyard.

Amélie slapped the rag against the window sill. There *was* an attachment between Clarice and the most infamous servant at Longwood. No matter their animosity, she dreaded to think of Clarice involved in this alleged conspiracy.

An hour later, Amélie returned to her room. Napoleon was still with Doctor O'Meara. The two men had taken a last ride around the island together, and now enjoyed a brandy in Napoleon's study. In the library she sat on her bed, rereading a letter from her brother Théo. As slow as the mail was, the news of their father's death would take more weeks to reach France.

A floorboard creaked outside her room, then again. She rose, picked up the candle, and eased her door open. A shadow crept along the wall near the alcove where the wine cabinet stood. Her pulse trebled and she stepped out to peer around the corner. She started when someone stood and moved into her light.

"Surprised, *mignonne*? Are you spying on me again?" Jules frowned, squinting. He clutched a bottle of wine to his chest. His clothes were rumpled and his hair in disarray with a few pieces of straw, as if he was just returning from his tryst.

"What are you doing here? His Majesty ordered the count this morning to forbid you from his wine cabinet." Amélie stiffened, breathless with anger.

Marchand hurried out of the drawing room, as if hiding there. "Now I've caught you, Jules, don't deny this again." He spoke with unfamiliar sharpness. "I've kept you under watch."

Jules's gaze slid between them both. "My master told His Majesty I was helping him inventory, and never forbade me access. What is this game?"

"I think your master was covering up the fact you were caught." Amélie jerked the candle and the flame wavered. "Now you both have disobeyed Napoleon."

Jules shrugged, then half smiled. "It's not what you think."

"Then what are you up to?" Marchand demanded. "Confess it now, *sur l'heure*."

Jules leaned toward Marchand with a conspiratorial wink, his lower lip stuck out to its limits. "If you must know, since you dog my steps, I take the wine to the Count de Montholon. He puts a special tonic in it for the emperor, and—"

"What sort of tonic?" Amélie's heart lurched and she tightened her fingers on the candlestick. Her fears were correct!

"You're aware the emperor shuns medicinals. The count is looking out for his health." Jules turned to Marchand. "You shouldn't say a word, though I doubt *she* will keep quiet."

"Where does the count get this tonic?" She shoved her flame near his face.

Jules cast her an insolent look. "From Doctor O'Meara."

Not the mild, ineffectual doctor whose innocence she'd defended? "How could… and you've been doing this one bottle at a time?"

"O'Meara gives my master a small ration at a time, but today was another waste. There seems to be as many bottles as before, as if the wine isn't being drunk very often."

Napoleon admitted he frequently forgot to request the wine. "You will stop this at once," she warned.

"Someone will speak with your master about this tonic." Marchand snatched the bottle from Jules. "Give me the keys."

Jules grimaced and held the keys aloft. Marchand twisted them from his hand.

"*Peste*! The Count de Montholon will hear of this." The man slunk out of the room toward the front door.

"Napoleon will have to see the complicity now. He's already agitated because O'Meara leaves Longwood for good tomorrow. The doctor can't be involved. There has to be a rational explanation," Amélie said as she and the chief valet stood before her door. She told him of Napoleon's interrogation earlier. "We need to question Doctor O'Meara in the morning."

"I'm sorry if I doubted you before this. I'm used to so much slander here, I disliked making a rash judgment." Marchand rocked on his feet and jangled the keys.

"I understand, Louis. Good night." Amélie shut her door, the candle now wavering in her hands, the flame dancing. She mused on her willingness to give O'Meara the benefit of the doubt, but not so the Count de Montholon.

* * * *

Amélie left her half-eaten breakfast and hurried outside. Marchand waited near the doctor's door in Longwood's right wing, more a line of connected sheds. She stifled a nervous yawn, having spent a tormented night stewing over O'Meara's alleged involvement.

The doctor invited them in with a smile. He removed things from his dresser and placed them in a battered valise already overflowing with clothes.

"To what do I owe this great honor?" he asked, always the amiable Irishman.

"We won't waste too much of your time, Doctor." Amélie clenched her fingers together, her words even. "I know you're readying to leave Longwood today."

"Lowe demanded I not speak to anyone when he ordered my dismissal. I insisted I be allowed to pack my own possessions, and say goodbye to Napoleon." O'Meara shoved a brush into the clothes, conversing in the bad French he'd learned since living here, so Marchand understood him.

"Doctor, it's come to our attention that the Count de Montholon," she emphasized the name, bitter in her mouth, "may be adulterating the emperor's wine."

"We caught Jules at the cabinet last evening." Marchand crossed his arms. "He admitted to a tonic he says came from you."

Amélie studied O'Meara for a guilty response, a sign of fear or anger at being discovered. To her relief he gave an amused smile and chuckled softly.

"The count did ask me for a tonic, to improve Napoleon's health. It's harmless really. Montholon said he was concerned his sovereign wasn't getting enough exercise. This was before you came along, Amélie, to shake him out of his self-imposed inactivity." The doctor wiped mold off a pair of shoes and wedged them in his case, his manner relaxed and congenial.

"You say the tonic's completely harmless?" She wasn't convinced, yet let out a tense breath.

"Aye, some believe in its rejuvenating qualities, but I was sworn to secrecy. Napoleon says chicken broth or fasting and hot baths are the only true cures. He's usually spurned everything I prescribed for him." O'Meara tried to shut his valise, clothes poking out the sides. Amélie stepped over and folded them neatly inside.

"Do you make this tonic?" Marchand asked.

"No, it's made by an elderly woman in Jamestown. She's known for her healing herbs and potions. Don't worry, I checked her out thoroughly beforehand."

"Even so, this practice will be halted immediately," Amélie said. "I'd like the name of this woman. I hope there's no chance something...toxic was ever used."

O'Meara's round face sagged. "You know me better than that. I've always had a profound respect for Napoleon, but I can't speak for the other British on this island. I'd recommend being...careful." He grasped Amélie's shoulders, giving them a light shake, his crooked smile sad. "You must look after him for me. It's not by choice I'm leaving. Lowe is a petty, little man, yet so contradictory. Did you know he's freed the children who will be born of slaves beginning next December? Slavery is repugnant to him, but he treats Napoleon with inhumanity."

"I'm sorry you're being sent away, Doctor. The emperor will miss you." Amélie's knotted muscles relaxed. "I promise to take excellent care of your patient."

"I trust you will, lass. I deeply regret having to go. I must take my leave of Napoleon before Lowe musters his troops to haul me off. I'm afraid Lowe attacked my pride and insulted me. I had no choice but to defy him."

"The governor seems to bring that out in us all," Amélie said, sad that Lowe proved triumphant in having O'Meara desert Napoleon.

"Aye, well, maybe it's time for me to return to Europe." O'Meara brushed a hand through his wooly brown hair and pointed down at a splintered drawer. "Lowe had his soldiers break into my desk and rifle through my papers. They stole gifts Napoleon had given me, which Lowe refuses to return."

Amélie sighed at the governor's cruel raid on their lives as they said farewell to the doctor.

"Doctor O'Meara seems to be telling the truth," Marchand said as they walked back around the house. "His Majesty will still be furious to know they added something to the wine."

"I did have faith in him, but I'm positive something else was put there, and it's *not* for the emperor's health. Now the count has purposely ignored his orders."

* * * *

Two hours later, Amélie observed with sorrow as Napoleon watched the doctor ride away, escorted by the governor's soldiers.

He shut the salon door, took her arm, and walked her back to his study. "Lowe would stoop to anything. Here he's a little sovereign with absolute power, but I have my revenge. I told O'Meara to seek out my family. To gather all the letters the sovereigns addressed to me when I was in power and have them published to bring shame upon them. These emperors and kings once begged for my favors and to leave them on their thrones. Now they scheme to crush me."

"To send O'Meara away is so unfair. I'll brew you a cup of my calming sage tea. Please sit." She shivered at the anger on his face. Amélie understood his Corsican temperament intensified his desire for revenge. Napoleon's upset might force her to wait before bringing up Montholon's perfidious actions.

"The *Edinburgh Review* published articles on Lowe's foul behavior here, and I managed to obtain a copy. Lowe accused O'Meara of providing it to me. That meant the ax for him." Napoleon followed her into the preparation area where she'd left her box of sage.

Amélie scooped out the herb, then realized she was being the "good little wife," the protector of her man's serenity, something she'd railed against in the past. She stiffened her neck and had to strike a balance between two extremes.

"Napoleon, you need to speak immediately to the Count de Montholon. Marchand and I discovered he's been putting a tonic into your wine behind your back. This behavior can't be tolerated. We caught Jules in the act after you ordered the count to keep him away."

"O'Meara mentioned something about you and Marchand's inquiry, *without* my knowledge. Also the tonic, which enrages me. Montholon disobeyed a direct order? This will be his final disabuse of my authority," Napoleon clinked together teacups on the preparation table. "The disharmony in this place never ends and everyone strives to become a part of it."

"I'm trying to help you, because I love you." She looked at him over her shoulder, and didn't add that he dismissed things he didn't wish to see.

"I laid awake half the night, turning these events over, and now there's more. I need some peace." Napoleon moved up behind her and ran his hands over her shoulders. "Oh, Amée, I'm not angry at you. Yes, at my own stubbornness. You see right through me, *mon amour*."

Amélie felt the warmth of his body so close to hers, his fingers unnerving on her flesh. A crackling sensation traveled up her spine to her neck, like the electricity that hangs in the air before a storm breaks. She turned and put her arms around him. The vulnerability in his eyes drew her further. He had been through so much and she, too, wished their troubles would disappear. "Speak to the count this afternoon. That's all I ask."

Napoleon kissed her cheek. "I'd much rather speak with you, alone." He caught her mouth with his and she let him kiss away their distress. He parted her lips and their tongues touched for the first time, fomenting that lush fullness inside her.

She caressed the back of his neck, her mouth hungry on his. He pressed his body into her and fumbled with the hooks of her dress.

Warmth simmered deep inside her and she molded herself against him. To her surprise, he lifted her up onto the table, clattering dishes. He kissed her chest, pushing down her bodice, shifting himself between her knees.

"In the middle of the day, in here, how scandalous." Her flesh tingled and she sighed with the forbidden pleasure. She glanced about, to see if anyone might come in, until Napoleon's sweet kisses dissolved her senses.

"We need to consummate our relationship, Amée." Napoleon ran his lips across the top of her breasts. He reached along her thighs and tugged at her undergarments. His fingers slipped into her drawers, stroking her. "...Forget our burdens."

Amélie gasped at his intimate invasion, her breath sharp in her lungs. Smelling sage and the heady scent of desire, she unbuttoned his waistcoat. "Forget our burdens, *vraiment*."

Napoleon kissed her exposed nipple. "You're right though, not here." He lifted her down and pulled her toward his study, his eyes burning with fever, face flushed.

Heat radiated like molten lava through her every limb. Her body demanded release. "I am more than ready."

In his bedroom, Napoleon took her in his arms again. "I want to prove my love to you, unselfishly if I can. I feel out of control, like a boy at his first time." He traced his fingers down her neck, his hesitancy endearing.

"Teach me…everything," she whispered. Bashful without the experience, she'd learn to be his only source of pleasure.

Napoleon caressed her skin as he removed each item of clothing. Amélie quivered in expectation. He laid her across the bed and slipped off her drawers and stockings. Once naked, she covered her breasts, vulnerable when he appraised her with his luminous eyes. He tenderly dislodged her hands, kissing each palm and the insides of her wrists.

"You're so desirable, like no one else." Napoleon undressed and climbed in beside her. His caressing fingers and hot lingering kisses made her writhe and moan.

She met his kisses, taking his breath deep inside her, her hands rubbing over his smooth skin. Her extended nipples brushed sensually against his chest. The musky scent of their flesh mingled.

Stroking between her thighs, he probed his fingers deeper, forcing her to cry out. His lips savored her breasts and Amélie arched her back, her blood and nerves about to explode. Her body sheathed in moisture, she wanted him to open her up, like a bud.

Again kissing her mouth, Napoleon entered her, gentle at first, then with more insistence. She whimpered in pain and then succumbed to a throbbing where even pain became pleasure.

Chapter Thirty-Three

...Nature is in a state of tension so painful that the outbreak of the storm is desirable...—N.B.

Amélie awoke in Napoleon's arms, her back against his chest, hearing his gentle breathing. Late afternoon light filtered through the shutters. She felt soreness between her legs, and the stickiness of blood. She almost stretched like a cat, satisfied in the warmth, and purred along his body. Turning her head briefly, she watched him sleep. How much younger he looked since they had grown close—his healthier complexion, the weight loss. Now he belonged to her.

She smiled. No one loved him as well as she. Both his wives, the first indifferent, the second shallow, had been unworthy of him. Neither equaled Amélie's genuine passion, her caring devotion. She loved the man, not the rising young general, nor the great conqueror of Europe. Though his enemies had stripped him of his empire and banished him to the bottom of the world, he was still a proud, imposing, and fascinating human being.

Amélie felt Napoleon's lips on her neck and rolled over to face him. She grinned, half amazed to be in his bed, modestly covering her nakedness with the blanket.

"I never slept so sound and had the most tender dreams." He brushed her hair from her cheek. "You knew this was the way it was supposed to be, and I kept resisting. You're much wiser than I."

"I knew how I felt about you," she whispered, reaching up to touch his face.

"How wonderful to wake with you here." Napoleon dipped his head and kissed her lips, then drew back. "Don't ever conceal your charms from me." He tugged down the blanket, revealing her breasts. Kissing down her chest, he languidly savored each nipple until she tingled with pleasure. "Your skin is so sweet, the softness, the taste of you. Clean."

Amélie abandoned her shyness and urged him on with another kiss. She caressed his reddish-brown hair, as silky as she'd once imagined when she watched him from afar. Her hands trailed down his body—she'd explore every inch of him. She kissed his chest as her fingers felt the deep scar on the inside of his left thigh, where a bayonet had gouged him at the battle of Toulon.

She devoured his kisses, his touches, as if she'd discovered a glorious new ritual. She starved for him, and he behaved just as needful. He directed her hand, and she stroked him, enjoying the desire on his face. Their lips and breath steamed together, Napoleon pushed inside her, moving slowly. She allowed her body to take over, rising and falling with his, the heat infusing her. She arched her back and moaned with pleasure.

Afterwards, Amélie lay in his arms, unable to suppress a smile that went beyond contentment. Her sister-in-law once said you only "sleep" with your husband to please *him*. How untrue a statement. A woman could enjoy this intimate aspect of life as well as a man. Not to mention she now had the sensual details she needed for her writing.

* * * *

Fresh from a hot, soaking bath, Napoleon told Marchand to bring Montholon to his study. He wished he could indulge in pleasure with Amée for weeks until Sully's return—how luscious to lose himself in her supple body, and to experience these sweet sensations from his youth—but business must prevail. Clad in his best uniform, trying to erase the slaked smile from his face, he took a chair before the study fireplace.

"Your Majesty, you asked to see me," Montholon said in the effusive tone he reserved for him. "I hope our relationship is not harmed by my earlier perceived misconduct."

"Perceived?" Napoleon couldn't help but chuckle—a good way to smooth down his aggravation. "O'Meara related something very interesting to me before he left."

"Let me express my deep sorrow at his untimely departure." Montholon bowed.

"You always told me you thought my doctor to be intrusive." Napoleon spoke in a forced languid voice. "It is a great loss to me, but O'Meara informed me that you've been putting an herb tonic in my wine. Your manservant, Jules, admitted as much."

"Before you scold me about Jules, as you have every right, let me say I did not know he was at the cabinet yesterday. I have chastised him." Montholon stood at attention, looking like a tin soldier in his blue uniform and tarnished gold epaulets. "The tonic was perfectly safe, Sire, but if I've displeased you, I'm certain I can explain."

"You did this without my permission, tampering with my personal wine. You know how I feel about medicine, and still you initiated this. Your behavior angers me." Napoleon strained for an indolent tone, leaving the man before him to guess where this led.

"O'Meara brought me the herbs. I saw no harm in looking out for your well-being, Sire. You take herbs when the kit…Mademoiselle Perrault prescribes them." Montholon cleared his throat. "About Mademoiselle, if I may be so bold, don't you fear the malicious slander relayed to Europe? The English papers already talk of your *amourette*. Dare you continue to pay attention to a girl of her low station?"

"Never mention her in that way! Do I care anymore what Europe thinks of me? I am above their petty slurs." Napoleon hid his disgust that Montholon hadn't learned any respect for Amée after their last confrontation, and he now blamed O'Meara for the wine. His relaxed mood wore thin. "Low station? What does that mean, my good man? My father was a humble lawyer on a small island. I started out as only a soldier. You, on the other hand, were born to the aristocracy. Does that make you any more prominent than I?" He raised a brow at Montholon, allowing a hint of menace to slip in. "Events have proved otherwise, haven't they?"

"You misinterpret, I only wanted—"

"You want to malign a beautiful, intelligent young lady, who cares for me above all others." Napoleon gripped his chair arms. He would rid himself of this man who refused to respect his wishes. "The only person without fail who is straightforward with me. You will cease *all* your household meddling immediately."

"Of course I will, as your obedient servant. I have so missed our friendly discussions together here." The count's condescending manner brittle, he stepped toward the door. "A soothing glass of wine will calm our tempers. Shall we have some of your Constantia? I'm certain I can find a bottle that has not been touched."

Napoleon hesitated, amazed at the man's audacity, disgusted by his confirmed treachery. Was Montholon desperate enough to risk sipping a poisonous beverage to accomplish his underhanded aims? "I don't feel like any wine. You may have a glass, however. Help yourself."

"That's fine, if you don't care to join me." The count *sounded* disappointed. He stiffened back to attention. The light slipping through the shutters formed stripes on his shiny boots. "I only wish to make your cruel exile more comfortable."

"Is that why you came with me?" Napoleon's anger simmered He wanted to be certain he had the correct adversary, but now it didn't matter. The count betrayed him with the tonic. "You behave like a man who can't be trusted in too many things."

"You've given me the privilege of accompanying you. I thought that meant I'd have a say, as far as decorum, on what goes on in our court." Montholon appeared to struggle with his courtier's mask, his mouth pinched. "I do need to know one thing. Marchand confiscated the keys to the wine cabinet. If Jules misbehaved, this is still an insult to my personal staff. Am I to have these back, as—"

"Out of the question, you can't be trusted to ensure the sanctity of my wine." Napoleon sat up straighter in the chair to deliver his *coup de grace*. "Albine has expressed an urgent desire to return to Europe with your children. I agreed it was a sensible idea."

"When did you speak with her?" Montholon's eyes widened for an instant. "She has been unhappy, Sire. I think it's more from your apathy towards her than any compulsion to return to Europe. *En vérité*, we have felt neglected. You and Albine were so dear to one another."

"It's preferable you go home with her." Napoleon ignored that inference. "A family needs to remain intact. Albine's doctor at the camp says she needs to take waters for her health. Now you should make preparations—"

"*Mais non*, Your Majesty. Pardon my rude interruption. I wish to remain here to serve you. That's completely out of the question." The count tugged at his high collar. "If Albine desires to go, I will consent to her leaving without me."

"I am dictating that you leave with her." Napoleon clenched a fist on his thigh. "I will, of course, give you a settlement, as was promised in the beginning."

"Sire, I know I have displeased you, but I'll never be so foolish again. I feel it's my honorable duty to stay." The count's voice anxious, his posture almost sagged. "You're well aware that Governor Lowe won't let us leave without reason. Albine and I both signed the paper swearing to stay with you as long as you remained on the island."

"The governor will not stop you if your wife's health is at stake. Depart Saint Helena with your family. Make certain that manservant of yours, Jules, accompanies you." Given the discomforts of the island, his courtier should be relieved to go. Amée appeared to be right. The unmitigated gall of this *aristo*. Napoleon sank back into his chair, his shoulder muscles tightening. "Speak with Albine and I'll have Bertrand make the appropriate arrangements for your departure. Not another word! You will leave with your wife and children. You're dismissed."

* * * *

Amélie soaked in rose-scented water in Napoleon's tub, luxuriating in the size of it. Toweling off, she dressed and joined him at the study table where Saint-Denis served them dinner.

"From now on we must lock up our food supplies. That old cabinet in the butler's pantry has a hasp, we just need to put a lock on it." She took a bite of braised beef, stringy and tough—her father prepared meat better. Another thought upset her more. "I wish the count and his entourage would move to Jamestown to await a ship. I know I insisted on your confrontation, and it was necessary, but this dismissal may make him desperate."

"Much of the guilt does point to Montholon." Napoleon stroked his hand along her arm, ignoring his food. "Bertrand reminded me about his embezzling of army pay under the first Bourbon Restoration, and that he was never brought to court-martial for such a serious crime. His stepfather is close to the Count d'Artois, the king's nefarious younger brother." He grimaced. "I suspected Artois of planning assassination attempts on my life."

"At least we found out in time." Amélie pulled his hand to her breast. "I realize the count's attention meant much to you. Is there anything I can do to make this easier?"

"Having you with me makes many things easier." He smiled tenderly, caressing her breast. "What a monumental blunder trusting him. Perhaps I thought having an actual blue blood with me would be a bridge for my return to power."

"The count acted indispensable when you needed support." Amélie removed Napoleon's hand from her tingling nipple and kissed his fingers. "Try to eat something."

"He might have poisoned Cipriani. My poor, loyal Cipriani. He must have been suspicious, too close to the truth." Napoleon poured himself half a glass of Madeira and filled the other half with water as was his habit. "The Royalists are behind this, of course."

She watched him sip the wine, but was that even safe? "Cipriani had managed the food, another excellent reason to have...removed him. I know this is extremely painful for you."

"To think I promised this *aristo* a significant reward in my will." He chuckled dryly, swirling the wine. "Imagine, offering personal wealth to the rogue plotting your death."

With a shiver, Amélie nudged her plate aside, her ap*petite* gone. She sipped her Madeira, concentrating on the rich flavor that held no aftertaste.

Napoleon pushed his chair beside hers and squeezed his arm around her. "Don't worry. I've already told Marchand to take over the household food management." He kissed her mouth. "I've too long succumbed to the ennui of this island."

"Let's forget food and sit on the sofa." She kissed back, her lips lingering. She'd initiate their ardor. Slowly blowing out the table candles, she clasped his hand and they moved over to the lumpy cushions.

"Maybe you're the only person I can depend on." He lifted her hair and kissed her nape, holding her thick locks to his face as if the scent intoxicated him. "No woman ever gave herself to me so selflessly. This cold, barren place is now inviting and warm, as you are."

"You often read my thoughts—it's unnerving." She laughed and ran her fingers along his thighs. His tender expression melted into that sensual yearning that fueled her ache for his touch.

"Can you read mine...now?" He unfastened her dress, his hands roving over her, his lips hot on her bare shoulder. "I've been accused of being abrupt in my amours, but not when I felt genuine passion."

Amélie quivered with his kisses. Her breath quickened at his face full of desire, his mouth eager for hers. They tossed their clothes aside. She stretched out on the cushions and pulled him down on her naked flesh. Napoleon entered her slow and steady and she fit her body around his, like a flower clutching its stamen. She moaned.

* * * *

A warm February rain beat down on their bleak patch of earth, turning the courtyard to red mud. Amélie darted into the kitchen, a basket with five turnips in her grasp.

"Here, Chef Gascon. These are the last in the garden, but they're rather puny." She swiped back her wet hair and put the basket down on the table.

"I'll try to do something with them, before we wash away. The stores are low again, so anything will do." Gascon didn't look at her as he made this blasé comment. He shuffled around the kitchen, absently wiping a rag across the greasy stove.

Amélie stepped in crumbs, then rinsed mud from her hands in a bucket of water floating with ants. The table was sticky with dough. She hated to see the kitchen in such deterioration. Her father would have been mortified.

"*Eh bien*, Amélie, so you finally surrendered?" Saint-Denis entered through the door, one eyebrow cocked. He shook the rain from his coat sleeves and black hair.

"None of your brazen mouth," Amélie warned, only half serious, drying her hands over the stove. Ali still had to have his amusements no matter how her status rose.

"You looked so content at dinner last night. Oh, yes, quite the fatted calf." He fixed her with his mischievous glare.

"We shouldn't discuss such things." Chef Gascon, his flabby face wobbling, banged pots around, clanking them onto hooks. "Where is that Clarice? She's been of little help to me." He groaned. "Hopefully the soldiers will bring some mackerel tomorrow, to stretch our resources. Ah, me, this rain makes my bones stiff. I'll be back for dinner." He met Amélie's eyes briefly, and traipsed from the kitchen.

"You embarrassed the man. He obviously doesn't approve of my 'surrender.'" Amélie picked up the bucket, opened the door, and sloshed the water into the courtyard. She set it just outside to catch fresh rainwater. Then she reached high and checked her herbs hanging from the rafters. "I've heard you find the Bertrand's new governess, Miss Mary Hall, quite the *belle*. Is this true?"

"Such a pretty, bright new face." Ali's broad grin revealed a crooked tooth on the left side he must have taken great pains to hide in the past. "Don't change the subject."

"I'm certain the whole island knows about me. Though I was falsely accused long ago." Amélie put vinegar in a bowl with a splash of rainwater and scrubbed down the kitchen table and stovetop—spicy over musty. "Which flag should display from Alarm House stating the cook's daughter has officially taken up residence in the imperial bed?" She squished the cloth and blinked away the idea of what her father would have said to this.

"Now *I* surrender, your ribald tongue cuts me to ribbons. Are you taking lessons from Clarice?" Saint-Denis threw up his hands in mock supplication. "Do you have any mint left to make tea? Jules has an upset stomach. He's very irritated, now that His Majesty is sending him and the Montholons off."

"The issue is between Napoleon and the Count de Montholon." She scrubbed hard on a mildew spot on the wall, trying to redirect her anxiety.

"I thought nothing of it at the time, but Jules wasn't in his quarters the night of your attack. Clarice asked me if I'd seen him. She said she'd looked all over Longwood. She was sniffing him out for a beau. They've had a liaison now." Ali shoved his hands in his waistcoat pockets and hung his head for a moment. "Jules is a rogue. I'd stay away from him."

"I wish you *had* spoken up. Please, keep a watch on Jules until they leave." Amélie strangled every drop of moisture from the rag. Jules fingers around her throat? He must be the culprit. His and the Montholons' removal couldn't be swift enough for her. Now that Napoleon revealed their suspicions, she feared what the scoundrels might be forced to do.

Chapter Thirty-Four

It is my fate that I should be betrayed again and again by the horrible ingratitude of the people to whom I have shown the most kindness—N.B.

Amélie's apprehension drained from her body when Count Bertrand handed Napoleon the papers of official release for the Montholons.

"Lowe pretended to give me a difficult time, but now it's finally arranged, Your Majesty," Bertrand said, his smile satisfied.

Napoleon didn't even glance at them and dismissed the grand marshal from his study.

"I wonder if Governor Lowe is curious about why you're sending such close companions away. I'm glad they've cowered in their quarters these past days." Amélie spread her mother's doily on top of Napoleon's bookcase. She'd transferred her personal items into his chamber. Since their intimacy, she slept in his bed. A few of the servants winked, while others wouldn't meet her eyes, as she carried possessions back and forth. Amélie, full of love and sensual gratification, felt proud of her position. "I'll have to keep some things in the library. There isn't enough room." She bent and put her arms around Napoleon as he sat at his writing desk. "I hope there's a ship for Europe in port now."

"I'm afraid there are some unfortunate developments." Napoleon sounded far too solemn, and didn't turn to look at her. He wiped his quill on his breeches, a bad habit from his days of glory when he had unlimited access to clothes to replace the ones he ruined.

"What do you mean?" She fingered his frayed collar, wary.

"Montholon says he can't make the next sailing. Albine is ill and needs complete bed rest. He's called for the army surgeon to look at her."

"You're not teasing me, are you?" Her strained remark didn't wring a smile from him. "We have to remove those people from here. The countess wanted to leave for some time. Why would she change her mind?"

"It's hardly her fault, Amée, and it won't be long. Probably two more days and they can move to Jamestown." He patted her arm. "I gave permission to let the doctor examine her."

She straightened, digging her fingers into his shoulders a little. "I can't help but wonder if she's faking on purpose."

"You don't think *she* is in on any of this? If so, she most likely has been duped by her husband." Napoleon played with his inkstand, acting too cavalier.

"After my recital, she seemed terribly anxious for me to walk off alone." Amélie stepped away from him and gripped her elbows, not happy that he defended his past mistress. "Don't you think it's a threat to have these people under the same roof?"

"They'll move to Jamestown when the doctor says she's better, *je te promets.*"

Napoleon stood, his expression weary. "Lunch will be here any moment. Let's sit and relax."

"This is a convenient solution to being sent away. I worry about your safety." Amélie shivered, though kept her voice even. Jules still lurking around the premises—her own safety.

"We're taking every precaution to ensure our food isn't tampered with." He walked close and caressed her cheek.

"The Montholons are expert manipulators." Amélie turned away and almost chewed on her thumbnail. "Taking all this precaution isn't foolproof if you allow the rats to run free in the garden."

"I'm exasperated with arguing." Napoleon threw up his hands. "I haven't had any adverse symptoms in some time. Will there never be an end? I bear enough hostility from my situation on this island alone."

"*Mon Dieu*, are you still under her spell?" She stared askance at him, all her fears bunching up again inside. "You've let them influence you. I can't believe it."

"Your lack of sympathy for an ailing woman is fueled by your unfounded hatred for her." His anger startled her. For a moment she beheld the emperor who must have intimidated his foes back in Europe. "They will be gone in another day or so. Why keep adding to the problem?"

Amélie stalked from the room for the library, wounded by his accusation. The unrelenting tension had taken its toll. He'd never directed anger at her before and she feared his attachment to the Montholons. She locked the door and stewed over this latest obstacle.

Just prior to dusk, restless, she went out to her neglected garden and weeded and pruned: her old routine for alleviating frustration. In the kitchen she stirred up a bowl of soapsuds then sprinkled the foamy mixture over the vegetables to repel pests. She should splash some over the Montholons' sheets.

"Your father would be very disappointed, Amélie." Madame Cloubert suddenly hovered over her like a tree rat. "You wasted little time after that good man's death. This place has become even more scandalous. My husband is appalled."

"My father is in a better place than this, Madame." Amélie's voice cracked. She plopped down the bowl, crouched, and dug her fingers deeper into the earth as if she'd stop her world from spinning. "He understood my wishes."

"If you become with child, what will you do then? Have you thought that out?" Madame Cloubert poked down with her long nose as if pecking for evidence.

"Then I'll have a *child*." Tears formed in Amélie's downcast eyes. Her and Napoleon's baby? Even illegitimate, she longed for that. If they all weren't soon poisoned. Dislodging a clump of weeds, she splattered mud across her arms. A caterpillar wriggled by her hand.

"I'm concerned about you with no guidance. You're heading for ruin. You should have left the island after the funeral." The harridan sprang upright and crossed her skinny arms over her flat chest. "What idiocy has His Majesty convinced you of? Ha! He can never marry you."

"I do appreciate your concern." Amélie squirmed with disgust that she couldn't find solace in her own garden—and that Madame spoke the cruel truth. Pests came in many forms. "Women need to be stronger and direct their own lives. Even if it means—for one spectacular reason—following your heart and not your head." Amélie sighed and dragged herself up. "Excuse me, Madame, I'm finished here."

"*Attends*. Tell me why you now lock up the staples. What is happening? Aren't the rest of us entitled to know?" Madame Cloubert's gaze darted around the courtyard. Her shabby dress flapped about her bony frame—a flag on a pole.

Amélie couldn't upset the household any further. She pressed the woman's shoulder, leaving a smudge of mud. "No, not yet. Again, good evening."

Later, she immersed herself in a warm chamomile bath in Napoleon's tub, he nowhere around. She soaped her flesh and rallied herself for the emerging battle. She still felt odd in his quarters, behaving as mistress in more ways than one.

Afterwards, she sat on the sofa in the study, her well-worn book on gardening in her lap. He entered a short time later. She pretended not to notice and struggled not to glance up from her reading.

* * * *

Napoleon poured two glasses of brandy at the sideboard. He'd allowed his impatience over not hearing from Europe to infect his relationship with Amée. By his calculations, he should have received word by now. He must remain positive that O'Sullivan wouldn't have a change of heart toward aiding his escape.

"We're all under a tremendous strain." He sat beside her and waved the snifter under her nose. "I'm sorry I snapped at you earlier. You didn't deserve that. Can you forgive a sour-tempered man who loves you?"

She met his gaze with her large brown eyes, a sad smile. "I'm frightened about what might happen because of my love for you." She accepted the glass.

He slipped his arm around her. Her hair smelled fresh. "Bertrand is negotiating for our unwelcome tenants to rent a suitable lodging. The boarding house is full of soldiers and their wives because of a flea infestation at Deadwood. In the meantime we'll be vigilant."

Amélie took a sip of brandy. "Can I ask for one more promise?"

"Please do." Napoleon kissed her earlobe, tasting the sweetness of her cleaned skin.

"Don't let the Montholons ingratiate themselves with you again."

"I haven't. Never allow those people to come between us. What we have is too precious." He sipped the burning brandy and nestled her against him. After denying pleasures of the flesh for months once he tired of Albine, Napoleon felt the stirrings constantly with Amée. He never cared for clever women—they made him uncomfortable—but she seemed a perfect blend of honesty and intelligence. He trailed a finger across her cheek, her loving face. He hoped he wouldn't yet get her with child, not with impending events.

"I'd never allow anyone to come between us." She set down her glass and snuggled her head on his shoulder. "I'm not very experienced. I'm still learning how to behave like a refined woman."

"Just don't grow cynical or jaded." Napoleon kissed the top of her head. Tilting up her face, he kissed her lips, tart and sticky with brandy. "I'll teach you refinement, as long as you only practice with me."

Amélie gazed up, her damp honey-colored hair curling around her cheeks, and smiled. "How can I resist, when just your touch seduces me?"

Napoleon kissed her again. If he was forced to languish on this island, could he remain happy? Stay content with her long-term? With the British breathing down his neck, dictating his every move? He reached into her robe and caressed her soft breast, and knew he definitely could not.

* * * *

A horrible retching sounded from the bathroom. Amélie hurried in and found Napoleon bent over the tub, shivering. She banged on the duty chamber door. "Marchand, fetch a doctor! Napoleon is ill. He's vomiting, shaking. Please do something! *Rapidement!*"

"I'll run to Deadwood for the surgeon." The chief valet jerked into his frock coat and sprinted out as Ali rushed in.

The valet helped Napoleon from the bathroom to his bed, where he collapsed, his face like pasty dough. Tremors racked his body and Ali wrapped him in blankets. Amélie blinked back tears. She heated a hot water bottle and placed the warmth under his feet.

"What has the emperor eaten?" Ali asked.

"Everything I have. A light supper last night, breakfast this morning." She stood by the bed holding Napoleon's cold hand. Had the Montholons, or Jules, managed their goal, and now she'd lose him, their future together? She kissed his hand and choked down a sob.

Over the mantel, Frederick the Great's clock ticked by twenty minutes. Amélie stroked Napoleon's brow. Her stomach flipped as if she might retch herself.

Marchand finally brought in the army surgeon. From the bedroom doorway Amélie nibbled her lip while he examined Napoleon.

Her fears roiling, she rushed outside to the butler's pantry and unlocked the cabinet. She snatched out her bottle of oil she'd made recently of distilled young rue shoots in water. With honey slopped in a bowl, she stirred in the oil. She hurried back across the courtyard, almost bumping into Chef Gascon. He stared at her with his droopy face. His son was killed at Waterloo. Gascon had free access to their food. *Was she chasing off the wrong person?*

Her father would have known though, working so closely, and reported him to Count Bertrand. She gulped a breath and must trust her instincts.

Amélie gripped the bowl, fetched a spoon, and scurried back to the bedchamber, her heart in her throat. "How is he, Doctor?"

The tall skinny officer, his red uniform an intrusion in the emperor's sacred chambers, frowned. "Who are you?" he asked in stilted French.

Amélie rushed and sat on the bed beside Napoleon. His skin looked like yellow wax, his breathing shallow. Teeth clenched, she lifted Napoleon's head from the pillow. "I want you to swallow this." She spooned her oil and honey into this mouth.

"Just what do you think you're doing? Move away, miss." The doctor glared at her. "What is that concoction?"

"What is your diagnosis, Doctor?" Marchand stepped forward, his eyes wide with concern.

The man sighed. "The patient seems to have had an acute attack of the bowels. I'm going to give him tartar emetic to clean out his ills, induce more vomiting."

"*Mais non!*" Amélie gasped, terrified when she thought of Cipriani's similar diagnosis right before his death. "He's been poisoned, can't you see? This is a cure." She *must* cure him. She prayed to believe in her restorative powers. Her love couldn't slip away now.

"That's not my opinion. Stop this instant. You'll only make him worse."

"I trust her," Napoleon rasped, his voice so feeble. He accepted another spoonful of the rue mixture. "Tastes awful."

Amélie smiled and set the bowl aside.

"I really must object to this unorthodox procedure." The doctor pulled a vial from his bag. "Now let me—"

"What more can you do for him than give him more poisons?" Amélie sobbed, pressing her forehead against Napoleon's clammy one. She eased his head back down.

The Bertrands bustled into the chamber. Ali had run to Hutt's Gate to inform them.

"How is His Majesty?" Count Bertrand stepped to the bed and the doctor immediately complained about Amélie's actions. Bertrand nodded to her, then clasped the doctor's arm and led him away. "Is there any more you can do for him, Doctor? Herbal tinctures have been known to work."

"Do you suspect Napoleon's been poisoned?" Fanny asked after Amélie told her what she'd done. "Where are Charles and Albine?"

"I wonder that myself." Amélie caressed the stray lock of hair on Napoleon's pale forehead. He closed his eyes, his breathing easier. "I panicked and had Marchand bring the doctor. I hope my remedy works if it is poison. Fanny, please sit with him until I return."

The countess sat down by the camp bed, her black eyes distressed. Amélie kissed Napoleon's cheek and hurried out, through the house, out the front door, and along the right wing of Longwood. More tears blurred her vision, her body seething with fear and anger.

She pounded on the Montholons' door, but no one answered. Furious, she jerked the knob and the door opened. The empty chamber smelled of stale perfume. Amélie stepped inside. Shoddy furniture filled the small bedroom and sitting room. The countess's clothes press slumped in a corner, overstuffed with clothes. Where were they, these vermin of Longwood?

She opened drawers and searched dresser tops, with no idea of what she hoped to find. In the drawer of a small table beside the bed, under some lace handkerchiefs, Amélie pulled out a book. About to toss it aside, she read the title.

Memoire du procez extraordinaire contre la dame de Brinvilliers, the story of Madame de Brinvilliers. She'd read this book a few years before about Marie-Madeleine d'Aubray, Marquise de Brinvilliers, a woman beheaded for poisoning her father, her brothers, and several other people with arsenic in the 1600s.

Heart thumping, Amélie rushed back into the house and showed Fanny the book.

Countess Bertrand sucked in her breath as she flipped through the sticking pages.

Amélie sat down beside Napoleon and kissed the sweet honey from his lips. She pulled the taffeta curtains close and stretched out beside him in the bed, her arm hugging his chest. Count Bertrand and his wife left, shutting the bedroom door.

* * * *

"The milk will coat your stomach." Amélie held up the glass, urging Napoleon to drink the following morning. Propped up in bed, some color had returned to his cheeks. "Did you eat or drink anything separate from me before your illness?"

"A cup of coffee, but the coffee was locked up. No one unauthorized could have interfered with it." He coughed, his voice still raspy, and set aside the milk. "Then you try to poison me with your own wicked brew, and dare to bring a doctor I don't know in here."

Amélie breathed easier, relieved at his teasing. "What could it have been? I was so frightened."

Napoleon held out his arms and she slid into them, cuddling him through his flannel nightshirt. "I wouldn't dare leave you...by dying, after at last finding you," he murmured into her ear.

Brushing her cheek against his bristly one, she sat back, wiped away her tears, and smiled. "I'll prepare *soupe à la reine* for your lunch."

Napoleon smiled back, then frowned. "Where has Montholon been throughout this?"

"He'd apparently disappeared." Amélie sighed in irritation. "However, he's outside now demanding to see you, and I told him you were resting."

"No, let him in. I want to speak to him." He scooted up taller in the bed.

Amélie reluctantly opened the bedroom door, stared into the count's smug face, and informed him that the emperor would receive him.

"Your Majesty, Albine and I have been overcome with sorrow at your illness." Montholon oozed into the room, not a hair out of place, his uniform pressed. His medals reflected the sun streaming in through the window. "*Grâce à dieu,* you've recovered. What could have caused this relapse? More of those annoying island maladies, I'm certain."

"Bertrand has secured a cottage for you and your family in Jamestown. You can await a ship from there. You have Lowe's permission to depart the island," Napoleon said in a frigid voice, "but more important, you have mine."

Montholon stood stiff at attention. "Again, Sire. I lament that I've vexed you. The wine tonic was an insolent blunder." The count flicked a glance at Amélie. "I will make amends with the young lady, anything to honor you."

Make amends with her? The man had to be frantic. She stifled a scoff as she observed from the fireplace.

"That won't be necessary, as you are departing Longwood today." Napoleon smoothed the blanket over his chest. "Have your servants pack your things."

"Sire, I am an indispensable member of your court. My guidance and advice to you has always been sincere. That's why I request to stay and serve you."

Amélie clenched her teeth and pressed her fingers along the mantel's gray paint.

"Serve your family, and give Albine back her book." Napoleon pulled the Brinvilliers book from his night table and held it up. "Interesting story, this poisoning."

Montholon accepted the book. Turning the item over in his hands, he barely glanced at it. "I...haven't read the story. If I could only convince you not to change your once warm affections for me."

Napoleon pinned the count with his chiseling gaze. "Retire to the cottage Bertrand selected. Be free to move around the island, away from the cordon of sentries. Then we will talk again." He coughed and reached for his glass of orange water. "This is my command and I expect you to obey it."

Amélie stepped toward the bed at Napoleon's aggravated tone and clasped her hand on his shoulder. "Count, you should go. You're tiring him. You've heard the emperor's wishes." She quivered at the man's desperation. If he had an important mission to accomplish and bungled it, he'd return to France in disgrace.

"I'll send my dear wife off with my blessing and remain with you, Sire, as I dedicated myself to in the beginning." Montholon cast Amélie a derisive glare. He fingered his left epaulet, scratching with his fingernails until he stopped himself. "My manservant *is* the one who behaved badly, but he will go with Albine."

Amélie held her breath. Would Montholon admit that Jules assaulted her?

"I won't argue with you anymore." Napoleon turned from the count and patted her hand. "Amée, pull the bell cord, tell Marchand I wish to shave."

Marchand entered a minute later, as if always at the ready, with a basin of warm water and a mug of shaving soap. Napoleon shaved himself while the valet held the mirror, always wary of anyone near his throat with a sharp object.

"As I said in Plymouth," Montholon's voice squeaked out, before he tamed it, his distress clinging to him like sweat, "I am the only true aristocrat left in your entourage."

"Basta!" Napoleon leaned forward, his eyes afire. He shook the razor blade, flinging soap across the blanket. "I won't hear any more. You sorely try my patience. True *aristo*, indeed, as if my Empire meant nothing. As I already told you, I'll see that you're compensated financially for your time here. The solution for all concerned is for you to leave with your family. Now go!"

The count bowed out the door. Amélie shut it, and clicked the key in the lock. Marchand handed his sovereign a towel to wipe his face before being dismissed.

She kissed Napoleon's silky, sweet-smelling cheek, regretting his spiritual depletion at this showdown with a false friend. "You're still providing him money?"

"I won't give him a sou." He kissed her on the mouth. "Neither will I speak to him again." He trailed his fingers up her bodice. "I have better attentions to provide."

"I think you need someone to keep you warm." Her flesh tingling, she lifted the blanket and climbed into the bed.

* * * *

Amélie glared out the salon window. Near the garden, Jules wrapped rope around the Montholons' trunks and heaved them in the waiting cart. He whistled and waved, acting unperturbed by this departure. Her muscles clenched.

The nurse climbed in the cart with the infant Helene-Napoleone, while Tristan made a final visit with the emperor in the drawing room.

Ali walked up beside Amélie. "The count and countess ranted at each other all day. We hear much through our attic floorboards." He waved at Jules. "I'm glad the troublemaker is going."

"Do you mean Jules or Montholon?" She fingered a hole in the shutters. The sun dipped toward the shrouded summit of Diana's Peak.

"Both. Montholon is livid at his discharge, but the countess wants to go home."

"The count stalled most of the day. I'll have to throw away our precious food supplies and begin again to make sure there was no last minute tampering." Amélie slammed the shutter closed.

"I'm still injured that you kept all this skullduggery from me." Ali put his hand over his heart, but he did sound a trifle upset. "I want to protect His Majesty, too, don't forget."

"You neglected to tell me about Jules." She wagged a finger at him. "At least the supply ship came today. I told Napoleon not to eat or drink anything until the soldiers bring replacements. I'm starting in the butler's pantry."

Amélie left the house and bustled across the courtyard, grinning in reprieve after so much turmoil. She rippled her shoulders to shed off her anxiety.

Inside the pantry, she plucked the key from her apron pocket and unlocked the cabinet. She'd discard everything, secured or not, to be safe. Again, she fought doubts about Chef Gascon, but he'd spoken of his son's army service, and how proud he was of him, how he'd died a hero's death in Belgium.

"Mademoiselle Perrault, *tres fortune*, only the two of us here."

Amélie flinched. She turned to face the Count de Montholon, who stood in the doorway.

Her skin prickling, she raised her chin. "Count. You should be boarding the cart with your family."

"First things first. A word with you." Every word he uttered dripped in menace from his small mouth. He didn't bother to clip on his courtly smile.

"I have nothing to say that the emperor hasn't already said." Amélie strained to keep her tone nonchalant. She fisted the key and half-turned back to the cabinet.

"You're quite satisfied with yourself...locking away the food, undermining my influence with His Majesty." He slid one step inside the pantry.

Amélie picked up a large tin of flour. "You had no business tampering with the emperor's wine and conniving in other deceits behind his back."

"You're forcing His Majesty to dismiss me. Everything progressed splendidly until you interfered. The great Napoleon under the thumb of his kitchen whore." He advanced farther into the room. His jaw jutted out with lower teeth showing.

Amélie's pulse vibrated in her chest. She gripped the tin before her. "You should be happy to leave this existence, and not be separated from your wife and children."

"What business is that of yours?" He tugged at a curly sideburn with his slender fingers. "I had promised...promised to stay until the end."

"The end?" She swallowed hard. "That could be twenty years from now." She forced her breath to move slowly, inside and out. "Could it not?"

A flicker in his icy blue eyes made her hands tighten around the cool, smooth tin.

"Nothing I say persuades him to my remaining. How can a simple maid replace a courtier and loyal soldier such as I? Regardless of how...inviting her favors are." His cold monotone alarmed her more than outright anger would have.

"Loyal, are you? Your time here is done. Why can't you accept it?" Her stomach churned. "Don't come any closer. One shout and I'll have several servants in here. Now leave."

"His Majesty won't be able to function without me. He's grown too soft, too obtuse." Montholon gave a slick smile, another step forward. "How much money would you accept to persuade him to change his mind?"

"You are a *fool*, Count." Amélie's anger burned up her throat. Edging back a step, her heel bumped the cabinet. She jerked off the tin's lid. "Napoleon doesn't need a courtier such as you. Get out of here."

"You will never understand my importance." Montholon reached out, long fingers groping for her arm. "Stop behaving like a stupid little girl." His hand grazed her, like a claw. "Gold always entices whores."

"*C'est odieux!*" Amélie threw the lid at his face and slammed the tin into the side of his head. In a cloud of flour, she ran from the pantry, across the courtyard, and into Longwood where she called for Napoleon.

"Captain Blakeney!" Napoleon stomped out the back door with Amélie beside him and shouted for the orderly officer, much to that soldier's surprise. "Remove the Count de Montholon from these premises at once!"

Chapter Thirty-Five

What is love?...the feeling that he is at the same time powerless and immortal—N.B.

"Why don't you and your family move into the Montholons' old quarters?" How gratifying to say that. Amélie picked up two silver candlesticks from the new dining room sideboard. "There's rat droppings back here."

"I wouldn't mind leaving the attic." Madame Cloubert swiped her polishing cloth over the inlaid ebony. The linseed scent thickened the air. "Now, you must give me time to grow used to you being mistress of the house." The woman snorted. "I never thought I'd admit this, but it's too quiet around here. Except for Gascon whining about his ills and his dull cooking. So many people have gone from when we first arrived."

"I'm enjoying the calm." Amélie laughed. She walked toward the back door. "No one picking quarrels or flaunting their importance. No more fits of jealousy." She'd felt especially relieved when she watched the ship carrying the Montholons and Jules sail away from the island that afternoon, three days after they'd left Longwood.

"I'm off to bed." Madame Cloubert tossed down her cloth and climbed the attic stairs. "I wonder if my lazy husband is already snoring. I'll ask him about the move, not that he gives a damn."

Amélie opened the door, the breeze on her face. Napoleon was occupied at his desk, so she stepped out for a moment. The fleeting dusk retreated from their yard in ever darkening shadows. The frogs grunted along with the inherent blowing of the wind. Even in the twilight she saw the mess the Chinese were making, digging furrows close around the house in which to place more plants at Napoleon's recent behest.

The evening chilly, she pulled her shawl close around her and strolled toward the wall. Lights glittered at the Deadwood Camp. Oxen drawn carts rolled over the plain in that direction, carrying women with boxes on their laps. They would be attending a Regimental ball, wearing their traveling clothes for the rough journey along the twisting road, their dancing gowns preserved in the boxes. Slaves hurried beside them bearing lanterns as the wind flapped the canvas covers of the carts. Such fetes were a separate world from Longwood, but Amélie didn't mind her exclusion. She smiled and swayed in the breeze. She had everything she needed right here.

She'd even snuck off to the library a few times to work on her treatise—the sensual details—but hadn't worked up the nerve to tell Napoleon of her endeavor.

A discordant noise close by diverted her attention. Hiccupping sobs and sputtering drifted from behind the kitchen. She stepped over, next to that building, touching the splintered wooden side for guidance. As she walked around through the murkiness, the sobs grew more distinct.

At the back, Amélie dimly made out a figure hunched near the wall. "What's the matter?" she asked. "Who is there...can I do anything?"

The figure moved, sniffing loudly, but didn't answer.

Amélie edged closer. "Do you need help?"

"Nooo...go away." A female's angry, pathetic wail.

Amélie hesitated, then slipped inside the kitchen to retrieve a lantern. She lit it and retraced her steps. The light splashed over the figure. The person jerked up her hands to shield her face, scrunching down farther.

Amélie hovered close, holding the lantern aloft as a woman squinted up.

"Let me…" Amélie caught her breath. She stared into the blotchy face of Clarice. After setting the lantern down, she crouched beside her. "What is it? What has happened?"

"You don't care. Go away!" Clarice's sobs turned to anger. Her auburn hair clung like rust to her damp cheeks.

Amélie wasn't sure if she cared or not. Clarice had caused her a lot of misery, but she had too much heart to desert her in this tragic mood. "Shall I get your mother?"

Clarice reached up and grabbed her by both arms. "*No*, you can't do that."

"All right, I won't." Amélie shifted her feet to regain balance, before pulling at the other woman's fingers to loosen her grip. "Tell me what's wrong."

Clarice let go and swiped her sleeve under her nose with a sniff, her white cap drooping over her forehead. Her hazel eyes looked like red wounds in the lantern light. "Everyone will know soon enough. I'm going to have a baby." She spewed it with bitter loathing.

Amélie said the first thing that entered her mind. "Is it Jules's?"

"*Merde*! That jackass. He wanted to have his way, but when I told him I was expecting, he became irritated. As if it were all my fault and he had nothing to do with it."

"You let him leave the island...without marrying you?" Amélie grimaced, torn in her wishes. Madame Cloubert would be outraged when she found out, but Amélie reveled in Jules's departure.

"He wanted me to rid myself of the embarrassment." Clarice gripped her arms around her knees. "Then he refused to admit it was even his. He couldn't wait to flee to Europe with the Montholons."

"If you had told me, I could have had Napoleon force Jules to marry you." She shivered in dismay. "Then you might have sailed with them."

"I'd never marry that imbecile. He didn't love me." Clarice raised her head, her voice steadier. "You can help me, Amélie. I need money. You can get funds from the emperor."

"For what?" Amélie narrowed her eyes and fidgeted in her cramped position.

"I want to go to town, pay my way on the first ship out of here." Clarice wheezed in a deep breath. "Before my mother sees me swelling."

"You can't simply leave." Amélie gaped at the other woman's fantasy after all they had endured on Saint Helena. "The governor must approve it."

"The hell with that man. Just get me the money. I'll find a way off. I know what to do." Clarice grabbed Amélie's arms once more. "Don't mention this to anyone. If you help me, I have a secret Jules told me about the Count de Montholon, but if you betray me, you'll hear nothing."

"Not Montholon again?" Amélie gritted her teeth and shook off Clarice. "I, all right, I promise not to tell. Go into the kitchen and clean yourself up. I'll think of something." She rose and staggered back toward the house in an agitated daze. She'd so hoped to be done with the Montholons.

She felt compassion for wretched, selfish, pregnant Clarice, even after harsh treatment by her hands. If Amélie did give her money, she had to know what deviousness Clarice planned. She couldn't risk her actions further damaging Napoleon's relations with Lowe, and she must hear this secret about the count.

* * * *

Napoleon heard her enter the study and he stuffed the letter to his banker in his desk cubby hole. "Did you enjoy the evening air?"

"A little. A cold wind is blowing." Amélie walked up beside him and caressed his shoulder. "What are you writing?"

"Nothing important." Napoleon pulled her onto his lap, embraced her, and smoothed her hair. She smelled fresh, like a breeze off the Alps. "You look upset. Is everything all right?"

"I'm very happy to be here with you." She smiled, softening the disturbance on her face, and kissed his cheek.

"You realize, Amée, if I had met you years earlier, as I might have wished, if our youths could ever match, I would have loved you and left. I was too busy with my own affairs, rushing to my next battle, searching to further my ambition and power. I never took the time to really love anyone." He kissed her mouth, using his honest confession to cover up his remorse at the subterfuge. Did she suspect his plans and how much longer could he hide them from her? "I'd never have given myself the chance to discover you."

"That's a sweet, lovely sentiment." She settled into the comfort of his thighs and leaned her cheek against his. "You've been writing a lot lately. I heard you wrote Josephine very erotic love letters."

Napoleon laughed, remembering that lovesick young man who had romanticized Josephine into something she wasn't. He liked that he could laugh and put aside the humiliation. Might he recapture that now, toward someone who deserved his affection? He stroked her face. "Once I aspired to become a writer. Can you believe that? A man who had spent most of his life on the battlefield, pondering such a gentle pursuit."

"I am surprised, but you stayed a soldier instead?" Amélie rested her head on his shoulder.

"I wrote in journals constantly in school. I thought if I had no success as a soldier, I would try composing novels." He stared into the fire for a moment. Her bottom on his lap stirred other desires.

"Did you ever write anything fictional?" she asked.

"I wrote some allegories. A few small novels: *La Nouvelle Corse, Le Comte d'Essex,* and *Masque prophète.*" His spoke with dreamy pride about that idealistic youth.

"You should try writing again, here. What better place to be a writer than on a remote island?" She fingered one of the gold buttons on his waistcoat.

"I've written plenty on this island that never passed through Plantation House, many which were published in England and France. Remember the *Remonstrance* and *Letters from the Cape*, venting my spleen against the governor and his superiors for the world to see? Not that I signed my own name to those." Napoleon cuddled her closer. His mood drooped a little. "I also...wrote a poem about my son."

"*Vraiment*?" She raised her head to look at him. "Can you recite it for me?"

He sighed, opened a small door to the right on his desk, and pulled out a creased slip of paper. Unfolding the paper, he rubbed it with his fingers. "'My wrongs my cares, should be forgot with thee, my power Imperial, dignities renown. This rock itself would be a heaven to me, Thine arms more cherished than the victor's crown. O, in thine arms, my son, I could forget that fame...'" Napoleon's voice thickened. He saw tears spring to her eyes and hugged her head to his face to rub off his own tears in her hair.

"That's so beautiful." Amélie embraced his shoulders. "I hope my arms make this a heaven for you as well."

"They do. I wrote this back before I found such glory in your sweet touch." Napoleon kissed the tip of her nose, her cheek, earlobe, then trailed his fingers over her breasts.

"What about writing more novels?" Amélie moaned and nestled closer.

"You're determined to make me content on this rock." He unfastened the back of her dress, yet his mind brimmed with worries: O'Sullivan's return, his uncle's success in finding his double. He tugged down her bodice and kissed her bare shoulder. "I spent so much time on the writing of my life with Las Cases, re-creating my campaigns, recording my contributions to France."

"Now you could write anything you desired. Let your imagination run wild, manipulate your characters as you would wish in real life." She unbuttoned his waistcoat. "Write of the exciting places you've been, such as Egypt."

"Many would say I've already tried that, the running wild and manipulating of people—my head in the Ossian clouds." He chuckled because he wasn't done yet. Only death would keep him from his dreams. "You'd think I'd learn not to confess these things to you."

Amélie chewed on her lip for a moment. "I've been writing myself. On women needing to be better educated. A discourse...on sex for women so they aren't ignorant or helpless the first time."

Napoleon laughed again, certain she jested. "You aren't serious, of course?"

"Why shouldn't women be as informed as men?" Amélie sat up straighter, rearranged her bodice. "I know this shocks your male sensibilities, but I think it's important."

"Amée, you're talking insanity." He scowled. The little minx did want to shock him. He'd convince her not to even attempt it. "A man likes his woman innocent. As you were our first time. The man wants to be the teacher of intimacy."

"Please, read what I've written before condemning it. I've described the act as tastefully as possible."

He gripped the chair arms, shifting beneath her. "You are serious. You're using *our* relationship for your sordid details?"

"You could assist me with your power of intellect." She slid off his lap. "I'm also addressing other matters. Women alone are punished in adultery. I asked you to protect me in our relationship, but all women should have similar protection by law, especially if they have illegitimate children. If marriage isn't possible, we common women need legal recourse."

Napoleon grimaced, thinking of his once innocent Marie Louise bearing Neipperg's illegitimate child. No one would condemn her because of her status. "A husband needs to know if the children his wife has are his and not someone else's. That's why women have been punished and not men." He stood and paced the room to contain his irritation. This isn't the way he'd expected the evening to progress. "I'm not comfortable with you writing intimate details about me."

"I don't mention names, of course. It's more a 'general' description. Women are more vulnerable to a man's attentions, the way things are. If the man is a cad and deserts her, she should be legally protected."

"The legalities are fine. You have some interesting points, but this other...you would create a scandal. I don't like it. It would encourage women to be forward. They would lose their gentleness." Napoleon strode back and slipped his arms around her. "Rousseau says 'A woman should never be made to feel independent, she should be a coquettish slave to render her alluring, an object of desire, a sweeter companion to man.' Don't look at me like that. I'm only quoting."

"Women are left with passive obedience without sufficient character to manage a household or family." She smiled up at him, trying to cajole no doubt. "If her husband is weak, they both fail. If a man has an intelligent partner and friend, they both benefit."

"*En vérité.* You have valid issues, but you must forget these other outrageous ideas." He pinched her cheek, treating her like a naughty child. "My Civil Code provided for women after divorce. A husband had to support her if she hadn't the money, and whatever she owned prior to the marriage she retained afterwards."

"The divorcing husband chooses where she resides. An adulterous wife can be sent to prison, and only the husband's consent to take her back frees her. Children born of an adulterous liaison can't be legitimized. All that's in the Civil Code."

Napoleon shook his head. Sitting on the sofa, he dragged her onto his lap again. "I have always preferred docile, submissive women, and look who I fall in love with." His smile faded at her serious expression. "I would marry you, Amée, if it were possible." He surprised himself with these words. "Divorces are still frowned upon in many countries. I worry about my son's future."

"Shhh. Don't you understand here something as mundane as being wed to an Austrian archduchess doesn't apply?" She stroked his face and kissed him. "The rest of the world is too far away for its rules and regulations to matter. On this island, I am your wife."

"On this island, my sweet..." Where after this? His bold protégé must have the courage to follow in his wake. "Despite your women's issues, will you be my comfort, my coquettish slave?" He nibbled on her neck, like silk against his lips, and massaged his hands along her thighs.

"Of course I will, if you'll be mine." She ran her hands over his chest.

"With no campaigns to plan, no countries to administer...all I desire is enticing you back to bed. If you promise *not* to write of it." Napoleon slid his hands inside her bodice to stroke her soft skin. He'd deter her from these foolish ideas later. "Perhaps it's that sinful ginseng, an herb renown for stimulation, didn't you say? Be aware, record one action in which I recognize myself and I will burn your licentious words."

* * * *

Amélie gripped the cart seat, sitting beside Clarice as they trundled down the steep Side Path into Jamestown. She'd told Napoleon she needed money to go shopping with her the following day. He seemed surprised at this sudden friendship, but acquiesced. Amélie hated to tell him the truth. He'd force someone to marry Clarice—an intolerable situation for both her and any hapless bridegroom—but she disliked keeping secrets.

Archambault dropped them off in front of Solomon's Shop on the main street, where everyone bought their jewels and Chinese trinkets. He ambled off to find amusement elsewhere. Amélie had counted on the groom drinking in one of the sleazy cafes, ignoring his duty as chaperone.

Passersby glared as the two women stood before the shop. People whispered and cast sly looks. In this insular community, everyone knew they were the French who cohabited with *him*, the infamous prisoner of Saint Helena.

"I feel like a freak on parade the few times I've come here," Amélie whispered, trying to ease the tension. The sultry air smelled of rot, reminding her of her first moment on the island. She twinged at the idea of her father beside her. "I'm surprised the governor lets us shop now."

"There's nothing worth buying," Clarice groused, staring at the package Amélie held. "You didn't have to come into town with me."

A phaeton pulled by four black ponies rambled by. A woman sat inside, wearing a fuchsia gown much too garish for her middle age. Nose in the air, she preened as the feathers in her hat bobbed.

"Yes, I did. Look at that haughty Lady Lowe." Amélie watched the arrogant woman, married to their jailor. If she had a trace of compassion, Lady Lowe could do much with her husband to ease Napoleon's situation.

"She looks like a silly goose pretending to be a peacock." Clarice grumbled and hunched her shoulders. "Have you heard the verse invented by her? 'God save the King, God save the Queen, but damn the Neighbor?' The Neighbor, that's what these stupid Yamstocks call His Majesty."

"How unkind of her." Amélie inhaled and squeezed the parcel under her arm. "I have the money. Now what do you intend to do?"

"If you insist on following, let's walk." Clarice strode off down the street paved with small stones. Whitewashed houses with narrow verandas decorated in bright flowers lined both sides. A parakeet screeched from a window.

Amélie shivered despite the humidity seeping into her clothes. The ochre-colored cliffs that loomed on both sides of the town imprisoned the tropical air. They passed the soldiers' barracks which stood next to a tiny plot, called the Company's Garden, at the south end of the street. The East India Company's storehouses sat on the other side of the square—the hub of Saint Helena's confined world.

"Now hand me the money, I can manage alone," Clarice snapped as she sat on a bench in the park with its cypress, fig trees, and tangled foliage.

"I need to know what you're planning." Amélie sat beside her. "Also, what's this secret Jules told you about his employer?" A man so despicable he tried to bribe her at the end.

"The *ganache* made me promise not to tell. I'll take that." Clarice snatched the package and smoothed it over in her lap, the contents clicking inside. "He said the count came here for monetary reasons, and you had ruined it all."

"That much I know. Did he say his master was on a paid mission?" Amélie plucked at her dress skirt, sticky on her thighs. "A scheme to prevent Napoleon from ever rising to power again?"

"Something like that. You know how Jules enjoyed boasting. He said he managed to sprinkle arsenic in His Majesty's snuff. That probably caused the emperor's last illness." Clarice whispered this final part as if ashamed.

"Did you have knowledge of *any* of this beforehand?" Amélie gripped the splintered bench to resist jerking the other woman's arm.

"*No*, of course not. I would have warned the emperor." Clarice sounded a shade contrite, if a resentfully expressed weakness.

"Did Jules tell you anything else?" Amélie lowered her voice as two soldiers strutted by, chuckling behind their hands as they gawked. "Was Montholon's stepfather involved? Did his wife know of this plot? Was my assault part of it?"

Clarice hopped to her feet, her auburn hair damp on her forehead. "Jules said the count forced him to do it...the attack. That's all I know. Now I have to take care of things. Go back to the shop, return to Longwood, leave me here."

"I must know your plans. You can't get off the island without papers and Governor Lowe's permission." Amélie stood. "If you cause problems, it will reflect on Napoleon."

"You're still so naïve. I'm not leaving, just this *thing* inside me is! I have the name of a doctor who'll dispose of it for me." She clutched the package to her breast. Her eyes darted wild above fat cheeks, lips trembling, as if she wasn't altogether comfortable with her decision.

"Clarice, you can't commit such a terrible act, and it's dangerous for you as well." Amélie reached out a hand to touch her shoulder, then flicked her gaze down the street.

Clarice pushed her fingers aside. "*Aller*. You may be screwing our emperor, but you need to grow up! Jules was right about getting rid of the problem."

"You may not understand now, but I wanted to help you. Anything you did here would cause a furor and damage us all. You need guidance." Amélie again glanced down the street. "I couldn't risk allowing you any money."

Clarice glared at her, then at the package. She ripped it open and bits of worthless metal spilled out onto the grass. "I can't believe you tricked me, you horrid witch!"

A few townspeople gathered, whispering and gesturing in their direction.

"*Ma pauvre fille!*" The bulky form of *Monsieur* Cloubert plodded down the street as Clarice stared in shock. "Bless you for warning me, Amélie." The man reached out plump arms to embrace his daughter, who hid her face in her hands and burst into tears.

Amélie sighed with relief and scooped up the metal.

* * * *

Amélie returned to Longwood, shaking over her confrontation with Clarice and the validation of Count de Montholon's and Jules's treachery.

Napoleon met her in the salon with a huge grin on his face, distracting her.

"Aha, Amée, it has finally happened!" He thrust a letter in the air. "These English fools have relented. They've allowed my mother to send out three companions to join us in our exile. Uncle Fesch has succeeded!" Napoleon swept her up and twirled her around the room, the paper crushed at her back. "They're only a few weeks behind this letter. Now things will change, and quickly!"

"Why would the governor allow more people to come? He always insists on restricting visitors from Longwood." She stumbled back to her feet. She didn't want newcomers invading her sanctuary, her time with Napoleon. His fevered expression almost frightened her.

Chapter Thirty-Six

It did me little good to be holding the helm; no matter how strong my hands, the sudden and numerous waves were stronger still—N.B.

British soldiers escorted a cart with three people and a Chinese driver through Longwood's front gate. Amélie stood on the veranda under the arch of green trellis work, suspicious that Napoleon's mother and her brother, Cardinal Fesch, had been allowed to choose these additions to the household: a priest, a cook, and a doctor.

She returned to the preparation room where Marchand arranged orange slices, figs, and almonds on a plate.

"With the British fixation on controlling every aspect of our lives, I don't understand how they gave official permission for these outsiders." Amélie picked up the plate of cold ham. "Napoleon acts as if it's a supreme honor, not an intrusion." Napoleon's excitement pricked her jealousy and curiosity. She carried the food toward the dining room.

"His Majesty might be interested in seeing new faces." Marchand shrugged and this unsettled her more. He carried a salad and curried chicken to the sideboard. The chief valet then placed silverware and linen napkins on the long table.

Amélie stared past him impatiently, awaiting these guests who were being set up in the former quarters of Las Cases and the Montholons in the back wing.

"I'm not comfortable. Your valets knew about it, before me." She tossed rosemary in the corners of the mildewed room. She finally had things exactly the way she wanted, and now the status quo would be disturbed. What would the priest think of the great Napoleon sleeping with his kitchen wench?

"We do need a doctor, since His Majesty lost Doctor O'Meara and he refuses to accept any doctor not of his own choosing." Not that much time had passed. How did Napoleon's mother—who'd paid all the visitors' expenses—anticipate O'Meara's recall?

"We've always needed a priest." Gascon slumped in with a plate of lemon slices and a jug of tea. "They insult me, however, by sending another cook." He blinked his hound dog eyes through the tart fragrance, his clothes rumpled as if he'd just crawled from bed.

"An assistant cook will be of great help to you, Chef Gascon." Amélie forced a smile over the sadness that no one could replace her father.

Gascon needed help now that he didn't have Clarice to work in the kitchen. Madame Cloubert had hustled her family off the island as soon as she learned of her daughter's condition and found a ship bound for the Cape.

"The governor was anxious enough to shed himself of the Clouberts." Amélie bustled around the table straightening the utensils, the napkins, trying to calm her frustration that Napoleon kept these people a secret.

"Maybe the British are feeling a little sympathy for His Majesty, in allowing these people to come." Marchand squeezed her shoulder and strode toward the salon.

Wasn't it more a confirmation that their emperor might be imprisoned here forever? If she felt relieved their cloister would stay intact, she didn't understand Napoleon's enthusiasm.

The front door opened to a rumbling of voices. She smoothed down her hair, her skirt, and stepped into the drawing room. Napoleon, his smile warm, left Count Bertrand and clasped her arm. When the guests filed in after Bertrand, her heart sank.

"This is Abbé Vignali," Bertrand said, standing back as if he loathed to touch him."

A man in priest garb ambled in, ducking his head and wringing his hands. His hair wild and unkempt, his clothes disheveled, he greeted the room at large in a Corsican accent. "The end of February and such heat," the priest moaned, fanning his face.

A second man with wavy black hair, who looked Corsican as well, swaggered in behind Vignali, his sharp features full of scorn.

Bertrand grimaced. "Doctor Antommarchi, from a hospital in Florence, a coroner by trade."

A pale, thin young man hung back from the group, leaning against the wall, his pasty face sweaty. He looked about to slide down in a faint.

"Over there is the new cook," Bertrand said in a deadpan voice, his chagrin over their visitors obvious.

Amélie stared at these inadequate additions. The doctor and priest scrutinized her with ill-concealed contempt. She grasped Napoleon's arm to hold him close, overcome with the creeping fear that he drifted away from her.

* * * *

He acts his part well—an illiterate country bumpkin, Napoleon mused. His anxiety lifting almost made him giddy with eagerness for the next phase of his scheme. The priest brought word that O'Sullivan prepared to sail shortly after their departure.

Napoleon paced around his study, unable to sit after an hour of refreshments and conversation with their guests.

"Why would your mother send such people here?" Amélie watched him, her expression troubled.

"What is the matter, my sweet?" He stopped before her and caressed her cheek. Soon he would have to let her in on this charade, the escape. She'd be upset and try to talk him out of it.

"That cook is ill, and the priest seems like a backward peasant." She eyed him with skepticism as she closed the study door. "Your mother sent you a coroner for a doctor?"

"Madame *Mere* had her reasons. The chef cooked for my sister Pauline in Rome. Abbé Vignali has a small intelligence. I met him on Elba. As for Antommarchi, a doctor of cadavers? Quite amusing." Napoleon laughed. The governor must be pleased with these *bouffons*—no suspicions on *that* front. Soon—very soon—what doctor attended him here wouldn't be an issue.

"Why didn't you tell me they were on their way?"

"I wasn't sure." Napoleon turned from her scrutiny and opened the box the visitors had brought from his family. He smiled as he unwrapped each item. His sister Pauline sent a silver-backed mirror, hairbrush, scissors, and an ivory comb. From his mother were newspapers, books, and an oil painting of the King of Rome in a white satin coat descending a staircase. He clutched the picture close, fingering the gilt frame, his breath catching. "Maybe someday, *mon fils*."

"Here is a lovely medallion of your mother." Amélie held up the portrait with its pearl encrusted frame, as if to distract him from gazing on his lost little boy.

"Ah, yes." Napoleon smiled at his mother's likeness. Would he ever see her again, this woman who'd shaped his life, grown old?

He glanced up at a sharp knock. Amélie opened the door to Count Bertrand.

"What is it?" Napoleon asked his grand marshal, a man already frustrated by these consuming events. Another voice of reason he didn't need.

"Sorry to interrupt, Your Majesty. One of Lowe's officers just brought this to me at Hutt's Gate." Bertrand bowed and held out several pieces of paper. "This is the edict from the allied powers meeting at Aix-la-Chapelle that we've awaited. I'm afraid…please read it for yourself."

Napoleon snatched the papers from him. He surmised it was bad news by Bertrand's gloomy expression. The man needed to learn the art of the impassive face. "Bah! This is nothing I don't already know." Napoleon scanned the French translation. "Apparently Lord Amherst told his British superiors I have it too easy here. They've voted unanimously to keep me exiled on Saint Helena for the remainder of my life. The rigid policy toward the ex-emperor was approved." These written words, their disdain, angered him, and he strained for his own impassive face. He clenched his jaw. He'd have the final triumph on them all.

"I'm so sorry. This is very unfair." Amélie pressed her hand on his arm, yet didn't look overly aggrieved. She wanted him happy on this island, but entrapment wasn't happiness.

Napoleon chuckled and threw the paper on his desk. "These scoundrels with their arbitrary pronouncements have no power over me. To think Russia, my one-time ally, wrote the strongest slander. Czar Alexander and his false worship when I held the reins, he'll see I'm not a man to simply be discarded." Napoleon turned from them to hide his sly grin.

* * * *

The Chinese, heads bent in their mushroom hats, set up a little wooden fence in front of the thickening boxwood sprouting around the house. Amélie scrutinized the activity as she picked a few straggling strawberries. The English had continued to bring plants to Longwood and she tended them. Napoleon's insistence on the hedges and now the fence seemed a ring of camouflage to push the night patrol farther from Longwood's walls.

Since the guests arrived, Amélie felt excluded. The place vibrated with an uneasy energy and more of Napoleon's evasions. His off-handed reaction to the edict from Aix-la-Chapelle confirmed her fears.

She entered the coolness of the house and walked with her basket into the dining room. Marchand and Ali had their heads together, talking low. They saw her and moved apart. With a distracted nod, Marchand left the room.

Similar actions involving the newcomers had happened on several occasions.

"I hope you plan to supervise the kitchen, fair empress." Ali strutted over, his grin too broad, Napoleon's green riding coat draped over his arm. "Chef Gascon just dragged himself up the attic stairs, saying his life is over. He complains constantly about the new cook."

"Is that what you two are whispering about? Cooks?" Amélie tried to soften the irritation in her voice. She set her basket on the preparation table. She hated to let him know that Napoleon excluded her from anything. "You find too much pleasure in this farce."

"Farce?" The valet shook out the emperor's coat, picking lint from its faded lapels. "His Majesty says a German soothsayer convinced his mother he was no longer on Saint Helena, that angels had carried him off to safer environs."

"Yes, he told me that's why she sent such ineffective people here." Amélie tapped the strawberries, releasing their sweet scent. She studied Ali's face, her frustration simmering. "These weak 'additions' might compromise your intrigues."

"I have no intrigues." Ali shrugged, though a mischievous grin flitted across his face. "Are there enough strawberries so I can take some to my wife?"

"You certainly hurried to marry your mistress before the priest arrived." Amélie rinsed the fruit, snatched up a knife, and sliced through the berries. "How can you trust these guests, when the British approved them?"

"Madame Bertrand isn't happy I stole away her governess." Ali smirked, but his pleasure bloomed through. "We promised she would still work for Madame. Isn't it time I settled down? Mary is so lovely."

"Does she approve of your scheming? Isn't it dangerous?" Amélie sprinkled sugar on the fruit, refusing to stand on the outside again. Did Napoleon still contemplate escape?

"Amélie, you are *la premiere femme*." Ali continued as if she hadn't spoken. "Stealing our emperor from the clutches of harm, releasing that great mind that's keenest when all is lost. I never thought His Majesty would rise above his misery here." The towering valet bent down and kissed her cheek. "No matter what happens, you must believe how happy you've made him."

"What if something terrible happens?" She shivered in dismay. If she *had* released that great mind, to what purpose would Napoleon put it? She almost grabbed the valet's collar to shake him, but Ali slipped like a shadow out of the room.

She clenched her fist around the knife handle, determined to discover what all the whispering was about.

* * * *

On Sunday Amélie dressed in her blue silk gown, a fichu tucked in its square-necked bodice. Her heart quivered when she looked at Napoleon attired in his full uniform, medals gleaming, cocked hat slipped under his arm. The grand emperor once again.

"Come, my sweet, we have a Mass to attend." He extended his other arm.

"I am honored." Amélie smiled and almost added "your majesty." She stroked his sleeve, proud to be his consort, and they strolled together into the dining room.

The emperor allowed Abbé Vignali to transform this chamber into a place to hold Mass. Napoleon was not very devout, and took the fuss with amused indulgence.

Their mahogany sideboard, used for an altar, had its sides draped with red satin hangings fixed to the ceiling with gold hooks. White satin fringed with gold lace was used as an altar cloth. The priest had brought two silver crucifixes, scented candles, and lamps for burning incense. A chalice and paten, a font for holy water, and a vessel for the holy wine—all made of silver lined with gold—provided the ritual with dignity in the shabby room.

The numerous candles burning were reminiscent of the stuffy formal meals where the courtiers had forced food and perspired in the heat. She adjusted her fichu in the growing humidity and smelled the smoky-sweet incense, which brought back memories of her childhood.

With imperial ceremony, the priest welcomed Napoleon. Count and Countess Bertrand, in full court dress, bowed, along with the servants decked out in livery. Did the new additions notice the frayed, mended condition of their clothing?

Napoleon assumed his regal bearing as he nodded to his subjects. Amélie sighed, knees weak. Her insecurity at not being of his class flared up.

She stepped back and joined Countess Bertrand.

"Abbé Vignali appears almost priestly now, but he always averts his face when I'm near," Fanny whispered. "How strange they were even allowed to come. Henri never said a word." She frowned, then caressed the heads of her two children. "I am happy to show my son and daughter this ceremony. Our religion was too long neglected."

"The abbé doesn't look pious to me. He's avoided me so far. It *is* odd that our men kept this from us." Amélie saw Napoleon and the priest exchange a furtive glance. She stiffened. Something about the abbé's face looked familiar now that he'd cleaned himself up. Fidgeting in her clammy dress, she worried that the entire ceremony seemed uncomfortably staged.

* * * *

Amélie shook the jar of rosemary and thyme until the pungent fragrance floated out. She placed the jar in their bedroom grate to mask the smell of the coal they were forced to use lately.

Napoleon sat in the study with Abbé Vignali and Doctor Antommarchi. She listened at the adjoining door, but they talked in what she perceived to be a Corsican dialect that she had trouble following.

Finally, she opened the door and all three men stared over at the same time. The priest glanced down, the doctor sneered. Napoleon stuffed papers in his desk drawer and turned the lock. He dropped the tiny key into his waistcoat pocket.

"That will be all, gentlemen." Napoleon stood. The others rose, bowed, and left the room. Antommarchi gave her an arrogant, measuring look when he passed.

"What are you three conspiring about?" Amélie kept her voice light, walked to the open window, and pushed open the shutters. The warm early autumn air drifted in scented with boxwood.

"Conspiring? What an odd choice of words." Napoleon stepped to the window and closed the shutters tight. "We're planning work in the garden."

She sighed. "This is the third time I've walked in on your little group, and you immediately adjourn and scatter." She peered out the shutter holes. The latest orderly officer lurked out front, a harried look on his face. "*Il me confond*. Lord Bathurst finally relaxes the restrictions, saying you can move about the island more freely, but you take pleasure in irritating the orderly officer and being reclusive again."

"That made Lowe livid, countermanding those previous orders he's tried so hard to impose on me." Napoleon chuckled, but it sounded forced. "With Lowe in charge, this so-called freedom will only erupt in more problems and squabbles. I don't want them to think they have any influence to change my habits at will."

"If you won't ride or take walks...what about your exercise?" She straightened books in the green-painted bookcase and swiped a cloth over the dust. The servants were reluctant to intrude on their privacy since they'd rarely gone out in the week since Mass. She relished acting as mistress of these once forbidden quarters, and especially mistress of this man, but his behavior disturbed her. "Why won't you tell me what you're *really* planning? Don't I have a right to know?"

"Indeed, my sweet." Napoleon stared out the shutter hole. "The orderly officer runs all over the grounds trying to catch sight of me. It keeps Lowe wondering if I'm still here. I hope it prevents him from savoring his meals and sleeping at night." He stalked over and cupped her chin just as she reached his desk with her cloth. "I enjoy plenty of exercise, with you, in bed."

"I'm grateful for that." Amélie trembled under his touch. She leaned into him, his warmth. He evaded her questions, as always. She tried a seductive smile. "Don't punish your health with stubbornness. What are those letters you're hiding away?"

"They're nothing...business. Maybe I'm punishing you for keeping that Clarice affair a secret, and those dirty little tales about Montholon again—but he's out of our lives. His servant is fortunate to have left the island, or I'd have thrashed him for hurting you." He traced his fingers over her cheekbones and jaw. She fought her sensual reaction, because he redirected her curiosity.

"What about you, not a word about these people sailing to join us?" She met his penetrating gaze. "You've been agitated since they've arrived."

"You're nagging again, too willful for your own good." Napoleon kissed her lips and she felt that twinge of pleasure deep inside. "Often events must follow their course."

She gasped when he kissed her, deeper. The heat rose to fog her concerns, but she pulled apart from him and shook off the effect. "Tell me of these events... please."

Then the realization he might be dealing in illusion, dreaming of things beyond reason, struck her once more. Her mouth went dry. Was this another game to make his life on Saint Helena bearable?

"As I say, when it is appropriate, my love." Napoleon clasped his hands behind his back and stepped away from her.

She hugged herself, wanting to hug him, to chase away his sorrows. He needed to remain satisfied here. She stared at the ugly, rumpled sofa where once an awestruck girl and overweight man discussed opera. "Do you know I think I fell in love with you the first time in this room?"

"The first time…doing what?" Now he sounded distracted.

She walked close and slipped her arms around him. "When you invited me in, the day after I had sung for you."

"Ah, when you showed me your opera book, and refused to sit beside me until I insisted?" He broke into a sweet smile and embraced her.

"Yes, that auspicious occasion." She pressed against him, feeling his heat along her body. A sudden urge overwhelmed her to draw him inside her to make certain he stayed near.

He laughed. "As I remember, you were a little petrified of me. What makes you recall that as love?" He smiled tenderly, despite his skepticism.

"Not petrified…intimidated, a bit." She kissed his mouth, tasting the wine he'd shared with the others. The *others*. She wished to send them off the island. "I had a definite feeling that day. Something that exuded from you to me…my innermost self."

"I understand. A feeling intangible, yet thoroughly tangible." He eased back from her, his gaze almost sad. He traced his thumb along her lower lip. "You are a woman of many facets, though I hope I've discouraged you in your radical writing." He walked away, not waiting for a reply.

Her arms drooped to her sides as she struggled to gage his changing moods.

Napoleon strode into the bedroom and she followed. She sat on the camp bed as he walked to his chest of drawers.

"That young and presumptuous idiot of a doctor says I, the once Emperor of the French, should work in the garden for exercise." Napoleon jerked open a dresser drawer.

"I agree with him there." She slipped off her shoes, and rubbed one foot over the other. "Antommarchi dislikes me and shows it. He thinks I'm beneath you, I suppose?"

"He wouldn't dare say that to me. I'll have a word with him. He'll only be interested in me when I've stopped breathing." Napoleon rummaged through the drawer's contents. "I asked for a French doctor, but the Vatican told my uncle they want to weaken, not strengthen, my ties with France, so he was forced to appoint this ill-mannered Corsican."

"Are you ashamed of your own countrymen?" Amélie inhaled the herbal scent from the grate, her spirits low because he harbored too many secrets.

"I was raised a Frenchman from the age of nine. Unfortunately, my enemies always point out that I'm a foreigner, a Corsican, even after I brought France to her greatest distinction. Our island does have a barbarous reputation." Napoleon pulled out an old shirt and shook it.

"Now you give this island distinction." She ran her hand along the mattress where they shared so many sensual nights. Was she strong enough to keep him slaked?

"True. Chateaubriand wrote that I cannot stir on this rock without the world feeling a shock from it." He faced her, his gaze intense.

"I wish you would confide in me. I could offer advice, help you." Her throat thickened and she took a slow breath. Even if his plotting *was* delusional, she yearned to be a part of it. She might entice his body, but his thoughts were too often his own.

Napoleon grabbed a large straw hat from a peg. "The Abbé and I are about to perform an experiment. He's close to my height and build. We're going to dress in drab gardener clothing and work in the garden, keeping our faces hidden. I want to see if the orderly officer will be fooled by our subterfuge."

Napoleon enjoyed such gambles, so she said nothing about this caprice. She sympathized with his need to play these games to retain his sanity, yet this particular ruse added to her qualms.

Napoleon donned the shirt and planter's hat, pulling it low, and walked out into the dining room. She returned to the study and peered out the shutter holes until two men in large straw hats entered the garden. Waiting a few minutes more, she turned to the desk.

Unable to stop herself, she probed the desk drawer's tiny keyhole with a letter opener. She jiggled at the lock, the drawer groaned. Her guilt made her jump at each noise. After a last frustrated jerk, the lock clicked and the little drawer fell open. Amélie groped in and snatched out two folded letters.

* * * *

The letters stashed between the pages of a book on the cushion beside her, Amélie sat on the study sofa with Napoleon. With the cool evening breeze trapped outside the shutters, her dress already stuck under her arms. Her supper churned inside her.

"What do you discuss with this priest, whom you accused of having only a 'small' intelligence? What do you whisper about with your ill-mannered doctor?" she asked, forcing a nonchalance.

"Mostly boring political talk. The sad situation in Europe. What will be France's destiny? They have an uncertain king who rules with half measures, a shadow government without force or talent. Their prince of the blood heads the opposition, so what troubles lay ahead?" He kissed her cheek and tugged her earlobe. "Now, let's you and I speak of more pleasant topics."

"No, I insist you tell me what you are scheming. Please don't treat me as if I'm not important enough to know the truth." She glared at him, yet quivered under his scrutiny. "I had hoped we'd share everything."

"Still nagging, I see." Napoleon sighed, his words soft. He pressed a knuckle to his upper lip. "I'm only thinking of your peace of mind."

"I'm sorry to have done this." Amélie slipped the letters out and raised them up, her fingers trembling. "You have a letter to your banker Laffitte, asking for funds to be deposited to a *Monsieur* Bonheur on the island of Corsica. A name that means 'good luck.' Then this other, to an account in Ireland. Ireland? I can't help it if you're angry over my—"

"You broke into my desk, Amée? I had no idea what a little spy you are." Napoleon took the letters, his vivid gaze troubled. Laying them aside, he gripped her hands in his. He pressed them to his chest and his heartbeat reverberated through her flesh. "Those letters are only copies of what has already been mailed."

Tears clouded her eyes. "I'm afraid for you." Did he deal in delusion or reality? Either way, she was terrified of losing him. "Please, I beg you to tell me."

"Oh, *mon amour*. If…if all goes right, there is something incredible about to take place." He squeezed her hands so tight, she feared her bones might crack. "Now it awaits a particular ship arriving. Give me a few more days. I will be asking you to do something very difficult and undoubtedly dangerous."

* * * *

Two mornings later, Amélie awoke alone in the camp bed. She jumped up and searched Napoleon's interior quarters, but with her pulse skittering up her throat, she choked back a sob and knew he'd gone.

Chapter Thirty-Seven

I find it ridiculous that a man should not be able to have more than one legitimate wife—N.B.

"Climb in, *Signorina*." The Italian standing beside her grasped her arm. Amélie clutched her bundle and inched forward on the pier, stepping down into the boat. She tried not to stare at the tiny vessel's other occupants. Huddled inside her cloak, the yellow bandanna wrapped tight around her head, she shivered in the cutting wind and mist.

"Sit over there," the Italian said in his laconic voice. His pock-marked face held its usual implacable expression.

She crammed between two obese women who scowled at her presence. The stench of rotting fish off their bodies roiled her stomach. The Italian remained on the pier and spoke in a whisper to a skinny man who balanced at the bow holding a long pole. The younger man nodded and tipped his hat to the Italian. Then he dug the pole deep into the water and shoved off from the ramshackle pier.

The others around Amélie began to converse, gesturing with vigorous hands and bobbing heads. She might as well have been invisible—but wasn't that the intention? Their local Italian strange to her ears, she only picked up a word here and there. At such an unfamiliar dialect she felt adrift, as if she'd be lost among these strangers, unable to communicate. A captive of hostile rabble dressed in shabby, peasant garb. She gripped the rough wood of the bench.

The boat undulated along the coastline and she cast a quick glance over her shoulder at the shore. The Italian stood there, arms crossed, watching.

"Don't speak to anyone," he had instructed. "No matter what happens. When you reach the next destination, someone will meet you."

With the relentless rain of the past two days, she chafed damp and uncomfortable in her layers of clothing. Her feet squished in muddy shoes and her fingers were red and freezing. For comfort, she felt the belt around her waist under her corset, where she hid the pink topaz necklace, along with several coins. Shoulders hunched, she tried to blot out her anxiety, yet it seeped back in. What else could she do but think if forbidden to interact?

She swallowed a sigh. Each day she found it strange to no longer be on Saint Helena, or even her brother's home in Lyon. The secretive fashion in which she'd traveled these last two weeks since leaving France stripped her raw.

The huge woman to her left jabbed her in the ribs for more room. Amélie winced and edged away, but had nowhere to go except the fleshy bulwark of her other seatmate. Two dusky men pulling on the oars laughed, their voices harsh on the gray water. She slumped over, hiding her face, resting her forehead on her knees.

An hour must have passed as the voices babbled around her. Amélie pretended to sleep, but never once reached that state of oblivion. Besides, if she dared let down her guard, they might rob her of what little she had, rip the precious necklace from her person. She was a meaningless entity to them—they cared nothing for her desperate quest.

Soon, another shoreline appeared on the horizon. Another tiny island in the Mediterranean. Amélie straightened up, aching for this journey to be over. She had no notion of where she sailed, or how long it took to get there. This ambivalence flustered her, but she understood the necessity.

Their vessel skimmed closer to the hump of land with the steady dipping of oars. The drizzle stopped. A pink-hued beach glistened in the sienna rays of a fading sun. The people around her raised their voices, shrill and excited. Amélie shrank away from them. The abrupt movement toppled her backwards onto the wet, slimy floor of the boat.

The oarsmen snickered again.

"*Stupido*!" one of the women said with a spitting gesture.

Amélie understood that well enough, but bit her tongue. She drew up her legs and wiped squishy fish parts from her hands.

As soon as the boat bumped against a weathered pier, her fellow travelers scrambled to disembark up a short ladder, rocking the tiny craft. Amélie stumbled after them. Now who was she to meet? The Italian had been easy to spot: the man with the red and black madras kerchief knotted at his throat. She'd received no such instructions for this leg of her journey. If the Italian had forgotten to inform her, it was too late now.

She stood on the humble quay, the wind whipping her hair, before trudging up the beach. She had no idea where she was. One more island with quaint whitewashed villages and swarthy inhabitants. Goats and sheep ambled on rocky slopes. The rich fragrance of lavender, lemon, and verbena permeated the air.

She strode past three barrels on the upper edge of the wharf. Her stomach growled in hunger. The Italian had assured her someone would be waiting.

"*Kalispèra*." A dark, stocky man of at least fifty years spoke a foreign greeting as he leaned on a barrel.

Almost replying *bonsoir*, she sucked in the word. Not only warned to be silent, her explicit instructions were "no French at any time."

She solemnly nodded and walked on, scanning the area.

The man fell in step behind her. Irritation, then fear prickled her skin.

"Please, *despinis*," he whispered, crowding to her side and clasping her arm. "Are you the one?" His clothes stank of smoke and body odor.

She flinched, about to pull away. Then she scrutinized him, searching for any indication this stranger could be her contact.

"Yellow bandanna, gold hair, and brown eyes? *Né*, you must be. I have seen no one else like this. No one so pretty." He spoke in heavily accented Italian.

His uncertainty troubled her. She nodded cautiously, anxious for relief.

"I am *Il Greco*." His smile broad, he had remarkably good teeth in his leathery face. A thick black moustache, flecked with gray, obscured his top lip.

Amélie again nodded. The Greek. The last had been the Italian, and now the Greek. How many nationalities would she experience before reaching her journey's end?

"Are you hungry?" The Greek still held her arm and they walked together, entering the ivory-cubed village near the water's edge. Down a dirt road made slippery by the rain, they stepped into a tiny dwelling crammed with two tables and a counter.

Amélie scraped mud from her shoes before entering and shutting the door. Strings of garlic bulbs and red peppers hung from hooks on the plaster walls. Her stomach growled again at the delicious smells.

"What is your pleasure?" the short, round woman behind the counter asked. Her Italian bore a closer resemblance to what Amélie was accustomed to.

"Food for us, *parakaló*." The man pointed to several items on the counter and beneath the glass casing.

Amélie dropped in a chair at a wobbly table, her bundle in her lap. Her escort sat opposite her. A dead fly lay in the dust on the window ledge.

"I have seen you around here? You are Greek, eh?" The proprietress slapped down two plates of sliced onions and tomatoes floating in pungent olive oil, a hunk of goat cheese, and a basket of brown bread.

"I come from many places, so who is to know?" The man leaned back in the chair and chuckled. He pushed up his cap brim. "Do not forget, we want the chicken too."

Amélie sopped a piece of bread in the oil and nibbled, savoring the crisp and tart flavors.

"I bring it, *lo prendero*. No patience, eh? Too many Greeks on this island now." The woman cast him a severe look, then waddled to the kitchen, returned, and placed a platter of boiled chicken in tomato sauce before them, followed by a bottle of wine. "This is *vino Italiano*...not that swill you call wine." She pursed her lips in distaste. A dark down of hair shaded the upper one.

"What is wrong with Greeks? You don't give us a chance." He again laughed, his mouth wide open, bread crumbs trapped in his moustache. He turned to Amélie. "Eat, eat, you are too thin. A woman should be plump with a lot to hold on to."

Amélie quivered at his rudeness. She had lost weight in the turmoil of these past months. She bit into the creamy cheese, tasted a piece of bland chicken, but barely sipped the fruity wine.

"I hope she is your daughter, because she is too young for you, *signore impaziente*." The proprietress continued to glare at him and Amélie prayed for him to be silent.

"*Ochi*, more wine? Ahhh, have some. It is not bad for Italian grapes." The eager Greek refilled Amélie's glass, but she nudged the glass aside. A clear head remained crucial.

After finishing their meal, her escort consuming more wine than food, they returned outside to a bracing wind.

"November is such a foul time of year to travel. What a nosey old *moulari* she was. Not good for us, uh?" The Greek turned up his coat collar, then jauntily clasped her arm and they traipsed through the village.

"We will stay in a hotel at the end of town," he told her. "A nice quiet place, *né*?"

She fought the urge to jerk free. Her aching muscles longed for rest.

The sun had almost set by the time they ascended a sloping path to a plain, square building in a grove of lemon trees. The Greek procured two gloomy rooms in the back.

* * * *

In the sparse chamber, Amélie undressed, draping her damp clothes over a chair. From the small bundle she extracted a wrinkled nightgown. With no water to wash, she threw on the nightgown and climbed into bed. Stinking like sea kelp, she tucked the covers snug around her. She absently moved her thumb toward her mouth, but stared instead at the strong, fine nail she hadn't chewed in months. She massaged the anxious knots from her stomach, desperate to hold on to any mark of courage.

She prayed to be almost there. Her loneliness for Napoleon pierced her like a pain she never knew existed. Ten months had elapsed since he slipped from his exile. Her body ached for his touch, her soul for his smile. She felt as much his wife as if she'd stood in a cathedral and been blessed by a priest. "For all my bravado about strong, intelligent women, I'm still a silly lovesick girl." She laughed to herself, burrowing under the thin bedclothes.

A sudden knock startled her. Always afraid of discovery, she dragged the blanket from the bed, wrapped herself, and crept to the door to listen above her racing heart.

"Open please, *despinis*," came the Greek's voice.

Amélie opened the door a crack, staring at him in question.

"May I come in for a moment?"

She shook her head and didn't budge, refusing to allow him into her dark little room.

"I thought...you might want company." He smiled, holding up a bottle of wine and two glasses in the shadowy hall.

Amélie's eyes widened. She thrust up a hand. The door gripped tight, she jerked out her finger and pointed down the hall toward his room. She bristled at his insulting behavior. She feared this was the payment he expected for helping her.

"I was mistaken...*signomi*." He shrugged his shoulders, tapping his forehead with the bottle. He slunk down the passage without protest.

Amélie shut the door, wishing it locked. She wedged a chair under the knob, surprised and repulsed by the men who found her attractive. She heaved a sigh and only desired *one* man.

* * * *

Over breakfast the next morning, Amélie glared at her companion. The Greek remained unflappable, never losing his amiable countenance.

They walked north out of the village. She hugged her arms close to her body, staying a few feet away from him. Past olive trees and rustic huts, they followed a rocky trail up a hill where crimson ice-daisies sprouted from between stones. A boy herded goats that grazed on one slope. Their bells tinkled sweetly in the morning breeze.

"I am glad the rain is gone." The Greek stopped and stretched at the crest of the hill.

She plucked at her bandanna. A few clouds scattered in the blue-gray sky—the color of Napoleon's eyes.

"I don't know who you are, or why I am even doing this." He shrugged. "I'm a man who doesn't mind performing favors, and I keep my mouth shut."

Amélie bit at her lip. She suppressed her rising anger, her urge to demand that he perform his duty and leave personal feelings out of it.

"They told me you wouldn't speak, because you could not. Have you no tongue?"

She turned away, moving her tongue inside her mouth as she pinched the ends of her scarf. She glared at him once more and thrust up one hand in a gesture of *where do we go now?*

He slapped his cap against his knee. "I am taking you down to the opposite port, over there."

Below, a group of fishing boats huddled together in an inlet of deep blue water. This no-name island shimmered in shades of green and bronze, with pink sandy beaches lining a restless sea. She swayed in the gentle breeze, far from the rough trade winds of Saint Helena. Though Saint Helena had been paradise to her for a time, her Elysium.

The Greek started down the other side of the hill, scattering pebbles. He glanced occasionally over his shoulder as she trailed behind.

They passed under Judas trees down to the shore. Fishermen repaired huge fishing nets laid out on the sand. Women wearing dark scarves and plain black dresses, their faces weary from a lifetime of hard labor, toted baskets of food to the men. Brown children skirted the surf, laughing and arguing playfully.

"Wait here for a moment." The Greek touched her shoulder, his hand almost lingering. "I'll see if this is the right man."

Amélie stood on the loose sand, yearning to take off her shoes and stockings and feel the warmth between her toes. Her companion approached one of the boats, and after a short interval returned to her.

"This fisherman on that boat, his name is Lorenzo. He is the one who will take you across." The Greek removed and fingered his battered cap.

She almost laughed as at last she learned someone's name. She searched her escort's face, eager to hear a destination, but knew that would be dangerous.

The Greek leaned close and kissed her cheek before she could back away. "Safe voyage, *despinis*."

Amélie hurried off, rubbing the end of her scarf over her face. She reached the boat where a bare-chested man in tight gray breeches waited. Lorenzo stood tall and muscular, proudly displaying his copper physique. A deep scar rippled down his left temple.

"Come, *ragazza*, quickly." He gave her an impatient hand into the vessel. "We have to catch the tide or it's all for nothing."

Bundle clutched, Amélie stumbled onto the deck. Demoted to "girl" she wished she could hire her own boat and travel alone, but the risk for a lone woman prevented such an endeavor.

At Lorenzo's order, the crew of five men rushed to raise the sails of the small two-masted craft. One or two threw curious stares in her direction.

Lorenzo opened a hatch and directed Amélie into a tiny cabin below.

The stink of fish filled her nostrils as she fumbled around in the dim chamber. She found a spot behind the ladder, where she hunkered down in her dirty clothes. Covering her face with her scarf, she struggled to ignore the rocking boat, the stench. Her head on her knees, fingers digging into her calves, she dismissed the chaos, and concentrated on her own thoughts. She relived her last night with Napoleon as she had nearly every night since. That shattering moment when he'd revealed the reason behind the whispering and overt secrecy.

Chapter Thirty-Eight

There are things written in the great book of destiny that must be accomplished whatever one does—N.B.

Napoleon sipped the chamomile tea in an effort to calm his stomach. His entire body raged, as if cannon fire struck him and burned around inside fighting for a way out. The moment he awaited hovered just hours away.

He sloshed aside the cup and stared over at Amée as she readied for bed. Down to her shift, she slipped the garment over her head, her firm young body with full breasts enticing. With regret he let her shrug into her nightgown. Since she'd found the letters, she remained perturbed.

"Amée, sit with me." Napoleon sat on the bed and pulled her down beside him. "I realize I've put off your concerns these last few days, but I know I can rely on your courage. What I have to tell you is both alarming and exhilarating."

"Finally, you'll explain. What is it?" Her dark eyes sharp, expression leery, she still caressed his shoulder.

"I am attempting an escape." He squeezed her hand, feeling the pulse in her wrist jump.

"You can't mean that," she said with a nervous laugh. "It's just a game, harmless plotting, isn't it?"

Napoleon drew her close, kissing her lips, avoiding her startled eyes. He smelled the sweetness of her and tried to relax. "I regret not being able to confide in you before, but everything had to be planned to the tiniest detail. I couldn't risk your reaction being a hindrance."

"You're taunting me. Admit that you are." She pulled back and glared at him as if he'd lost his sanity. "I knew you and your Corsican guests were scheming about something, but I don't believe it's possible from here. I can't—"

"Don't despair, *mon amour*. I wanted to make things easier for you...if I could." Napoleon stroked her thick hair, regretting the misery on her face. He hoped to survive his ordeal and rediscover the love and pleasure he shared with her. Something he'd enjoyed far more than he thought he would at this stage in his life. "Your upset only proves your devotion to me. When I arrive at my destination, if things remain calm, I'll instantly send for you."

"*Send* for me?" Amélie pressed her hands on both sides of her skull, as if attempting to absorb and hold this in. "*Mon Dieu*. Where will you go, how...?"

"I can't divulge where I'm going, nor give you much knowledge of the plan, for that may prove dangerous to you, as well as me." He waited for her to compose herself, reassured by the adoration she felt for him. "Amée, I can no longer tolerate this situation—the eyes of the world upon me only to watch me fade. I want more, my freedom, and you beside me, living life to the fullest."

"If you're caught, they may execute you." Her lips quivered, her voice rising in pitch. "You can't take that risk, please."

"Shhh. I will be all right." He ran his fingers along her silky neck. "Maybe now is the time for me to go to America. If I had gone in the beginning, I may never have grown close to you. Fate directed me to you." Napoleon hugged her to his chest, but she stiffened, resisting. "Now the world mourns my unfair incarceration, so let them ponder my next move when they discover I've slipped away."

"How can you throw all we have away?" Amélie pinched at the material of his nightshirt, a mock inflicting of pain. Tears pooled in her fawn's eyes and dripped down her cheeks. "I wanted you to pursue a different life here, not go back to what was before. How can I forgive you for…? Do you want to start a war? You can't do all that again."

"No, no. My destiny has changed. We'll have far more, you've shown me that. I no longer want to be a warrior, but a thinker, a philosopher, and theorist. Never doubt me on this." He strained to squelch his own doubts. He captured her hands and kissed them, then kissed away her salty tears. "I also need to make certain my son has a future. Marie Louise is too weak to ensure he's advised by the right people, that he's brought up the French way. You and I will see to it, through people I trust. I was foolish to think she could provide his future, or that by remaining true to her I protected it. I don't need that connection of ancient blood. My blood is more vibrant, fresher. My son's heritage is me, not a Hapsburg."

"I've always believed so." Amélie clung to him, wiping her face on his nightshirt. Her whole body trembled like a frightened bird. "Yes, I want to do that, but take me with you. *Please.*"

"Not yet." Napoleon massaged the back of her head, the delicate bones. She must remain brave after his departure. "It would make it harder for both of us. We have to follow the plan."

"The…" She stared up again, sniffing. "When will you go?"

"Before tomorrow's dawn." He hoped he sounded apologetic, but his muscles thrummed, blood hot, the confident general, excited on the eve of battle.

"*Before dawn? Mon Dieu.*" She gasped, jerked from his arms, and left the bed. Striding the length of the room, she gripped her elbows. "Are you certain it's safe, what you're doing? How could you be?"

"Listen. You remember that merchant captain who called at the island a few times? He's a trusted man in the East India Company, but he condemns my treatment here. He's helping me." Napoleon would prove his trust in her by revealing this much. "If I'm successful, and I believe I will be, you and I will reunite in several months time."

"Several months, so long?" She heaved a breath. Her nipples poked through the thin material of her gown. "I can't believe you kept this from me."

Napoleon smiled over the sadness of leaving her. She'd never understand his nature, his thrashing at the bars in this cage. "I kept this secret because I knew you would try to talk me out of it and I might have listened, as your powers of persuasion are legendary." He said this to placate her. He'd never allowed anyone to direct his wishes.

"Can I stop you now? I'm afraid—"

"*Non*, don't be afraid. Others have gone before me to pave the way." He held out his hand. "You gave me back my strength, my determination. The luck that I thought I'd lost after I put aside Josephine."

"Then I can blame myself if anything goes wrong." She blinked, sat on the mattress edge, and raked her fingers through her hair. "What was that letter for funds to be sent to Ireland? I assume Bonheur is someone who will funnel money to you...somewhere? You can't think of returning to Corsica."

"No, not that island. This man who is risking everything to help me has family in Ireland. Many Irish have little love for the English. You are right about Bonheur." Napoleon caressed her neck and shoulders, her soft, smooth skin. His desire throbbed. "I don't wish to abandon you either. That part tears at my heart."

"How will we here explain...your disappearance?" She sniffed and put her arms around him. "We'll have to cover it up, to give you time."

"Shhh. All this is taken care of, my sweet." He traced his fingers around her ear, down her neck, and across the quivering pulse in her throat. "Let's only think of our love tonight, and how much we'll store for when we reunite." Napoleon eased her down in the bed, kissing her savory lips, his hands stroking under her nightgown. He caressed and kissed every inch of her. At first Amée resisted, her breathing erratic, almost a sob, but soon she responded to him, and he reveled in the slow tender melding of their bodies. He'd carry her essence with him on his journey.

* * * *

In the morning, Amélie awoke alone in the bed. Napoleon hadn't attempted awakening her to bid farewell. Determined not to sleep, she'd fallen into an enervated slumber. He'd stolen away, possibly to great danger or death. She muffled weeping into her pillow, smelling him on the sheets.

When she mastered her emotions, it struck her that these others he mentioned must have been the Count de Las Cases, the various footmen, even Doctor O'Meara, all sent off the island at different intervals. All, as she'd witnessed, devoted to Napoleon. What finer rallying of support than the eloquent Las Cases singing the Great Man's praises to all and sundry. O'Meara, whom she'd heard was discharged from the navy over his defense of Napoleon—and disparagement against Lowe.

Had her astute lover been wise to Montholon from the beginning and not entrusted him with this stratagem?

The young priest, Abbé Vignali, immediately assumed the identity of the escaped prisoner. He was the same height, basic bone structure and build, and had blurred this resemblance with his scruffy hair, disheveled robes and slouching manner.

Vignali dressed in Napoleon's clothes and frequently worked in the garden under a broad hat that shadowed his face. He walked with Amélie some mornings, just enough so as not to arouse suspicion. Occasionally they rode the horses, but that was rare. As long as none of the British came too near, they hoped no one noticed the difference. Still it was a complex orchestration to keep the orderly officer fooled. Vignali proved adept at subterfuge, portraying both the young priest and the notorious general under the same roof. He wasn't at all the ignorant peasant he'd first affected.

As Napoleon had told her that last night, his screen against Governor Lowe and the orderly officer, his habit of evading them in the past, leant itself to deception.

"Colonel Bingham is here," Ali said to her after a month passed. He sooty eyes held no amusement. "He insists on seeing the emperor. He says he has something important to convey."

"Oh, no. The colonel has had enough close contact with Napoleon to know the difference." Nausea rose in Amélie's throat. Their plan couldn't go awry this soon. "We can't even summon Count Bertrand to smooth the way. Fanny says he's down with dysentery. Tell the colonel His Majesty is ill. Send Marchand to tell him." She rushed to peek out the shutter hole at Bingham standing on the front porch. Marchand walked out and the two men conversed, but she couldn't hear over her hammering heart.

Finally, Bingham left and strode out the front gate. Marchand came back in.

"I suggested he talk to Count Bertrand, who will probably crawl from bed to protect our emperor," Marchand said, his expression grave. "I said His Majesty is ill from the same affliction and can't be disturbed."

"How long can we put off these high-ranking officials?" Amélie shivered and went to their bedroom where she slept alone in the camp bed, mourning the man who once shared it with her. Vignali slept in the adjacent study to preserve the illusion of intimacy. She suffered in this deceit, her arms empty each night. Even working in her garden didn't bring much solace. Each day she agonized over Napoleon's safety and the idea that Governor Lowe, or someone like Bingham, might demand an audience.

* * * *

After three more tense, mind-numbing months, Marchand spoke with Amélie alone.

"Everything seems to have gone smoothly," he told her in the privacy of her bedchamber. "Of course, we had the long wait for a letter to come back to inform us. The next step is to have you removed from the island. We must be careful not to make anything obvious."

"You've heard about him. *From* him?" Amélie almost flung herself on the chief valet. "Is he well and—?"

"I can't go into details." Marchand steadied her with firm hands, his smile indulgent. "Yes, I was informed that he's well."

"Oh, Louis, if you knew how I've worried over him." She choked back a sob, her heart flopping. "He's safe, *grâce à dieu*. Now how do you propose to remove me?"

"Count Bertrand will go to Plantation House and inform the governor that his wife wishes to return to the mainland with her children and she's taking you on as their governess." Marchand gazed around this room where he'd taken such tender care of his master. "I wish I could join you, but we'll proceed from there."

"He's safe." Amélie fluttered her hand down the camp bed's curtains, staring at the stern eagle atop who had observed her lonely nights. "Fanny wants to leave? Without her husband?"

"The countess wishes to put her children in school, and has wanted to go for some time. This is the perfect opportunity. Count Bertrand will follow, probably by next year." Marchand studied her expression. "Madame Bertrand was only let in on this when you were."

"Lowe might still suspect something. He knows how devoted I've been to the emperor, by rumors or conjecture." She pressed her fingers over her quaking chest. "How do we explain my forsaking him?"

"We planned for that also. Hints have been dropped about your relationship souring...and now mutually ended. That our emperor has taken up with another servant, the lovely Mary Hall-Saint-Denis." Marchand winked. "A major reason you're anxious to accompany the countess, and for her to seek a new governess."

"A...good plan. I hope there are no obstacles. You know how awful I've felt since he left. All this anxiety, night and day, wondering if I'd ever see him again." Amélie walked to the mantelpiece. Frederick the Great's clock ticked out the time—time that had weighed too heavily on her.

"Don't say that. You will reunite." Marchand stepped over and squeezed her shoulders in brotherly affection. "In Europe you will be notified of the next action to take."

"At least now I'll feel I'm making progress." She sighed and smiled. "What does this mean for those of you who stay? Can you be sure the servants, or anyone, won't gossip?"

"No gossipers, we're all loyal. Also, a monetary bribe didn't hurt. We have several plans. Only time will tell which one we'll be forced to use." Marchand moved toward the door.

"Will you stay on here indefinitely with your Jamestown mistress?"

"We do have a fine son. I don't know yet what I'm going to do." He hesitated before opening the door. "His Majesty wouldn't allow me to marry her. He wants to elevate me to a more acceptable marriage. A daughter of one of his old guard. He thinks that highly of me."

Still, Napoleon lowered himself to love his kitchen wench. Amélie had to attribute that to her own force of personality. She rubbed her forehead as another situation jumped into her mind. "Louis, I need to take my father's...body back to France. I promised him I would." Tears gathered in her eyes. "I could never leave him here, without me."

Marchand nodded, his smile sympathetic. "*Bien sûr*, we'll arrange that for you. Everything will be all right. My one regret is, *I* may never see the emperor again. Though I do hope, in a few years, to join you...with my new wife, whoever she may be."

"I hope for that too. You'll be most welcome. Promise me you'll provide well for your mistress and son here before you leave." Amélie hated to see him abandon his island family, but the valet would never defy Napoleon. She followed him out into the study where Napoleon's other camp bed was made up for Vignali. Not much longer! Excitement, a purpose, careened through her. Some of the tension eased from her clenched muscles.

* * * *

Following two weeks of negotiations with Governor Lowe, Amélie and Fanny Bertrand, with her children, were granted permission to return to Europe. François Perrault's body would be removed from the cemetery at St. Paul's, to be placed in the hold of a ship for transfer home.

Amélie prayed each night for Napoleon's safekeeping. When the day came for her departure from Longwood, she had the odd feeling of desertion. Deserting the place where she'd won his love and rallied his soul. The place where she'd grown into a mature, sensual woman, and...where she'd lost her father. She'd leave behind, however, a house that had echoed like an empty shell without its formidable master. Where was Napoleon now? Had his escape been rough and perilous? Was he ever sick or lonely? *Had* enough time elapsed for him to be secure somewhere else?

"Say hello to Versailles, my birthplace, and Paris for me," Ali said when he'd told her goodbye, standing beside his pretty blond wife—the rumored new imperial mistress. "Give my deepest respect to our emperor."

"Amélie, have a safe voyage. What will I do without your special herbs? My head will fall off, *je m'inquiéte*." Chef Gascon hugged her, his cheeks jiggling. "Put your father to rest. We'll have none here."

After the long voyage home, they were detained in England until the authorities received permission for them to reenter France. Arriving in Lyon in late September, Amélie absorbed the early autumn weather, but for some reason missed the clinging damp and mists of the Deadwood Plain. She'd seen to her father's interment in the cemetery near St. Nizier's, beside her mother. She hoped eternity would mend the break between her parents.

Staying in that city with her brother Théo and his wife, she kept in touch with Fanny Bertrand. Back in the land of plenty, she had little interest in her surroundings. She only noted the political unrest under the Bourbons.

Another month crawled by and Fanny asked her to come and stay with her at the countess's home on the outskirts of Paris. Amélie had quickly obeyed, impatient for any news that brought her closer to Napoleon.

"Everything is ready for you to travel. I haven't been given all the details, no one has. It's necessary for secrecy. Amazing how they kept this from us for so long on Saint Helena. I have yet to totally forgive my husband," Fanny said with a wry smile. Her complexion looked healthy, pinker, now she was back on French soil. "*Ma foi*, Abbé Vignali was really Eugene Robeaud. A man who used to impersonate the emperor in France, at his request, in certain official situations when Napoleon wanted or needed to be elsewhere."

"No wonder he was so skilled at it. Our quiet, rumpled priest." Amélie shook her head. "I didn't appreciate being excluded either, but if it's been successful..."

"With the network of Bonapartists anxious to free their idol, and other sympathizers, it appears to be." Fanny stepped to the window of her little parlor, which showed a cool autumn day. "I enjoy having our seasons back in the right order, and look, not *one* red-coated soldier in sight near my garden." Her shoulders sagged. "I only wish Henri was here."

"We're both missing our men. It's all right to miss them, as long as we persevere." Amélie rallied her strength each morning with that mantra. She glanced at the gloomy sky, but saw a turbulent sea, that other October two years past, when the *Northumberland* had sailed into Jamestown harbor and she'd compared herself to a little moth that yearned to be a butterfly.

Fanny turned, her black eyes mischievous. "While the children are at school, let's discuss this other matter. Your manuscript on sexual education for women."

"I finished it in Lyon. My sister-in-law, Suzanne, thinks it's wonderful. Read it and see if you agree." Amélie pulled out a package from her portmanteau. "You said you knew a publisher in Paris who might be interested. Publish it under the name Madame Carolina, the name of the first opera character whose aria I sang for Napoleon. See that it's distributed for all women to read. The information is important."

"I definitely will, *je te promets*. I can't wait to see it stir up all the self-righteous males around here." Fanny took the package and crackled the paper as if dying to peek inside. "I'll be discreet so nothing can be traced back to me. Henri would be scandalized."

"So will Napoleon." She twinged with guilt, her underhandedness, but maybe she'd never tell him. "I have money he left me. Give this amount to the publisher. It should be sufficient." Amélie handed her a small purse of coins. She embraced the older woman. "I value your help, Fanny. Now I have to concentrate on continuing my 'grand adventure.'"

Amélie laughed to soften her worries at this reverse *Odyssey*. She wasn't the nymph Calypso, but the brave wife Penelope, trying to find her way to rescue Odysseus, her husband-soldier.

Chapter Thirty-Nine

*There are only two powers in the world—the sword and the spirit...
the sword is always beaten by the spirit—N.B.*

"Now, just where will you sleep tonight?" Lorenzo bounded down the ladder. He stood with hands on his slim hips, his muscled body framed in the fading light from the open hatch.

Amélie squinted up at him from the place she had burrowed since setting sail, the darkness and fish smell a cloying shroud around her. Hadn't *Il Greco* informed him of her incapacity to speak? She stood and stretched her cramped legs.

"I'll have someone bring you food, but we have nothing fancy here." Lorenzo lit a lantern, revealing coiled ropes, buckets, and extra sails. He then tossed her a blanket. "Sleep in that."

She wrapped the dirty blanket around her, anxious for the food.

"Now stay below, I want no trouble." He glared at her as if he resented the information she yearned to know.

She gripped the smelly wool, nodding. The ship heaved and she stumbled.

"Crawl back in your corner, sleep. I have my own problems." He sprinted up the ladder, dropping the hatch cover with a bang.

Amélie staggered back and curled up behind the ladder, determined not to despair. How much longer? The ship's fabric creaked and swayed. The air turned frigid and she shivered. She stiffened in her cocoon each time a fisherman traipsed down the ladder to fetch something. One man brought her a bowl of fishy soup and a slice of hard bread that she choked down with gratitude. Her stomach sloshed with the soup, as chaos surrounded her. Would she be fortunate enough to be taken unscathed to the correct locale? Would she survive long enough to reach Napoleon?

* * * *

A storm swept up on the second day. A fierce gale, and a lashing rain, battered the small vessel. Amélie gripped the ladder as the boat groaned and jounced her about. She pushed open the hatch and poked out her head to gulp for fresh air, the water soothing her face.

Lorenzo and his crew fought with the flapping sails. "I warned you to stay below!" he yelled at her.

Slumped on the ladder under the closed hatch, nauseous, she heard the rain slow. The boat stopped listing. Desperate for air, she crawled out onto the deck. The drizzle refreshed her. The lighter wind swirled her hair. She stumbled to the rail.

The sky pushed down coarse and gray. Another boat loomed out of the mist in their path. This larger boat sailed up on their port side, crew shouting. Amélie couldn't decipher their language. The Italians she traveled with shouted back. The other boat lowered a dingy into the sea.

"Didn't I command that you stay in the cabin?" Lorenzo grabbed her shoulder. "Lower the rope ladder!" he ordered one of his men. "Make certain of their business."

Amélie pulled from his grip. The ladder flopped over the side with a *thunk*. Two men climbed up from the dingy and conversed with Lorenzo's crew.

"Damned Greeks, they think they own this sea." Lorenzo poked at a small pistol in his waistband. "If these aren't the right people, I'll shoot them. You, *ragazza*, get below!"

She shuddered, stepping away from him on the slippery deck. The boat heaved. She stumbled toward the hatch. The two strangers hurried toward Lorenzo.

Amélie slipped and smacked onto her bottom, the air knocked from her lungs. She gasped for breath, crawled for the hatchway, and trampled back down the ladder.

Moments later, two men swarmed into the cabin behind her and she staggered into a corner. Pressed against the bulkhead she trembled, confused.

One man, in a filthy red cap and dark coat, rushed toward her and pointed up the ladder. He snatched her arm, trying to steer her onto the bottom rung. She stifled a groan, then gestured toward her bundle of meager belongings. Did he mean to harm or save her? She ached to speak, to demand answers.

The man shook his head, shoving her up and out on deck into an increasing rain. Amélie tried to jerk away. She stared around, swiping wet hair from her eyes. Lorenzo was at the bow, his back to her.

Redcap dragged her to the rail. Grasping her by both shoulders, he leaned her over, his fingers digging into her flesh. "Climb down, you must! *Parakaló!*"

Below her, the small dingy bobbed in the churning sea. A man with oars sat on its bench. Amélie gripped the rail, her thoughts in turmoil. Were these men her next contacts?

"Get in boat, you must!" Redcap ordered in broken Italian, his accent similar to *Il Greco's*. The other man joined him and these two strangers wrestled with her, finally forcing her over the rail. She crawled down the wobbly ladder and stumbled into the dingy. The two jumped in after, almost capsizing them.

Half blinded by rain, Amélie sat rigid on the soaked bench and hugged bruised arms around her shaking body. If they weren't saviors, had she been found out? Would they demand she tell them where Napoleon was, when she had no idea herself? She bit down on her lip, tasting blood.

Her captors rowed away from the fishing boats, conversing in their Greek tongue. They seemed to study her with sinister smiles. Amélie squeezed her elbows, trying to steady her breathing. She whispered a prayer, her mind spinning with ideas of escape. She shuffled her feet in an inch of water on the boat's floor and prayed not to drown.

Another landfall rose into view, wavering in the gray mist. The boat touched shore on a narrow beach. Redcap hopped out and reached down to assist her. Amélie gave him her hand, anxious for solid ground. The man still in the boat pressed on her bottom, fingers groping. She cringed.

The instant her feet felt earth, she pushed Redcap away and he slipped and toppled back into the boat. The others cried out.

Amélie lurched up a slope of slick grass. She ran down a narrow lane that led to an ancient-looking village clinging to a hillside. She slogged through muddy streets already peppered in footprints, and ducked into an alley to crouch behind a cart. Why would they molest her if their intentions were honest?

After remaining hidden for quite some time, she crept from the alley and peered out onto the main road. A fat man driving a donkey cart squelched by. She slumped against the wall. The alley was a dead end. She had to risk the main thoroughfare.

She rushed along the narrow, crooked lane that split this village in half, glancing over her shoulder every few minutes. Cracked stone walls loomed up on both sides. Whitewashed houses, amid locust and lemon tree branches, peeked over the tops. She'd lost her assailants, but was now lost herself.

The rain stopped. Amélie's soaked clothes stuck to her legs, chafed against her skin. Her drenched body stunk. Her feet squished in the mud. She traversed a steep hill and an old woman in black passed her carrying a basket, a small kid goat trotting at her heels. The oldster, her shriveled lips sunk in a toothless mouth, stared in disapproval at this water wraith.

Amélie sucked down a whimper and swore she was a victim of a nightmare. Now she had second thoughts about those men. Lorenzo had let her leave with them, but was *he* reliable?

She trembled. She might be stranded here with no hope of rescue, wandering these islands forever in search of her lover.

Teeth clenched, she trudged up the road, unsure where to go. Unfamiliar stringed music drifted from beyond where the wall stopped. On the corner, elderly men sat outside a taverna at spindly tables under a dripping awning. As they talked in animation, throwing back glasses of wine, they scrutinized her progress.

The street veered sharply to the left, but a smaller path led up another incline to the right, ending in a set of stone steps. Above that was a small, covered terrace with a few tables and chairs, a low-slung building on the far side.

Silence lingered around the area, yet she felt drawn in that direction as if she heard a call pertaining to her. Her knees ready to collapse, she dragged up the steps, passing fig and cypress trees on banks of scented green maquis. She entered the terrace and dropped with a squish into one of the chairs.

The evening bore down, chilled, and a young girl strolled the perimeter of the taverna's terrace, lighting lanterns that dangled from poles.

Another dark-haired girl with a long face approached Amélie's table. She asked a question, undeniably in Greek.

Amélie motioned as if eating. She needed her strength, to plan her next strategy. She pulled out a few of the coins she had left, laying them on the table. The girl nodded and returned to the building. Amélie had no idea if she'd communicated her wants or not.

The girl brought her a glass of thick, red liquid. Amélie sipped the sweet cherry flavor, quenching her thirst, trying to soothe a now scratchy throat. Her cheeks and forehead simmered with heat, despite the chilly air.

Through the spill of lantern light, three men entered the terrace. Her stomach lurched. Redcap strode toward her table and she cringed. He grinned with a slight shrug, as if nothing adverse had happened between them.

Amélie stood, scraping back the chair. Redcap raised his hands in a gesture meant to calm her, but Amélie backed away, needing space, to think. She bumped into the long-faced girl who held a plate of oily fish. The girl glared at the advancing man.

Amélie staggered across the terrace toward the opposite side, which overlooked the foot of a hill. *What do you want?* she longed to shout. *Tell me your purpose!*

The man shook his head, speaking to the girl in Greek, and continued to walk toward Amélie. Amélie stared out into the darkness beyond the lantern's reach. Her breath rasped in her throat.

Redcap stepped within a few feet of her. He again put up his hands. "No, no, I do not harm," he whispered in his bad Italian. "I help."

Amélie bristled with anger, her distrust so long gnawing inside her. Her head grew dizzy. Redcap reached out for her and she jerked back, anxious for further explanation. Her heel felt nothing and she toppled off the terrace.

Sprawled on her hands and knees on the stony earth, she moaned. Amélie scrambled to her feet and brushed off pebbles and mud. She hiked up her soaked skirt and faced the hill that thrust up in the blackness. Instinct pulled her and she tripped up the slope.

Footsteps rushed behind her. Firm hands grabbed her shoulders.

She stifled a scream and twisted away.

"*Per favore, sia calmo,*" a soft Italian voice urged in her ear. "You are all right now, I promise. Be so good to come with me, this way."

This man smelled of spice, not fish and damp wool. Amélie still stiffened.

The man tugged her forward, the direction she'd already intended. "I have come to help…sent to find you. Were you not treated kindly? I scolded those Greek cretins at the taverna. Did they scare you?"

Amélie sucked back oaths, but jerked her shoulders and elbows against his body. Her head thick and burning, frustration burst inside her. "Where are you *taking* me?" she hissed in Italian, thrilled to use her voice. They stumbled several feet up the slope in the murky night.

"Do not worry, you are meant to go with me, Amélie." The man's small hands remained firm, dragging her along. "*Appena un momento.*"

She coughed and wheezed. He'd used her name. She almost melted against him, but fear kept her rigid, cautious. Could she finally have reached her destination?

The man halted, bracing her tight at his side. A metal gate creaked.

"We're here. I'll just pull the cord. Everything will make sense." His soft voice was encouraging. "My cousin waits for you with impatience."

His cousin…*him*? A bell rang in the distance. The man released her. Amélie found herself gripping iron bars. She rested her throbbing head against the cool metal. Another voice joined her escort's, but they both sounded a thousand leagues away. When her legs buckled, she slumped to the ground.

Chapter Forty

What is history, but a fable agreed upon?—N.B.

"Bring brandy, quickly." Napoleon brushed damp hair from Amée's forehead, feeling the heat on her skin. "What have these fools done to you? This is what comes from entrusting to strangers." He sat near the massive hearth of this castle gatehouse, the fire crackling and snapping, Amée cuddled in his arms. Wrapped in a blanket, she continued to shiver, her wan face tinged pink with fever. He'd stripped her of her reeking clothes and slipped one of his shirts over her body.

His cousin Ernesto handed him a pewter cup. Napoleon eased her up to prop her head on his shoulder. "Amée, try to drink this," he whispered into her blond tresses that smelled of the sea. How his arms had ached to hold her, surprising him at the intensity of his feelings during these months of anxiety and hardship. Not that he was a stranger to the rigors of travel, the long march through a hostile landscape. He might be free, but the danger of exposure always clung to him.

She groaned and her eyelids fluttered. He put the cup to her lips and she sipped, then coughed and pulled her head back. She opened her eyes and squinted as if he might be an illusion. "Let me sleep," she murmured, burrowing down into the blanket. "I have places to travel in the morning."

Napoleon chuckled and kissed her hot forehead. "No, you're safe now, my sweet." Would either of them ever be safe? "No more traveling alone anymore. We're together as before, to love one another." He smiled. He meant that word—love. So elusive to him before, now not just an empty promise.

She opened her eyes and studied him, the wary woodland creature. "Napoleon? *Mon Dieu!* At last." She wriggled from her cocoon and flung her arms around him, sobbing into his shirt. Breath rasping, she leaned back and stroked her hand along his face. "I can't believe...so long I've...You've grown a beard."

"What better disguise. Drink more brandy." He raised the cup again and she sipped. Her sinuous body stirred baser emotions within him. After experiencing so much pleasure with her, this year of celibacy had been agonizing. He'd behaved his best, eschewing any female companionship, concentrating on the day-to-day machinations of escape. He caressed his fingers over her soft cheeks. "I want to put you to bed...to sleep."

Amée mumbled in protest, but he rose and carried her into the other room and tucked her beneath a heavy quilt in the four-poster bed. After a long kiss on her lips, Napoleon returned to the fire.

"We won't be able to stay here much longer, after the commotion at the taverna." Ernesto stepped over and leaned against the stone mantel. "I'll see if the others are prepared to set sail earlier than we planned."

"Always be prepared for the unexpected," Napoleon called after him as Ernesto strode from the room. In his thirties, totally trustworthy, the swarthy young man—a relation from his father's side—had proved invaluable.

Napoleon sighed and settled back in the chair. He stroked the silky beard he still thought strange each time he glanced into a mirror. His muscles relaxed at this stage accomplished, but he tensed again when he thought of what lay ahead. So much yet to do. A man needed a purpose in life…and a woman to love, who loved him. Power and riches all faded in the battle for self-preservation. "That's what keeps life interesting," he said into the warm flames, "the hunt, the parry, the unexpected, the ultimate victory over your opponents."

* * * *

Amélie awoke to a sun-drenched morning. A warm breeze wafted through the open window above her. She sat up, stretched her limbs, and looked out. A vineyard and farmland spread beyond this modest villa, or Dammuso, as they called it here.

Half woozy with fever, she'd been bundled up three days ago and bounced on a small fishing boat to this island of Pantelleria, south of Sicily. Napoleon told her they needed to keep moving, especially if the situation grew uncomfortable where they were.

"Amée, rise up, you sleepy one, the coffee is getting cold." Napoleon entered the room with a smile that drew her own. He had lost more weight in all this maneuvering, the stress of the escape. He sat on the bed, tracing a finger under her chin.

"Why don't you come back to bed?" She slid her arms around his neck and kissed him. The beard she'd yet to resign herself to tickled her lips. He tasted like the strong coffee they brewed here.

Napoleon reached over and closed the window shutters. He shrugged off his dressing gown, lifted the covers, and slipped in nude beside her.

She pressed her naked body along the length of his.

"We'll leave on a major sail soon." He stroked his hand over her breast, tingling her nipple. "I'm used to such changes. It brings back my days on the battlefield, rushing from one place to another, planning my strategy." He kissed her deeply.

"You're enjoying this, aren't you…the moving about I mean." She laughed, nestling into him and the cotton sheets. His eyes hazy with desire quickened her breathing.

"I'm enjoying having you with me again." He rubbed his stomach and pelvis against hers.

"I intend to keep you that way." She quivered inside and caressed his chest. She'd have to be clever and alluring to accomplish this.

"I would like to be settled somewhere. We plan to travel to New Orleans, live incognito for a time, see what my enemies are doing to search for me—if Robeaud is found out. One of my exiled generals—prevented from accompanying me to Saint Helena, Charles Lallemand—has done much preparation for me there." He kissed her throat.

"New Orleans sounds exciting." She struggled not to show her worries over his safety. She'd prefer someplace isolated, a private island.

"We could get married under this disguise, if that wouldn't trouble you. Then our children would have a semblance of legitimacy."

"I would be honored to be your wife. Names don't matter." She brushed her fingers over his whiskers, basking in his radiant smile. She wasn't so naïve to believe he'd stay satisfied in obscurity. "How long could you live as someone other than yourself?"

He chuckled and kissed her ear. "We'll follow the safest route for now. In my heart, I will always be Napoleon. Nothing can change that."

"What will you do in America?" Amélie stretched beneath him, their skin hot in contact. She longed to be like a cat, without worries, contented in the sun.

"I'll ponder the great thinkers of history, Goethe…I met him once, Diderot, Voltaire, Rousseau, and add my own ideas. Maybe study theology. Look for ways through the sciences to improve life. There are many things I've wanted to explore in depth—industry, commerce—but never had time. Do you realize that a canal in Suez would open up trade? I was there. I saw it." His expression turned thoughtful. "I'll stay in touch with people who will see that my son receives the proper care. Someday, I may be able to reveal myself. Time will tell. My son as a young man, beyond the treachery of the Austrians, will meet his father once more."

"He'll be very proud." Amélie sighed as he continued to caress her, his fingers probing. She dismissed the sadness that he may never see his son again. She'd give him more sons, arrange a life they'd savor. "I'll search for interesting herbs in America. Make my tinctures and potions for the deprived women of New Orleans." She didn't mention her writing on sex. Was her manuscript ever published in Paris? Each day she gathered more details for another book.

Napoleon kissed both her nipples. "Most important, you and I will pleasure ourselves to the utmost."

Amélie moaned as their bodies slid together in a perfect fit. She arched her back and would face anything with him beside her.

The end of her journey shimmered into the beginning.

About the Author:

Diane Parkinson grew up in the San Francisco Bay Area, joined the navy at nineteen, and has written and edited freelance since high school. She married in Greece and raised two sons in Puerto Rico, California, Guam, and Virginia. She writes book reviews for the Historical Novels Review and worked at The Wild Rose Press from 2007 to 2010 as a historical editor. Diane served as president of the Riverside Writers from 2007 to 2008. Her debut novel, *The False Light*—adventure and romance in eighteenth-century England—was released in April 2010.

She writes as Diane Scott Lewis and lives with her husband and dachshund in Locust Grove, VA.

Visit her online at:
http://www.dianescottlewis.com

Also by Diane Scott Lewis:

The False Light
by Diane Scott Lewis

eBook ISBN: 9781770650596
Print ISBN: 9781770650657

Romance Historical
Novel of 124,316 words

Forced away from France by her devious guardian on the eve of the French Revolution, Countess Lisbette Jonquiere must deliver an important package to further the royalist cause. In England, she discovers the package is full of blank papers, the address is false, and she's penniless. Stranded in a Cornish village, Lisbette toils in a bawdy tavern and falls in love with a man who lives under the shadow of his missing wife.

Immersed in poverty, Lisbette realizes what sparked the revolution in her homeland. Her past catches up to her when desperate men hunt her down: they demand the money her deceased father embezzled from the revolutionaries. Lisbette learns the truth of her father's death, and her lover's involvement in his wife's murder.

Once again, Lisbette faces the threat of losing everything.

Also from Eternal Press:

White Heart, Lakota Spirit
by Ginger Simpson

eBook ISBN: 9781615722501
Print ISBN: 9781615722518

Romance Historical
Short Novel of 58,000 words

Caught between the world of red and white, how will Grace Cummings choose?

A normal morning turns to disaster when a small war party attacks Grace Cummings' family and slaughters everyone but her. She returns to the Lakota camp filled with hatred, anger and fear, but through the help of another white woman in camp, learns the Lakota way.

When white soldiers invade the camp and presume to rescue Grace, she must decide where her heart lies.

CPSIA information can be obtained at www.ICGtesting.com
Printed in the USA
LVOW091015261111

256542LV00005B/199/P